Characters

- Logan — main character, hired to work on undercover to look for terrorists
- Sam — his daughter

- Casey — guide. Having problems w/ H.S. sweetheart
- Megan — his high school sweetheart

- Hank O'Leary — Big guy, expert fly tyer + guide
- Jackie — concert violinist. Met Hank @ Fly Tying Expo.

Ernie — old guy hurt in fire

John Kincaid — hiding stuff along river

- Zulfo — bad guy
- Peter Bolden — bad guy

Judd Boone = Mike McLucas from the Oasis.

RIVER *in the* SUN

by SCOTT RICHMOND

Copyright ©2012
Scott Richmond

Library of Congress
Cataloguing-in-Publication Data

Richmond, Scott.
River in the Sun
Scott Richmond.
−1st ed.

LCCN 2012947219
ISBN 0-9633067-2-2

Published by
4Rivers Press

5   4Rivers Press
4   West Linn, OR
3   www.4riverspress.com

2   *Cover painting and interior
    pencil drawings*:
1   Guy Jacobson

Design:
Eric Hillerns

Printed in USA

Set in Paperback and
Clarendon.

First Edition
First Printing

**For Barbara,
Heather, and Holly.**
Family trumps
everything.

and

**For Major, Gabe,
Ty, and Mataan.**
Thanks for the
ride, guys.

Also by Scott Richmond

Acknowledgements

Kathy Lesley, for her many astute suggestions about plot, character, and style. Karen Brattain, for bringing order and consistency to my otherwise anarchistic use of commas, semicolons, em dashes, etc. Shirley Blume, Craig Lesley, Marie Morgan, Chris O'Donnell, Hugh O'Donnell, John Smeraglio, and Bernie Taylor for early readings of the text and many useful suggestions for improving it. Dolores D'Aigle, Dr. Jeff Hall, Amy Hazel, Mark Malefyt, Dr. Dan Sager, and Dr. Miranda Wilkerson for technical information and fact checking. Eric Hillerns for cover and book design. Guy Jacobson for cover art and interior pencil drawings. The gang at Westfly for not lynching me while I worked on the book and neglected the website. And above all to Barbara Richmond, Heather Richmond, and Holly Richmond Woods—my wife and daughters, respectively—for their repeated readings, insightful suggestions, encouragement, patience, and refusal to roll their eyeballs, at least when I was looking.

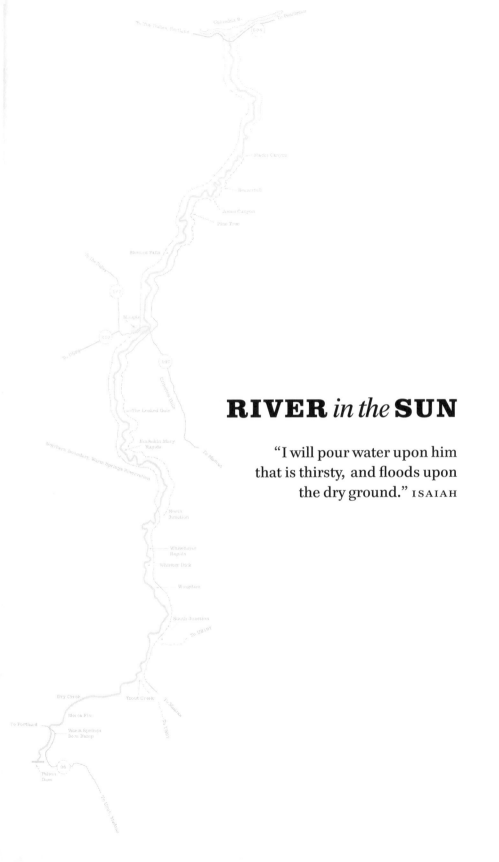

RIVER *in the* SUN

"I will pour water upon him
that is thirsty, and floods upon
the dry ground." ISAIAH

North Central Oregon

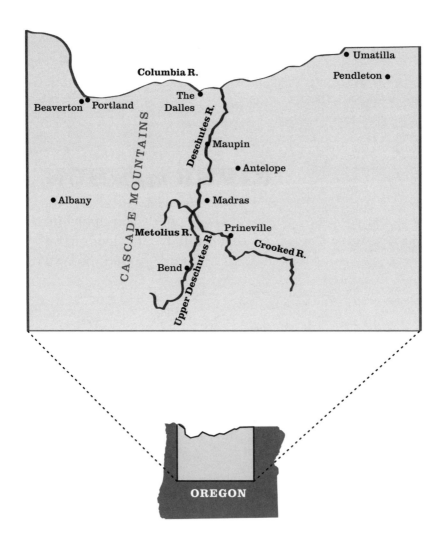

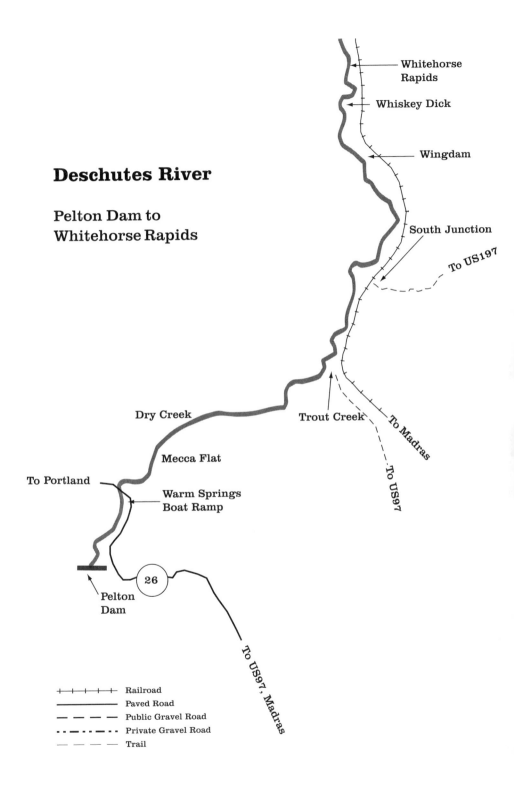

Deschutes River

Pelton Dam to Whitehorse Rapids

Whitehorse Rapids

Whiskey Dick

Wingdam

South Junction

To US197

Dry Creek

Trout Creek

To Madras

To US97

Mecca Flat

To Portland

Warm Springs
Boat Ramp

26

Pelton
Dam

To US97, Madras

+++++++	Railroad
————	Paved Road
— — —	Public Gravel Road
·—··—··—··	Private Gravel Road
— — —	Trail

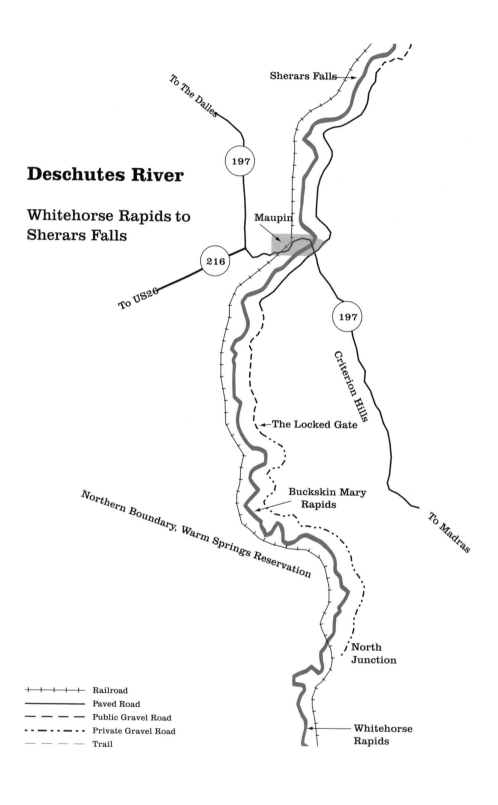

Deschutes River

Whitehorse Rapids to Sherars Falls

To The Dalles

Sherars Falls

197

Maupin

216

To US26

197

Criterion Hills

The Locked Gate

Buckskin Mary Rapids

Northern Boundary, Warm Springs Reservation

To Madras

North Junction

Whitehorse Rapids

┼┼┼┼┼	Railroad
———	Paved Road
— — —	Public Gravel Road
·—·—·—	Private Gravel Road
– – –	Trail

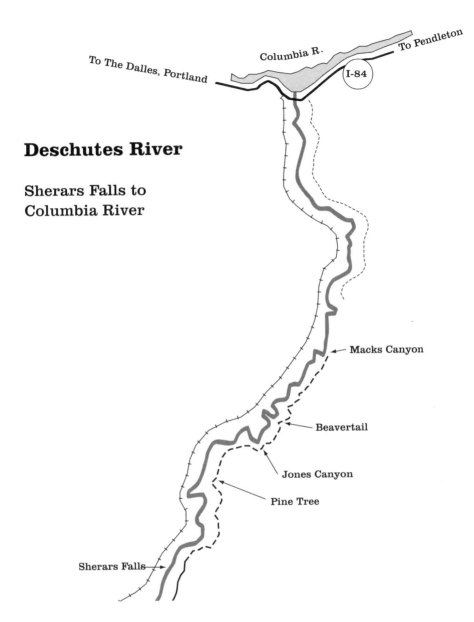

Deschutes River

Sherars Falls to Columbia River

To The Dalles, Portland

Columbia R.

To Pendleton

I-84

Macks Canyon

Beavertail

Jones Canyon

Pine Tree

Sherars Falls

+ + + + + +	Railroad
———————	Paved Road
— — — —	Public Gravel Road
·— ·— ·— ··	Private Gravel Road
— — — —	Trail

1: Confluence

1

THE DESCHUTES IS A RIVER OF GRACE IN AN ARID LAND.
The mainstem begins at the eastern base of the Cascade Range, meanders south, then makes a U-turn and flows north with a purpose. It is joined by the pure, transparent waters of the Metolius. Another tributary, the Crooked, drops out of the rugged Ochocos—cowboy country. These three rivers spring from sources deep within the earth. Commingled, they make up the lower hundred miles of the Deschutes.

Over the last million years the Deschutes has sliced through a thousand feet of hard basalt, creating a deep canyon that hides the river from casual view. You can travel across central Oregon's high desert and swear it's nothing but barren hills. Then your journey takes you to the rimrock, and suddenly you see it, wide and powerful—an unexpected revelation.

Rainbow trout thrive in the Deschutes' rich waters. In May you can see them taking salmonflies near the riverbank. By June they're sipping caddis and mayflies in the backeddies and below the alders. Anglers love the rainbows for the way they rise to a dry fly. Graceful as their name implies, they bring hope to winter-weary hearts.

In July the rainbows are joined by steelhead. They look like very big trout, but don't be misled: as the name implies, steelhead have been tempered by a dangerous journey through dark waters. Unlike rainbows, they seldom reveal themselves. You need different tactics—and unwavering faith—to draw them to a fly.

Anglers revere the Deschutes. Many come to enjoy the scenery and to catch the beautiful, strong fish. Others come not for what they can take from the river but for what the river gives them.

2

April 16, 5:47 a.m.: Near Maupin, Oregon

CASEY WILLIAMS WAS PROUD of himself. It wasn't even 6:00, and he was almost to Maupin. Another hour and he'd pull into the Trout Creek boat ramp to meet his boss, Judd Boone. He'd be half an hour early. Judd would be impressed—or at least he wouldn't think Casey was as big a screw-up as usual.

He could have left earlier from his winter rental on the Oregon coast, but Amanda had wanted a proper farewell dinner. And dessert. And.

It wasn't love. Casey knew the difference. So did Amanda. But each was convenient for the other through the long, gray drip of a coastal winter. On days when Casey didn't have clients to guide for winter steelhead, or stormy weather rendered the rivers unfishable, they'd helped each other pass the time.

His real love lay in Maupin, where he'd been born and where he'd graduated from high school ten years ago. Fly fishing and guiding on the Deschutes were his passions. The coast, like Amanda, was a diversion.

Casey was an independent fishing guide in the winter, but summers he worked for Judd Boone's Rainbow Anglers. Today was "First Float," an annual drift from Trout Creek to Maupin. Their guiding season started at the end of the week, so Casey and Judd needed to see how winter flows had altered their favorite fishing spots and whether the campsites were in good shape.

He stopped at the end of US 216, then turned right onto 197—four more miles to Maupin, then on to Trout Creek. The two-lane road dropped below the rimrock and began its winding descent. A few turns above Maupin, he saw a pickup truck with a horse trailer behind. The truck had come the other way, through town, and was pulled over just past the end of the guardrail.

A man in his late thirties or early forties stood beside the truck. He was looking at the river twisting through the canyon 700 feet below. Suddenly he doubled over, as if in pain.

Casey was about to stop and ask if he needed help, but headlights were coming up the hill through the tight S curves. He angled toward the narrow shoulder. A Ford pickup—probably Hank O'Leary's—rumbled past.

Then, before he could find a place to pull over, he saw a plume of thick, black smoke rising from the river's east bank. The OK Cafe? He stomped on the accelerator and sped through Maupin's deserted main street.

At the bottom of the hill, as he crossed the Deschutes bridge, he could see the OK Cafe, serene and intact. But three buildings down, smoke poured sluggishly from the eaves of the Drift Inn, an old hotel and restaurant that had seen better days. As he watched, a window shattered, and flames poured out.

A beat-up Toyota sat crooked in the parking lot. Casey knew the car: it belonged to Ernie Doyle, the janitor and backup breakfast cook. Casey skidded to a stop and jumped out. He looked in the car; Joey, Ernie's dog, barked frantically. "Ernie!" Casey yelled. No answer. Again: "Ernie!"

A glimmer of light came from a nearby window—not the

flickering orange of flames but a steady yellow glow of electric light filtered through a gray haze. Ernie must be inside.

Casey ran to the window and scanned the room. All he could see was smoke. He found the door and touched the knob. Cold—no fire here, yet. The knob turned, but the door was deadbolted. Casey looked for Ernie's keys. *Why no keys?* he wondered. Why would Ernie have locked himself inside? He stepped back five feet and threw himself at the door. It gave way, and he burst into the hall. Air rushed in behind him. Smoke swirled, and the fire suddenly sounded louder. He closed the door to block the inflow of air.

It was impossible to see or breathe. He coughed, then dropped to his hands and knees. At floor level, breathing was difficult but possible. Casey pulled a bandana from his hip pocket and held it over his mouth and nose. Through the smoke, he spotted a pair of shoes down the hall at the edge of the kitchen. Ernie, prostrate. A cast-iron frying pan lay nearby.

Coughing and choking, Casey crawled toward Ernie.

3

April 16, 5:47 a.m.: Near Maupin

LOGAN MCCREA PARKED HIS pickup just past the end of the guardrail above Maupin and walked to the edge of the canyon. He shivered slightly in the cool, faint breeze.

Barren hills rolled endlessly before him. A thin band of predawn light wedged through a crack between the horizon and the gray, snow-threatening clouds.

The river's roar was plain, even this far away, and he could just make out the dark, winding water. The sight of the river awakened pleasant memories—that first overnight fishing trip in his new driftboat seven years ago, when he and Trudy were a happy couple with their pretty daughter, Samantha, who loved camping and horses.

That was when he was successful and confident in his career—when he would feel free to take an occasional day off from work and sneak over to the Deschutes for some fly fishing.

Those memories quickly spiraled into despair. He was unemployed and heavily in debt. His daughter, now nineteen, was lamed and scarred from the accident that killed her mother. Worse, she'd withdrawn into a dark silence that excluded him and everyone else.

He doubled up, clutching his stomach, and retched without issue. This wasn't unusual; since last August, he'd started every morning with dry heaves, usually within the first hour or two after waking.

Two vehicles passed him, one going up the hill, the other headed down and accelerating quickly. *Why the sudden hurry?*

Logan bent over as his stomach convulsed again. Three heaves later, it stopped. He breathed heavily, eyes closed, and wondered if this was the day he'd kill himself. It was a speculation, not a decision; the thought, like the dry heaves, came nearly every morning.

"Dear God," he sighed as his breath came back to him, "please let this be a better day." This, too, was typical—a sentence he repeated most mornings, always rhetorically. But today he was so desperate that he meant every word.

4

April 16, 5:47 a.m.: Near Maupin

HANK O'LEARY SQUEEZED himself into his fifteen-year-old dark blue pickup truck. At six foot four and 245 pounds, he was a tight fit. He ran his fingers through his thick, curly hair, once bright red but now more auburn and tinged with gray. He scratched his chin—hidden deep within his heavy beard—and headed out of Maupin.

Hank's truck sported two large decals in the rear window. One proclaimed his membership in the National Rifle Association. The other was a replica of the yellow-red-and-green Vietnam campaign ribbon.

As he wound through the tight curves above town, he spied a pickup and horse trailer pulled over just past the end of the guard-rail. Near it, a man suddenly bent over at the waist. Hank's main focus, though, was on the trailer; he wondered if there were any horses in it.

A truck pulling a driftboat—Casey Williams?—came down the hill. His attention shifted back to the road, and he steered carefully between the two rigs.

Two miles farther, Hank turned his Ford F-250 onto Highway 216 and headed west through the long, straight stretch known as Juniper Flat. He tuned the radio to a country music station. A twangy up-tempo song filled the truck. He tapped rhythmically on the steering wheel and sang along. His resonant baritone—honest and unembellished, gentle and reassuring but with a hint of steel—was accustomed to country music: he sang and played harmonica with Water Dawgs, a local band.

The radio changed to a love ballad. Hank grimaced and turned it off. He mentally reviewed the flies he would demonstrate this afternoon at the Northwest Fly Fishing and Tyers Expo in Albany.

He didn't mind sitting in front of a dozen or so anglers for three hours while he showed them how to tie a few of his more famous creations. But other than public demonstrations, he could no longer bear to sit at the tying vise.

This problem began a few months ago. He'd had an eye infection that had stopped him from tying. After the infection cleared up, he had no desire to tie; half a dozen flies and—wham!—he was out of his chair and looking for something else to do. He'd been a disciplined professional tyer for over thirty years. Now he couldn't tie a dozen flies a day.

He had a restless sense of anticipation—for what, he didn't know. The feeling reminded him of that first step into an unknown steelhead run: promising, but it's a tough wade over slippery rocks, with trees at your back so it's hard to cast. You feel like anything could happen—good or bad—but you don't know what to expect.

Hank sighed deeply. Somehow he'd get through this. He shrugged his shoulders a few times and did a neck roll. He stretched his right hand over the truck's worn seat covers to reassure himself that he had everything he needed for the day. Lunch—two peanut butter-and-pickle sandwiches, apple, bag of Fritos. Water bottle. Coffee thermos. Fly tying kit. Smith and Wesson .38 Special snub-nosed revolver. Yup, everything he needed.

5

April 16, 8:30 a.m.: Newberg, Oregon

LOGAN MCCREA PULLED INTO his driveway, the empty horse trailer rattling behind. The weather was cool and cloudy, the same as he'd seen in Maupin. The terrain, however, was completely different.

While Maupin perched in a desert canyon above a river, Newberg lay in gentle fir-covered hills, dotted with pastures and hobby farms like his.

Logan parked by the barn. His daughter Samantha—"Sam"—was in the corral, cleaning up after the horses. Pretty and on the tall side, Sam wore jeans; a denim jacket covered a flannel shirt. Her blonde ponytail spilled from the back of a baseball hat. She moved awkwardly, stopping often to rest her bad leg. Sam paused as she neared Major, the gray two-year-old gelding, then moved on. Logan winced.

Sam scooped a pile of manure and dumped it into the wheelbarrow. "You're back early," she said to Logan without looking at him.

"I slept in the truck, then hit the road first thing." He forced a smile. "One more horse sold and delivered. Only two more to go."

Sam glanced behind her at Major, then turned to Mataan, the 14.2-hand Arabian she'd ridden in horse shows until the car accident shattered her right leg.

"Or not," Logan said gently, although he didn't know where he was going to get the money to feed Mataan and Major.

He saw Sam's head turn toward the road. Logan followed the look. A car moved tentatively down the long gravel driveway. Sam shrugged and resumed cleaning the corral.

A white Ford Taurus pulled up, and a middle-aged man, plump and a bit jowly, got out and walked stiffly to Logan. "Mr. Logan McCrea?" he said, offering his right hand. "I'm Bill Short. Can we talk?"

Logan shook Short's hand. He led him inside the house and waved him to a seat at the kitchen table. The kitchen, like the rest of the house, was large but had the barest minimum of furnishings.

Bill Short was about five foot five, with a sagging face and baggy eyes. Logan speculated on his line of work: repo man, bank manager, or lawyer? He'd seen more than his share of each in the last few months. But while Short had the look of bureaucracy about him, his manner suggested he wanted a favor, not money or possessions.

Logan fetched two coffee mugs from the cupboard and held them up.

"Coffee? Sure," Short said without enthusiasm.

Logan walked to his La Marzocco espresso machine, gleaming grandly on the granite counter.

"Whoa!" said Short. "Fancy stuff! Well then, if you're making lattes, I'd like a double shot skinny low foam." He cleared his throat. "I mean, if it's not too much trouble." Short pointed at the La Marzocco. "Heck of a machine," he said admiringly. "Double spigot, commercial quality. Not many of those in a private home."

Logan smiled thinly. *And probably not in mine much longer,* he thought. His mind turned briefly to how much he could get for it on eBay and how long that might keep Sam and him going. After the La Marzocco and the two remaining horses, he'd sell his driftboat. Then his fishing gear. Then what? His stomach went tight, and his hand shook as he ground some beans.

He pulled a latte for Short, then a double regular for himself. He sat down opposite Short, expressionless.

Short sipped his latte. "Mmm. You do good work!"

Logan nodded but said nothing.

Short pulled a manila file folder from his attaché case and laid it on the table. He cleared his throat. "I'll get right to it. I'm from Langley." He took something from the inside breast pocket of his suit coat. It had the appearance of a blue Central Intelligence Agency ID badge. "Bill Short" it said under a photo of him wearing a navy blue suit and red tie; it could have been the same suit and tie he wore now. "Walter Dietz sent me," Short said.

Logan couldn't help but blink once, but he showed no other expression. Inside, he was blown away. That was the last name he expected to hear today. And how come Short didn't call and make an appointment? How did he know Logan would even be home today?

Oh, right, if you carry a cell phone, someone knows where you are—and whom you're with.

Short shook his head, then put on black half-height reading glasses and opened the folder. "Logan McCrea," he intoned, reading from some papers inside the folder. "Grew up in Portland, went to Cleveland High School. Graduated *magna cum laude* from Oregon State University with a bachelor's in computer science twenty-two years ago at the age of twenty-one. Double major in English Literature, focus on the romantic poets." He looked up. "Unusual combination."

Head back down, Short went on. "Master's degree in computer science from Stanford two years later. Married Trudy Pitman while at graduate school. Following university, worked for Electronic Defense Laboratories, Inc., in Mountain View, California, for four years, all with Walter Dietz as manager ..."

Working for Dietz had been a good move after college, Logan reflected. The man was smart and charismatic, with a fine technical mind. In the 80s Dietz had been a lead engineer on the CKTAW hardware, a big intelligence coup at the time. Logan had learned a lot from Dietz.

"... came with Dietz when he moved to the National Security Agency at Fort Mead. Worked as a designer of collection systems. Clearances: secret, top secret, crypto, special intelligence, and various sensitive compartmented and need-to-know projects." Short looked up again.

Logan eyed him impassively.

Short's head went back down, and he continued. "Left NSA eight years ago when Dietz transferred to CIA. Moved to Beaverton, Oregon, to do ... to *manage* custom software development for Transept Corporation. Four years ago joined Med-Rec, a start-up, to do the same job."

Logan looked out the window at the two horses.

"Divorced from Trudy two years ago this month. One daughter, Samantha, now aged nineteen, who lived with her mother, then with you after … after … " Short cleared his throat. "Samantha seriously injured last August in an automobile accident. Broken femur, ribs, head injuries. Six months in the hospital and physical therapy. Trudy killed in the same accident. Sorry."

Short continued. "Med-Rec in deep trouble. Core product has serious problems. Stock price plummets. Med-Rec now being bought by General Medical, Inc. Deal still in limbo, but GMI wants the $237,000 that Med-Rec loaned you to buy stock, which is now nearly worthless."

Bill paused, a bit triumphantly. Logan gave him a cold stare. It wasn't his fault Med-Rec had failed. He'd managed custom software add-ons, not the core product. And it had seemed like a good idea at the time—to borrow money to buy stock. Every exec in the company did it, and as a VP he could borrow more than most. And it had worked out. For a while. The company made its Initial Public Offering, and the stock zoomed to $35. Logan's half-million shares were worth a lot of money—enough that he felt confident in buying the Newberg horse farm, mostly as a way to win back Trudy and Sam. But he couldn't sell his Med-Rec shares—SEC rules: six-month lock-out for pre-IPO stock. Four months after the IPO, the bubble burst, and Med-Rec shares dropped like a rock in a vacuum. Then it became clear that Med-Rec had cash flow problems. And product problems. Wall Street's sharks smelled blood, and the stock fell to pennies a share. And Logan owed Med-Rec a quarter mil. And he had taken out a big mortgage on 20 acres in Newberg at the peak of the real estate market. And the property was now worth much less than he owed on it—not that he'd made any payments in the last five months. And his 401-K plan and all his other equity—a lifetime of saving and investing—went to Sam's medical bills because Trudy hadn't set up the insurance correctly after their divorce.

At least he hadn't fallen into a credit card trap. At the first sign of trouble, he'd canceled all but one, which he kept in the safe deposit box for an emergency. But even if he sold the La Marzocco coffee machine and everything else, it would only delay the inevitable.

Another two months—three at the most—and he'd have to dig out
that card and rack up bills he knew he'd never repay. He hated debt,
hated owing something to other people.

Logan felt his stomach churn, and a too-familiar vertigo swept
over him. Panic set in. He worried he'd faint, sprawled over Bill
Short's manila folder. Was he having a heart attack? What would
happen to Sam if he died? Logan stood up and paced.

"Here's the deal," Short said. "We need someone to do a little
work for us. Nothing major. Just need some eyes peeled. Probably
no real threat, but we have to check it out. Don't have the manpower.
They're all off in Iraq or Afghanistan or some other 'stan.' Hiring
freeze. Can't hire anyone new. We need a *consultant*. Dietz wants
you."

Logan continued to pace.

"You're probably wondering, 'Why me?'"

Logan ignored him.

"Dietz said you could be like this," Short muttered. He took out
a handkerchief and mopped his forehead, looking exasperated. He
shuffled some papers in the folder. "You've got the right qualities.
According to Dietz, 'Logan McCrea has wide-ranging knowledge and
is willing to share his learning with others.'"

Logan tensed and stopped pacing.

Short went on, reading from the report in front of him. "'Lively
sense of humor.'" He paused briefly. "Not that we've seen much of it
today," he said softly to himself. Short cleared his throat and went on.
"'Uses both sides of his brain. Not afraid to think outside the box.
Observant. Writes well. Loves to fly fish. Knows the Deschutes River.
Good in a crisis.'"

Logan faced Short, arms across his chest. "Look, Bill Short,"
he said. "Or whatever your name is. Who are you really, and what
do you want?"

"Oh my goodness!" Short said in mock amazement. "He has
the power of speech!"

"So you did a little digging and got the outline of my life. Any clever person could put that together. You've never met Walter Dietz. Who are you?"

"I'm Bill Short!" He fished the blue ID badge from his pocket and wiggled it back and forth.

"You're some guy who knows how to use Photoshop and got your fake badge laminated in plastic at the corner print shop." Logan pointed at Short's folder. "Dietz doesn't talk like that."

"Well … I … I paraphrased," Short said, looking down at his papers.

Because he was standing, Logan could see a little of what Short was reading. It looked like a transcript, with handwritten margin notes. "You know … 'Bill' … you must need a trip to the boy's room after that coffee. There's a bathroom down the hall."

Short stared at Logan. "Well, maybe a little break is in order," he finally said. He stood up and put the transcript in the folder, ready to take it with him.

"You won't need that," Logan said off-handedly. "You can leave it on the table."

"It's classified!"

"You just told me I'm cleared from here to doomsday. And it's about me."

The two men locked eyes, then Short put the folder back on the table. He moved toward the hall. "This way?"

Logan nodded. "Take your time. There's some *National Geo-graphics* in there. The one with the cover story on Paris is pretty interesting."

Logan waited for Short to close the door, then slid behind the table and opened the folder. He found a margin note that said *Wide-ranging knowledge and enjoys sharing his learning with others.* It was next to an underlined part of the transcript that read *Pedantic know-it-all.* Dietz had often called him that.

Logan read further. Next to a handwritten *Lively sense of humor* the transcript read *Smart-ass.*

And so it went. *Uses both sides of his brain* was opposite *Takes forever to make a decision. Analyzes every detail to death. Then does a Vulcan mind meld and goes with his intuition.* That was pure Dietz, even down to getting the wrong sense of Vulcan mind meld.

At the end, the transcript read *Keeps his head when the going gets tough, but pees his pants over little things. Nice guy, though. I like him and respect him, even though he can be a pain in the butt.*

Logan restored the folder to its original state and resumed his seat at the other side of the table. "Learned enough about Paris?" he called down the hall.

There was a hesitation, then a click as the door opened. Bill emerged looking tentative.

"Give Dietz my regards," Logan said. He motioned for Bill to take a seat. "So, what does the old crow want me to do?"

"He wants you to go fishing on the Deschutes and keep your eyes open."

"I see. And the government is going to pay me for taking this fishing trip. Is this part of an economic stimulus package?"

Bill took a big breath. "Here's the deal. NSA picked up an open cell phone call from an Islamist terrorist group in Germany. The caller referred to some other group—one we'd never heard of—doing something big on the Deschutes River. We don't know which group they were talking about, or what they're planning, or even if it's real. We're flying blind, and we have no resources to spare. We can't connect the dots because we have only one dot, and it's not a very good one. We need someone to spend time on the Deschutes and see if there are any more dots. Dietz thought of a cover story: you're working on a guidebook for the river. So you spend six months poking around the Deschutes, asking questions and keeping your eyes peeled. Report to us if you see anything unusual."

Logan admitted the cover story was plausible, but he seriously doubted the assignment. Islamist terrorists on the Deschutes? Absurd! The country was paranoid. Then he remembered Round Butte and Pelton Dams, and the entire Columbia River hydropower system. Maybe it wasn't so far fetched. But he had other concerns.

"I'm not a field agent," he said. "I'm a computer wonk. Or was. I have no field skills whatsoever. I sat in an office and designed computer systems to process SIGINT—Signal Intelligence."

"I know what SIGINT is," Bill said testily. He waved a hand over the manila folder. "And I know what you did. We have a possible domestic threat from possible foreign terrorists. But it's low probability, and we have no resources. We're looking for someone to check it out, freelance. For a modest—very modest—compensation."

The word *compensation* caught Logan's attention, but he had other questions first. "Doesn't this fall under the FBI's jurisdiction?" he asked.

"From the nature of the source, it's not clear whose purview it's under. Anyway, FBI didn't want it. Dietz put up his hand and volunteered to take it. Then he asked me to contact you."

"So you don't need Rambo at this point. Just some guy to hang out and see if anything is really going down."

"That's the deal."

Logan thought for a minute. "Show me what you picked up."

Bill wordlessly fished a sheet of paper from his folder and handed it to Logan. It was stamped *Top Secret* at the top and bottom, plus a codename that Logan didn't recognize. The content said simply "Cell phone call: A group in Oregon might pull off a spectacular mission. They need some help putting the 'stuff' in place. There was a mention of the Deschutes River." The date of the intercept was three days ago.

"That's it?" said Logan. "Can I see the verbatim?"

"It's an NSA intercept," Bill said. "They don't give out verbatims." He tapped the manila folder slowly. "You were there. You know how they are."

THEY HAMMERED OUT A DEAL in a two-latte, nonstop negotiation. First, the government would assume Logan's home mortgage and make the back payments. "We anticipated that," Short said. "Someone in Treasury owed Dietz a favor. It's just one more bad loan to heap on the government's pile. No one will even notice." So Logan was out from under that obligation but had no equity.

Second, the CIA would pay him through October while he scoured the Deschutes looking for terrorists. He'd get money to cover his living expenses, but it was skimpy at best. They'd buy him a new laptop and fund his internet and smart phone. Logan and Sam would have health insurance, but only until the end of October.

However, the feds wouldn't touch the loan he'd taken with Med-Rec. So he still owed $237,000, but he got to keep his half-million shares of stock—technically worth about a nickel a share but practically unsellable.

The stickiest part of their negotiation was the two horses, Mataan and Major. Logan pushed the point that he could use Mataan, the older horse, for surveillance. "You can see a lot on horseback," he insisted. "And I need both horses because Mataan will get lonely if it's just him. They're herd animals, you know." His real motivation was that he thought the horses might be a way to reestablish a relationship with his daughter—to get her out of her sullen silence. They could also be used for physical therapy.

Eventually, he got Bill to agree to pay an extra $100 a month for keeping the horses. "You're worse than Dietz," Bill said, mopping his forehead.

"It is a poor student who is not better than his master."

"Thank you, Confucius," Bill muttered.

Logan ignored the remark. "What kind of surveillance equipment are you going to provide?"

Bill fetched a money clip from his pocket and peeled off three fifties. He stacked them neatly in front of Logan. "Here's $150. Buy yourself some really good binoculars."

Logan slid the fifties back to Bill. "$150 gets you 'barely adequate,' not 'really good.'"

Bill picked up the money, then restacked it in front of Logan. "Well, then," he said. "Here's $150. Buy yourself some barely adequate binoculars."

Logan scowled and put the money in his shirt pocket. "Who," he said, "will be my handler?"

"Me."

"You're ... a case officer?" It seemed unlikely.

"No. I'm in administration. Mostly I do accounting work. Keep track of the money, make sure the bills are paid. That kind of stuff. Plus a few odd jobs. Like this."

Logan mulled this over. It was crystal clear how important this intercept was: no one wanted it except Dietz, and he only took it as a way to help Logan—a welfare project. As further proof, his "handler" was a bean counter and general dogsbody, not a trained agent. But beggars couldn't be choosers; he needed the money, so he'd play the game. "Management," he said slowly, putting the best spin possible on Bill's job. "So what's our covert communications plan?"

Bill wrote something on a piece of paper and handed it to Logan.

Logan looked at it, puzzled. Encryption key? Not enough digits.

"That's my cell phone number," Bill said.

"I don't have a secure cell phone."

"Neither do I," said Bill. "That's an open line. We're talking Maupin, not Moscow in the height of the Cold War, and these people— if there are any people—are not exactly the KGB." His voice became sarcastic. "We don't think you'll need any one-time encryption pads sewn inside a dead rat and dropped in an alley." Bill stood to go. "There's a secure videophone link in Beaverton that you can use in case you find anything important. I'll give you instructions on how to use it. Anything else, call me or send an email."

6

April 16: Near Maupin, Oregon

TWO MEN MET ON A DESERTED gravel road near Maupin. One
was thin and in his early forties. His neatly trimmed dark hair was
going gray at the temples. He wore wire-framed glasses and had an
intelligent, educated appearance. His name was Peter Bolton,
although that wasn't what his driver's license and credit cards said.

The other man, Zulfo Osmanović, was a few years older. Stocky,
he looked like someone who was once a bodybuilder but had stopped
working out. A prominent scar ran across his forehead. His head
was shaved.

"Did you take care of the old guy?" Bolton asked.

"Maybe," said Zulfo. His English was good, but he spoke with
an accent.

"What do you mean, maybe?"

The scarred man looked away. "I started the fire in the grill
vent. It was thick with grease. But just when the fire was going good,
some kid ran in and pulled him out. They took him away in an ambu-
lance." Zulfo shrugged. "He'll probably die."

Bolton eyed Zulfo coldly. "*Probably?* Now we'll have to wait."

"Oh, let's just do it."

"Patience. Patience will win for us. We need to know if the
old man can talk. And the fire will stir up people. We'll wait until
everything settles down."

Zulfo chewed his lip. "I don't like waiting," he said.

"Patience," Bolton repeated.

"The Russian has been on my property in Antelope again."

"Is he getting close?"

The scarred man shook his head. "It's forty acres, and he hasn't
got a clue where we buried the stuff. But he might get lucky."

"We'll have to take the risk," Bolton said.

"How long?"

"A couple of weeks. Maybe a month."

"I don't trust that guy who's going to cache it for us."

Bolton removed his glasses and idly polished them. "You don't trust anyone," he said. "That's to your credit. My contact says Kincaid is very good at what he does. Others concur." He replaced his glasses. "It's a calculated risk, but I don't see any other choices. We have to move it sooner or later, now that the Russian is prowling around. Kincaid is the best option we have. The people in Munich agree."

"There are too many people on that river."

"Kincaid says it's worked for him before, and I believe him. It's the best we can do under the circumstances. Like I said, it's a calculated risk, but the odds are very much in our favor. When the time comes, we'll distract the Russian while Kincaid hides the stuff."

"It's too bad the FBI picked up our friends in Michigan last fall. We'd have had it all done by now. Do you think they'll talk?"

"First," said Bolton, "they're not our friends. They're merely people who were going to do something for us while we did something for them. But I doubt they'll talk, and that's the main thing. And now that we're set up with the cell in Munich, we don't need our Michigan *friends* any more."

Zulfo nodded. "They should have everything arranged in a few more months."

"Then we'll get our stash and take the next step."

"What if we fail?" said the scarred man.

Bolton shrugged. "What if we succeed?"

7

April 16: Albany, Oregon

HANK O'LEARY WAS MILDLY DEPRESSED. And a little ticked off. He felt that way every time he drove to, through, or anywhere near Albany. The town didn't bother him; it was the closure of Lenny Burk's Mid-Valley Fly Angler, an Albany fixture for two decades, that made him feel this way. Hank liked Lenny and had enjoyed going to his shop and talking about fly tying and fishing. But Lenny's, like most fly shops, had been a shoestring operation and hadn't survived the tough economy.

While the demise of Lenny's shop depressed Hank, what got him ticked was that it had been replaced with a Starbucks. Hank didn't like Starbucks. More exactly, he didn't like the idea of Starbucks. He'd never had a latte, but he knew they were expensive and that the people who bought them were pretentious yuppies. A simple strong brew ought to be enough, not some five-dollar cup of froth.

He turned off Knox Butte Road and into the Linn County Expo Center. He parked his pickup and zipped the fleece vest that covered his khaki work shirt, placed the oiled-cotton "packer" hat squarely on his head, and stepped out. Last, he slipped the snub-nosed .38 into its pocket holster in his jeans.

A light drizzle was falling, and people walked quickly across the wet asphalt. They divided into two groups. One, mostly men, moved quietly toward the Northwest Fly Fishing and Tying Expo in the conference center. The other flowed like a noisy creek and was mainly women going to a quilting show in the Santiam Building just beyond. Hank joined the flow of men.

As he approached the flagpole in the courtyard, he saw a dark-haired woman in her early forties, looking like a lost dog. She had a classy look. Someone who spent most of her time indoors.

Probably came from the quilt show. Had a striking face. Not beautiful exactly, but unusual. A mix of ethnicities. Something about the eyes and cheekbones. Asian background, maybe even Southeast Asian. But her skin was more olive, Mediterranean perhaps. Dark eyes with considerable flash. Intelligent looking. On the short side, but well proportioned. She was wearing black slacks and black flat shoes. A brown leather vest covered a black turtleneck sweater. Her left forearm was in a cast and rested in a navy blue sling.

Hank was suddenly aware of two things. First, he'd been staring at her for a full minute. Second, she'd been staring back at him that whole time. She seemed no more able to take her eyes off him than he could look away from her. She shook her head and blinked her eyes. "Do you know where I can get some coffee?" she asked. Her accent was unusual: vaguely European but hard to place.

The conference center had coffee, but you needed a ticket to get in. There was the thermos in Hank's truck, but she didn't look like someone who drank that kind of coffee. Finally he said, "You mean like a Starbucks?"

"Starbucks works," she said.

"There's one down the street. A ways. About a mile. Maybe a mile and a half. In the mall."

"Which way?"

Hank pointed. "Under the freeway, then west. And south."

"I'm not from here. I don't know my way around. Can I walk there?"

"Not really. Not in this drizzle." Hank shifted uneasily. "I'm … going that way myself. Thought I'd get a latte or something." *Right,* he thought. *What an idiot.* "I could give you a ride." He had no idea where this notion came from.

She looked him over—top to bottom and back up again. Put her tongue in her cheek and a finger on her lips. Looked him straight in the eyes. Finally she said, "Okay. You're not some gun-toting killer, are you?"

Hank managed a thin smile. "Not today," he said airily.

ON THE RIDE TO STARBUCKS, she introduced herself as Jackie but didn't give Hank her last name. She was visiting a distant cousin who lived in Albany and enjoyed sewing, hence the quilt show; but Jackie didn't care much for quilts.

At the Starbucks counter, Jackie gave a complicated string of commands to the barista. Hank said, "Same here." He had no idea what he'd ordered. With tip, it cost him almost five dollars. He winced.

High prices weren't the only source of pain. The last time Hank was in this space, it was Lenny Burk's fly shop. Pastries were displayed where the fishing flies used to be. Three women sat on a sofa sipping drinks and chatting; the rod rack once stood there. A bearded man typed on a laptop computer where Lenny had kept his stock of chest waders.

They sipped their drinks in silence for a few minutes, then Hank said, "Excuse me, but you look like you have some Southeast Asian background. Sorry to be so ... curious."

"That's okay. I have a mixed background. French, Chinese, and Vietnamese. I lived in France when I was young, then moved to the US when I was sixteen. You were in Vietnam? I saw the decal on your truck."

"Yes. I was there."

She nodded. They were silent a little longer, then Hank asked what she did for a living. "I'm a professional musician," she told him. "A fiddler. Or at least I used to be." She pointed at her left arm, the one in a sling.

"Really! I'm in a country band—Water Dawgs. I play chromatic harmonica and write some music for them. How'd you hurt your arm?"

"Fell down the backstage stairs after my gig."

"Will that affect your fiddle playing?"

"I broke my arm a few weeks ago. I'll get the cast off in early May, then do some rehab. It's not a bad break. They're optimistic that I'll have a complete recovery." She sighed, looking uneasy. "But they don't know for sure. It's possible I won't be able to play professionally again—at least not at the same level. My bookings have been cancelled for the next year." She straightened and looked at him. "What do you do? Other than the band?"

"I'm a professional fly tyer—fishing flies. Or used to be. I had an eye infection. I couldn't tie for a while."

"Are your eyes okay now?"

"Yes." He paused and rubbed his chin, looking at her, wondering if he should go on. He leaned forward slightly and looked straight into her dark brown eyes. "Truth is, I can tie just fine," he said. "But I'm having trouble staying … It's like I want to do something else," Hank said. "Something different."

"Like what?"

Hank leaned back and spread his hands. "I don't know. It's all I've ever done. Except the Army. And ranch work when I was growing up."

"All I've ever done," Jackie said, "is the violin. I started when I was three. Played professionally since my early twenties. I practice six or seven hours a day, then play concerts. Or used to."

"You don't exactly play fiddle in a bluegrass band, do you? Something more … formal."

"I'm a classical violinist. I tour America, Europe, and parts of Asia doing concerts. This winter I was doing the Sibelius concerto. I was in Amsterdam when I tripped on the back stairs and …" She looked at her bad arm.

"Are you famous?" Hank asked. "Sorry, but I never listen to classical music. I don't know these things."

Jackie hesitated, then said, "Yes. In my world. My full name is Jacqueline Moreau." She paused. When Hank showed no sign of recognition she asked, "Are you a famous fly tyer?"

Hank laughed. "Trust me, my world is a lot smaller than yours. But … among western fly anglers, I'm … well, pretty well known. They talked me into doing a book a few years ago. It's still selling."

Jackie gave an understanding nod.

"So," Hank said, "the world thinks of you only as a violinist because that's all ..."

"... all I've ever done! Just like they only think of you as a fly tyer. I think there's more ..."

"... more to me—us—than that!"

"But what?"

They both shrugged.

"So who are you when you don't tie flies?" she said. "And who am I when I don't play the violin?"

"Beats me. But I think I—we—need to figure it out."

"I've tried to talk to other musicians about it," she said, "but they ..."

"... don't get it because you're tops in your field, and they ..."

"... want to be where you are, and they can't understand why you'd want to do something else!"

Soon it was lunchtime, and she wondered where to eat. "I don't usually eat out," Hank said. "I've got sandwiches in my truck, but ..."

"What kind of sandwiches?"

"Peanut butter. With, ummm, pickles. Everyone thinks that's weird, but—"

"Dill or sweet?"

"Sweet."

"I love peanut butter with sweet pickles! Most people go, 'Yuk!' But peanuts go great with vegetables. Maybe it's my Southeast Asian background—peanut sauce, sweet-and-sour, all that. I haven't had peanut butter and pickles in months."

"You're welcome to share mine," Hank offered.

They sat in Hank's truck and shared his sandwiches. Then he drove her back to the Expo Center, and she went to the quilt show.

He liked Jackie and was sorry to see her leave. They seemed to have some connection, despite their obvious differences. He spent the rest of the day at the Fly Tying Expo, but he kept thinking about her. It was pointless, though; he'd probably never see her again.

HANK SLEPT IN HIS TRUCK THAT night; motels cost money he didn't have. More exactly, he *tried* to sleep in his truck. He couldn't get Jacqueline Moreau out of his mind. He wanted to see her again. But how?

He was up by 6:30 the next morning and drove to a gas station. He washed up and brushed his teeth in the men's room, then stood by his truck wondering what to do next. A thought came, and he drove to the Starbucks where he'd taken Jackie.

Hank pushed open the glass door and walked slowly to the newspaper rack. He feigned interest in the headlines, but his eyes were scanning the room. In a corner, nervously sipping from a white and green paper cup, was Jackie. She looked up and saw him. And smiled broadly.

He walked over and sat at her table.

"I was hoping you'd come here," she said, "looking for a latte."

"I never go to Starbucks," Hank confessed. "Before yesterday I'd never had a latte. I came here looking for you."

"I came here hoping you'd be looking for me." She paused and looked at him quizzically. "Really? You'd never been in a Starbucks before? Never had a latte?"

"Never had a latte. Went into a Starbucks once, though. I got a hot chocolate for my wife." Noting a hint of disappointment in Jackie's face, he added, "Ex-wife."

Jackie nodded thoughtfully, then looked at him sidelong. "Was that a good trade?" she said slyly. "To get a hot chocolate for your ex-wife?"

Hank thought for a moment, got the joke, and snorted. "That would have been a good trade, alright. For me, not Starbucks!"

Jackie looked sheepish. "I shouldn't imply bad things about someone I've never met. I'm sure she had some good assets."

"If you'd left the '-ets' off the end of that sentence," Hank said wryly, "you'd have described her perfectly."

Jackie suppressed a giggle, then said, "Any current wives?"

"Two exes, none current. Lots of ex-girlfriends but none current. You?"

"One ex-husband. No one current."

Hank nodded thoughtfully, then said, "What's it like touring around and doing concerts?"

Jackie told him about her last year as they shared coffee drinks and pastries. Then she asked him about fishing, and rivers, and fly tying.

"Come with me to the Fly Tying Expo," Hank said, "and I'll show you."

~

LONG ROWS OF FOLDING TABLES filled the hall. Behind every table, a tyer worked on a fly, usually a personal design. Several attendees sat in front of each tyer, watching and asking questions. There were dozens and dozens of tyers, and hundreds of attendees.

"Hey, Hank," said a voice from a nearby table.

Hank turned to the voice. "Caddisman! How are you? How's Caddiswoman?"

"She's good."

Hank turned to Jackie. "Jackie, this is Art Cadbury, known as Caddisman. Art, this is Jackie."

Hank and Jackie sat down in folding chairs across from Art. Hank peered at the work surface: long olive-dyed feathers and dubbing, dark red thread in the bobbin, long-shanked hooks. "Damselfly pattern?"

"Yup." As he worked on the fly, Art said, "I see they're using a Jonzie for the pin this year. Nice." He turned to Jackie. "Hank invented it. When it comes to flies, he's the Wizard of the West."

Jackie gave Hank a soft punch on the shoulder. "I knew you were famous," she said.

Hank shrugged but smiled. Every year the Expo made metal pins featuring a fly pattern or aquatic insect; collectors loved them. Thirty years ago Hank created the Jones Canyon, called a "Jonzie" by most anglers. It became one of the most popular flies used by Northwest steelhead anglers, especially those fishing the Deschutes.

"In the world of fly tying," Art said, "Hank is king. His book, *True Flies: Practical Patterns for the Western Fly Angler,* is a classic."

"And fifteen years old," Hank said. "As old as the hills and twice as dusty. Like me."

"Classics never go out of style," Jackie said. "That's what makes them classics." She stood up. "I'm off to the ladies room," she said quietly to Hank. "I'll be right back."

After she left, Hank said to Art, "I've got a new steelhead fly. Might be even better than the Jonzie."

"You say that every year."

Hank reached into a shirt pocket and pulled out a Ziploc bag with some purple-hued flies. He tossed one in front of Art. "Try it. The Plum Dandy. Took a lot of fish for me last year."

Art examined the fly and nodded approvingly. "Three kinds of feathers. Each one will move at a different current speed. Perfect for transition water."

Hank nodded. "Movement is key."

Art whip-finished the head of the fly he was working on, then swept back the dubbing toward the tail.

"Nice damselfly," Hank said.

"Thanks. Speaking of damsels, apparently you're not with Ginny anymore."

Hank shook his head vigorously and rolled his eyes. "Noooo. No no no. Nope. She left over a year ago. Uh-uh." He shivered like he'd just stepped into a deep freeze. "I've given up on women. And vice versa. Never had a relationship go more than a year and a half."

"Yet here you are with a new lady friend. Jackie."

"We … just met," Hank said. "Yesterday."

Art nodded. "Well, I hope she lasts longer than …" Art looked up.

Hank followed his gaze. Jackie was coming back.

Jackie seemed fascinated by Art's damselfly. "How did you do that?" she asked. For the next hour, Hank and Art showed her how to tie a fly. As they left Art's table, Jackie said, "That's not easy, is it?"

"No," Hank said. "The little ones are even tougher. And tying them fast—like when you're doing it for a living—is … " He closed his mouth. No sense making a big deal out of himself.

"Don't be so modest," Jackie said. "I could show you some notes on a violin and how to hold a bow. But you're not going to walk on stage and play the Bruch concerto by the end of the week. Skill takes time and practice. And talent."

~

AFTER LUNCH JACKIE TOOK HANK to some art galleries. It was more interesting than he thought it would be. Then they walked in the park. Conversation centered on what they would do if they weren't busy with their respective careers. Neither had a clue, but both were open to anything.

By dinner, Hank knew he was smitten. He liked being with Jackie; she was so easy to talk to and understood where he was coming from. She was completely different from any woman he'd ever met. And he was different when he was around her. Softer, somehow. More open to whatever came his way. All he could think about was spending more time with her.

Love. God almighty. At his age. Practically at first sight. He'd never been hit with anything like this. Lust at first sight, yes. Hell yes— plenty of times. That was how his relationships with women always started: not from the heart, but from organs farther south, and while in a bar.

But he worried about their differences. A rough-hewn 58-year -old, six-foot-four professional fly tyer, Vietnam combat vet, lifelong trout bum, poor-as-dirt, barely educated, harmonica-playing son of a buckeroo; and a five-foot-three, sixteen-years-his-junior, classical violinist who spoke four languages and spent most of her time in a rarefied artsy world. How was that supposed to work?

But love. Good God.

AFTER DINNER HE DROVE JACKIE to her cousin's. As he parked in front of the house, he said, "Look, Jackie, I'd like to see more of you, starting tomorrow, if that's okay. But first there's a couple of things you need to know about me. And if you don't want to see me again … well, we'll each move on."

"Yes …" she said cautiously.

"First, I have a concealed weapons permit, and I'm armed."

Fear flooded Jackie's face.

"It's okay," Hank said. "I'm cool. I'm just kinda … Ever since Vietnam I've carried a gun. It makes me feel more secure." He managed a weak smile. "At least I don't sleep with it under my pillow anymore."

"Glad to know it!" Her expression eased somewhat.

Hank ran his fingers through his thick, curly hair and did a neck roll. "Another thing is … I've never been good with women— for the long run. I do and say stupid things. The only thing I'm good at is tying flies. And I was good in the Army." He wagged his head. "I was damn good in the Army. I was a Green Beret and a Lurp in Vietnam."

"A Lurp?"

"Long Range Reconnaissance Patrol—LRRP. We went on extended missions. Weeks in the field, deep in enemy territory. Recon, intelligence. Ambushes. We kicked some serious butt."

She looked at him questioningly. "You mean you killed a bunch of people."

"Yes." He shrugged. "It was a war. They were the enemy. And they were trying to kill me and my friends." Hank shook his head. " I was a kid, young and ignorant. I grew up near the Ochoco Mountains in eastern Oregon. To me, war was like elk hunting, only warmer. And the elk could shoot back, which made it more interesting."

"You were fighting for your country."

"Thanks for the thought, but not really," Hank said dismissively. "I *enlisted* for my country. After that I fought for my unit, for my buddies. I had no more understanding of why we were there than I had about global finance. Still don't. Fact was, I loved combat. It was an adrenaline rush. I was a crack shot—still am—and I was a natural warrior with nothing else to do at the time. I was in Vietnam for one year, then spent two years doing the same job in Laos and Cambodia—that's a secret, although everyone knows we did it."

"Shot anyone lately?"

"Not since 1973. We were disbanded in '74. Once I was state-side I could see that it would be a long time before we had any more wars; the public wouldn't stand for it. So I left the Army."

Jackie smiled at him. "Thanks for telling me. It was a long time ago. Like you said, you were a kid. And as for the other … let's not think too far ahead."

~

WHEN THE DOOR CLOSED BEHIND Jackie, Hank called his friend Lenny Burk. "Lenny," he said. "It's Hank. Can I crash on your sofa for a couple of nights?"

"Of course. You could have stayed here last night, you know."

"I didn't want to bother you for one night. But I've got some things I want to check out in town. It will take me a day or two. Maybe longer, if it goes well."

8

April 18: Maupin

CASEY WILLIAMS PARKED IN the OK Cafe's gravel lot and got out of his truck. Twenty-nine, blue-eyed, and with a compact build, he sported a sandy-colored beard on his square chin. He coughed a couple of times and rubbed his left shoulder—still tender from breaking down the Drift Inn door—and walked into the cafe.

While most of Maupin rested on a gentle slope midway between the river and the rimrock, the OK Cafe lay down the hill on the Deschutes' east bank—close to the river whose patrons it had served for over seventy-five years, most of that in the hands of the Boone family. More than a cafe, the OK rented simple cabins to anglers and sold T-shirts and other tourist items in a building next door. And it was home to Judd Boone's Rainbow Anglers, the outfitter that Casey guided for in the summer.

Some folks described the OK as funky, but Casey thought of it as homey. A false-fronted wooden building, built early in another century, housed the cafe. Small but not cramped, old without being tacky, the OK served simple food: burgers and other grilled fare, sandwiches, milkshakes. Near the door, three picnic tables with umbrellas awaited customers. When weather or desire ruled out *al fresco* dining, four high-backed brown-painted wooden booths—built by Judd in his workshop—could be found inside. Six swiveling stools, upholstered with green vinyl, stood on a riser in front of the counter.

Pictures mounted on the walls and the ceiling showed Maupin and the OK from the early 1900s to current times. Over Casey's favorite booth, two anglers in baggy pants squinted from a faded, sepia-toned photo; they stood in front of a Model A, each holding two big fish. Casey knew what the casual visitor did not: the men in the photo were Judd's father and grandfather. Next to them hung a recent color photo of Judd running Whitehorse Rapids in a driftboat.

"Hey!" said a voice from behind the counter. "It's the Hero of the Year!" Judd's wife, Susan—dark, short, and ever friendly—walked over and gave Casey a hug. "Good work, kid!" she said kindly. She returned to her place behind the counter. "What can I get you? It's on the house."

Casey slid into a wooden booth. "A Double Burger with fries. And two glasses of water." This was his first day back in Maupin. After he'd hauled Ernie from the burning Drift Inn, they'd treated him for smoke inhalation and kept him overnight for observation. Ernie was not so lucky; he was comatose at a hospital in The Dalles.

A younger version of Susan slipped into the booth, opposite Casey. It was her daughter, Helen, who helped at the OK when she wasn't working in the school's administrative department. Helen took Casey's hands in her own. "Glad you're okay," she said. "That was some thing you did."

"Anyone else would have done it. I was just there at the right time."

"No. Not everyone would have done it." She looked down at the tabletop. "Casey," she said quietly. "There's something you should know ... "

Casey heard a screen door slam, then Judd Boone's voice in the kitchen. "Later," said Helen with a squeeze of his hands. She returned to her place behind the counter.

Judd Boone strode into the room. He was skinny below the waist but had the wide shoulders, sinewy forearms, and big, calloused hands of someone who has spent most of his adult life rowing a boat on a river. He tipped back his sweat-stained Stetson and took the pipe from his mouth. "Got any good stuff left for me?" he said in a hearty voice to Helen.

"Here," Helen said, handing him a plate with the remains of a hamburger bun and two cold French fries. "Eat this up, and you can have seconds. And a glass of water for dessert. And sir? This is a no-smoking restaurant."

Judd inhaled loudly through his nose. "Ooo, feisty women around here tonight." He clenched the pipe back in his mouth and put the plate in the sink with the dirty dishes. He turned to his wife, Susan, who was wiping down the counter with a dish towel. "How about you?" he said to her, arching his eyebrows suggestively. "Have you got any good stuff left for me?"

Susan snapped the dish towel on his butt.

"Ow! Ow! Ow!" Judd said in mock injury. He faced Casey, "Watch out for these women, young Casey. They're dangerous. Especially the old one. She's cocky because last fall she got the biggest elk in Wasco County." Casey knew this to be true, although he was already on the Coast when it happened. "You know why she's such a good hunter?" Judd said, rocking back on the heels of his cowboy boots.

Casey smiled and spread his hands. "Why?"

"Because after flipping burgers around this place all summer, she's ready to *kill* something. Watch out she doesn't get you in her sights."

Susan pointed her index finger at Judd and jerked it like she'd just fired a gun.

"Dangerous!" Judd said. "Dangerous women around here!" He took off his Stetson, smoothed out his few remaining gray hairs, and scratched his bearded chin. "Casey ..." Judd's voice dropped to a more serious tone. "Good job saving Ernie from the Drift Inn. Hell of a thing to rush into a burning building and pull out some old geezer." Judd put the Stetson back on and took another puff from his pipe. "They figure out what started the fire?"

"Nope."

"I have a theory. Started in the kitchen. *Grease* fire."

Casey laughed. The Drift Inn had been notorious for its poor food. "Could've been," he said. Casey had nagging doubts about the fire's origin, but the investigators didn't share his suspicions. Anyway, he didn't want to talk about the fire. "When I came in," he said, "a young lady was leaving. A blonde girl. Is she new?"

"Diana. She's the summer hire. She's from Redmond."

Casey nodded. "Diana," he repeated. He leaned back in the booth and cocked his head. "So, what'd you find on the river?"

"Everything looks good. That snag that gave us fits in Old Reliable? It washed out with high water, so the run will be easier to fish this year. Grass is tall and growing well, so there'll be lots of ticks.

And of course it also means we could have wildfire problems when it dries out. BLM set up more of those high-tech outhouses. Too bad you couldn't go with us."

"Sorry."

"Well," Judd said, "you had a reasonable excuse." He pointed his finger at Casey and put on a tone of mock sternness. "But it's only good once!"

Helen came over and put some broken plastic knobs on the table. "While you were gone," she said, "the knobs fell off again. I think it's time to get a new microwave."

"Oh, I think there's a simpler solution than that," Judd said. He disappeared for a couple of minutes and came back with two vise-grip pliers. He clamped them to the microwave's control stems. "That ought to do it," he said proudly. "Just twist those. Better than new. Gives you extra leverage."

Helen looked dubious. "I think we need a new oven. With a digital pad. Something made in this millennium."

"Just try this for a while. It'll work fine." Judd walked toward the kitchen, headed for the back door. Directing his voice to no one in particular he said, "If there're a couple of pork chops left, I'd appreciate it if Thelma and Louise here would whup 'em up while I'm hosing down my boat." Just before the screen door slammed, Casey heard him say loudly, "You know, there really ought to be a Society for the Prevention of Cruelty to Old Fishing Guides."

Casey smiled and shook his head. When he was fourteen, his father died in a logging accident. Casey went through a difficult, angry time, and was often in trouble. School—never his strong suit due to his dyslexia—became a battleground. By the time he was seventeen he was failing all his classes, his mother was distraught, his older sister wouldn't talk to him, and most people in town had written him off. Then Judd took him under his wing. He gave Casey useful jobs, took him fishing, and issued a few pointers about life. Thanks to help from Judd and a few others, Casey got himself together. He loved Judd like a father, even though Casey often screwed up when he was around him.

When Susan disappeared into the food storage area to get some chops for Judd, Helen slid quickly into Casey's booth. "Look," she said, "you need to know something." She looked back over her shoulder, then at Casey. "Megan's coming back. In a couple of weeks."

Casey's blood went cold. He'd rather run back into the burning Drift Inn than hear this.

"We have a pregnant teacher at the school. She's due in two months and has taken a leave for the rest of the year. Megan's been hired as the substitute. Through the rest of the year. Maybe permanent. She's rented a house in town."

"Is she still living with that guy in Portland?"

"Dumped him last December." Helen shook the hair from her eyes. "She wanted this job. She lobbied hard to get it. She'll be here a lot. You're going to have to deal with it." She squeezed his hands. "I thought you should know so you could … you know … be ready."

Casey closed his eyes, breathing heavily. *Be ready? Not if I had a million years.*

2: Rainbows

9

May 10: Maupin

LOGAN MCCREA SLID *The Complete Works of Shakespeare* into the bookcase beside two linear feet of computer references. Then he flattened the cardboard box and tossed it onto the stack with the others.

He scanned the living room of the small rental house in Maupin; it was starting to look homey. In another week or so his affairs in Newberg would be wrapped up, and he and Sam would shift their lives to this new place.

Since his meeting with Bill Short, Logan had been to Maupin five times—twice to find the rental house, then three more, including today, pulling a horse trailer filled with boxes, clothes, and furniture. Over the last six months he'd sold nearly everything he owned on eBay and Craigslist, so it was easy work.

He'd used some of his precious cash reserves to buy curtains and other cheery accessories so the rental would look good to Sam. Her bad leg ruled out heavy lifting, so she'd stayed home and hadn't yet seen the house. If Sam had an opinion about the move—or thoughts or emotions of any other sort—she hadn't shared them with Logan.

Besides the piecemeal relocation of his household, Logan's official purpose for these trips was "reconnaissance." After unloading the trailer he'd go to the river, splitting his attention between trout fishing and looking for suspicious people. He hadn't spotted any terrorists, a fact he dutifully reported to Bill Short. He'd also caught some nice rainbow trout on dry flies, but he left that out.

~

HIS FINAL MOVING CHORE COMPLETED, Logan drove up the bumpy access road and parked at the Locked Gate six miles upstream from Maupin. He checked the time: 12:30—the blue-winged olive hatch would start in an hour or so.

The temperature was cool, and the somber, gray sky occasionally spat rain. These were perfect conditions for a spring hatch, and Logan felt a tingle of anticipation as he donned his waders and jacket. He walked upstream to a favorite spot, then sat on a rock and waited.

When fishing the blue-wing hatch, Logan preferred backeddies—places where the river creates a large circulating counter-current downstream from a point of land. The Deschutes is backeddy-rich; some are hundreds of feet long and extend across half the river.

Logan knew from experience that the little blue-winged olive mayflies would emerge in the water upstream, then drift into this backeddy. They would go round and round until ready to fly off. The current concentrated the insects, which made it a perfect place for trout to feed—a giant lazy Susan delivering a steady supply of fresh food.

Logan spotted a few blue-wings in the backeddy but resisted the temptation to cast. More floated in. Then a small ring appeared, and a blue-wing was gone, eaten by a trout. Another rise ring, then another. He could see dark, shifting shadows half a foot below the surface. These were trout, waiting for insects to drift into their feeding lanes.

Logan rose and prepared to cast. He waited until he knew where a trout was lying, made two false casts to work out line, and let his fly drop gently onto the water. There was no response, and he cast again. Still no response, and he made a third cast.

Backeddy fishing is tricky. Logan's floating flyline lay across bands of current moving in different directions. The opposing forces pulled at his line and made his fly drag unnaturally. He knew that if he imposed his will, heedless of conflicting currents, he'd never connect with a rainbow. To avoid this problem, Logan knew a few special casts that would give his leader enough slack so the fly would drift more naturally.

Sometimes, however, he would have the wrong fly. Other times the fly would be right, but the cast would be to the wrong place. Or the trout would move. Or his leader wouldn't be supple enough. Or, more likely, he'd have the wrong standpoint. It was vital to be in the right place, a spot that gave his fly the best chance of a natural, trout-enticing drift.

Logan stopped casting and studied the water. He shifted his standpoint and cast again. He gave slack when needed and waited patiently. This time he was rewarded with the sight of a rising rainbow. He was connected.

He caught six more trout before the hatch faded; each trout was carefully returned to the river.

It had been a good day, a hopeful day. How appropriate, he thought, to be on this river of grace and catching rainbows. Such a beautiful fish and such a beautiful name. Rainbow: the sign of promise, of clearing after the storm, of hope for a new life and a brighter day.

Perhaps, he reflected, his life had finally returned to a positive trajectory. The rental house was small and old, but it would be adequate for Sam and him. He had employment through October and would spend the summer on the river he loved more than any other. Some of his debts were cleared.

But what about the $237,000 he owed Med-Rec? What would he do when this temporary job was over? Where would they live then? Where would the money come from? What about Sam's college?

What about Sam?

These worries seized his mind, and an afternoon that had been buoyant and hopeful sank into anxiety and despair.

10

May 16: On the Road to Maupin

ON A SUNDAY IN MID-MAY LOGAN and Sam loaded the two horses in the trailer and left Newberg for good. It had been a cool, wet May—shaping up to be one of the wettest on record—and there was a threat of snow on Highway 26 as it crossed a shoulder of Mt. Hood. Leery of pulling a horse trailer on a snowy road, Logan took the longer but lower route up the Columbia River. He turned onto Highway 197 at The Dalles; Maupin lay forty-some miles to the south.

The land rolled on, big and empty—wheat country. Almost halfway to Maupin, some antique farm machinery quietly rusted on the left side of the road. A faded sign invited people to "Come to the Dufur Threshing Bee" but didn't say when to come. A mileage sign announced "Tygh Valley 16 / Maupin 26."

"So I'm going to live in a town called Maupin," said Sam, "and my nearest neighbors will be in Dufus and Tiggy Valley? Is Dufus where you go for fun?"

"Dufur, rhymes with two-fer. Tygh, rhymes with fly. Tygh Valley is smaller than Maupin. Dufur's a little bigger. Maupin has about 500 people. The business district is two blocks long. Parts of town look pretty good, and some parts … are how they looked fifty years ago, which was the last time they saw a coat of paint."

"Dufur and Tygh Valley and Maupin," she mused, emphasizing the DOO in Dufur and popping the *p* in Maupin. "Who am I going to talk to?"

This was a major concern for Logan. Sam's close friends had left for college. She was headed for Stanford, but the accident changed everything. First she was in the hospital, then physical therapy. And now there was no money. Logan knew Sam felt trapped and lonely. She spent far too much time in her room listening to music that was angry and depressing, at least to Logan's ear. He hoped the change of scenery would stir both of them to new life.

"You'll find somebody," Logan said.

"I don't know how to talk to country people."

"They're just people. Make small talk as an opener. You know, the weather, the food. Stuff."

"You mean like, 'Nice shirt! Did you get it in DOOfer or Maup!-in?'"

Logan smiled. It was the closest to humor she'd come in months. "Yeah, like that. As for what to do, why don't you come on the river with me while I work on this guidebook?"

"It's not a guidebook, is it?" She said, suddenly serious. "You're doing something for that Dietz guy."

Logan didn't reply.

"Is it dangerous?"

He chewed his lip. "No," he said. "It's probably a boondoggle. Dietz is paying me back for when I saved his bacon in Germany."

~

As HE PARKED THE TRUCK in front of their rental house, Logan felt he should prepare Sam. "The house is not what you're used to," he said. "The best way to describe it is 'cozy, quaint, and nostalgic.'"

"In other words," Sam said, "the house is small, old, and the wallpaper dates from the Johnson administration."

"That's about right. Except the wallpaper is more Truman era."

"What are those trees around it?" Sam asked.

"A mix of pine, locust, elm, and oak. They'll provide shade during the heat of the summer." He pointed toward a house about 200 yards away. "Same as around the Deckers' house. Ty Decker is our landlord. Most of his land is used for growing alfalfa and wheat, and he keeps a few cattle." Logan pointed south. "He stores grain in those silos until the prices are good." He moved his finger to the east. "The greenhouses are for his organic produce business. He and his wife go to farmer's markets. They also run a CSA—Community-Supported Agriculture."

Sam looked around at the scattering of outbuildings, farm machinery, and old cars. "It's very … country," she said.

Logan unloaded the horses, then led Sam to the house. After looking around—it didn't take long—she put her hands on her hips and said, "It'll do. When's lunch?"

"The grocery store is closed for remodeling. I thought we'd go to the OK Cafe. It has good burgers and milkshakes. After lunch we can drive back to The Dalles and load up on groceries."

~

ONCE IN THE OK CAFE, LOGAN thought he'd show Sam how to talk to local people. They entered and sat on the counter stools. A dark-haired middle-aged woman was barely visible around the corner, doing food preparation. A young pretty waitress was wiping down the counter in front of Logan. A nametag identified her as Diana. As she worked, Diana's apron and blouse fell open and revealed an expanse of tanned and jiggling bosom. But Logan wasn't focused on her. He was looking over her shoulder at the microwave; the plastic knobs had been replaced with a pair of vise-grip pliers.

"Hi, Diana," he said. He cocked his head toward the microwave. "Nice knobs."

Diana sprang back red-faced and put her arms to her neck, covering her chest. Logan hadn't expected this reaction. He looked at Sam. Her face was strained, her eyes bright and bulging. She began to cough, but it sounded fake.

What had he said? His mind rummaged over the images of the last few seconds. The microwave. Peripherally, the waitress wiping the counter. His remark. Suddenly his face felt very warm. He pointed a finger at the microwave. "The vise-grips." He jabbed a finger for emphasis. "On the microwave. Nice … controls."

The waitress relaxed her shoulders. "Oh, yeah." She turned and looked at the vise-grips, then back to Logan. "Gotta replace that thing. Judd's pretty frugal. 'Make it. Make it do. Do without.' I guess that's 'make it do.'"

They ate their burgers in silence, but occasionally Sam looked down and shook her head. Back in the truck, she said, "Yeah, Dad, you're really good at that country talk. I can hardly wait to hear more of it."

Logan looked sheepish and shrugged. At least it got Sam talking. And laughing. He hadn't seen her so light-hearted since before the accident. This move to Maupin was going to be good for both of them. A new beginning, *tabula rasa*.

~

THE MICROWAVE INCIDENT WAS on Sunday. Monday morning Logan got his camping and fishing gear together and prepared his driftboat. He planned to float the river from Warm Springs to Maupin starting the next day—more "reconnaissance" with a lot of fly fishing on the side. In preparation, he went to get a fishing report from a local fly shop.

Maupin boasted two fly shops: Deschutes River Fly and Tackle, which was up the hill in the main business district, and Deschutes

River Fly Shop, down the hill near the OK Cafe. The first was owned by Dave Jansen, the other by Dave Tindal. Logan had no problem keeping them straight, but Sam tended to mix them up because the shop names were so similar and the owners were both named Dave. So for clarity, Logan called them Upper Dave and Lower Dave, from the location of their shops.

Logan went to Lower Dave's for his report. Sam limped into the store with him. Two men were talking to Lower Dave. One was an older man, late middle age, tall with thick curly hair and a reddish beard. The other was a young sandy-haired guy, maybe late twenties—average height, with a patch of beard on his chin. He was permanently tanned, a bit stocky, and had powerful shoulders; Logan pegged him as a fishing guide. The two men stopped talking when Logan entered.

"Good morning," Logan said to Lower Dave. "I'm starting a float trip tomorrow. Warm Springs to Maupin. What's hatching, and what flies do I need?"

"Blue-winged olives are mostly done," said Lower Dave. "But the salmonflies are out, and the golden stones are starting to hatch."

"Isn't that early? I wouldn't expect them for another week or two."

"There's a new mixing tower at the dam," said the sandy-haired man. "They take more water from the surface in the spring, and that makes the river a couple of degrees warmer than usual."

"Then in the summer, they'll take cooler water from the bottom," said the tall bearded man. "We don't know how that will affect the steelhead."

"Stoneflies start hatching when the water temp hits 52 degrees," said Dave. "Everything's early. Most people haven't caught on. Between the early hatch and the crummy weather, you'll have the river to yourself. As the day warms up, the adult salmonflies and golden stones get active and land on the river. So nymphs in the morning, dry flies in the afternoon and evening."

Dave went to the fly bins. "Use a two-nymph rig with a Soft

Rock …" he held up a stonefly nymph imitation "… and an SDP. For an adult, you can't go wrong with an O Stone."

"Don't use those," said the bearded man. "They're crap. Worthless. Designed by an idiot, tied by an old geezer with ten left thumbs."

"Thumbs?" said the young guy. "I thought he tied them with his toes."

"Don't listen to them," said Lower Dave. "They're just locals who hang around the shop because they're too lazy to get real jobs."

"Hear that, Casey?" said the bearded man. "We've been insulted. We'll have to go somewhere else for our free coffee." His voice was surprisingly soft and slow-cadenced for a man of his commanding size, and Logan suspected he'd been raised around large, skittish animals—probably cattle and horses, maybe sheep.

"This is Casey Williams," said Dave, pointing at the young man. "He's a guide. Works for Judd Boone." Dave's finger shifted to the bearded man. "And this hunk of meat is Hank O'Leary. He played Chewbacca in the first *Star Wars* movie because he didn't need any makeup and came with his own bandolier. He's dumb as a post, but he ties good flies. He invented the Soft Rock, SDP, and O Stone. He tied these."

Logan shook hands with both men and introduced Sam. He tried to act cool, but he was really impressed. Hank O'Leary was famous. Like every serious fly fisher, Logan owned his classic fly tying book, *True Flies: Practical Patterns for the Western Fly Angler*, but he'd never met the man.

"Dave's right," said Casey. "I just finished a Trout Creek-to-Maupin trip, and those were the killer flies. Soft Rock for the big nymph and an SDP for a caddis pupa and—"

"SDP?" Logan asked.

Dave seemed suddenly distracted, and his face took on a hard look. At first Logan wondered if he'd asked a dumb question, but then he saw Dave's focus was outside, beyond the glass door. Logan turned and saw a pickup pass by—scruffy and pulling an equally scruffy red-and-blue aluminum driftboat. "SDP?" Logan repeated.

"Oh. Excuse me," Dave said, his focus back inside his shop. "Supa Dupa Pupa. And the O Stone for an adult pattern."

"You might want a few of the O Stone Layers, too," said Hank. "It imitates the egg-laying females when they come back to the water."

Logan bought a dozen of each; he could expense it to Bill Short. As he and Sam headed out the door, a fortyish Asian-looking woman came into the shop, walked up to Hank, and hung on his arm. She looked familiar to Logan.

Back in the truck Logan said to Sam, "I know that woman from somewhere. Who is she?" He had a thought and thumbed through some album covers on his smart phone. He stopped at one, then showed it to Sam. "She looks exactly like Jacqueline Moreau," Logan said, "except for the fancy hairdo and dress in the photo."

"Who's Jacqueline Moreau?" asked Sam.

"One of the top classical violinists in the world. I have several of her CDs and a bunch of downloads off iTunes. Her recording of the Sibelius concerto is sublime."

"What would she be doing in a fly shop in Maupin?"

Logan waved his hand dismissively. "Oh, it isn't her. Remarkable resemblance, though."

11

May 17: Highway 197 South of Maupin

JOHN KINCAID CHECKED HIS rearview mirror to see if anyone was following him. He saw an empty road behind his red-and-blue driftboat. Still, he couldn't shake the feeling that someone was watching him. But then, he always felt that way.

He planned to launch his boat at Trout Creek and carefully make his way downriver, camping at a few favorite spots. He had his fly rods and would make a show of fishing. If anyone saw him, he'd just look like another angler making a three- or four-day fishing trip. Then at night when no one was around, he'd bury the stash given him by the neatly dressed man with the wire-framed glasses.

Kincaid didn't know what the man with the glasses had given him, nor did he know his name. No doubt it was drugs, and the man was some sort of dealer selling to suburban users. No matter. He'd get his money, and their stash would be well hidden.

Kincaid was proud of his ability to hide things where no one could find them. This was the fifth time in three years that he'd done this kind of job and the third time he'd used the Deschutes as the hiding place. It seemed to be the last place anyone thought of looking. He was just another driftboat floating down the river, making occasional stops to catch some trout. No one would suspect the truth.

Near Criterion Summit, a car appeared in his rearview mirror and followed him for several minutes. Kincaid slowed to let it pass. It didn't. Could be a cautious driver. Or …

He noted the make and color, then pulled onto the shoulder. The car passed him. Still, Kincaid lingered. He pretended to check his tires, then his trailer lights. After five minutes he pulled back onto the highway. He drove on, looking ahead for the car he'd seen earlier, looking behind for anyone else that might be following him.

12

May 17: The Dalles, Oregon

MONDAY AFTERNOON CASEY Williams drove to The Dalles, a mid-sized town on the Columbia River. He needed groceries, and he wanted to see Ernie Doyle, the man he'd pulled from the fire at the Drift Inn.

Ernie's dog, a yellow Labrador named Joey, sat next to Casey. Casey had been taking care of Joey while Ernie was in the hospital. Since the fire, Ernie had been in a coma. TBI—Traumatic Brain Injury—the doctors said; in addition to the smoke inhalation, Ernie had suffered a serious blow to the head.

Casey went into Ernie's hospital room. It looked the same as when he'd been there two weeks ago: tubes and wires hooked up to Ernie, and Ernie lying still, eyes closed. "I'm taking care of your dog," Casey said. "The kid next door looks after him when I'm on the river." There was no response.

A nurse came in. "Any change?" Casey asked her.

"No," she said. "He could be like this for a long time." She paused. "Maybe forever. There's been brain swelling, and it takes a while for that to go down. Could be weeks, maybe months. He was hit pretty hard."

"Will he be okay when ... if ... he wakes up?"

"We don't know. We can only wait and see." She gave him a sympathetic look. "Good friend or relative of yours?"

"Sort of a friend."

~

IT WAS ALMOST DARK WHEN Casey headed back to Maupin. He thought about the fire and Old Ernie as he drove. The whole thing bothered him—not just that Ernie was in such a state but that no one knew for sure what had happened.

They knew that a beam had broken in the fire and fallen down, but the beam was in the kitchen, and Casey had found Ernie in the hall. The theory was that Ernie had tried to cook up some bacon for himself, but the grease flared up and started a fire in the grill vent. Ernie was hit by something—the falling beam?—and staggered into the hall before collapsing.

Casey wasn't so sure. When he'd found Ernie, a cast-iron skillet lay near him. Further, Casey didn't think the beam had fallen down yet. And then there was the matter of Ernie's keys. When Casey had arrived at the fire, the Drift Inn's door had been dead-bolted shut. Ernie would have left it unlocked. Even if he'd locked it, he'd have left his keys on the table by the back door. But Ernie's keys were never found. It was like the door had been locked from the outside. But by whom?

Something else irked Casey. The authorities, along with most of the town, had written Ernie off as an alcoholic. "He got drunk and did something stupid," people said. "Sure it doesn't make sense, but you know Old Ernie; he could have done anything." That seemed to be enough.

But Casey wasn't satisfied. Ernie had been trying to sober up, and no one had seen him drunk for a year. Every time Ernie had an overwhelming urge to drink, he took Joey for a walk. Sometimes he took three or four walks a day, long ones. Casey often saw them striding along the Deschutes access roads, Ernie looking resolute, Joey happy and with his tongue hanging out. Last fall, when most of his guide trips were one-day floats near town, Casey would go up to the road and ask Ernie who was catching fish and where. Ernie saw it all. He was lucid and observant, not drunk and stupid.

When Casey had expressed doubts about the official version of the fire, people told him he'd been gone all winter and hadn't seen Ernie, that Ernie had probably fallen off the wagon. No one had seen him drunk that winter, but they knew his past. It didn't seem fair that

Ernie was getting his life together, then this happened to him. And that everyone wrote him off because of the way he used to be, not how he was now. Besides, why would anyone try to kill a harmless old coot like Ernie?

By the time he reached Maupin, Casey decided he was just imagining things, had seen too many TV shows. The official explanation made the most sense.

~

CASEY DIDN'T FEEL LIKE GOING home and eating dinner alone. So he headed for the OK, hoping to be around some people.

There was only one car in the parking lot. Through the window he could see someone sipping coffee in a booth: shortish, late twenties, dark hair that was mostly straight but with a few unruly curls, navy turtleneck stretched over a trim but perky figure, black-framed glasses in the current style. He hadn't seen her in nine years, but there was no mistaking her. She was Megan Boone—Susan and Judd's daughter, Helen's sister, the first and strongest love of Casey's life, the woman who'd hurt him more than anyone on earth.

Megan had been back in town over a week, but Casey had been on multi-day float trips and hadn't seen her. He took a few deep breaths. He had to see her sometime. He couldn't avoid her. But what would it be like? What would they say to each other? They couldn't pick up where they'd left off, with her telling him she didn't want to be with him anymore—with her telling him he was an immature small-town screw-up who would never amount to anything and was totally beneath her intellectual level and had no sophistication and no taste for the finer things in life and only wanted to play computer games and go fly fishing and she no longer had anything in common with him and couldn't understand why she'd ever thought she was in love with him and when would he grow up—probably never. Well, she hadn't said it in those exact words. But she'd said it.

His self-esteem was fragile at that time of his life, and she'd shattered what little he possessed. It had taken him years to get over the things she'd said. Now all the pain and inadequacy flooded back. And, tell the truth, the anger. He wanted to ask her—demand from her—if she really thought he was that bad.

He opened the truck door and got out, but stood unmoving in the dark. More questions came. *If the great big world is so wonderful, how come so many people go to the Deschutes to get away from it? Those other guys you were with, were they better than me? Or just different? I've changed; I'm not the unreliable, self-centered, computer-gaming, joke-playing dude I used to be. Can you see it? Sure, I don't sit around and read Shakespeare and stuff; I'm dyslexic, remember? It's hard for me to read, damn hard, and I was never any good at school. But that doesn't mean I'm stupid and worthless. Don't you see the difference in me? Or do you just see me the way I used to be?*

Those were the questions he wanted to ask but couldn't, shouldn't. He walked toward the OK and stood with his hand on the doorknob and thought of bigger questions, gentler questions. *How are you? What have you been doing? What do you think about … everything? I've changed; have you?*

And the question behind all the other questions: *Are you going to break my heart all over again?*

He took another big breath and walked into the OK. Helen, Megan's sister, was cleaning the grill. When she saw Casey she left the room.

Megan looked up from her table. A cup of coffee sat in front of her. "Oh. Casey. Hi." She wrapped a lock of hair around her right forefinger.

"Megan." He looked around the room, then back at her. "How's it going?"

"Good." Megan put a spoon in her coffee and stirred it carefully, although she always drank it black. "And you?"

"Oh, you know, guiding. For your father." He forced a smile and waved a hand. "But I guess you knew that." He tried to act casual, like they'd seen each other last week. "Just got back from a three-day trip. Salmonfly season you know."

"Yeah." She brought the coffee to her lips, but the spoon hit her cheek. She put the cup back down and slowly removed the spoon. "I hear they're early this year." She put an elbow on the table, then raised the cup again and took a slow sip. "Not their usual time."

Casey nodded. "Yup. Early." He kept nodding. "A couple of weeks early. Most people haven't figured it out yet. There's some good fishing now."

"Dad got a new microwave for the restaurant," Megan said. "Helen and Diana insisted. Diana's the new girl, the summer help."

"A new microwave!" Casey said like one of them had just won the lottery. "That's terrific." He rocked back on his heels and folded his arms across his chest, then pointed a finger at her. "I hear you're teaching at the school."

"Uh-huh. High school English. The rest of the year. Tutoring and summer school, too." She was nodding her head. They were both nodding their heads.

"Yeah, high school." Casey looked reflective. "English," he said thoughtfully. He reached up to run his hand through his hair, forgetting he was wearing a hat. The hat thunked to the floor. He reached down slowly to pick it up. "Well, nice to see you again." He straightened up and put the hat back on. "I'd better get my stuff ready. Back-to-back three-day floats starting Wednesday." He headed for the door. "See you around."

"You too. Bye."

He got into his truck and slammed his fist on the steering wheel, making the horn honk. He saw Megan look up, startled at the sound. He waved to say it was okay—just an accidental toot—then realized she couldn't see him. He drove off, swallowed whole by the black night.

THE NEXT MORNING CASEY WENT in search of a cup of coffee and someone to talk to. Normally he'd have gone to the OK, but he didn't want to go there because … well, just because. So he went into Lower Dave's fly shop; Dave always kept a pot handy.

The shop was empty, which was not unusual for a weekday at this time of year. "Morning, Dave," Casey hollered up to the loft where Dave worked when no one was in the shop.

"Hey, Casey, what can I get you?"

"Nothing. I came for a cup of your free coffee. Got any other free stuff?"

"Sure, take a couple of spey rods and some high-end reels. Load up your truck with waders while you're at it." There were footsteps on the stairs, and Dave appeared, hand outstretched. "How are you?"

"Oh, I'm okay."

Apparently Casey said it with as much conviction as he felt, which wasn't much. "Trouble in Casey-land?" Dave asked.

Casey paused, then told Dave the details of last night's awkward encounter with Megan Boone. "I don't know what to do next," he said when he was finished.

"Well, Casey, if you're looking for advice about women, I'm not your man." The shop door opened, and Hank O'Leary came in. "And neither is he," Dave said, pointing at Hank. "Casey's got woman troubles," Dave said to Hank. "Megan's back in town, you know."

Hank held up both hands in a back-off gesture. "Don't look to me for advice," he said. "Or better yet, watch what I do, then do the opposite."

"I don't know about that," said Dave. "I see you've got a new lady staying with you. Pretty classy lassie. Not like the usual bimbos you hook up with."

"Do I have a reputation?" Hank said.

Dave was silent. Casey feigned interest in the rack of spey rods.

"Look," Hank said. "I've never been Mr. Touchy-Feely-Sensitive-Guy when it comes to women, but Jackie's really good at these things. Maybe she can help." He went to his truck and returned with Jackie.

Casey was extremely uneasy. He didn't want the whole town involved in his love life, or lack of it. It was only a moment of despair that made him tell Dave. Now Hank was in on it, and then his ladyfriend would know. If he wasn't careful, they'd organize a betting pool at the Rainbow Tavern: "Pick the date that Megan Boone dumps Casey. Again." There'd be fierce competition for the earliest possible date.

Casey stood by uneasily while Dave told Jackie the brief and ancient history of Casey and Megan. "And now she's back in town," Dave concluded.

"Hmm," Jackie said. "Very interesting." She looked deep in thought. "I wonder why she came back?"

Casey shrugged.

"I am very discreet," said Jackie. "I will speak to no one."

This made Casey feel better. He liked Jackie, with her vaguely foreign accent, exotic looks, and friendly manner. And she seemed to understand his unease.

"You knew her in high school?" Jackie said. "Went with her then?"

"And for a year after. Until her second year of college."

"Ah, and she broke it off then. No fight, just ended it?" She paused, looking thoughtful. "Did you …?" She looked expectant.

Boy, did they. After graduation. And all summer. And when she came home for breaks. Did Judd know? Would he have killed him if he did? Casey felt embarrassed. He looked everywhere but at Jackie. He said nothing.

"I see," Jackie said knowingly. She cocked her head slightly. "And your meeting last night was the first time you'd seen each other since the breakup?"

Casey nodded.

"And it was awkward?"

Casey nodded again.

"For both of you?"

This last question seemed to be important. Casey thought about it a little while. "I think so."

"That is a good sign for you," said Jackie.

"Why is that a good sign?"

"It means she has many questions and didn't know where to start. If she didn't care, she'd have blown you off." She held her hand near her mouth and blew across it. "Poof. 'Leave me alone. You are my past, not my future.'"

Casey looked at Hank, who was giving him an I-told-you-she-was-good look. He turned back to Jackie. "So what should I do?"

"Be a friend. Build a new relationship, a different kind of relationship. If you can't get to friendship, you have no hope. But from friendship, you can go many places, all of them good. You are both older, different. You need to learn about each other all over again. You may not get to where you want to be, but it's better than where you are now. You may not want to risk your heart, but you will have to. You must have patience. Go slowly. And forget the past."

"How can I forget the past?"

"You will have to find a way." She cocked her head to one side and looked at Casey with narrowed eyes. "Another thing. We women like our mysteries. We will reveal them to you when we feel comfortable. Maybe never. Do not force our secrets from us."

Casey wasn't sure what this last bit meant, but he nodded his head anyway.

13

May 18: Deschutes River

TUESDAY NEAR NOON, LOGAN and Sam launched at Warm Springs. Temperatures hovered in the mid-50s, and the wind blew lightly. The clouds were close and moving, the sky a shifting mix of blue, white, and gray. The hills were the luminous green that comes from a rainy spring.

That young guide—Casey?—was right. No other boats plied the river, no trailers cluttered the parking lot by the boat ramp. And salmonflies were thick in the bankside grasses and alder trees. Logan showed one to Sam.

"It's huge!" she said.

"Biggest bug on the river. Over two inches long. Three and a half if you count the antennae and tails. After living in the river for three years, the nymph crawls underwater to shore and climbs up on the rocks or grass stems. The back splits open, then the adult emerges, unfurls its wings, and flies off." He pointed to some empty exoskeletons on a rock.

"So they leave the old world, and suddenly they're a completely different creature!" she said.

Kind of like us, Logan thought. *I hope.*

He let the current carry them downriver, occasionally pulling on the oars to keep the boat in the best part of the flow. Logan used a sixteen-foot driftboat, a craft ubiquitous on western rivers. Sometimes called McKenzie boats, they are wide-bottomed dories modified for whitewater. Logan's boat had no motor; power was not allowed on this part of the Deschutes.

Shortly after the Highway 26 bridge, he anchored off the west side of an island. "The nymphs drift in the current in the morning," he said to Sam, "and the adults are active in the afternoon. So we'll start with nymphs." He handed her a fly rod.

"No, I'll just watch," she said. "It's been a long time since I cast a fly. And I'm not sure my leg is strong enough for wading. You fish."

Logan nodded. He stepped out of the boat and picked a rod with the two-nymph rig Lower Dave had suggested. He tied a puff of white yarn to the leader for an indicator. The nymphs would drift near the river bottom, and the yarn would float on the surface. If the yarn went under, it meant a fish had grabbed one of the flies—or that he'd snagged a rock.

He waded upstream from the boat and cast his flies into a narrow seam between fast and slow water, favoring the slower side. His strategy was to make four casts, each landing in a slightly different place, then wade upstream about ten feet and do it again. And so on, until he'd covered all the good water alongside the island.

Crickets chirped in the grass. The sawmill on the Indian side of the river made faint industrial sounds. The sun played peek-a-boo through the clouds, making Logan first hot, then cool. An osprey circled high above the river. A line of verse came to mind: "What hovering, taloned fate/waits to drop on me?" He shook off the feeling of imminent doom and took a deep breath, reveling in the scent of sagebrush and juniper.

It wasn't long before his indicator went down. He set the hook and met solid resistance. Too solid. "Rock," he said over his shoulder to Sam. He worked the flies loose and resumed casting. The indicator went down again, and this time it was a fish. It ripped for mid-river, then headed downstream, taking line from the reel. Logan worked the trout into quiet water and soon had it to hand.

The rainbow was thirteen inches long, respectable but not large. And fat! Like all Deschutes' trout, it was a wild, native fish; no hatchery-raised trout were stocked in the river. He gently removed the hook from its jaw and released it. Logan caught two more fish alongside the island before returning to the boat.

"Well, done, Dad!" said Sam. "Looks like you know what you're doing."

"I know this hatch really well. I used to fish it every year. And this is the stretch of river I know best, from Warm Springs to Trout Creek. My ignorance will become obvious when we get below Trout Creek. I've never fished that part of the river except around South Junction."

"You haven't floated below Trout Creek?"

He shook his head. Truth to tell, he was worried about it. Some tricky and dangerous rapids awaited them, Whitehorse in particular. He'd never run it, and his boating skills felt rusty.

They left the island and drifted downstream about a mile. "How come you're not fishing the west bank?" Sam asked.

"That's the Warm Springs Reservation—officially the Indians are the Confederated Tribes of the Warm Springs Reservation. They're actually three tribes: Wasco, Warm Springs, and a Paiute band. The Reservation borders the Deschutes for almost thirty miles below the boat ramp. You can get a permit to fish seven miles between Dry Creek and Trout Creek, but the rest of it is off-limits to non-tribal members."

"And you're not fishing from the boat because … ?"

"Because the regulations don't allow it. It's a fish conservation thing."

An extensive area of flat land came into view on the east side. "Mecca Flat," said Logan. "There's an island at the upper end that can be good." He anchored at the lower tip of the island, planning to fish his way to the top, as at the previous stop.

He took another trout on the nymph rig about mid-island. As he neared the island's headend, he sensed something on the back of his neck. He grabbed and looked. It was a salmonfly. He tossed the bug in the air. A clumsy flier, it fell onto the water and floated downstream about ten feet before disappearing in a sudden splash—devoured by a trout. "Hmmm," Logan said with mingled curiosity and anticipation.

Logan watched another salmonfly land on the water. Instantly a trout rose and swallowed it. Out of his left eye, he could see long antennae wiggling along the edge his baseball hat. A salmonfly soon peeked over the edge and looked at him. Clearly the day had warmed enough to get the insects active, and trout were looking for them. Logan went back for his dry-fly rod.

Starting where he'd left off, he cast an O Stone into the fast seam of water as it poured around the island. A trout rose up and grabbed his fly with a head-and-tail rise, then raced down and across at a rapid clip. Logan's reel spun, and his rod bent in a deep arc. The fish leaped from the water. "You're a fat bugger!" he said to the trout. It took several minutes to bring it to hand. He measured the trout against his rod—sixteen inches and over two pounds. He let the fish go.

Two casts later, he had another fish, slightly smaller. Then another. And another. The trout were plump, sassy, and eager for his dry fly. And he shared the river with no one.

At the next stop, he encouraged Sam to get out and fish. He supported her as she waded and coached her as she cast. Soon she could throw a fly forty feet with reasonable accuracy. When she started catching trout, she got excited.

For the rest of Tuesday, Sam would fish for a while, then Logan, then they'd float to the next good spot.

They camped a couple of miles below Trout Creek. Over dinner, Sam said, "Didn't we camp at Trout Creek when I was a kid?"

"We did. You, me, and … and Mom." They were silent for a minute, then Logan said, "I miss your mother. So much. She was a saint. Kind, generous to a fault, upbeat, full of life. Loved animals and being outdoors."

"I miss her too," Sam said, looking out to the river. "Dad …" she said. She opened her mouth like she was about to say something more, then closed it.

"Yes?"

"Nothing."

WEDNESDAY WAS TUESDAY'S clone, offering plentiful trout and no people. Logan couldn't believe his good fortune: back on the river he loved more than any other, epic fishing, Sam talking to him and in a good mood. And he was going to do this all summer. "Bless you, CIA," he said under his breath. "And bless you, Paranoid America."

The depression and anxiety that had clung to him like caked mud began to wash away. It was noon Wednesday before he realized that it had been two days since he'd experienced his usual dry heaves.

~

THEY ARRIVED AT THE WHISKEY Dick campsite around 3:00. The landscape had changed from gentle to rugged as the Mutton Mountains rose 2,000 feet above the river. Whitehorse, an infamous rapids, was a mile beyond in a narrow cleft as the river passed through the mountains.

He anchored the boat and selected a campsite on sandy soil near a big ponderosa pine. Logan thought he heard thunder in the distance. Clouds had been gathering throughout the afternoon, and the sky was now dark and threatening.

As he and Sam erected the tent, Logan contemplated its shortcomings. In a strong wind, it could flap like a flag in a gale, and the rainfly was dodgy at best. Further, the stakes didn't feel secure in the sandy soil. But he figured the weight of the sleeping bags would hold the tent down when he and Sam weren't in it.

Once the tent was up, he showed Sam where the outhouse was located. It was a new two-story fiberglass structure with a short flight of steps that led to the business part. The outhouse was large enough for a wheelchair, although you couldn't have gotten one up the stairs. Sam's leg was tired from climbing in and out of the boat, so Logan helped her up the steps. "See the solar panel on the roof?" he said. "It generates electricity that composts waste. Saves a lot of maintenance headaches."

A skylight brightened the room. A fancy shelf ran along the

other side. Someone had left a section of the previous day's *Wall Street Journal* on it. "Even comes with reading material," Logan said.

Back at camp, they found a guide boat had pulled in with two clients. The guide was setting up a tent as Logan and Sam walked past. "How'd those flies work for you?" said the guide, standing up. "It's Casey Williams. We met at the fly shop a couple of days ago."

"Oh, yeah. Nice to see you, Casey. The flies are great! Fishing's been super! Thanks for the advice." Lightning flashed. Logan counted to twenty before he heard thunder. The storm was moving closer but could still miss them. "I'm going to try for a couple more fish before this weather rolls in."

"Better be quick," said Casey as he pounded in another tent stake.

Logan waded in and worked his way up a fifty-yard stretch near a bank overhung with grass stems and alder branches—what anglers call *junglewater*. After catching a couple of fish, it occurred to him that he should stake down his tent a little better, like he'd seen Casey doing. That notion turned to conviction when a wind gust hit him like a hammer. He'd forgotten how hard it could blow on the Deschutes. He waded toward camp.

As he neared his boat, something large tumbled across the flat and splashed into the river. It was his tent. He ran as fast as he could toward it, but the water slowed him down. Taking a shortcut past the end of his boat, he tripped over the anchor line and bellyflopped into the river. He came up sputtering and staggered on toward the tent, which was drifting downstream.

Too late. It drifted into the main current and spun slowly while gathering speed. A quarter mile away and mid-river, his tent sank from sight in deep water.

Logan ran back to camp. Sam was biting her lip. She looked like she might cry. "Don't blame me," she said. "I tried to catch it, but the wind was too strong. You should have staked it down better. Why are you so wet?"

"Tripped over the anchor rope." He looked around. "The sleeping bags were in the tent?"

Sam nodded without looking at him. She was quivering.

Casey came up to them. "Dude. That's too bad." Rain hit them hard and sideways. "You need to get out of those wet clothes," Casey said. "Do you have extra?"

Logan nodded. "What are—"

"Get into your dry clothes. Make yourselves as warm as you can. Spend the night in there." He was pointing at the outhouse. "I've got a portable toilet that my guys can use."

Logan felt a little better once he got into dry clothes, and even better once he and Sam were out of the storm, sitting on the floor of the outhouse with their backs against the wall. But Sam looked deeply unhappy. "It wasn't my fault," she said.

"No, it wasn't your fault," he said. "I should have staked the tent better." Logan got down the newspaper that had been left on the shelf. He offered it to Sam. "Want some bedtime reading?" he said, trying to make a little joke.

Sam turned away from him.

~

"How did that work out?" Casey asked when they saw him the next morning.

"We survived," Logan said. "We're headed for town." He looked at his boat, then back to Casey. "Any advice about running Whitehorse Rapids?"

"You haven't been down it before?"

Logan shook his head.

Casey pointed downstream. "Go around this point. You'll see some cliffs, maybe 150 feet high, on river-right. There's a 90-degree left bend, a short straight stretch, then another 90 left. After the second left, you'll see some whitewater—a line of rocks that goes most of the way across the river. Passage is on the left side—"

"Got it. Left turn, then left turn, then pass through Whitehorse on the left."

"That's not Whitehorse," Casey said firmly. "After that whitewater, the river starts a long right turn. The current isn't very fast. Move to river-right. You'll see some trails going up the bank to the railroad tracks. Anchor your boat and walk up to the flat ground next to the tracks. Go downstream until you see the rapids. I'll be along in a little bit, so wait for me if it's not clear what to do."

Logan nodded and headed back to camp. Fifty feet from Sam he heard her scream. He instantly knew the cause. "Step back very slowly," he said. "They're not aggressive. They just want to be left alone." He could see the rattlesnake stretched out below a sagebrush, tail vibrating, mouth open, fangs showing.

Sam stepped back. The snake slithered away. Sam shuddered, sneezed, and blew her nose. "I don't feel good," she said.

"I'll get you home as soon as I can," Logan said, trying to sound comforting. He calculated the time to Maupin. Twenty-one miles to the Harpham Flat take-out. Average flow of maybe three miles per hour. Might make five with rowing, but can't row all the time. The trip would take at least six hours.

Logan was about to go when he saw Casey staring at the river. Logan followed his eyes and saw an old red-and-blue aluminum driftboat. It was the same rig that had caught Lower Dave's attention on Monday. The rower—a gaunt man with a scraggly beard and unkempt hair—was alone. "Who's that?" Logan asked.

"No one you want to know," Casey said, his voice edged in disgust. "His name is John Kincaid."

~

LOGAN ANCHORED THE BOAT and walked up the trail to the scouting point. His first view of Whitehorse Rapids terrified him. It was all rocks and whitewater and noise. He tried to pick out the best route. He thought he should go down the middle, then veer off to the left, but he wasn't sure.

He spotted a faded photo in a plastic frame sitting on a rock. It was a picture of a teenage girl who'd drowned in Whitehorse a couple of years ago. A small metal pail held dried flowers. Sam came up to Logan and looked at the memorial soberly. "Do you know how to do this?" she asked nervously.

Logan shook his head. "We'll wait for Casey."

Casey arrived half an hour later, and Logan asked him if the correct line was down the center, then move quickly to the left.

"Uh-uh. See that rock? The pointy one under the wave?"

Logan's eyes followed Casey's finger. He could just make out a gray shape under the wave. He nodded.

"That's The Canopener," Casey said. "That next one below it? That's Oh Shit Rock. That's what you say when you hit it. There's a strong right-to-left current. Wants to push you onto The Canopener and Oh Shit. If you hit either rock your boat will go over, and you'll be in the river. Whitehorse sinks about two dozen boats every year. People have drowned here."

He pointed to the middle, then farther right. "There are two entries. Center and right side. See that V-slick near the right bank? At this flow, you're best off to enter there, facing downstream. It's less risky than the center entry. Slip between those two rocks that are just below the surface. You'll get a big bounce over that standing wave at the bottom of the V-slick. Once you're through the entry, keep going straight. You hardly need to touch the oars." He pointed to a large rock rising in mid-river. "That's House Rock. Pass it on the left. After House Rock, it's a mile of technical water. Not hard, but you have to pay attention and stay on the oars. The hard part is the entry. Get it right, and it's a piece of cake. Get it wrong and …" He drew a finger across his throat.

"You can follow me," Casey said. He turned to go, then apparently thought of more that needed saying. "Put your anchor inside the boat so it doesn't bang around. Tie everything down. And you really need better life jackets. Those ones you've got are not good enough for serious whitewater."

Logan nodded. He was scared as hell. Sam came up to him. "Dad, my arms are all itchy," she said like it was an accusation. She pushed up a sleeve. Small red blisters dotted her right forearm.

Logan's heart sank. "Are you allergic to poison oak or ivy?"

"I don't know."

Poison oak grew in many areas near the river. Logan was mildly allergic. Apparently Sam was more so.

Casey looked at her arm. "I've got some stuff for that," he said gently. "It takes off the oil. It's not a cure, but it'll keep your skin from getting worse." He was now looking at the back of Sam's neck. "Umm, I'll get the tick kit, too."

"I've got a *tick*?" Sam said. She looked ready to puke.

They took care of Sam and got in their boats. Logan thought he knew what line to row through Whitehorse; from the scouting point it seemed obvious once you saw it. But on the water everything looked different, and it wasn't clear at all. With his heart in his throat, he followed Casey.

The entry was a rush of water and noise. His boat sped through faster than he would have thought. There was hardly time to do anything. He saw Casey spin his boat and row hard to the left. He followed suit. Soon they were past House Rock, then through the technical water; the tough part was over.

Casey rowed for the right bank. Logan followed. "We did it!" Logan said.

"Don't get cocky!" Casey answered. "We're going to fish here for a while. See you in Maupin! And be careful in Buckskin Mary Rapids. It's just big standing waves—no problem if you ride down center-left. There's a scouting point on river-right."

Logan and Sam were soon around a bend and couldn't see Casey. Logan relaxed on the oars. Sam twisted in her seat and looked behind them. Logan turned the boat sideways so she could see the water they'd come through. He let the oars slide down until the collars stopped on the oarlocks. *Without Casey,* he thought, *I'd have done it wrong and probably sunk the boat. Nice kid, seems to know the river well, and ...*

As they drifted, the downstream oar blade hit a rock. The oar pushed into the boat at just the moment Sam stood for a better view. The oar handle shot up like a blunt spear and hit her leg. It was a glancing blow, not a direct hit, but it was near where the femur had been broken.

Sam dropped into her seat, white-faced and clutching her leg. She was saying words Logan didn't like to hear her say.

"Sam! Are you okay?" he said, rowing for shore.

"Do I look okay?" she said through clenched teeth.

Logan anchored the boat and tried to comfort her. She shook him off. A quarter of an hour later, Sam's teeth were still clenched. Logan said, "We're going to get you some help."

"How? We're in the middle of nowhere."

"Not as much as you'd think. It's only two miles to North Junction. There are vacation houses on a private gravel road that goes back to Maupin. Maybe we'll find someone with a car. Does it still hurt?"

"I'm feeling a little better," Sam said. "I think I'll be fine."

"We should get someone to look at your leg," Logan said. A minute later: "Is it getting better?"

"It still hurts, but not as much. Just give me some time. Please stop asking."

Logan up-anchored and rowed hard until they reached North Junction. He spied a man mowing the lawn around his cabin. A car was visible. He pulled over and asked the man if he would take Sam to town. He was an older gentleman, polite and understanding. He agreed to take her to Maupin, and even to a hospital in The Dalles if needed.

"You don't need to do this," Sam said. "Let the man enjoy his time on the river."

"No! Let's get you to town for an X-ray. I'll go with you," Logan said.

"Okay, I'll go to town. But you don't need to go with me."

"It's no trouble," Logan insisted. "The boat's in a secure place. It'll be safe."

"I can do this on my own," Sam said. "I spent six months in a hospital and out-patient care. I don't need someone to hold my hand."

Logan shook his head. "I don't know. Are you really feeling better?"

Sam sighed heavily and closed her eyes. "Stop hovering!" she said, sounding exasperated. "I'm sick of people worrying about me! You don't need to go with me!"

Logan was frustrated. He was concerned about Sam, and she kept brushing him off. She was probably angry with him because of all the things that went wrong yesterday and this morning. "Look," he said firmly but apologetically, "I'm sorry all this happened to you. You have a right to be mad at me. I admit that I made some mistakes on this trip. I haven't done this for a while. Things happen. We'll learn from it and move on. Next time it will be better." He motioned Sam toward the front seat, then opened the rear door and made a move to get in. "Let's go."

Sam gave him a look familiar to any adult who's been around teenagers. "I'm not mad at you about the trip! Just let me go into town by myself and stop treating me like a ten-year-old!" Then she added sharply, "What part of 'No' don't you understand?"

"Don't talk back to me, young lady," Logan snapped. "And what part of 'I'm sorry' don't *you* understand? Sometimes accidents just happen. You can't blame me for everything that went wrong."

Sam sucked in her breath. "The trip is not the problem!" she said evenly but strongly. Then her posture changed, and she exploded with, "Do accidents just happen? Or does someone *make* them happen? Someone's always to blame!"

"What's that supposed to mean?" Logan yelled back. "Yes, I

should have staked down the tent better. We'll get a new tent and sleeping bags. I shouldn't have let the oar drag. I'm sorry—"

Sam threw up her hands. "Okay! I agree! You're right!" she shouted. "The trip is the problem! You fucked it up! Just like you fuck up everything. But I accept your apology." She gave him a mock bow of magnanimous courtesy. When she straightened up, she said loudly, "Now will you shut up and let me go to town by myself?"

She turned away for a few seconds, then rounded back on him, "It would be nice if you could just say you're sorry and have everything go back to the way it used to be! Some things can't be fixed by saying you're sorry! I wish they could be! You have no idea how much I wish they could be! But that's not how the world works! Sometimes 'Sorry' isn't enough! Get that into your thick goddam head!"

Sam grabbed the door Logan was holding and slammed it shut. She slumped into the front seat. "Go!" she said to the driver.

The driver, thoroughly embarrassed, looked at Logan for direction.

Logan clamped his jaw shut and turned his head away. He waved them on. The car left, spewing dust and gravel onto him.

~

AS HE WALKED TO HIS BOAT, Logan was convinced that this fight was all Sam's fault. She was being irrational and willful. A typical teenager. What could you expect? But as he thought about it he admitted that he'd been partly to blame. And as he thought further, he saw that he'd been almost entirely to blame. He'd been pushy, insensitive, and even more willful than Sam. As the adult, he should have acted with more wisdom and patience. Further, he should have taken the trip more seriously and been better prepared—taken it in easy stages as he got used to rowing and camping again. Instead, he'd rushed into it and put Sam in harm's way.

He sat heavily in the rower's seat and jerked up the anchor.

"Well, Logan," he sighed to himself as he took up the oars, "you certainly could have handled that better." As he rowed, he obsessed over his mistakes, both on this trip and in the past. Sam was right. He'd failed her. He'd failed Trudy. He was failing at everything.

Logan was soon in a familiar state of deep anxiety about his situation and uncertain future. He'd spent much of the last nine months in this condition. For most of his life he'd kept his emotions under a tight rein, but now his mental state seemed beyond control. He lived in a black hole that devoured all joy, that sucked all the light out of the world and sent it God knows where. He felt like he was possessed by a demon. Every time he tried to get his head together, the old feelings would flood back. The world would turn gray and threatening, filled with ugly, unhappy people. And the demon would whisper in his ear: *There's no hope for you. I can overwhelm you with fear and depression any time I want. I can make you dance like a puppet on a string. You're going to be like this the rest of your life. There's only one way out. You know what it is.*

By the time Logan dropped the anchor at the Buckskin Mary scouting point, he was a mess. He dragged himself up the steps, life vest still on, to see the rapids. The river plunged through a narrow slot in the rocks, dropping about ten feet and forming big standing waves at the bottom. But, as Casey had said, it was not a difficult rapids if you passed through on center-left.

Logan was turning to leave the scouting point when he saw a boat coming through the rapids. He figured he'd watch to see what line the rower took, and maybe pick up some tips. The boat was just like his. In fact, it was his; somehow it had come free of the anchor.

He watched, horrified, as his driftboat turned crosswise at the right side of the entry, hit a large rock, and tipped onto its side. The boat filled with water and sank. Everything—rods, flies, the works—was tied down tight and went to the bottom with the boat.

Logan couldn't believe this was happening. The trip had started so well. For the first time in months, he'd felt a glimmer of hope. And in less than twenty-four hours he'd screwed the pooch:

the tent, the snake, the poison oak, the tick, the injury to Sam's leg, their big fight. And now the boat and all his gear were gone.

He doubled over in a spasm of dry heaves that went on and on. When the fit finally ended, Logan stared at the rushing water. It would be easy, so easy. Toss the life jacket into the water, then himself. People would think he was just another unfortunate boater. "Too bad," they'd say. "Didn't take the rapids seriously enough to put on his life jacket. Got into trouble, sank the boat, was pulled under." They'd shake their heads. "People should be more careful," they'd say. "Sad," they'd say. Then they'd go back to the minutiae of their lives and forget he'd ever existed. They'd never know the truth: that it was no accident. Maybe Dietz would feel sorry for Sam—pull some strings and set her up with a college scholarship. She was better off without him. The world would be better off without him. One jump from this rock and all his pain would be over.

He became aware of a movement on his left. A boat had entered the rapids. It was Hank the fly tier and the lady who looked like Jacqueline Moreau. They waved. He'd been spotted—no hiding it now.

Logan's shoulders sagged in resignation, and he began the long walk to Maupin.

14

May 20: Deschutes River at Buckskin Mary Rapids

"DIDN'T WE SEE HIM AT THE fly shop?" Jackie asked after she and Hank bounced through Buckskin Mary Rapids. "He has a pretty daughter, maybe nineteen or twenty, who limps?"

"Logan," said Hank. "Sam is the daughter. I didn't see her at the scouting point. I thought she was going with him. Didn't see his boat either. Weird."

They were on a two-day float from Trout Creek to Maupin in Hank's driftboat. Hank was having a good time showing Jackie the river. She'd oohed and ahhed at the canyon's rock formations, pointed excitedly at every osprey, giggled and whooped through each rapids. And when they came upon a family of river otters, she acted like she'd never seen anything so cool in her life. Jackie was having a ball doing things she'd never done before, and Hank was loving every minute of it. They'd camped at Wingdam, a few miles upstream from Whiskey Dick. It was Jackie's first night in a tent.

She hadn't done any fly fishing because of her arm. The cast was now gone, and she went to Portland a couple of times a week for physical therapy. The time for fishing would come. Meanwhile, there were other things Hank wanted them to do together. "There's a blues concert in Portland over the Fourth of July," he said. "Would you like to go?"

"Love to!" Jackie looked pensive for a moment. "Hank, honey, you've been showing me the river, and it's been wonderful. I'd like to show you more of my world."

"Like what?"

"I saw in the paper that the Oregon Bach Festival starts June 25. It's in Eugene. I can see my cousin in Albany while I'm there."

Hank had deep reservations about this. First, he'd never cottoned to classical music. But Jackie was eager to go to a blues and bluegrass festival with him, so it seemed fair that he should open his mind and go with her. "Classical music? Umm, okay."

"I'll tell you how to listen to it. Once you understand a little, I think you'll like it better."

Hank nodded agreement, although he was uneasy about it. "Before we go there," he said, "maybe we can drive over to eastern Oregon. I'll show you the ranch where I grew up."

"I'd like that," Jackie said.

Hank pulled the boat to river-left. "Put your life jacket back on," he said. "Four Chutes coming up." He set up for the first and trickiest of the chutes. The entry was a V-slick between two large rocks as the river made a right turn—not dangerous as long as he split the space between the two rocks.

"And Hank?" Jackie said, "I'll buy the tickets for the Bach Festival."

This was the second and biggest of Hank's concerns: money. The O'Leary piggy bank was an undernourished critter. "I'm not comfortable with you paying," he said. "It's not right."

"It's the twenty-first century, my darling. Let me do it." She took a deep breath. "You wouldn't believe what I get paid for a concert. When I'm home in New York, I live simply and teach an occasional master class—fun and lucrative. My recording royalties keep going into the bank. My grandfather was a wealthy man who left all his money to me. And I have a very savvy financial advisor. Frankly, I have more money than I know what to do with."

"I don't care if you've got enough money to burn a wet mule," Hank said. "It doesn't feel right." He'd switched to his firm voice, the one he used around recalcitrant livestock and as an Army sergeant.

Jackie was quiet, then said, "Hank, have you ever worked as a fishing guide?" She spoke off-handedly.

"No. That's a different set of skills. Guiding takes a lot of patience. You're always teaching, keeping all kinds of people happy no matter what. Why?"

"I just wondered. So what does a Deschutes guide like Casey get for a trip?"

"The client pays about $450 a day. But there are fees, shuttle drivers, food, and other expenses. And Judd Boone, the outfitter, gets a cut. Casey nets about $250 a day, plus tips. He's not guiding every day, and he only guides on the Deschutes half the year. It's a hard way to make a living."

"So it would have cost me $900 for a two-day camping trip on the river? Plus tips?"

Hank could see he'd just been finessed. He opened and closed his mouth a few times, but no words came out.

"We're just trading your skills for mine," Jackie said.

He grunted as he pulled on the oars to line up the boat between the two rocks. "It's a deal," he said. They shot through the first chute and bounced over the standing waves at the bottom. Hank pulled hard to the right. "Second chute coming up."

"Hank," Jackie said. "There was something upriver that bothered you. In a cove by that big rock. You looked at something with your binoculars, something that made you angry. It was near that place with the funny name. 'Whiskey Bill's?'"

"Whiskey Dick. There was a boat on the Reservation side. Belongs to John Kincaid. 'Nearly Honest John,' they call him in town—behind his back of course. He'd covered the boat with a camouflage tarp, but when the wind blew I could see a bit of the bow. It's an old red-and-blue aluminum boat. I'd know it in an instant."

"Why don't you like him?"

"He'll do anything for money. He's done prison for growing marijuana. Lots of folks think he's selling meth, and maybe cooking it; you hear things in town. I believe it. He looks like a meth user— super skinny, doesn't take care of himself. He used to be a fishing guide, a pretty good one. He still guides some—illegally because he can't get a permit. He shouldn't have been on Reservation land. That side of the river is closed to anyone who isn't a tribal member. And the fact that he was trying to hide the boat means he was up to no good."

They passed through the second chute. As Hank lined up for the third, he spoke in a low voice. "Jackie, it bothers you that I carry a concealed weapon, doesn't it? Be honest, straight up."

"It bothers me," she sighed. "But I understand why you do it." She looked at the sky, then back at Hank. "No, I don't understand why you do it. I couldn't possibly understand what you went through in Vietnam. How old were you?"

"Nineteen when I started my tour."

"You were a boy! How could they send you to a war?"

"I was typical. The average age of a Nam grunt was nineteen. Almost half the combat deaths were teenagers."

"An army of children! No wonder so many of you had problems when you came home." She shook her head. "What were they thinking?"

Hank shrugged. "You do what ya gotta." He had a thought. "Come with me to the pistol range. Shoot a few rounds."

Jackie looked uncertain and worried.

"You said you'd teach me what to listen for in classical music, and that would help me appreciate it. Maybe if you knew a little about firearms you'd be more comfortable around them."

She nodded. "Deal."

They rocked through the third chute, and Hank set up for the fourth and last, a minor rapids on a left bend—easy, but dangerous if you passed too close to the right bank. "Hank?" Jackie said. "I don't want you to tell people who I am. Introduce me as *Jackie Riviera*."

"Whatever you want. But—"

"I just want to … I'm not sure I'm going back to the violin. I want the space to think about it, without being reminded of my professional life."

"Is it your arm?"

"The arm is fine. The doctor and the therapist agree that it's healed well and there's no permanent damage. With practice, I should be as good as ever. It's just that …" She paused, and her mouth took a serious set. "The violin is all I've ever done in my life. You can't believe the grind and discipline it takes to get to this level. And to stay there." She brushed her hair from her eyes and faced Hank straight on. "I'm afraid of burning out. And if I burn out, then what? Without …"

"… the violin, who are you?" Hank said, completing her sentence. "And what do you …"

"…do with my life? You've got it."

Hank nodded. "You need to find out who you are when you're not Jacqueline Moreau the violinist."

"Just like you need to find out who you are when you're not Hank O'Leary the fly tyer."

15

May 20: Antelope, Oregon

SERGEI KALINNIKOV THREW down his shovel and cursed in Russian. That Balkan bastard Zulfo had screwed him. He'd tricked him into believing this was his hiding place, then made a show of leaving Oregon so Sergei would have time to poke around his Antelope acreage. And there was nothing here. For two days he'd been chasing the wild goose.

Sergei had tracked down Zulfo at his job in Pendleton, then discovered his recently purchased 40-acre property in Antelope, a small town southeast of Maupin. You had to love America: all kinds of information was readily available to anyone who bothered to look. That's how Sergei uncovered the Antelope purchase. And how he'd found that Zulfo had paid cash for it. That was the key. Zulfo's salary as a diesel mechanic never would have given him that much money. Clearly he'd had help. And just as clearly he'd bought the property for the sole purpose of hiding something—probably for the benefit of the people who'd given him the money to buy the old farm. Just what he was hiding, Sergei didn't know. It had to be important, or he wouldn't have gone to so much trouble and expense. But now it was clear that Zulfo was on to him.

Sergei wiped the sweat off his pudgy face and tried to think what this meant, and especially whether it meant he was in any danger. He knew from experience that it was one thing to be clever and another thing to be clever enough to stay out of trouble. "Turkey was thinking," Sergei mumbled to himself, "just before they lopped off his head and put him into soup." He'd have to be extra careful now.

Another thing was clear: while Sergei had spent two days digging up half of Antelope, Zulfo had probably moved the stash somewhere else. Otherwise, he wouldn't have given Sergei free rein.

So whatever Zulfo was hiding was very important. And it used to be here in Antelope but wasn't any longer.

Further, Zulfo couldn't have carried this off alone. He had an accomplice. Maybe more than one. And they had hidden the stash somewhere else while Sergei was breaking his back in this village.

He had to return to Moscow at the end of the week and give his superiors a report. He'd tell them that he was on the trail of something big and was very close to finding it. He'd leave out a few details, like two days of fruitless shovelwork in Antelope. His story would corroborate the flimsy intelligence they'd received, and while it proved nothing conclusively, it should be enough to earn him a return trip to Oregon.

16

May 26: Maupin

A WEEK AFTER LOGAN'S DISASTROUS float trip, there was good news and bad news.

Sam's leg was bruised but fine after a few day's rest. However, they were back where they'd been for months: Sam silent and withdrawn, Logan staggering under a heavy weight of anxiety and depression.

Whitewater Salvage had recovered most of Logan's fishing gear. But the river's powerful hydraulics had pushed his aluminum driftboat through some nasty underwater rocks, and it was damaged beyond repair.

Bill Short, his CIA contact, reluctantly provided money for a new boat. Instead of a driftboat, Logan bought a used inflatable raft. The raft would be more forgiving in whitewater, and therefore safer. It was also less money, and Logan put aside the extra. Better to have a few bucks under the mattress, he figured, and spend it on his "mission" than to risk Bill telling him no.

The new raft needed oars, and the nearest supplier was in Bend, a little over an hour away. Logan drove there and bought the oars. After loading them into his truck, he found himself dreading the return trip to Maupin. Two weeks ago this assignment felt like a lark: almost half a year on the Deschutes, floating the river and fly fishing; it was a paid vacation, like he'd won the lottery. Now Maupin and the river were a prison. He was sentenced to five more months of Sam's unresponsive silence; five months of constant reminders of his failures as a husband, a father, a provider; five months of being trapped in a bleak present leading to a bleaker future.

Logan slumped over the steering wheel for several minutes before mustering the courage to start the truck and head for home. Home? What a joke.

When he reached the north edge of Bend, he turned off the road to Maupin and onto the Cascade Lakes Highway. He had no idea where he wanted to go—only where he didn't want to go.

The road climbed over the shoulder of Mt. Bachelor, then down the west side. Logan passed lakes he'd fished in the past: Sparks, Todd, Hosmer, Elk. The next sign pointed to Lava Lake. He was drawn to it and turned off. Then he followed the dirt spur to Little Lava Lake, the big lake's smaller brother just to the south.

There were no people at Little Lava. He parked and emerged slowly from his truck. The sun shone, and a gentle breeze rustled the trees. Logan took a deep breath of clean, pine-scented air, then walked down the trail to the lake's outflow.

A creek issued from Little Lava and meandered through a mix of grassy meadows and pine trees. The creek was two or three feet deep and about thirty feet across. Fed by underground springs, the water was pure—clear as crystal. The flow was unvarying, regardless of season or drought, because it came from an inexhaustible source deep within the earth.

Large trout—some over five pounds—were visible in the current. But there were no anglers: the creek was closed to fishing at this time of year to protect the wild trout that moved out of Crane Prairie Reservoir and came here to spawn.

This peaceful little stream was the beginning of all things: the origin of the Deschutes River. The humble creek would wander south, gathering waters to itself. It would pass through the big reservoirs of Crane Prairie and Wickiup, then make a U-turn and head north. Below Bend, the Metolius and Crooked would add their flows, and it would become an unstoppable force carving a deep canyon through solid rock. But here, it was just an innocent little creek, twisting prettily through the grass and the pines, sparkling in the sunshine, offering no hint of what it would become.

Logan sat with his back against a pine tree, his arms wrapped around his knees. He hadn't come to the source for years. He breathed deeply a few times, then thought about his fight with Sam. What an asshole he'd been! His beautiful daughter—hiding behind her wall of silence and resentment and God knows what—needed his patience and his help. And what had he done? He'd been pushy, inflexible, insensitive … the list went on.

Then there was Trudy. He'd let his work stress take over their relationship and had treated her terribly—short tempered, hypercritical, impossible to please. What a self-centered bastard! And now she was dead, and he could never make it up to her. Sam was right: sometimes "Sorry" isn't enough.

And Sam and Trudy weren't the only ones. It wasn't like he'd been a monster, but he could have been so much better. Throughout his life he'd said and done things that seemed clever and oh-so-smart at the time, but in hindsight it was clear that he'd just been arrogant and self-absorbed.

Logan tipped his head into his arms and wept bitterly.

After several minutes, he stopped and caught his breath. He was conscious only of the pure river, the river of grace, eternally flowing.

Logan slipped into the river and stood knee deep, not feeling the cold. He looked upstream. The river flowed toward him. No matter how long he stood there, the river would continue to come— bringing all that was good, washing away all that was not, turning resistant rocks to tiny grains of sand washing softly to the sea.

He dipped his right hand into the river and stirred the water, sensing its currents. He cupped water in his palm and let it run through his fingers. Then both hands, holding the water. Another double handful, bigger than the last. Again, hands into the river. He lifted the water high, like an offering, then returned it to the river.

A firm resolve formed in his mind: from this moment forward, everything he would do—everything—would be for Sam. He would devote all his thought and energy toward her. He would find strength to resist his depression and overcome his fears—not for himself, but so he could help Sam. He would find a way.

17

May 26: Near Madras, Oregon

JOHN KINCAID CHECKED OVER his left shoulder, then his right shoulder, then snapped his head back to the left to see if he could catch somebody sneaking up on him. For good measure he looked in all his closets and made a quick tour around his yard. He couldn't be too careful; there might be someone spying on him, peeking in a window. There might even be someone on a hill looking at him with a spotting scope. He glassed the hills with his binoculars. It didn't look like anyone was there, but he couldn't be sure.

He returned to his house, pulled all the shades, and counted out the money they'd paid him, plunking each $100 bill on the kitchen counter. He counted it three more times to make sure they hadn't cheated him. Then he stuffed the bills into a Ziploc bag and put the bag in the freezer. He'd bury it tonight.

It was easy money—just float down the Deschutes and quickly do the deed when no one was around. He'd had a close call when Hank O'Leary floated by, but he'd covered up his boat with a camo tarp. He was sure the big fly tyer hadn't seen him.

The Deschutes was perfect, the last place anyone would think to look because it was so obvious. But if you picked the right time of year, when the river traffic was low, you could hide almost anything from a suitcase to a boxcar and no one would know. He didn't want to overdo it, though. Once every year or two was often enough.

Kincaid knew that the guy who'd paid him—not the neatly dressed man with the glasses but the man with the accent and the nasty scar—didn't trust him. But he should. Nobody had found any of his hiding places yet. That was the key: know how to hide things, trust no one, and be reliable.

That's why people kept coming back to him. He didn't need to know what it was: coke, pot, meth, you name it. He'd hide it without peeking, get his money, and be set for months.

18

June 3: Maupin

"WHOA! THE OK'S GONE YUPPIE! What's the deal, Judd?"
Casey's eyes were fixed on the shiny La Marzocco espresso machine
in a corner of the cafe.

"Well, young Casey," said Judd, "you nailed it. We've gone
yuppie." Judd was standing near the cash register peering at
yesterday's receipts through his half-height reading glasses. His wife,
Susan, was working the grill. "Yes," Judd went on, "espresso is just
the beginning. Next, we're going to sell iPhones and BMWs. It's part
of our expansion program. How was your three-day?" He slipped his
glasses into a shirt pocket and jammed the receipts onto a spindle.

"Good," Casey said. "Fishing was decent, clients were pleasant.
River's getting crowded now that folks have figured out that the
salmonfly hatch is early." He slid into a booth and relaxed against the
high back. "Tell me about the espresso machine."

"Did those people tip well?"

"Yes, very well. This is the third year I've guided them, and they
booked a trip for next May. Now tell me about … " He pointed at the
La Marzocco.

"How well did they tip?"

"Twenty percent. When did you get this thing?"

"Nice. Decent fly casters, were they?"

"Well enough. One guy especially. He was pretty good at
getting his fly under the alders. Really got the notion of fishing
junglewater." Clearly Judd wasn't ready to tell him about the OK's
new addition.

"We booked some more trips while you were gone," Judd said.
"Four one-day trout trips from Warm Springs to Trout Creek and a
couple of four-day steelhead trips from Macks to the mouth. One of

the four-days is four anglers. I've got a string of one-day trips, so Brandon will be the second guide on your four-day."

Casey hid his reaction. Just before the start of the season, Judd's two other employees had suddenly left, one to take a "real" job in Portland, the other to work in Alaska. Judd had to scramble to come up with another guide and someone to row the bag boat. Brandon Muckenhirn was the new backup guide. He was working about half time.

Casey didn't like the new guy one bit. First, Brandon was a trust-fund guide: he came from a wealthy southern California family and worked the river more for fun than as a job. Brandon could be pleasant and knew the river well enough, but Casey suspected that Brandon was a class-A jerk.

Second, Brandon was Casey's age and very good-looking; he was afraid Brandon might get interested in Megan.

"Who's going to row the bag boat?" Casey asked. The bag boat carried all the camping gear and food. On multi-day trips, the bagger goes ahead and sets up the next camp while the guide stays with the clients and focuses on the fishing. Casey had no bagger for his May trips, which made a lot of extra work for him.

"I've asked Willie to be the bagger this summer," said Judd. "He did it a few times last year. I think he's ready for fulltime."

Casey bit his lip. He couldn't hide his reaction this time. Judd had had a distant cousin from the boondocks near Enterprise, in northeast Oregon—a kind of ne'er-do-well rodeo rider and small-time rancher. Somehow the cousin and his wife both ended up dead; there was something there that no one talked about. Their son, Willie, came to live with Judd and Susan; that was the year after Megan broke up with Casey. Willie was fifteen at the time. Fifteen and illiterate. They'd tried him in the Maupin school, but Willie never got the knack of being educated. Casey doubted he would ever learn to read, or tell time, or a lot of other things. At least he was living on his own now.

"Willie, huh," Casey said with zero enthusiasm.

"You got a problem with that?" Judd said defensively. "Willie's quiet around people and knows how to row a boat and set up camp." Judd took off his Stetson and smoothed back his gray hairs. "Besides, that group is two couples."

That explained it, at least partly. For reasons that were obscure to Casey, women loved Willie. They'd coo and cluck over him, while Willie would stand there with a shy grin and nod his head or give one-word replies. He might as well have been a poodle. But at least he was a poodle who could row a boat and set up camp. Willie could do the bag boat job, and the women would like him, and Casey would get a nice tip. And Brandon would do the cooking, which Casey had to admit was always superb. Whatever else you said about Brandon, he knew his way around food.

"Nope," Casey said. "I don't have a problem with any of that. Now when can I get a latte from that shiny hunk of metal over there?"

"You get your latte late–r," Judd said, clearly pleased with his little word play. "The guy's coming in to finish the installation and teach us how to use it. His daughter's going to be the espresso maker. The *barista*, as they say in Portland. Have you met him? Logan. His daughter is Samantha, goes by Sam. Young, pretty. Has a limp—some kind of accident."

"I met them at the fly shop, then saw them at Whiskey Dick two weeks ago. I heard he lost his boat in Buckskin Mary." Casey left out the part about the tent blowing into the river.

"Yup. The anchor was attached with a non-locking carabiner. He dropped the anchor, and a rock popped open the carabiner. Went to scout the rapids, and his boat drifted off. Bye-bye boat."

"Classic."

"We've all been there," Judd said. "He bought a raft. He's going to be here all summer and fall. He's writing a guidebook for the river." Judd headed for the door. "A *fishing* guide book," he said over his shoulder.

As Judd went out the door, Megan came in. Casey saw her hesitate when she spotted him. He'd already thought this through: do what Hank's ladyfriend told him. Be cool, be a friend, get to know her all over again. "Hey, Megan," he said. "How's teaching?" He waved a hand at the empty seat across from him in the booth.

"Casey." She moved cautiously to the booth and sat opposite him. "School's fine. Good trip?" She twisted a lock of hair around her forefinger.

"Went well." He kept his voice calm and easygoing. *Remember, be a friend.* "So, are you going to start a second career? Barista?"

"Oh, that." She looked over at the La Marzocco, then back to Casey. "The guy talked Dad into it."

"It's hard to talk Judd into anything, especially if it involves spending money. He must have been a silver-tongued devil."

"He was very persuasive," Megan said. "He told Dad that a corner of the OK was underutilized and that if he put in an espresso machine he could get more people coming through the door. He *gave* him the machine. Then he did the installation, and he's paying for all the coffee and stuff."

"So what's he get out of it?"

"Half the income and all the tips. His daughter will be the chief espresso maker, and Dad doesn't have to pay her. She'll be here most days and will train Helen and Diana for the days she's off." Megan brushed back her hair and looked reflective. "His daughter's very quiet. I hope it works out. I'm not sure this was her idea."

"But she's going to do it?"

Megan shrugged. "I guess. Do you know them?"

"A little. Sam and Logan. Sam's the girl."

Megan leaned close to Casey. "About time we got something 'twenty-first century' in here," she whispered.

"You don't like the OK?" Casey whispered back.

"I love the OK. But the food … I have mixed feelings about hamburgers and French fries. They remind me of home and family …" She put a hand on her stomach. "But they don't always digest well." She looked around to see if anyone was near them. "I doubt

Mom and Dad are going to start serving Thai cuisine. Breakfast is fine. I can handle eggs and toast. I skip the hash browns."

"You like Thai restaurants?"

"Love them."

"Me too. There's a new one in The Dalles. We could go there sometime."

"Sounds fun."

And just like that, they were going to hang out together. *This is all right!* Casey thought. *Thank you, Jackie!*

Their voices returned to normal volume, and they discussed school and Megan's English classes. It was the last push before finals and summer vacation. Casey asked about her students, and Megan asked him about his clients. They slipped into an easy, natural conversation.

They each ordered a breakfast. The new girl, Diana, served it. She was pretty and about Casey's age, but there was something hard about her that he couldn't put a finger on.

"I don't know about her," Megan said quietly when Casey asked about Diana. "She's kind of ... kind of ... I don't know how to explain it." She pushed her scrambled eggs around with a fork. "On the prowl," she finally said, resuming her whisper. "Looking for a guy."

"I'd better be careful," Casey said with mock caution.

"I think she's looking for a guy to take care of her. Financially."

That left Casey out, as they both knew. Conversation died for a moment; then they were back to school talk and things that were happening around town. A new grocery store was going in. People were excited about it.

They talked for half an hour; then Megan left for school. As he watched her leave, Casey had to admit that this "friend" thing was kind of fun.

Logan came in ten minutes later with Sam. They headed for the espresso machine. "Hey, guys," Casey said, "can I be the first person to order a latte in the OK Cafe?" He emphasized each "ay."

"A few tweaks, and Sam will pull one for you." Logan flipped some switches. "It'll take a few minutes."

"I hear you're writing a guidebook for the Deschutes," Casey said. "About time someone did that. What are you going to cover?"

"Well, uh …" Logan hesitated. "You know, fishing. It's not a whitewater book."

"All fishing, or just fly fishing?"

"Um, just fly fishing. That's what most people do."

"Except on the lower river during steelhead season. Most of the gear guys fish down there. And there are the salmon fishermen at Sherars Falls, if we get a salmon season. And there are ways to use a spinning rod to catch trout."

"Just fly fishing," Logan said.

"Are you going to cover all the campsites?"

"Sure. Everything along the access roads."

"It would be good if you could do all the drift-in sites too. I see plenty of people floating the river who don't know where they are or where the next campsite is. You know, a lot of people have those waterproof GPS units. You could give the coordinates of landing points, describe the campsites. If you need any help with the hatches, Dave's pretty good."

"Which Dave?"

"Both. But Dave Tindal is especially good about entomology. I'd be happy to talk to you about it, but you should get someone else to review the text. Oh, and tell people how to take care of the river. That's real important."

"Well, uh … yeah … I planned to have a chapter about that. Taking care of the river. And the fish."

It seemed to Casey that Logan didn't have a very clear idea what his guidebook was going to be about. "Who's the publisher?" he asked.

"Uh … um. It will be … self-published." Logan looked at the espresso machine. "All warmed up," he said, with apparent relief.

"Sam, would you like to do the honors and pull a … what would you like, Casey?"

"A mocha. Sixteen ounce."

"… pull a mocha for Casey?"

Sam limped cautiously to the machine. She looked at the dials and levers, glanced around for the ingredients, and fixed a mocha for Casey. She put it in front of him without a word.

"Thank you, Sam." He took a sip. "Hey, this is really good! Thanks!"

Sam nodded, and a flicker of a smile crossed her face.

"First one's free," Logan said.

"Double thanks, but the barista gets a tip anyway. He pushed a dollar bill across the table. Logan put it in the tip jar next to the machine.

Logan left, and Sam sat down. She looked out the window, quiet and expressionless.

Casey sipped his drink and thought about the guidebook that Logan was writing. He had a lot of ideas about what should be in it. More ideas than Logan had, apparently. It seemed like Logan hadn't really thought about it much. His reaction was odd. Surprised? No, that wasn't it. Uncertain? No, that wasn't it either. If Megan were around, she would come up with the right word. Evasive? Sort of. Next time he saw Megan, he'd describe it to her. Shocked? No, no. He shrugged and drained the last of his mocha.

19

June 3: Maupin

LOGAN WAS NONPLUSSED. HE'D used his "guidebook" cover story to convince Judd he'd be around long enough to support the espresso machine. Now Casey was quizzing him about a nonexistent book project. Logan would have to go through the motions of doing a guidebook, or his cover story wouldn't be credible.

Pretending to work on a book would be a major-league bother, involving mock research and maybe even drafts of the text. Just floating the river and hanging around Maupin asking questions wasn't going to cut it.

It would be worth the extra effort, though, if it helped Sam. After that first float trip she wasn't about to accompany him on the river. And summer jobs were harder to find than he thought they'd be, especially for someone with a bum leg. But he couldn't leave her alone in Maupin, hunkered in her silence, listening to her depressing music day after day. She needed to be around people but in a situation where she could choose the depth of interaction. Barista at the OK was perfect. Sam rejected the idea at first, but eventually she came around.

The La Marzocco formed the first part of Logan's two-pronged plan. The second part was to work with the two horses: Mataan and Major—especially Major, the two-year-old.

Sam was a born horse nut. She'd ridden since the age of five, done 4-H since fourth grade, and for the last few years had also competed in "breed" shows with Mataan. She'd won countless trophies and had had a thriving business teaching riding to younger girls. She'd gotten Major as a weanling and had begun his ground training. Her plan had been to saddletrain him when he was three, an age he'd hit next February.

But after the accident, Sam did nothing—no teaching, no riding, no groundwork with Major. She'd clean the corrals, but that was it. Logan couldn't even get her to groom a horse with a brush. She used her bad leg as an excuse, but there was more to it than that, although he didn't know what.

So Logan decided to work with the horses in the evening when he wasn't floating the river. He wouldn't put any pressure on Sam to help, but he hoped she'd take an interest.

Ty Decker, their landlord, had a round pen that was perfect for working Major. He also had a large corral where Logan could ride Mataan under saddle. The surfaces were packed hard, so Logan harrowed them with Ty's tractor.

After harrowing he put a halter on Major and led him to the round pen. Like Mataan, Major was a purebred Arabian. At 14 hands, he was a little smaller, but he would probably add another inch or so in the next year. Mataan was a bay—brown with black mane and tail—but Major was dappled gray with a flaxen mane and tail, four black feet, and an appealing white blaze on his face. Neither horse came from expensive lineage.

Logan began by leading the two-year-old, reintroducing him to the idea of having a boss. Then he backed him up. And that was it. After fifteen minutes, he returned Major to his pasture. Then Logan repeated the drill with Mataan. Again, after a quarter hour of leading and backing, he slipped off the halter and pastured him.

When working with horses, Logan was a gradualist: he started slowly and never did too much at a time. It was about steady, gradual progress. Horses get confused and flighty if you throw too much at them. So Logan kept the workout short and simple, then left them to "think about it."

~

OVER THE NEXT TWO WEEKS, Logan made two float trips, one from Warm Springs to Maupin and another from Trout Creek to

Maupin. Because Sam now spent her days at the OK, she'd gotten to be friends with Judd's older daughter, Helen, and her husband Kevin. When Helen found out Sam would be home alone, she invited her to stay with them while Logan was on the river.

Between float trips he'd fished around town and worked Mataan and Major in the evenings. He was up to half-hour sessions with Major and an hour with Mataan, who was now being ridden under saddle. Both horses were improving nicely. Major's haunch and forehand turns were good, and Mataan's trot was beginning to settle out. Still no sign of Sam, though.

One evening he was about halfway through his session with Mataan when he sensed someone approaching the corral. It was Ty Decker, their landlord. Ty, a compact, wiry man in his late fifties, was wearing his usual dark brown shirt under tan overalls. He leaned against the corral. "Your gelding's coming along," he said. "Is he purebred Arabian?"

Logan stopped the horse near Ty. "Hundred percent," he said.

Ty removed his glasses, blew off the dust, and replaced them. Then he cocked his head and took a close look at Mataan, starting with the feet and working his way upward. He rubbed his reddish-blond beard and looked thoughtful. "He's leggy for his size. Egyptian breeding?"

Logan was impressed. Apparently Ty knew more about horses than he had realized. "He's all Egyptian. Not expensive Egyptian, though."

"I can see that," Ty said. "He's short-necked and heavy in front. Probably has a hard time keeping his head down and staying in frame at the canter. Did your daughter do well with him in horse shows?"

"Very well."

"Then she must be an excellent rider, because he's not going to make it easy, is he?"

"No, he didn't. And she is … was … a very good rider."

Ty considered Mataan further. "But he seems calm, steady, and willing. If you want to do some trail riding with him you could try the old Criterion Ranch. Bureau of Land Management bought it a few years ago. Thousands of acres. Goes right down to the river. Public access, but no motor vehicles. It's about twelve miles out of town on Highway 197. There's a parking area next to those big horn-looking things."

Logan knew the spot; there was a communications relay tower there.

Ty went on. "I know a guy—Ron Bauer—who's got property off 197 not far from the Shaniko junction. Gabe, his 15-hand Arab gelding, needs work. I bet he'd be delighted to have someone ride his horse for him. He'd let you ride on his land; you're someone who knows enough to close a gate behind himself. It's rugged country— over 1,200 vertical feet from the highway to the river. But it's pretty, if you like the high desert. If you're interested, I could talk to him."

"Thanks!" said Logan. "That would be cool. Then Sam and I could ride together."

After Ty left, Logan nudged Mataan into an easy lope on the left lead, went two full circuits of the round pen, then did a rollback and started the other direction on the right lead. He was concentrating on Mataan's headset, but his peripheral vision picked up movement near the corral gate.

He pulled up at the gate expecting Ty again. It was Sam. "Don't fiddle with his mouth so much," she said. "He doesn't like it when you do that. And you're really too heavy for him." Then she turned and went back to the house.

Well, it was something, and he was grateful for it.

~

TWO DAYS LATER LOGAN WENT to the OK for a latte and to visit his beloved and former possession, the La Marzocco espresso machine. Sam had just finished pulling a drink. She hadn't seen Logan come in and was talking quite naturally to the customer—not a flood of words, but enough to give Logan hope.

He ducked back outside so as not to intimidate her and walked to Lower Dave's fly shop to kill time. Casey was inside, talking to Dave about the fishing. "Caddisflies are everywhere," Casey said. "Two weeks early like everything else. The junglewater is fishing well. And back in the alders? Oh, man!"

"How busy is it?" Dave asked him.

"Like usual. Pretty crowded from Warm Springs to Trout Creek. Lots of dirtbag guides clogging up the river, you know." They both laughed; apparently it was an inside joke. "Hey, Logan!" Casey called out. "Your daughter's doing great with the coffee machine. Been out on the river lately?"

"Thanks. A couple of trips. Caddis are thick in the alders. Bankwater's fishing well, and backeddies in the evening. But I think the trout are getting wary. There are a lot of people out there."

"You ever hunted them in deep cover? Way back in the alders?"

"Well, I fish along bankwater and cast under the overhanging branches."

"That works. But when they're super spooky, the big fish go where you can't cast to them from the river. You have to sneak up on them from above."

This got Logan's interest. He loved hunting trout and would rather stalk a single hard-to-catch fish than cast to a dozen easy ones. "Sounds like fun. How do you do it?"

"I've got a free day tomorrow. Float the river with me from Warm Springs to Trout Creek and I'll show you. No charge, just two guys going fishing."

"Are you sure you want to fish on your day off?"

"Let me tell you how it is with guides," Casey said. "You're either working your butt off from pre-dawn to post-dark, or you're doing nothing. And when you have time off, there's no money to do anything other than fish. You can't plan anything, either; somebody might book a trip on a couple of hours notice. Besides, I've spent two weeks watching other people catch fish and never getting any myself. It's like being the photographer for *Playboy* centerfolds, but you're not allowed to have a girlfriend." He paused. "Sorry to be so blunt. Hope I didn't offend you."

Logan spread his hands. "I understand. I'll pay for the shuttle and bring lunch." This was easy for him; expenses like shuttle drivers were picked up by Bill Short.

~

THE NEXT MORNING, HE MET Casey at 7:30, and they headed for Warm Springs in Casey's truck, his driftboat on the trailer behind. After launching, Casey rowed hard downstream. "Since it's just us," he said, "I'd like to boogie downstream, hit some high points, then focus on the lower stretch before anyone gets there."

Logan looked around Casey's driftboat, noting its casual efficiency. Logan was pretty sure that if he surveyed everything Casey carried, he'd find exactly what anyone might need for a river trip, no more and no less: flies that matched the current hatches, tippet spools, a spare rod in case of breakage, wader repair kit, eyeglass repair kit, sunscreen, extra hat, dry clothes for someone who fell in, duct tape, electrical tape, needle and thread, superglue, snakebite kit, tick kit, first aid kit.

Logan also noticed that Casey's anchor was attached with a locking carabiner. Logan had lost his driftboat in Buckskin Mary Rapids because he'd used the non-locking type; a rock had popped it open when he'd dropped the anchor. Now that he was aware of the danger, he noticed how many people used the wrong kind.

After ten minutes of rowing, Casey rolled up his sleeves. The young guide had tattoos on both arms. On the left he sported a dry fly—an O Stone—on his upper arm near the elbow, and an open-mouthed rainbow trout on the lower arm. As Casey pulled on the oars, the tattoos came together, so the trout tattoo rose and devoured the fly tattoo. Similar tattoos were on his right arm, but they were a steelhead and a steelhead fly—a Jonzie.

They stopped at a backeddy a few miles downstream from the

boat ramp. Logan knew this spot. The biggest fish moved under the branches of a big alder that leaned over the river. On previous trips he'd seen trout sipping caddis, but you couldn't fling a fly without hanging up in the branches or scaring the trout, or both.

Instead of wading in and casting from the river, Casey took Logan up on the bank. He stopped just as they were about to enter the deep shade of the alder. "Go slow," Casey said. "No sudden moves. Keep your hands hidden as much as possible. If they see the flash of your hands, they'll spook."

"Really? Just from your hands?"

"Yours more than mine. Mine are tanned and dark. Yours are a lot whiter." They moved into the tree, first next to the trunk then out on a limb. "Don't push on any small branches. You don't want them to see the branches move. Be the tree." Casey was talking in a whisper. "They don't hear you," he said, "but if you talk quiet, then you'll move quiet. It's all about being sneaky." He peered into the water. "There's Herman."

"Herman?" Logan whispered.

"Yeah. I don't know if it's the same fish, but there's usually some big guy in here. If it isn't the same one each time, it's one just like him." He looked back at Logan. "Sometimes I call him Oscar."

Logan peered at the water. In a narrow opening through the alder branches, he saw a large dark shadow near the surface. The shadow moved to the surface and sipped a small bug. "He's big!"

"That's not him. That's the little guy. We don't want him to take the fly and scare Herman. Herman's to the right."

Logan looked right and saw an even bigger silhouette. "Wow!" was all he could say.

"We'll just watch," Casey whispered, "and learn his rhythm."

As they observed Herman, another driftboat slipped by outside the alders, oblivious to Casey and Logan. "You're really hidden in here, aren't you?" Logan whispered. "Anyone in a boat, or even walking by on the trail, wouldn't have a clue."

"It's every boy's dream," Casey said. "Or at least every *sneaky* boy's dream."

Casey set up his rod with only one foot of line past the rod tip. He had a ten-foot leader, just a little longer than the rod. He grabbed the fly in his left hand. "This works best with one of Hank O'Leary's XYZee Caddis. You can grab the Z-lon tail and not get the hook in your fingers." He pulled the fly back with his left hand and thrust his right hand—rod hand—forward. The rod tip bent like a bow. "Don't point the rod tip at the water. Otherwise it'll hit the surface. Then it's bye-bye trout." Casey held this pose for thirty seconds or more. "Only one shot. If you fail, the fish will spook and be gone."

Herman moved into a good position, and Casey released the fly. The rod unbent and propelled the fly toward the water. It landed gently about a foot from the fish. Herman moved casually forward, sipped the fly, and moved on—immediately hooking himself. Then all hell broke loose.

Casey dropped down from the tree, threading his rod through several branches. "Always have an exit strategy," he told Logan over his shoulder.

After several minutes Casey had Herman to hand. He was a good eighteen inches and deep bellied. Casey removed the hook without touching the fish or taking it from the water. "See you later, Herman," Casey said as the big trout swam off. Then he turned to Logan. "See how it's done? Now we'll go downstream, and you can get the next one."

They stalked three more fish in this manner. Casey was obviously more skilled than Logan, but Logan was getting the hang of it. At one stop, Logan noticed that Casey used his left hand as the rod hand; at the previous stop he'd used his right hand. Logan also noticed that when Casey rowed, he didn't favor one oar over another. That was unusual for rowers. Apparently Casey was ambidextrous.

THEY BROKE FOR LUNCH AROUND 1:00. While eating turkey wraps, Casey said, "Your daughter's a nice lady. I like her."

Logan looked at him suspiciously. Did Casey have designs on Sam? Was that what this trip was about?

"Don't get me wrong," Casey said, hands raised. "She's too young for me. Besides, my attention is elsewhere."

Logan relaxed. "Oh, right. Megan Boone. Hank told me. How's that going?"

Casey chewed thoughtfully. "I think it's going fine. Slow, but fine. I don't have a lot of free days. But I've noticed that she comes in for a latte on the days that I'm off—she knows where Judd keeps the guide schedule. Always comes at the same time. So I make sure I'm there at that time. It's gotten to be an unwritten, unmentioned sort of thing."

"A *tacit* understanding."

"I'll take your word for it. Anyway, we always pretend to be surprised to see each other; then we sit and chat over our drinks." He paused and looked thoughtful. "I'm finding out things I never knew or suspected. We had a relationship in the past, but we were just kids. What did we know about anything?"

"People change, but sometimes there's a connection at a very deep level, a connection you never lose. Sounds like you're making progress."

"Yeah, thanks to Sam's lattes!" Casey rummaged in the cooler and came up with a bag of corn chips. "Gotta keep up the salt intake when you're on the river," he said. After a few noisy bites he hesitated, then asked, "How did Sam hurt her leg?"

"Car accident. She and her mother were driving on a winding road. They hit some soft gravel on the shoulder and slid into a tree. They weren't seriously hurt. They got out and were standing nearby. A car came around the corner and … At least we think that's what happened. The other driver said Sam and Trudy were in the road and he swerved. His car went into a spin … and he … couldn't see them

… until … It's a little murky. Trudy—Sam's mother—was killed, and Sam was badly hurt, especially her leg."

"That's awful! I'm sorry about your wife."

"We were … divorced at the time." He paused for breath, then went on. "Sam was pretty banged up. Ribs. Head. And the leg. Her thigh—her femur—was fractured in several places, and the bone had broken through the skin. They had to insert a steel rod into the femur. Then they attached a metal frame that was pinned through the flesh into the bone above and below the fracture. And she needed treatment for low-grade infection."

Casey shuddered. "That sounds …" He shuddered again. "… like something from a horror movie!"

Logan sucked in his breath at the memory of it. "It was. And it was painful for her. Then she needed lots of physical therapy to re-strengthen her muscles."

Casey nodded. "Is she going to be alright?"

"We think so," Logan said. "Eventually. She still needs physical therapy and general exercise. Mostly she needs a boost in her spirits. Injuries like that can bring on emotional issues relating to the possible loss—permanent loss—of mobility and function. I'm more worried …" Logan paused, not sure if he should go on. But he liked Casey, and he wanted to unburden himself. "She needs to be around people. People other than me. That's why I did the deal with Judd—with the espresso machine."

"That should help. She makes good drinks. I love her mochas! And she'll see a lot of people at the OK."

"Sam won't talk about the accident. Or about her mother. Or much of anything. Not to me, not to anyone. She's been withdrawn and bottled up inside. She used to be so social and verbal. Like a typical teenager. Maybe being at the OK will help her open up a little."

"It's hard to lose a parent," Casey said thoughtfully. "My father was killed in a logging accident. He was falling trees."

"How old were you?" Logan asked.

"Fourteen," Casey said.

"I'm sorry."

Casey grimaced. "I didn't handle it well."

"You were fourteen."

"I was never good in school. I'm dyslexic, so reading was difficult."

Logan nodded. Being dyslexic explained Casey's ambidexterity.

"I started running with the wrong crowd. Got into a lot of trouble—theft, vandalism, dumb kid stuff. Fell a year behind in school, headed for Dropout City. Caused my mother a lot of grief when she already had enough to deal with. My older sister wouldn't have anything to do with me."

"Obviously you settled down."

"Judd," Casey said with a shrug. "When I was seventeen he hired me to clean boats and do some other useful jobs. He didn't need the help, and he doesn't like to spend money. But he hired me anyway. He took me fishing and got me out on the river. I loved the river, and the more time I spent there the better I got. I started to feel sorry for the way I'd treated my mother, the way I'd let down my father."

"Sometimes feeling sorry for what we've done—or not done—is the first step to getting better."

Casey laughed. "Well, if that's true," he said, "then I should be almost perfect. Anyway, I spent all my spare time fly fishing on the river; then I began tying. Judd bought flies from me." Casey shook his head. "Man, those were pretty sorry flies. Judd put them in the 75-cent bin—the pity box—in the OK. But Hank O'Leary took me under his wing and taught me to tie right, and after a few months I was tying for the two Daves, the fly shop guys. I know now that I was cutting into Hank's business, but nobody minded, least of all Hank."

Casey put a handful of corn chips into his mouth and crunched them for a while before going on. "Judd convinced one of the white-water rafting outfitters to take me on when I was eighteen. I spent the summer cleaning rafts and other gear, and loading and unloading them from the trailers. After a while I guided tourists on the river.

Then Judd had me rowing the bag boat for him. And here I am ten years later, a real live fishing guide."

"So you finished high school?"

"Yup. Got it together and graduated. A year late, but I made it. The good news is that it put me in Megan's class—she had been a year behind me—and we saw a lot of each other."

"How long did you go together?"

"Until her sophomore year of college." Casey's face tightened, and his smile disappeared. "She dumped me. I wasn't expecting it. I … it left me almost back where I'd started. But I got over it. In time."

Logan saw Casey's pain, so he changed the subject. "Was your mother okay financially? After the accident?"

"There was a settlement that helped. But money was always tight. She lives in Portland now, near my sister Margaret. Margaret went to college. She's a CPA and makes good money. I see her every few months. She has twin two-year-olds, Zack and Travis. I can hardly wait to take them fly fishing."

"Kids are fun, at all ages," Logan said. *But I sure wish I knew how to get through to mine,* he thought.

"Well," Casey said, "don't worry about me and Sam. I'll treat her good, but my romantic focus is on Megan. Now Brandon Muckenhirn, on the other hand … Brandon is Judd's other guide, and between you and me and this sagebrush here, I don't trust him. Not for one second. I saw him eyeing Sam the other day. But then Brandon eyes every good-looking lady."

"Should I be concerned?"

Casey looked thoughtful for a moment. "Probably not. I think Brandon's got his eye—his ogle—on Diana. She works at the OK. Diana's late twenties, bleached blond. Pleasant face." He looked sidelong at Logan. "Really nice boobs."

Logan remembered her. She was the recipient of the "knobs" remark when he first came to the OK with Sam. "Oh, yes," he said cautiously. "Diana."

Casey straightened up and stretched. "Actually, I think Brandon should watch out for Diana more than the other way around. I think she can take care of herself."

~

THAT NIGHT OVER DINNER, LOGAN casually mentioned Brandon Muckenhirn and asked Sam if she knew him. "Oh, him," Sam said dismissively. "Pretty boy. Muscle attached to a driftboat."

"How about that girl Diana? Do you know her well?"

"A little." Sam looked thoughtful. "I think she's after Brandon. Something about someone to take care of her."

"If Diana's looking for a sugardaddy, he'd be the guy. Brandon's a trust-fund guide. Not that that's a negative. His last name sounded familiar, so I googled it while dinner was cooking. His father was a big shot in southern California commercial real estate. Buckets of money. He died a few years ago, and his sons took over. Or at least two of his sons. Apparently they're pretty smart guys and managed to avoid most of the impact of the big crash."

"Brandon runs a real estate company?" Sam was incredulous.

"No. His two older brothers do. Sounds like they've got all the business sense, and they parked him on the Deschutes to get him out of the way. At least that's how I read it."

"Well, he's got the dumbest German shepherd I ever met," Sam said. "Have you seen it? Named 'Wapato.'"

Logan almost gagged on his broccoli. "Wapato? He has a dog named *Wapato*?"

"He said it's Indian for 'elk.'"

"That's *wapiti. Wapato* is the Chinook word for potato."

Sam laughed. "How do you know these things?" she said.

"I'm a pedantic know-it-all. Just ask Walter Dietz." Logan was glad for a light-hearted, easy moment with Sam. This was the best conversation they'd had since the Voyage of the Titanic, as he now referred to that first float trip. He took another bite of his dinner, then asked, "How are you getting along with the other people at the OK?"

"Good. Susan and Helen are very nice to me. Helen treats me like a friend, and Susan is … motherly." Sam's face clouded, and she opened her mouth like she was about to speak.

"Yes?" Logan said expectantly.

"Nothing," Sam said. The clouded look faded.

After a few more forkfuls of dinner, Sam said, "You know who I like? Hank and Jackie. They often come in for coffee drinks. Jackie and I talk a lot. They're funny. They're so different."

"I talked to Jackie the other day," Logan said. "I asked her if she was Jacqueline Moreau the violinist. She said she was. I was blown-away—she seems so normal and approachable. Still, she asked me not to tell anyone. Oops! I guess I just did."

"My lips are sealed."

"She's going by Jackie Riviera." Logan wanted to push for more, lots more, but he kept his mouth shut. *Don't force it. Let it come naturally. Support, don't push.*

"Are you going to ride Mataan tonight?" Sam asked as they cleaned up the dishes. "In the big corral?"

"Yes."

"I think I'll work with Major in the round pen. Maybe tomorrow we can swap horses."

20

June 17: The Paulina Highway, east of Prineville, Oregon

"Who the hell is Patrick Henry O'Leary IV?" Jackie asked. She and Hank had just left a drive-through coffee stand in Prineville, a town southeast of Maupin, and Hank had laid his wallet on the seat. Jackie was investigating the contents.

"Put that down! Snoop!" He grabbed for the wallet. The pickup lurched. A locket hanging from Jackie's neck swayed with the movement.

Jackie held the wallet at arm's length away from Hank. "The driver's license has a photo of you but says your name is Patrick Henry O'Leary. The Fourth." She made a gesture with her left hand. "Out with it!"

Hank shook his head. "It's not that interesting. My great-great grandfather was born in Ireland and ended up in California looking for—and not finding—gold. He loved American history, especially the Revolution against the English. So he named his son—my great-grandfather—Patrick Henry O'Leary. It combined the Irish saint with the American revolutionary. You know, the give-me-liber-ty-or-give-me-death guy. My great-grandfather was nicknamed 'Irish,' my grandfather was called 'Patrick,' my father went by 'Pat.' They called me Henry, but I insisted on 'Hank.'"

"Maybe I should call you Henry the Fourth."

"Don't even think about it."

Jackie rummaged through Hank's duffle bag and pulled out his harmonica. She put it to her lips and blew. "Yuk!" she said. "All the notes came out at once! How do you play this thing?"

"You're worse than a curious monkey! What's got into you today?"

"Really, how do you play it?"

"You use your tongue to cover the holes you don't want."

Jackie tried a few notes but soon put down the harmonica. She looked out the window at the high desert scenery east of Prineville: lava rock, sagebrush, juniper trees. Barbed-wire fencing ran alongside the road. Occasionally a clump of cattle appeared. The tires went tunk-tunk tunk-tunk as they crossed cracks in the two-lane blacktop.

Fifteen miles from Prineville, the Crooked River appeared. The river moved slowly between low banks of lush grass. In places you could have crossed it in two hops. "The river's not very big," Jackie said, "compared to the Deschutes."

"No," Hank said. "Especially this time of year. It's bigger closer to the Deschutes."

"Does it bubble up out of the ground, like the Metolius?"

"The South Fork is like that. The South Fork and Beaver Creek come together between Paulina and Post and make the Crooked."

"Paulina and Post are the two towns along this road?"

Hank laughed. "Towns? Post is a store. Paulina is store and about a dozen buildings. Prineville is the only incorporated city in the county."

"And it's about …?"

"About 10,000 people. Most of the county."

Jackie shook her head. "It's The Empty Quarter."

"Not really," Hank said. "Look, there's a person now!" A man in a white T-shirt and a red baseball hat was opening the gate to a gravel side road.

"Yes," Jackie said. "The first human being we've seen in twenty miles. There's nothing out here!"

"You've got that right!" Hank agreed.

"Your family came here from California? Why?" Jackie asked.

"My great-grandfather was good with horses and worked on ranches. He came to southeast Oregon when he was nineteen, in 1888, and worked on the P Ranch outside French Glenn—way south of here. My grandfather was born there in 1895. My grandfather didn't see a future for himself in that part of Oregon and moved north to the Crooked River country in the early 1920s."

"And he was a cowboy, too?"

"Yes. But he didn't call himself a cowboy. He was a *buckaroo.*"

"What's the difference?"

"Same job, different style. If you're from Texas or Montana, you're a cowboy. But in California or the Great Basin you're a buckaroo. The word has faded out of use. Too bad—I liked it."

"And your father was a … buckaroo?"

"Third generation."

"How come you're not a cowboy? Excuse me, a *buckaroo.*"

"I could have done the job. I grew up riding horses and working with livestock. But my father was a smart man. He figured out that we'd never have enough land to make a go of it. And the cowboy days were mostly over." Hank cocked his head in Jackie's direction. "Did I tell you I did rodeo when I was a teenager? I roped and rode broncs. I was too big to be any good as a bull rider. You remember Ty Decker? Has the property where Logan and Sam live? He used to rodeo, too—when he was a teenager, and into his twenties. We ran into each other at county fairs and the like. He was damn good. Better than me. He'd rather be working with horses than doing what he does. He and my grandfather would have gotten along well. They're horse people."

"But you went into the Army."

"I didn't know what else to do after high school. My father served during the war and figured the Army would be good for me. So I enlisted. My father died while I was in Vietnam. My mother sold the ranch and moved into Prineville. A couple of years later she remarried and moved to Arizona. So after the Army, I had no family around and no place to call home. I drifted around for a bit, fishing and tying flies to earn my grocery and gas money. Eventually I landed in Maupin."

Jackie was quiet for a couple of minutes, looking out the window.

"Can I ask a very personal question?" she said tentatively.

"Anything."

"When you were in the Army, were you afraid of dying?"

"No."

"Why not?"

"Because," Hank said, "if they killed me, that would have been it. Nothing I could do about it."

"So you weren't afraid?"

"I was plenty afraid. But not of dying."

"What was it then?"

"I had four big fears. The fourth biggest was being wounded and disabled—step on a land mine and blow my legs off; that sort of thing. Third biggest fear was being captured by the NVA. Second biggest was being wounded *and* captured."

"What was your biggest fear?"

"Number one fear? Letting down my buddies. That one's never left me. I worry that someone will need me, and I won't be there for them. Now I'm getting older … " His voice trailed off.

~

HANK PULLED OFF THE HIGHWAY onto a gravel road blocked by a gate. A pickup waited on the other side. A man got out of the pickup and opened the gate. "Derek!" Hank said as they shook hands. "Good to see you. Thanks for unlocking the gate."

"No problem," Derek said. Like Hank, Derek was a big man with a soft voice.

Hank waved a hand at Jackie. "This is Jackie Riviera."

Derek touched his right thumb and forefinger to the brim of his Stetson. "Nice to meet you, ma'am." He turned to Hank. "Well, you know your way around. I'd love to talk, but I got things to do." He faced Jackie and touched his hat again. "Ma'am."

Hank and Jackie drove up the gravel road. "Not much of a conversationalist, is he?" Jackie said.

"Derek? No, he's kind of a quiet guy."

After a couple of miles, Hank turned onto a narrow dirt road. They soon came to a small wooden house nestled against a hillside. An old hand-crank washing machine squatted in a corner of the porch. A medium-sized barn with faded red paint and a rusted tin roof stood near the house. "Here it is," Hank said. "Castle O'Leary. Ancestral home of the landed gentry."

He led Jackie to the house and pushed open the front door. The furniture was gone, and decades of hot summers, cold winters, and all-season aridity had sucked the color from the paint and wallpaper. Otherwise the house was as he remembered it. Hank closed his eyes and pictured his mother hovered over the woodstove in the kitchen, his father's boot heels clunking on the porch as he came in with his chaps over his arm, and himself as a ten-year-old boy. It seemed like yesterday.

Hank and Jackie walked up the narrow, steep stairs, and Hank opened the door to a small room. "This was my bedroom," Hank said. The blue wallpaper sported 1950s-style cowboys and horses, each encircled by a brown lariat. Worn linoleum covered the floor.

Jackie looked at the ceiling fixture. "Is that a gas lamp?" she said.

"Propane," Hank said. "Everything ran on propane: the refrigerator, the furnace, the lights. We didn't have electricity. Too expensive to bring it in. Didn't have indoor plumbing, either. One thing about it, I learned to live cheap and simple."

"Has anyone lived here since your mother sold the ranch?"

"No. Derek's dad bought the place. He picked up most of the small ranches like ours and consolidated them with his property."

"And you had …"

"Just over 2,000 acres."

"And it wasn't enough?"

"Not in country that gets ten inches of rain a year. Not when you don't have enough flat, irrigated land to grow hay for the winter."

~

THEY ATE LUNCH NEAR THE CREEK, sitting on the ground. "Where did you go to school?" Jackie asked.

"For grade school, I went up the road a piece, in Paulina. Then Prineville for high school."

"That's a long bus ride!"

Hank shook his head. "I boarded with a Prineville family during the week. That's what the ranch kids did back then. I came home on weekends. I learned to fly fish and tie flies in high school. The family had a son my age, and he knew how to do it. The Crooked River near Prineville was an outstanding trout stream—and at its best in the fall, winter, and spring, before the water gets too warm.

We'd go up there and … well, we'd fish, drink beer, talk about cars, and … uh, make out with the girls."

"Ooh," Jackie said in mock shock. "Quite the little *roué*, were you?"

"Girls, beer, cars, and fishing—in that order. That pretty much sums up my interests as a teenager."

"Same as now?"

"No. The order's shifted around a bit. Fishing is at the top. Beer is at the bottom. Cars don't even make the list."

"And girls?"

He turned to her and smiled broadly. "They come just after fishing. And only one girl."

"What did you do in the summer?"

"Helped my dad. We had grazing allotments on federal land, and he'd leave me to watch over the livestock. Usually cattle, but sometimes he had a sheep allotment and would take on someone's flock for the summer. If it ate grass, he could manage it."

"Wait," Jackie said, holding up a hand. "He'd *leave* you?"

"Yup. He'd leave me for days at a time, watching over the cattle. Or sheep."

"By yourself? How old were you when you started doing this?"

"Fourteen. It was what you did. I wasn't really alone; I had a dog and horse. And Dad would come up every four days or so and stay with me a couple of nights, then go back. His visits kept me from going nuts. I learned to play the harmonica then; it was easier to carry than a guitar. I did that until I was out of high school and joined the Army." He shrugged a shoulder. "I watched over the stock, moved them along when they needed more grass, and kept away the predators. I carried a thirty-ought-six rifle and shot coyotes—and sometimes cougars—if they got close. There were lots of coyotes, so I got lots of target practice. That's how I became a crack shot."

"So when you went to Vietnam it was …"

"… the same thing. Camp in the puckerbrush, watch out for my buddies, and take out coyotes."

"Except they were people, not coyotes."

"They were trying to kill my friends," Hank said strongly.

"It's not simple, is it?"

"No. And since you asked," he said after a hesitation, "ranch work was what kept me stable in—and after—Vietnam."

"How so?"

"I knew what a bullet did when it hit flesh. I'd butchered livestock. I'd shot elk and deer, and dressed them out. So I was better prepared for war than a lot of guys. I wasn't distracted by the carnage. I was …"

"… Hardened?"

"Tempered. I'm sorry to be so … so graphic. But you asked."

Jackie nodded. "I'm glad you told me. It's a part of you that's hard for me to understand."

They ate their sandwiches in silence; then Jackie pointed at the little creek, barely two feet across. "Are there fish in there?" she asked.

"Used to be. When I was a kid, I'd catch little trout. Native redband rainbows."

"Were you fly fishing?"

"That came later. When I was boarding in Prineville."

"Oh, right. You said earlier. Did you learn to tie flies when you boarded in Prineville?"

Hank nodded. "I liked making things. I liked working with feathers. They're soft."

"And water is soft. Lao Tzu said, 'Nothing is softer than water, yet it wears away the hardest thing.'"

"Lao Tzu?" Hank asked. "Is he that spey caster from the Skagit? No, that's …"

Jackie laughed. "Lao Tzu was a Chinese philosopher. He lived over two thousand years ago."

"Well, if he wasn't a fisherman, at least he knew something about rivers."

Jackie closed her eyes and breathed deeply. "It's peaceful up here," she said. "I love the sound of wind in the pines and junipers. And the smell of sagebrush."

"When I was a kid," Hank said, "I read cowboy books—Zane Grey, stuff like that. They talked about the smell of sage. 'Sagebrush doesn't smell,' I thought. 'This guy is nuts!' But when I came back from the Army, I took a whiff. 'What's that smell?'" He chuckled. "Sometimes you have to go away for a while. Then when you come back you understand things better."

Jackie nodded, then lay back and pushed her hat over her eyes. "Peaceful," she said dreamily, and floated into sleep.

Hank sat back, knees up and hands touching the earth. As Jackie's breathing slowed into a steady rhythm, he thought about his parents. His father was cowboy-tough. He was a kind man but had little patience—and no respect—for people who wilted when the going got hard. Whatever life threw at him, he took it like a rock. What would he have thought about Jackie? About Hank going to plays and Bach Festivals and art galleries? He'd have told Hank he was putting on airs and would probably turn into a candy-assed pansy. Hank would have told him to go screw a sheep. Then they'd have both laughed.

But Hank had to wonder: why did he want to be with Jackie? And she with him? She was so different from any woman he'd ever known, and he was a world apart from any man she'd been with.

During his teenage summers, when he was by himself taking care of livestock, he'd lie in his sleeping bag and look at the stars shining clear and bright in the desert sky. He'd wonder what more there was to the world. Not just the world away from the ranch, but the world right where he was. He'd wonder if there was more than what was on the surface. If the rocks were gone—if that basalt crust just crumbled to dust and blew away—what would he find?

It hit him: that was what Jackie did for him. Soft as water, yet wearing away the hardest rocks—showing what was beneath the surface, revealing new depths and dimensions. And, in a different way, he did the same for her.

But where was it going? How long could they go on like this?

Hank decided he didn't need to know just yet. He tipped his hat over his eyes and lay back on the earth. Jackie stirred and snuggled into his side. He wrapped his arm around her shoulders and held her close. Soft, so soft.

21

June 30: Beaverton, Oregon

THE RECEPTIONIST ROLLED HER EYES when Logan came through the door. On his first visit, she'd greeted him with a smile. A week later, he'd gotten a questioning look. Three days after, it was pursed lips and an audible sigh. Now she'd given him the eye-roll, followed by a headshake.

Logan ignored her. She didn't know what suspicious activities he'd witnessed on the Deschutes, what Evil Doers where skulking in the sagebrush. He might hold the one piece of intelligence that would save the world from a horrible fate. It wasn't her place to pass judgment on him—even if this was the fourth time in three weeks that he'd come to the nondescript office building on Beaverton's Nimbus Street. He stood tall and said, "Bill Short."

"I'll let him know," the receptionist said in a dutiful, if tired, voice.

A door in front of Logan buzzed, and he entered a short hall. He stood until the door behind him closed. He spoke his name into a speech recognition box. Another door unlocked. In the hall beyond there were several more doors. Logan went to the one on the right and put his eye up to the retinal scanner. The door opened to a windowless room with a secure audio/video connection. Bill Short's face was on the screen.

"Yes?" Bill said testily. "What is it this time?"

"I saw a person sitting on a rock taking photographs as people floated down the river," Logan said. "The person was there all day. It looked suspicious, like somebody doing surveillance and planning something. I thought I should report it immediately."

"Do you have a photograph of this suspicious person?"

"Um, no."

"Did you ask around? Do some little bit of investigation?"

"Uh …"

"No," Bill said. "You came straight to us without filtering, without thinking about it. Without any more effort on your part than to drive to Beaverton—on our gas money—and call me out of a meeting so you could dump this on my desk like it was the intelligence coup of the century."

Logan saw Bill Short crook his finger, and a young man quickly appeared. Bill scribbled something on a piece of paper and handed it to him. Then Bill spoke to Logan—slowly, as to a child. "We are very busy here. Our resources are stretched to the limit. That's why we hired you. And we expect you to *use your brain!*"

"I'm just trying to do my job," Logan said defensively. "I wasn't a field agent or an analyst; I was a computer wonk. I didn't have any surveillance training, or anything like it. Besides, that Kincaid guy could have been important." After his disastrous first float trip, when Casey had warned him about the skinny man in the red-and-blue driftboat, Logan had reported Kincaid to Bill Short. That was his first trip to the building in Beaverton.

Bill sighed. "Yes. Perhaps reporting Kincaid was the right thing to do. Marginally. But we checked him out, and he's just a small-time drug dealer. Hardly an Islamist terrorist. You could have asked around and discovered that on your own. But your next three reports …" Bill shook his head.

Well, yes: Logan's next three reports. There were the two

parked cars on a deserted road at midnight—which turned out to be a couple of middle-agers having a clandestine infidelity. Then there was the dark-skinned man with a peculiar accent—a Brazilian tourist. And the pair of non-Indians poking along the riverbank on the Reservation side—a team of consulting biologists studying trout habitat for the tribes. Perhaps, Logan thought, he'd been a little too eager to find something that would justify his existence.

"Okay," Logan said, raising his right hand. *"Mea culpa.* I was overzealous and should have thought it through a little more. I'll try to do better."

"Don't ignore things," Bill said. "But filter them before you call me."

The young man Logan had seen earlier reappeared and handed Bill a piece of paper. Bill studied it, then removed his glasses and rubbed his eyes. Glasses back on, he held the paper up to Logan to see. It was a printout of a web page. *See yourself going through Box Car Rapids!* it said. *Relive the thrill!* It showed a man with a camera sitting atop a big rock overlooking Box Car, a class IV rapids just upstream from Maupin.

Logan's heart sank as he remembered that there were people in town who shot photos and sold them to whitewater rafters. The weather had warmed, and the rafters were coming to the river in force. That's what he'd seen.

"Logan," Bill said, "is this your suspicious photographer?"

Logan nodded ever so slightly, eyes downcast, a lump in his throat. He wanted to sink into the floor.

"We figured that out in less than five minutes," Bill said. "And we're on the other side of the country." He shook his head in exasperation.

Logan felt he should say more in his defense. "Look, Bill, I could do this job if you just told me what I'm supposed to be watching for. People planting explosives? Saboteurs around high-voltage power lines? Arsonists starting wildfires?"

"We—"

"Midnight tank maneuvers in the desert? Cattle rustlers? Witches' covens?"

"Probably not witches' covens. Everything else ... " Bill's face became more avuncular and conciliatory. "Logan, we have no idea what you should be looking for. If we knew, we'd tell you. All we ask is that you keep an eye out for anything of a suspicious nature. Then use your cover and ask around. You're 'writing a guidebook.' People expect you to be curious and ask questions. You're a smart guy; use your head. And Logan?" Bill said, turning away and avoiding eye contact. "It would be ... highly unusual ... most unlikely ... that you'll find anything at all. So have pity for our limited resources. It's enough that Dietz is taking care of you and your daughter for six months. Just don't push us too hard. Understand?"

Logan nodded, and the conversation was over.

"See you next time," the receptionist droned as Logan left the facility.

~

ON THE TWO-HOUR DRIVE BACK to Maupin, Logan castigated himself. What had he been thinking? Not thinking much at all, apparently. The problem was that everything, seen in a certain way, looks suspicious and threatening—especially if you have no idea what you're looking for.

The intelligence world is one of vague shapes seen through per-petual fog. You made the best guesses you could, but you rarely knew anything for sure. In hindsight, events and their causes seemed clear if you picked out a dozen "dots" and connected them. But in the real world those dots were surrounded by thousands of other dots, nearly all of which were irrelevant. Even if you had what seemed to be hard information, you never knew anything for sure because the other guys could be spoofing you—feeding you bad intel in order to lead you astray or to test your weak points.

The Hollywood version of the intelligence community—supercompetent men and women who did dangerous things and shot people dead whenever they felt like it—well, it was entertainment but it was seldom reality.

Even so, Logan had quickly jumped to false conclusions. It was hard to admit, but he knew the reason: deep down, he felt worthless and unneeded; he was desperate for some shred of evidence that he was of value to the world.

Bill's parting comments—about it being enough that Dietz was taking care of him for six months—made it clear that they didn't expect him to find anything of a terrorist nature. In a sense, that was good news. He could relax, enjoy his time on the river, and focus on helping Sam. If he saw something unusual, he would check it out. But it would have to be a major deal before he'd make another trip to Beaverton and rattle Bill Short's cage.

22

June 30: Southeast Portland, Oregon

"THIS PLACE IS A REAL DUMP," said Zulfo, the scarred man. "Yes," said Peter Bolton. "But it's anonymous. One apartment among many. Not a place anyone would be looking for me."

"You're using a fake ID?"

"Of course."

"Why this part of town?"

"Because it's got … an eclectic mix of people, shall we say. That makes it an easy place to hide. It's live and let live. Everybody minds their own business."

"As far as I can see," Zulfo said, "it's all steers and queers." He snorted in disgust. "Mostly queers." He drummed his fingers nervously on the table. "Are you sure Kincaid did this right? Do we know where he hid them?"

"We know where he *told* us he hid everything. And I doubt he looked inside."

Zulfo smiled. "He seemed impressed with those gadgets you put on the cases. He thinks they're booby-trapped." Zulfo paused, thinking. "They're not, are they? Booby-trapped?"

"Of course not," said the thin man. He was exasperated but showed no sign of it and spoke coolly and evenly. "If you're so concerned, Zulfo, float down the river with him and check on things. Make sure it's all where he said it is. It'll put your mind at ease and make you feel like you're doing something. Don't open the cases; just see where he buried them. And if he's tampered with them … you know what to do. But don't do anything until you know for sure where he's hidden our stuff."

Zulfo nodded. "What about the Russian?"

"We'll distract him again. It's not hard. He's not the brightest bulb."

"Is he working alone?"

"Seems to be."

"Why don't I just take him out?"

"Because that would bring attention we don't need. Nobody's looking for us. Let's keep it that way."

"How come it's okay to take out Kincaid but not the Russian?"

Bolton couldn't resist a small sigh. *This guy can be so thick*, he thought. *To think he could have been my brother-in-law*. "If Kincaid is found dead," he said slowly, "no one will be surprised. They'll figure he pissed off some drug gang. But if the Russian shows up with a bullet in the back of his head, the FSB will be here in a microsecond. And some other people as well. Don't be so damned trigger happy."

"Yeah, yeah," Zulfo said grudgingly. "I hear you." He drummed his fingers some more. "So you think the Russian is with the FSB?"

"Odds are."

"It will be so sweet when we pull this off. Spectacular! They'll take us seriously after that!"

"Yes."

They were silent for several minutes. Bolton smoked a cigarette, occasionally blowing smoke rings. Zulfo flipped quickly through a magazine. Finally he said, "I'd feel better if I could see it. Can you set it up with Kincaid?"

"Yes," said Bolton. "It might take a couple of weeks to arrange everything and make sure the Russian is led astray. Let's aim for mid-July."

23

July 17, afternoon: Deschutes River below Trout Creek

LOGAN SHIPPED THE OARS AND let his raft drift in the current. The day was warm—into the mid-80s—although not as warm as usual. In a typical July, temperatures often hit the upper 90s or low 100s. But the spring-that-wouldn't-end had merged into the summer-that-couldn't-get-started, and mid-80s counted as "mild" weather.

A few caddisflies bounced off the river. Normally this would be prime time for caddis, but everything was at least two weeks early. The fishing was more like the end of July than the middle: good action in the very early morning and right at dusk, and not much happening in between.

For the trout, May's salmonfly feast had been followed by massive caddis hatches, supplemented by pale morning dun mayflies. These abundances had filled their bellies and dulled their appetites. Throw in nearly three months of constant angling pressure, and you had trout with no inclination to expose themselves to get a meal. So Logan decided to chase them back in the trees, as Casey had showed him a few weeks ago.

The sky was clear and blue as Logan drifted lazily downstream. He tipped his head back, closed his eyes, and let the sun warm his face. Face-warming took less time these days: he'd stopped shaving and had a full beard. When he'd started this follicle experiment, Sam had accused him of falling face-first onto a porcupine. But now she admitted that it looked good against his face, which, despite frequent slatherings of sunscreen, had grown a shade darker.

Logan had now floated all one hundred miles of the lower Deschutes several times and was a fixture on the access roads around Maupin. He knew many of the fishing guides on sight, and vice versa. He knew which campsites were best, where to find shade in the heat of the day, what to expect from trout in every hour. His clothes were faded from constant exposure to sun and wind. In short, he'd become a river rat.

He was also going through the motions of working on a guidebook. He'd drafted a few pages on campsites and fishing tactics, asked detailed questions, and took notes—not much, but enough to allay suspicion.

Logan heard the noise of an approaching small rapids. He opened his eyes and slid the oars back into the water. He set up the boat and rocked through the whitewater. He was now in a long straight stretch. He knew from experience that the current had a slight left-to-right push, so he pulled the boat to river-left, re-shipped the oars, and again turned his face to the sun and reflected on the last few weeks.

Since coming to the river his depression and anxiety had been slowly releasing their grip. This change hadn't happened all at once, and he was occasionally bedeviled by panic attacks and low spirits. But for the first time in months he felt a cautious hope. Some days it was like a rising sun that filled his soul with joy and well-being. Then life seemed easy, like hooking trout on his first float trip in May. On other days, hope was more elusive and had to be stalked carefully, like hunting rainbows back in the alders.

One reason for his improved spirits was Sam. For the last few weeks she'd been working the horses with him. The La Marzocco deal at the OK had worked out well, too. Besides the social contact with espresso customers, Sam had gotten to know Diana and Helen. One or the other would give her a lift home in the evening.

Lately, Sam would start out on foot, and they'd meet her down the road. At first Sam could only get a hundred yards on her own. But the exercise strengthened her leg, and she was walking farther each day. Now she was getting halfway to town before being picked up.

Her limp seemed to be fading, and she was opening up to other people and to him. Shortly after he'd first installed the espresso machine, Logan had overhead someone talk about the "Ice Queen" making lattes at the cafe. He doubted he'd hear that kind of talk again. Sam was on the road to recovery, in spirit as well as body. In fact, the last time he was at the OK he saw a couple of guys in their early twenties hanging around her. She was talking freely with them, almost flirting. He had a father's normal reaction but had to admit it was a good sign.

However, she wouldn't talk about her mother or the accident. It would come out eventually, Logan figured. He'd have to be patient.

~

BETWEEN SOUTH JUNCTION and Wingdam he rowed toward shore. The sun was just above the western rimrock; it would be dark in three hours. He waded downstream a hundred feet to where he could climb a tree and hunt for trout like Casey had showed him. He soon found a good fish and hooked it. Then without moving his boat, he waded downstream another two hundred yards to the next group of alders, a thicket even denser than the one he'd just been in.

He climbed stealthily until he had a good view of a large fish. Logan was pleased with his approach. He hadn't wiggled a branch or otherwise alerted the trout, which was confidently sipping caddis as they drifted into its turf.

The alders were a cool, dark refuge. He was invisible to anyone on the river, although he could see out very well. He decided to relax and observe the fish. Logan loved watching trout: the efficient, sinuous way they flexed in the water; the slow cruise a foot below the surface; the sure but unhurried move to drifting caddis; the quick rise to inhale an unlucky bug.

Logan watched for half an hour before taking out his camera—he always carried a waterproof point-and-click—to take a photo that he'd show to Sam and to Casey. Casey especially would appreciate the fish in the deep cover of the alders.

He switched off the automatic flash, figuring it would scare the trout, and snapped a photo. He adjusted the telephoto setting and tried different framings. After half a dozen pictures, he was waiting for the fish to come back into frame when he was conscious of a driftboat moving slowly past the alders. Two men spoke in low voices. The passenger was mid-fortyish, stocky, and had a wide, prominent scar beginning above his right eye and running diagonally across his forehead; his head was shaved. Logan couldn't see the rower yet.

"How much farther?" said the scarred man. He had a slight accent. Logan couldn't place it, but it sounded vaguely eastern European or Slavic. They were probably wondering about the next campsite.

"About half a mile. Relax," said another voice, pure American.

Logan took his photo. There was a faint click of the shutter. He didn't think it would be a good picture though; the people in the passing boat were in the frame. He adjusted the telephoto setting and snapped the shutter. Again, a faint click.

"What was that?" the accented voice said quickly.

"What! What did you hear?" The rower looked around wildly. He was an unkempt, skinny man in a red-and-blue driftboat. Logan recognized him immediately as John Kincaid, the man Casey had warned him about. Logan was instantly on guard.

"I heard something in those trees."

There was a pause, then Kincaid said, "We should check it out."

"Where's the guy who owns that raft up there?" said the scarred man. "Do you think it's that fisherman we passed a quarter mile upstream?

Kincaid seemed to consider this. "You're probably right." He settled down for a few seconds, then was suddenly animated again. "Put that thing away before someone sees you!" he hissed. "We'll stop below here until dark, then check on your stash. I hid it good. Sit down and don't get people looking at you."

Logan could now see the scar-faced man standing in the boat. He was holding a lethal-looking semi-automatic pistol, which he reluctantly put into a duffle bag. He remained standing, scanning the riverbank.

Logan's blood ran cold. He stayed perfectly still. *Be the tree*, he said over and over to himself.

The two men seemed to be having some sort of discussion as they drifted. They anchored their boat a quarter mile downstream. Logan saw them get out and start up the bank toward his hiding place.

His heart pounding, Logan quietly slipped down from the trees and into the water. Alder branches arched over him, extending ten feet past the bank, their tips dipping into the river, making little riffles whenever the wind blew. The water was halfway up his chest. He waded stealthily downstream, completely concealed. Caddis flitted through the branches. Occasionally one fell onto the water and was sipped by a waiting trout. He passed within six feet of a deer standing in the shade, yet he was so quiet the deer never saw him.

Logan stopped about two hundred feet below his original hiding place. He'd reached the end of the alder thicket. There was another thicket fifty feet below him, but no cover between. The two men were close now. He held onto a rock and scrunched as much of himself into the river as he dared. Water occasionally trickled over the top of his chest waders and ran inside, chilling him. Still, he didn't move a muscle. The men were opposite him now. Kincaid was saying, "Your stash is safe. Don't worry. I've done this before. No one thinks to look here. Hiding in plain sight works best." They kept going. They stopped near the tree where he'd first seen them, closely examining it. They disappeared into the thicket.

He calculated how long it would take him to float through the open water. *Current about three miles an hour, which is about … four feet per second … fifty feet … about twelve seconds.* He decided to risk it. He let go of the rock and lifted his feet from the river bottom, then floated motionless downstream. His waders slowly filled with water, making him cold and heavy but not—contrary to myth—pulling him under water. Now he was into the next group of overhanging alders, under their arch of branches. He turned upstream, breathless. The two men were coming out from the thicket where he'd been. They'd missed his float.

Now they were looking in the water. They paused at the edge of the thicket, where he'd started his drift, then moved on. As they passed his new hiding place, Kincaid said, "I guess it was nothing."

"It could have been the Russian," the other man said. "Or someone working with him. We were right to check it out."

"Who's the Russian?" Kincaid said.

There was no reply. As they passed, Logan could see the scar-faced man's back. The pistol was in his waistband.

Logan stayed in the water until dark, then crept slowly and silently to his boat. He thought about drifting in the night, then decided against it; that would make him look even more suspicious. Better to leave things ambiguous.

He opted to move inshore and found a place among some large rocks on the berm below the railroad tracks. He could see his boat but wouldn't be silhouetted against the night sky and would blend in with the rocks. Sleep was impossible.

About midnight, he saw movement near his raft—two shadows, dark against dark. The shadows stood near his boat for a while; then a flashlight slowly scanned it, as if someone wanted to remember what it looked like. The light flicked off, and the two shadows moved away.

These guys scared Logan spitless. They were clearly dangerous, but what was their game? He came to no conclusions except that this pair was bad news and he needed to be very careful.

~

LOGAN RETURNED TO HIS RAFT in the morning and rowed straight for Maupin, cutting his trip short. He searched far ahead for the red-and-blue driftboat, but he never saw it.

He arrived in the early afternoon and immediately went to the OK and checked on Sam. To his relief, everything was normal. He made an excuse for coming back so soon and chatted with Sam while she made him a double-shot latte.

As he left the OK with the drink in his hand, he was suddenly clapped on the back and nearly knocked over. "Well, Logan. *Dobroe utro*. I have come to Deschutes at last."

Logan turned around, and his jaw almost dropped to the gravel. Standing next to him, wearing a Stetson, was Sergei Kalin-nikov. "Umm, *Dobroe utro*, Sergei."

In the waning days of the Cold War, when Logan and Dietz worked for Electronic Defense Laboratories—before the two men went to NSA— they were stationed at a super-secret listening post in Bad Rosen, West Germany. Sergei used to hang around town trying to get someone to tell him what all those big antennas were for. Sergei was probably the most heavy-handed agent who ever worked for the KGB. He was incapable of subtlety or maintaining a credible cover story. Binge drinking seemed to be one of his chief talents: after several months of strict sobriety, he'd go on a five-day toot. Then he'd dry out, and it was business as usual.

Everyone at the listening post knew who he was; Sergei jokes were a staple. Yet they'd checked him out with the intelligence community and found that Sergei had a fair, if spotty, reputation.

Apparently he had an animal intelligence and dogged persistence that worked just often enough to keep him on the KGB payroll. But the Cold War had ended, and the KGB had morphed into the FSB. Logan doubted Sergei had survived the transition to the New World Order.

"What brings you to the Deschutes, Sergei?" Logan said. "Take a wrong turn coming out of the Moscow metro?"

Sergei laughed so his big belly shook. "No, I come here on purpose. I hear you talk once about Deschutes to Dietz. So I come see for myself, now that our countries are friends."

Logan doubted Sergei had ever heard him speak to Dietz about the Deschutes, but he waved that off.

Sergei looked knowingly at Logan. "So! How is our friend Dietz? Keeping it in his pants?"

Sergei had tried to blackmail Dietz into telling him about the listening post. Dietz, ever the womanizer, had a torrid affair going at the Gasthof Bihler where they stayed. Two affairs, really. First with the tall, athletic twenty-year-old au pair girl he referred to as The Amazon. Then after a couple of months he moved on to Frau Bihler, a late-thirties woman with the biggest breasts in Bavaria, which was saying something. The Amazon was a diversion, but Frau Bihler was more like love for Dietz.

Sergei got wind of the affair. One day he buttonholed Logan, Dietz's obvious acolyte, and told him about photos he would send to Dietz's wife if he didn't feed Sergei some intel. Logan coolly said that Dietz's wife knew all about the affairs and was doing the same thing back in California. This was a lie, but Sergei believed it. Dietz was grateful to Logan ever after. Not that he'd saved Dietz's marriage—it was beyond that—but he'd spared Frau Bihler some embarrassment.

"I haven't talked to Dietz in years, Sergei. Why are you really here?"

"For scenery and fishing! And ... how do you say? ... whitewater rafting! Why else? I have rented RV!" He seemed proud of the fact.

"I am camping out, like American. Then I will write article for magazine. I am journalist now!"

Sergei poked an elbow in Logan's ribs and dropped his voice. "We all must watch out for our brothers," he said conspiratorially. Then he gave Logan another hearty slap on the back. "The Balkans! The despair of tidy minds! Ha!"

This latter was an old Russian proverb, but Logan couldn't make out why Sergei had said it. It was a complete *non sequitur.*

Sergei was looking at Logan's latte. "You get that here?" he asked.

"No, up the road in the grocery store," Logan lied.

"You are so tricky," Sergei said, walking into the OK. "See ya, ... pilgrim," he signed off in a Russian-accented John Wayne impersonation.

Logan debated whether to follow Sergei into the OK or not. He didn't want the Russian hanging around Sam. But he could see plenty of customers in the cafe, and Helen was there. So he got in his truck and went to Upper Dave's fly shop.

He browsed through fishing gear for a while, waiting for customers to thin out. When the last one left the store, he said, "Hey, Dave, do you know a skinny guy with a red-and-blue aluminum driftboat?" Logan already knew it belonged to Kincaid, but he'd found you learned more if you pretend to know less.

"Old red-and-blue boat?" Dave said cautiously. "Kind of a lanky guy? Stringy hair and a ragged beard?"

"That's the one."

"That would be John Kincaid. Nearly Honest John, we call him. He was a fishing guide twelve years ago. A pretty good one. That was before ... before ..." There was a pause. "You should stay away from him."

"Hmmm. I wondered. I saw him on the river. He looked like ... well, not like who you usually see on the river."

Dave spoke in a low voice. "Drughead. Used to deal pot, then cocaine; they say. Prison time. Probably moved on to meth. Hell, probably cooks it. Someone said he's selling oxycodone now." Dave adopted a tone of sarcastic pride: "We're real proud of our boy John. He keeps up with the times."

"If everyone knows he's a dealer," Logan said, "how come he's not behind bars?"

"This is a big, empty part of Oregon," Dave said, "with very few law enforcement people. It's easy to hide, if you're clever. And Kincaid is very clever. He might look stupid, but he's stupid like a fox."

"Is he dangerous? Have any radical notions, perhaps?"

"Radical notions? I doubt it. Probably too drug-addled to have any political beliefs at all. But dangerous? Those meth guys all go a little wacko and paranoid. Although I'd worry more about some of the people he hangs out with."

Logan nodded. "Thanks for the advice. I'll stay clear of him."

~

LOGAN LEFT THE FLY SHOP AND went to work on his raft. Kincaid and Scarface, or the Dastardly Duo as he now thought of them, had examined it carefully in the night, so he tried to change how it looked. The raft had a blue-and-yellow grab-rope around the perimeter. He replaced it with a white one. That was all he could do. Anything else would take big bucks.

As he worked on his boat, Logan thought about his scary encounter on the river. It seemed likely that Kincaid and Scarface were part of a drug operation. Bill Short had told him—and Upper Dave had confirmed—that Kincaid was a low-level dealer. The Dastardly Duo weren't actively causing havoc; they were apparently picking something up. That was consistent with a drug operation.

In addition, the Dastardly Duo certainly didn't fit the profile of Islamist terrorists. Kincaid was pure American and hardly a religious zealot. Scarface? His English was perfect, albeit slightly accented, and he clearly wasn't from the Middle East. The probability of those two being Islamist terrorists "approached zero from below" as his former boss, Walter Dietz, would have put it.

The spoiler for this theory was Sergei Kalinnikov. What was he doing on the Deschutes? Was he "the Russian" that Scarface referred to? It was possible that Sergei had a role in the Russian mafia; it was a common career path for ex-KGB types. Scarface sounded vaguely Slavic; he could be Russian. Maybe they were all part of the same group, or perhaps rival gangs.

However, Sergei didn't seem to be hiding anything. He was as cheery and heavy-handed as usual. And what was that about "watch out for our brothers?" And the Balkans being "the despair of tidy minds?"

Logan decided that Sergei Kalinnikov was the key. He'd send Bill Short an encrypted email and ask him to find out if Sergei was with the FSB, and if so what he was doing in Maupin, Oregon?

In the meantime, he'd give Kincaid and Scarface the widest possible berth. If Logan inserted himself into a drug deal he could blow his cover, let alone put Sam and himself in danger. He would spend the next week floating from Buckhollow to Heritage Landing, more than forty miles from where he'd seen Kincaid and Scarface. Odds were their paths would never cross again.

24

July 20: Portland International Airport

WHAT A STROKE OF LUCK! Sergei Kalinnikov thought to himself. There he was, a day away from having to fly back to Moscow with nothing to show his bosses, and Logan McCrea appears out of nowhere.

He'd recognized the young man from his time watching the NSA listening post in Bad Rosen. After running into McCrea in Maupin, he'd snapped a few photos with his big telephoto lens. Sergei would show the photos to his superiors, but he wouldn't tell them that he knew McCrea from the old days. Instead, he'd tell them he thought this unknown person was acting in a suspicious way and might be working for the CIA, FBI, or some other secretive agency. McCrea was probably just on a fishing trip, but he wouldn't mention that.

His bosses would run some face recognition software on the photos, discover that McCrea used to work for NSA, and conclude—on their own and without any help from Sergei—that he was on a mission of some sort. *What you go looking for, you will find!* That should be enough for them to send him back to Oregon. It was all a load of sausage, of course, but it was better than being stuck in Moscow with his bosses standing over his shoulder.

His flight was called, and he boarded the plane a happy man.

3: Steelhead

25

August 15, pre-dawn: Deschutes below Macks Canyon

IT HAD BEEN A MONTH SINCE Logan McCrea had shifted his attention from trout to steelhead. Instead of a light nine-and-a-half-foot single-handed rod and three boxes of trout flies, he now carried a thirteen-foot two-handed spey rod and a single box of steelhead flies.

He also carried a pad of ruled yellow paper and a GPS unit, and he made a big show of asking questions, checking out campsites, and taking photos. This was part of his "guidebook" cover story. Logan had been doing it before, but he'd intensified his activities so as to deflect suspicion after his scary encounter last month.

He'd made several float trips since then, as well as day trips along the access roads. There had been no further sign of Nearly Honest John Kincaid and Scarface. No doubt he was right: they were part of a drug operation, and he'd never see them again. Still, he remained alert, if not anxious.

He was currently on a multi-day float trip. Yesterday he'd camped at a favorite one-tent site that had good shade. An excellent steelhead run lay just upstream, and a couple more below. Last evening he'd fished the downstream runs, hooking two steelhead and losing both. This morning he would fish the run above camp.

Rising before dawn, he slipped into his waders, then switched on his headlamp so he could see to tie his bootlaces. He picked up his spey rod, a water bottle, and a granola bar, and hiked the meandering trail to the head of the run.

Logan waded in and began casting. Being right-handed and on river-left, he was doing single-spey casts. He threw about ninety feet of line, aimed 45 degrees downstream. Then the fly swung across the current on a tight line until it was straight downstream. At the end of the swing, he'd let the fly "hangdown" for about ten seconds because steelhead often followed the fly without taking it; give the fish a little more time, and it might grab. After the hangdown, he'd step downstream about three feet and cast again. And so on until the entire run had been covered. Each cast and presentation needed to be fluid, precise, and consistent.

The goal of the swinging presentation is to sweep the water with a series of concentric arcs. Each cast/swing/hangdown/step typically took about fifty-five seconds. The run he'd chosen this morning was about 250 yards long—typical for the Deschutes—so he would make about 250 casts. At almost a minute per cast, that's nearly four hours to cover one run.

When trout fishing, you have a good idea where the fish are. If they're rising to an insect hatch, you can even see them. Not so with steelhead. First, there aren't very many of them. Second, you don't know where they are. You believe that a fish or two might be somewhere in the run because steelhead favor a certain current speed, and experience has proven that this is good water. You also know that they're likely to hold in front of a rock or in a slight depression along the bottom. But there are many runs, each with many rocks and depressions. So you have a small number of invisible fish that could be almost anywhere. Further, even if a steelhead sees your fly there's no guarantee it will bite; the odds are actually against you.

When a steelhead finally grabs your fly after hours (or days) of casting, the urge is to leap into the air and scream "Glory Hallelujah!" But no. The angler has to resist every human impulse and slowly, even nonchalantly, swing the rod toward the riverbank. This pulls the hook into the corner of the steelhead's jaw and makes a more secure hookup. Once a fish is hooked, the odds are only slightly better than 50-50 that the angler will land it. And if it's a wild fish, it must be released unharmed.

Sometimes—especially after eight or more hours of fruitless casting—Logan would find himself wondering, *Why would a rational person fish this way? Why do anglers put so much effort into something so rare and elusive?*

After much reflection, he'd concluded that the reason was deeply subconscious: steelhead make a hero's journey; anglers seek to connect with that journey.

When young, steelhead are nearly indistinguishable from rainbow trout. Not only do they look the same, but they live in the same places, eat the same food, and try to avoid the same predators. But when they are a year old and about seven inches long, steelhead do something a rainbow would never dream of doing: they migrate to the ocean.

The journey to the sea has profound implications. First, their bodies change so they can live in saltwater. Second, those that survive will become larger and more powerful. And third, most will not survive.

A Deschutes trout is content to spend its life in the same two-mile stretch of river. After all, there's plenty to eat, and once it reaches maturity it's safe from most predators except otters and osprey.

But a steelhead risks everything so it can become more than a trout. It migrates down the Deschutes, then the Columbia, and finally swims into that vast deep where all the rivers of the world empty their waters. It will wander for a year or more, going places a trout will never go, seeing things a trout will never see, facing dangers a trout could never imagine.

Those that survive return to the river transformed, tempered. They are bigger and stronger, of course—like a rainbow that never stopped growing. For many anglers that's enough. If you catch big strong fish, then you must be big and strong, right? That's angler psychology: you become what you catch.

Other anglers, however, see more and therefore become more. They see a survivor that has been through dark waters, that has risked all to go beyond what it was. When their flyline goes tight, the connection is not just the eighty or one hundred feet to a steelhead: it goes deep into the sea and touches every place the steelhead has been, everything it has seen, all that it knows about survival.

These anglers know that they, too, are on a journey, and they ask, *How do I become more than I am? How do I travel through dark waters and return safely home?*

Logan concluded that the pursuit of steelhead with a fly rod rivals any religious conviction—surpasses most religious convictions, really. For trout, you need hope. But for steelhead you need an abiding, persistent faith—faith in the invisible fish; faith that if you keep doing the right thing in the right place at the right time … It. Will. Happen. At any microsecond you could be connected to something magnificent and grand, wild and natural. Your faith is rewarded right here on earth.

Logan had also observed that steelheaders separate themselves by sects according to what they believe is the right way to pursue such a noble quarry. The biggest split is gear anglers versus fly anglers. Fly anglers view themselves as morally superior because they fish with more grace. Surprisingly, most gear anglers agree.

Fly anglers then self-segregate according to tackle and tactics. First, it's single-handed rods versus the long two-handed spey rods. Spey rods are felt to be superior because they are more elegant and graceful. But even spey rodders split: those who do the touch-and-go casts—single spey, snake roll, etc.—see those who do the less graceful double spey and circle casts as the equivalent of adults riding bicycles with training wheels (*Geez, man, stop the beginner stuff and learn to cast!*). Even the touch-and-go people have their dichotomy: anglers who can cast equally well with either hand up and those who can't.

At the top of the pyramid are the touch-and-go spey rod fly anglers whose best cast is a single spey with their non-dominant hand on top. It takes major skill to cast like that, and they know they are the elite of the elite—and therefore some of them are insufferably snobby. This is the group that Logan aspired to belong to. Not that he would be insufferably snobby. He just wanted to be good enough to have the option.

At the bottom of the fly rod hierarchy are the nymphers: those who use trout-like tactics with a single-handed rod to catch steelhead. This may seem strange to non-fly anglers. After all, even the spey rod swingers use a wet fly that rides a few inches below the water's surface, so the difference between nymphing and swinging is only a few feet in the water column. Further, Logan knew, it takes skill to be a good nympher. And at very low water temperature, or on rivers whose structure makes swinging flies less effective, nymphing is the most logical approach. He had to admit that nymphing is very effective—often more effective than swinging. What's more, most swingers have no problem using nymphing tactics to catch trout. They only balk when it comes to steelhead. Why is it different?

It's different because the fish is different—as different as faith is from hope.

The point is not just to catch a steelhead. The point is to connect to an invisible elegance and grace. Therefore, you should be visibly elegant and graceful. And nymphing is graceless. The long broad runs of the Deschutes were such perfect places to swing a fly that it seemed sacrilegious to do anything else.

This morning, Logan was blessed. He experienced that mystical moment when the line went tight—he was connected, and it all seemed worthwhile. He hooked a beautiful wild steelhead, a hen of about ten pounds that ran hard and cleared the water with half a dozen big jumps. Strong-shouldered and silver-bright with a red stripe starting to show on her sides (the stripe would grow redder as she spent more time in the river), she took his fly near the end of the run just before Logan was about to give up on the morning's fishing.

He released her into the river and returned to camp. By the time he'd finished breakfast, the sun was high over the canyon. In two hours it would be nearly a hundred degrees.

Logan shucked himself from his waders and hung them from a tree branch. He slipped on khaki shorts and a pair of sandals, then set up his chair under the shade of an alder, the legs in six inches of water. The chair had a footrest and was big enough to support his head when he leaned back.

This chair was an essential part of Logan's river gear because he could take naps in it. August steelheading starts pre-dawn and ends at dark, so anglers only sleep a few hours each night. During the midday hours, when the sun pounds the river like a hammer, fishing is slow. Wise anglers use this time to prepare their gear for the evening session and get some shut-eye.

Logan read a library book for about an hour, then went over his notes for the guidebook's section on Mecca Flat, which lay at the upstream end of the Deschutes canyon. He began with the road directions and wrote: "The road to Mecca Flat is dirt and has large potholes. Turn east just past the Rainbow Market. Three roads fork off this dirt road. Take the third road; there is no sign."

He paused and thought about his visits to Mecca. The flat is broad and open, but the canyon pulls in close, like an hourglass, as you walk downstream. You soon come to some backeddies that hold nice-sized trout. Those fish see anglers all day long and are easily spooked, so he'd learned to sneak up on his hands and knees so they wouldn't see him.

He looked at his road directions again, turned to a fresh sheet of paper, and wrote:

> *The road to Mecca is dirt*
> *and has large potholes.*
> *Turn east just past the rainbow*
> *and take the third fork—on faith*
> *because there is no sign.*
> *Let yourself be pulled to the river*
> *like sand flows through the glass*
> *and you will come to heaven.*
>
> *Approach on your knees*
> *or it slips away.*

Logan put down his papers and closed his eyes. Before dropping off to sleep, he thought about last month's strange encounter with Sergei Kalinnikov, the former KGB agent he knew from Germany. Sergei had said they must "look out for their brothers." Who were Sergei's brothers? Then he'd launched into a *non sequitur* about the Balkans being "the despair of tidy minds." None of it made sense to Logan, and that bothered him because it meant something was going on that he didn't understand. He hadn't seen Sergei since that brief encounter by the OK. Where was he? Why had he come to the Deschutes?

He'd reported the incident to Bill Short via encrypted email rather than the secure videophone link in Beaverton. Bill investigated and found that Sergei had been in the US three times since April, listing his profession as "journalist." Neither Bill nor Logan believed that; it was a common cover story for Soviet spies during the Cold

War. But the CIA couldn't determine if Sergei was with the Russian FSB or some other group. Although the CIA and the FSB sometimes cooperated in the New World Order, present relations between the two countries were at a low ebb. The CIA didn't want to pursue the matter further unless there was better evidence of a threat.

They'd decided that Logan should try to weasel something out of Sergei if he saw him again. In the meantime, he'd keep his eyes peeled.

Thoughts of Sergei eddied in Logan's mind as he drifted into sleep.

~

LOGAN AWOKE WITH A START. He looked at his watch; four o'clock in the afternoon. He'd been asleep almost two hours. Something was at the edge of memory, like a dream almost remembered. Something that seemed important. He tried to dredge it to the forefront of consciousness. A shard of a thought rose almost to recognition; then it was gone. *Relax; try again.* And there it was: Sarajevo, summer 1914.

That surprised him. He recalled what he knew about Sarajevo: capital of Bosnia-Herzegovina; in 1914, part of the Austro-Hungarian empire; a Serb nationalist steps from a crowd and assassinates the Archduke Ferdinand, heir to the Austrian throne. The event triggers The Great War, World War I. Millions die. Unresolved issues after the armistice lead to World War II. More millions die. Europe is in ruins.

Okay, that's middle school history. He was ready to dismiss it as random synapses firing during a dream. Meaningless. Or …

Why did the assassination trigger a war? Because the Austrians were seriously pissed and intended to declare war on Serbia. The German Kaiser backed his Austrian buddies. The French and British lined up on the other side. Why? Because they were allied with the Russian Tsar. The Tsar started mobilizing his troops. The Germans issued an ultimatum for them to cease, but the Russians wouldn't comply because they were so abysmally inefficient. Why did the Russians even care? Because the Russians saw themselves as protectors of the Serbs, who were fellow Slavs and Orthodox Christians.

It hit Logan between the eyes: the Russians viewed the Serbs as their brothers.

That might have been what Sergei meant when he said they must "watch out" for their brothers. His reference to the Balkans—how they were the despair of tidy minds—wasn't a *non sequitur* at all. It was perfectly logical. In that tricky part of the world, everyone was both villain and victim. It was ripe for conflict and rife with intrigue.

But what did that have to do with Sergei being on the Deschutes? Did the Russians still see the Serbs as brothers? Perhaps. Brotherhood aside, Russia needed allies to balance against the European powers. Serbia, their traditional proxy in southeast Europe, was strategic for them.

Logan recalled that Scarface, the pistol-packing part of the Dastardly Duo, had a vaguely Slavic accent. He could have been Russian. Or Serbian. Or Ukrainian, Polish, or any number of other kinds of Slav. It didn't follow that he was a Serb, or that he was a buddy of Sergei's. He might not even be a Slav.

And the biggest question of all: what—if anything—did Russia and Serbia have to do with him and his mission? Islamist terrorists did not fit any of those scenarios. Once again he was back to the drug gang theory.

Logan's head hurt from thinking about it. He was tense and frustrated because he felt like he'd solved a minor part of a big puzzle, but the rest was a complete muddle. He tried thinking about it a while longer, then gave up. Sergei was the key. If he saw the Russian again, he'd try to get something useful out of him.

26

August 19: Deschutes Access Road below Maupin

CASEY LEFT THE OK AT 4:00 IN the morning for a one-day float, Pine Tree to Macks Canyon. His clients were two brothers, Stan and Drew. Stan was from Portland and fished often. He hired Casey once or twice a year. Drew was visiting from out of town and only fly fished when he came to see Stan. This was his first steelhead trip, and his first time with Casey.

"So are steelhead like salmon?" Drew asked. Apparently he was a morning person; his brother Stan was asleep, head against the window.

"They're both anadromous fish," Casey explained. "That means they're born in fresh water, migrate to the ocean when they're young, and come back to the river to spawn. Salmon die after they spawn. Steelhead don't. They return to the ocean, and a few live long enough to come back and spawn again."

"I see," said Drew. "But they're big, like salmon."

"Not quite as big, but most Deschutes steelhead are five to ten pounds. This year we're seeing more big ones than usual."

"Stan says we can't keep the fish."

"You can keep a hatchery fish, but not a wild one."

"Are the hatchery fish full-grown when they're put in the river?"

"No. They're released when they're about five to seven inches long. They migrate to the ocean with the wild fish, but they don't survive as well."

"How come?"

"Part of it is that the hatchery broodstock comes from different river systems and isn't adapted to the Deschutes. Part of it is ocean conditions, which vary from one year to the next and seem to impact hatchery fish more than wild fish. Then there's the rearing conditions in hatcheries, and how they select fish for breeding. Also the native rainbow trout may play an important role in how wild stocks propagate. And maybe they need a lot more wild fish to maintain a healthy population … " Casey continued for several more minutes, trying not to get too detailed or technical.

Finally Drew raised a hand. "It's complicated, isn't it?" he said.

"Yes, and there's still so much we don't know. We think we understand how Mother Nature works, but we don't have a clue. Worse, we think we can do better, but obviously we don't."

"I guess," Drew said, "that people have trouble accepting the fact that they're not as smart—and as good at these things—as the Creator."

Casey laughed. "You've got that right. And the Powers-That-Be think that if they occasionally give a guy a hatchery fish for the BBQ, he won't notice how badly they've screwed things up. The one thing that should be crystal clear is that we need to protect the wild fish. If we lose them, we'll never understand how things are supposed to work."

~

THEY LAUNCHED AT PINE TREE and floated to the first run. Casey positioned Stan at the head of the run and got him started, then took Drew downstream and worked with him. Half an hour into the run, Stan hooked a fish. Casey waded up to him and gave advice while he played the steelhead. When it was tired, Stan pulled it close. Casey tailed the fish, then handed it to Stan without removing it from the water.

Casey took out a waterproof camera. "Okay, Stan, lift and grin. Only a couple of inches out of the water, though."

Stan took the fish from the water, supporting its head with one hand and gripping in front of the tail with the other. It was a wild, native buck, about six pounds—a typical Deschutes one-salt fish.

Casey snapped a quick photo. "Back into the water," he said to Stan. Then Casey made sure the fish was revived and released it. He and Stan did high fives.

After the first run, they floated downriver, stopping here and there to fish, but there were no more steelhead. Near noon, Casey pulled into a shady spot and served lunch.

They rested through the heat of the day, then started fishing again as the sun crept close to the western rimrock. They were in Ferry Canyon as dusk approached. Stan picked up another steelhead right away, and Drew even had a hookup, although he lost the fish. The canyon was growing dark, and the air was cooling. With about an hour of fishing left, Drew reeled up and went to the boat. Stan wanted to keep at it a little longer.

Casey waded out to him. "Stand thigh deep," Casey said. "As you step down the run, angle toward that big rock." He pointed downstream. "It's all good water, so you could hook a fish anywhere. The tailout is especially productive."

"What's a tailout? You told me last year, but I forgot."

"Steelhead runs typically go like this: riffle, pool, tailout. The riffle is where the run starts—just as the water deepens after a shallow spot. Then there's the pool; that's the main part of the run. The tailout is the end. The water shallows up, and steelhead find the current to their liking. The tailout here is pretty good. You don't want to miss it. The tailout merges into the next shallow riffle, which often starts the next run."

They'd fished about ten minutes when Casey asked Stan what sort of work he did.

"I'm a freelance consultant for medical aid agencies. I handle logistics for agencies that send doctors on mercy missions around the world."

"Are you a doctor?"

"No. I just make sure they have what they need. Sometimes I travel to remote places, but usually not." Stan shook his head. "It's incredible what the rest of the world is like. Crises and desperate situations in so many places."

"I can imagine. Poverty, lack of food, no medical care."

"It's not just that. It's the wars. Tribal conflicts, ethnic cleansing—that sort of thing. There are some really nasty people out there. They take bad situations and make them worse."

"Nice cast, but be sure to wait for your D-loop to form before your forward stroke."

"Oh, right. Thanks." A few more casts, then Stan said, "There's so much hatred and revenge in the world. Things we just can't imagine here. America has always been the country of new beginnings, but there are places where they can't get over the past—where people focus all their energy on avenging something that happened three centuries ago."

Stan made another cast, then went on. "I was in Pendleton a couple of years back, on business. Went into the hotel bar before going to bed—you know how it is when you're out of town and alone. Sat next to a guy who'd had a few drinks. He was from Umatilla. He asked what I did, and I told him. Then he started talking about this girl he'd known. A *grand passion*. I'm thinking, 'Oh man, I've got to listen to some drunk whine about lost love.' I wished I'd gone to my room to watch Letterman."

"I can understand that," Casey said. While listening to Stan, Casey's mind kept track of the story as a sequence of images. He saw Pendleton with its rodeo arena, and a bar with two people talking— one of them Stan, one of them an indistinct man. Then he saw Umatilla with the indistinct man, then Letterman telling jokes.

Stan went on. "But he got started on his story, so I figured I had to listen for a while to be polite. It was terrible. Awful. His girlfriend was from Yugoslavia, but she'd been in California since she was twelve. Her father worked in the Bay Area—electronics, I think.

Anyway, the guy showed me her photo. Gorgeous. Dark hair, pretty face, obviously full of life. She was in nursing school. Boston. He was some sort of engineer. They were going to be married after her graduation. When she was a senior, she and her brother went to the old country to visit family. While she was there, the war started. This was late 1991."

Casey saw more images: a pretty girl with dark hair, the Golden Gate Bridge, Paul Revere, a wedding, a generic village in Europe. He had a sense where Stan's story was going. It didn't sound good.

"Her family background was Muslim. She wasn't religious—it was culture and history for them, not theology. She was in eastern Bosnia when things started falling apart. The UN created a so-called safe area in Srebrenica. It was over-crowded, desperate. She was useful because of her nurse training, so she stayed and helped one of the medical aid teams that was there."

"Did this guy talk her into coming back to the States?"

"He tried. But there was so much suffering, and she wanted to help. She felt she'd found a calling."

"Very selfless. I'm sure it wasn't easy."

"Yes. Anyway, in summer 1995 the Bosnian Serb army attacked the safe area. The West bungled it every way possible. NATO, the UN, everyone. Just screwed it up royally. Did nothing. Stood by and let it happen. Didn't think it could get as bad as it did."

"How bad did it get."

"The Serbs rounded up many of the men and boys and let others go. They killed the ones they'd rounded up. Tied their hands behind their backs, blindfolded them, and shot them in the back of the head. Others they herded into an old warehouse and sprayed them with machine-gun fire. Those that had left were hunted down like animals. Over 7,000 people were killed, most of them civilians. Worst crime on European soil since World War II."

"What about the guy's fiancée? Was she shot?"

"The different medical agencies were allowed to leave. They

formed convoys and evacuated wounded people. But a few miles from the Muslim front lines, this woman's convoy was stopped at a Bosnian Serb checkpoint. The vehicles and supplies were confiscated. The wounded were forced to walk. And this guy's fiancée was singled out because she was Muslim. She was gang raped for several hours by Serb soldiers. She staggered into Muslim-held Bosnia, physically and mentally traumatized. She never recovered. A few weeks later she threw herself from a window and died."

More pictures filled Casey's head, all of them ugly and tinged in gray. He closed his eyes. How much time would he need on the river to flush these images from his memory? Maybe it wasn't true. Maybe it was just an exaggeration. "How did they know this?" he said.

"A reporter followed up on leads and broke the story about the massacre at Srebrenica. A lot of people didn't believe it, but there was too much evidence. I called one of our people in Europe and checked out the story. He confirmed it." Stan shook his head slowly. "Anyway, this guy in Pendleton hates the Serbs. All Serbs. Wasn't too keen on America and its allies, either. This happened years ago, and it was like yesterday to him. I never met anyone who hated like that. He pushed up his sleeve and showed me a tattoo: *Never Forget. Never Forgive.* I don't think he will, either. Fortunately he was meeting someone at the bar. The guy showed up—tough-looking hombre with a shaved head—and they went off somewhere. I wasn't sorry to see them go."

Stan hooked another steelhead right at dark, but the fish couldn't wipe the Bosnia story from Casey's mind. How would he feel if someone had done that to Megan? He knew what his first reaction would be: he'd want to kill, in the most painful way possible, every bastard that did it. He wouldn't, but he'd want to. Would he spread his hatred to an entire population? He hoped not. On the other hand, he knew that it was one thing to stand in the Deschutes and think about it hypothetically and something else to be faced with an atrocity against someone he loved.

27

August 20: Southeast Portland

SHE'D COME AGAIN IN THE NIGHT—urging, yearning for revenge, giving him strength and resolve.

Years ago, when she'd first appeared in his dreams, she was happy and carefree—as she'd been in their youth. Now, her face and body were exactly as they'd been when he'd last seen her, but her voice had changed as he had changed: angry, unrelenting, vengeful.

They'd dealt with her as if she were nothing human, with no more feeling than a rock. Soon, they would learn what it was like to be treated that way. Soon, there would be no remorse, no mercy, no compassion or feeling of any kind—only revenge against those who'd done this to her. And against those who'd stood by and let it happen.

In the last two years there were times when he'd wondered if this was the right course. He'd hesitated, letting his emotions get in his way, wondering if this was what she would have wanted. But there would be no more wavering or ambivalence. The course was set, and he would follow it to the end. The dreams told him he was right.

He rose from his bed, showered, and shaved. He carefully combed his dark hair, then put on his wire-framed glasses. He buttoned up the front of his plaid shirt, then the left cuff. Before fastening the right cuff he glanced at the tattoo on his forearm: *Never Forget. Never Forgive.* And he wouldn't.

Peter Bolton looked at her photo in the metal frame on his bureau. She was smiling and happy, as she'd been when she'd first appeared in his dreams. But he had a different image of her now. "Soon," he said to the latter image. "Patience, and it will happen."

28

August 20: On the Road to Macks Canyon

WHAT HAVE I DONE? LOGAN THOUGHT to himself. *What was I thinking?* For the first time since he and Trudy had split up, he was having dinner with another woman. Was it a date? Did people still talk about "dates"?

Her name was Lisa Albright, and she was this year's fish check lady. The fish check lady was temporary help, hired by the Fish and Wildlife department to ask anglers how many steelhead they'd hooked, how many they'd landed, whether they were wild or hatchery origin, etc. She (or he; some years it was a fish check guy) sat in a chair on the access road eighteen miles above Macks Canyon and tried not to go nuts with boredom. It was a lonely job with little to do except wait for an occasional car to come up the road. Then she'd ask a few questions and write the answers on a clipboard.

To Logan's surprise, he knew this year's fish check lady. Lisa was a former computer programmer from Med-Rec, the now-defunct start-up that Logan used to work for. Lisa was about ten years younger than Logan. She'd worked in a different group than his, but like nearly everyone else at Med-Rec, she'd been laid off when the company tanked. And like nearly everyone else, she hadn't yet found a regular job.

Each time he'd passed down the road, he'd stopped and talked to Lisa. It always started the same—"How's the fishing? Anybody catching steelhead?"—then moved on to various people from Med-Rec and how they were doing. A few times they'd worked together on the *New York Times* crossword puzzle, especially if it was Friday or Saturday, the hard days.

They'd talked more than an hour today, and as Logan was leaving he casually mentioned that maybe they should get together for dinner in a couple of days—to talk about Med-Rec and her job search, of course. The invitation just came out. She'd jumped on it.

Was it a date? Logan hadn't thought about another women in a romantic way for over two years. First, he was trying to win Trudy back. After the accident, he was focused on Sam, besides dealing with his own issues. Now he was going out to dinner with Lisa Albright. He told himself it was just to aid her job hunt and to talk about old times. But honestly, there was more to it than that. How did he feel about it? In general, scared to death. In particular, worried how Sam would react.

29

August 20: Ashland, Oregon

"WHAT ARE YOU READING?" Hank asked.

"The Bible," Jackie said.

"Liar. It's a comic book."

"It's a graphic novel of the book of Genesis." She pushed it across the table.

Hank thumbed through a couple of pages; then his eyes bugged out. "Holy … ! Have you seen this picture of Eve?"

"Kinda buxom, huh."

"That's not all." He tapped a finger on Eve's backside and slid the book back. "She must work out. You don't get glutes like that without a lot of heavy lifting."

They were having lunch at a brewpub in Ashland, near the Oregon-California border. They'd been in the town four days, staying at the Winchester Inn, a local bed-and-breakfast, and going to the Oregon Shakespeare Festival. Before that they'd floated the wild and scenic section of the Rogue River in Hank's driftboat, camping on the riverbank for three nights. They'd been doing this sort of thing since May.

Lunch arrived, and after a few bites Jackie said, "How was my rowing?"

"You did good. Amazing, really. You're learning to read the currents and work with them. And my knuckles are starting to get their color back."

"Your knuckles?"

"From sitting in the front of my boat while you rowed us through Blossom Bar Rapids. I think I left permanent fingerprints on the gunwales. Blossom Bar is a lot trickier than Whitehorse on the Deschutes."

"But I did well?"

"You did great. You have to be clever, though. You'll never be able to muscle it—a little thing like you."

Jackie clenched her fist and crooked her right arm. "Yeah? Feel that!" she said playfully.

Hank felt her bicep. "Wow! You should be on the Wheaties box. Pretty soon you'll look like that drawing of Eve in your comic book."

"It's a graphic novel. How are my glutes doing?" She turned slightly and pushed a hip toward Hank.

He cocked his head. "They look good to me."

"But are they firm?" she said.

"I'll check later."

Jackie took a couple of bites from her sandwich, then said thoughtfully, "Which was your favorite play?"

"My favorite?" Hank said reflectively. "Let me think about that. I'll tell you this, though. I had no idea what to expect. I thought they just did a few musty plays in an outdoor theater for a week in front of some artsy-fartsy types, and that was it."

"No, my dear, it's three stages, and it goes nine months of the year. It's one of the biggest theaters in the country, if you add up the number of tickets they sell." She closed her book and looked straight at Hank. "So *Twelfth Night*: what did you think of it?"

"Funny. Some of those people were kinda mean to each other. Hard to understand the language in some places, not so hard in others. A lot of music references." He ate a couple of French fries. "And more stories going on than I thought. It didn't just go … I don't know how to describe it."

"It wasn't linear—didn't go in a straight line. Shakespeare was a circular storyteller. He'd start a few stories and flip from one to the next. They're all connected and tie together by the end. Did that bother you?"

"Not once I got used to it. I just went with the flow."

"It *is* a flow, like a river. Does the Deschutes go straight to the Columbia?"

Hank shook his head. "Lots of twists and turns."

"And quite a few backeddies. But all that water ends up in one place. Now, tell me how you liked *Hamlet*."

"Wow. I thought they'd all be wearing, you know, old clothes. But Hamlet was in a business suit, and at the end he had on jeans and a T-shirt. Cool. I liked him, poor kid. He was trying to do what he thought he ought to, but he kept second-guessing himself."

For the rest of their meal they discussed *Hamlet*. Hank was trying to get at the reasons for Hamlet's indecision, why he hesitated to act. "Maybe he didn't believe in ghosts," Hank suggested. "Maybe he thought it was just his imagination."

"Or," Jackie said, "it wasn't in his nature to be vengeful. He was caught between his love of his father and his inclination to find a less violent solution."

"So he's just supposed to let it go—that his uncle murdered his father?"

"But if he avenges his father's death, then what? You have to think these things through."

"It's okay to think about things," Hank said. "But sometime you have to take action."

"Did you have deep thoughts when you were in combat?" Jackie asked.

"Hell no! You learn to put some things aside for another time. When bullets are snapping past your head, your training takes over. Hamlet didn't have that. He was a student, not a soldier. I can see why he couldn't make up his mind. It's amazing that he finally did anything at all. Of course it didn't work out well for him. Or for everyone else."

"It was a tragedy," Jackie said. "Tragedies end with everyone dead."

As she spoke, a locket hanging from her neck swung back and forth. Hank reached across the table and took the locket in his hand. "I haven't seen this before," he said. "What is it?"

"I don't usually wear it," Jackie said. She slipped the chain over her head and handed the open locket to Hank. Two small, faded photos were inside: one was a beautiful young Asian woman, maybe twenty years old; the other was a European man in his thirties. Names were engraved on the back of the locket, and a date: 1949. Hank looked quizzically at Jackie.

"My grandfather and grandmother," she said.

Hank saw her eyes grow misty. Lines appeared on her face.

"My grandfather was French, from a wealthy family with aristocratic ties," Jackie said. "During World War II he fought with de Gaulle and the Free French. After the war, in 1946, he came to Hanoi—French Indo-China—as a diplomat. He met my grandmother. She was ethnic Chinese, but her family had been in Vietnam for decades. They became lovers. Very much in love, very passionate. My grandfather was called back to France, but he vowed to return. He told her he would divorce his wife and marry her. He gave her this locket, and put their photos inside."

"Did he come back?"

Jackie shook her head. "He didn't know it, but she was

pregnant when he left. Before he could come back, she died. In child-birth. The baby was taken to a Catholic orphanage. My grandfather made inquiries. He was frantic to find my grandmother. They told him she was dead. They didn't tell him about the child."

"The child was your mother?"

Jackie nodded. "In 1954, when the Communists took over in the north, my mother was taken to Saigon. That's what most of the Catholics did—they fled for the south. My mother married when she was seventeen. My father was half French, half Vietnamese. He had an Army career and became an ARVN officer, a major. He died in the fighting in 1975."

"During the fall of Saigon."

"Yes."

"What did your mother do?"

"She had me and two sons. I was the oldest. The Communists had no use for half-Chinese, half-French widows of ARVN officers. There wasn't much food. My brothers …" She paused and wiped a tear from her cheek. "My brothers died of disease … brought on by malnutrition."

"They starved."

"Essentially. My mother was weak and sick. She was desperate to get me out of the country while I was still healthy. She had a close friend who was planning to leave. He took me with him. My mother gave me this locket and said to keep it safe. We left on a boat. It was very crowded."

"How old were you?"

"I was seven."

"Things didn't always work out for 'boat people.'"

"It did for us. My mother's friend got me to France, to Paris. He was an educated man, a schoolteacher who spoke fluent French. His aunt was a nun who'd worked at the orphanage and knew my mother's history. He searched the phone books for someone with my grandfather's name. He was very persistent. Eventually he found a recently retired diplomat living by himself—his wife had left him years ago, and his only son had just died. He was a lonely man. We showed him the locket and told him the story."

"The diplomat was your grandfather?"

"Yes. He took me in. You see, he never knew my grandmother had a child. He adored me and adopted me. It was a blessing for us both, a new life for us. That's when I got my name—my French name."

"And why you grew up in France."

Jackie nodded. "I learned French in a heartbeat." She pointed at her right ear. "Good ears. Perfect pitch. And a talent for imitation."

"And a hell of a lot of guts and discipline. Did you start the violin in France?"

Jackie shook her head. "In Vietnam. My mother taught piano and did recitals. She was very popular, very good. There was always classical music in our house, either her playing piano or on the stereo. She'd started me on the violin when I was three. When I arrived on my grandfather's doorstep, I had two possessions: the locket and a kid-sized violin in a battered case. My grandfather was an accomplished amateur cellist—apparently music ran in the family—and played regularly with a group of friends in a string quartet. The lead violinist was a well-known teacher, so my grandfather immediately started me in lessons. It was quickly clear that I had ambition and natural talent. When I was twelve, I won a national youth competition and got a scholarship with a top-tier teacher. The first day, he told my grandfather—he took me everywhere, did everything for me—to get the music for one of Bach's Unaccompanied Sonatas. When we met two days later, I played the first half from memory. I'd never seen it until we got the music. My teacher was stunned."

"I guess!"

"To make the story short, my grandfather and I moved to New York when I was sixteen, and I started at Julliard."

"Why didn't you stay in France?"

"Well," said Jackie ruefully, "by the time I was a teenager, I had almost no memory of Vietnam at all. I considered myself French. But the French did not share that opinion. To them I was a half-breed colonial, a reminder of an era they wanted to forget. My grandfather thought I'd be more accepted in the US."

"He moved with you?"

"Yes. I won the Naumburg Competition in my early twenties and started a solo career. He went with me when I was on tour. He taught me how to travel well and survive on the road."

"Your grandfather was something else!"

"He was the most wonderful person I ever knew." She gave Hank a sly smile. "You come close, though."

"I'm honored. So what happened to your grandfather?"

"My career started well. I was a 'sensation.' But I was young. I was technically brilliant, but something was missing. By the time I was twenty-five, the critics were starting to notice that I lacked that 'something special.' I was older, and more was expected of me. It wasn't there. Then my grandfather suddenly died. He was eighty-four. I took it very hard. 'How could God do this to me? It's my fault for being a bad girl.' I left off touring for six months. During that time my Vietnam memories flooded back—my mother and father, my little brothers, the panic when Saigon fell, the trip when they smuggled me out, the desperation and dread that consumed everyone on the boat. I'd repressed my Vietnam memories for years, but they flooded back—all the memories, all the emotions. They were vivid to me, like they were yesterday."

"What happened to your mother?"

"Of course my grandfather tried to find her as soon as I showed up in Paris. He used his diplomatic contacts, but ... " Jackie spread her hands wide and shook her head. "She was gone. No trace of her. So many died after Saigon fell."

Hank nodded. "And in Cambodia. Around two million, they figure."

Jackie took a deep breath. "I didn't know how I could go on

without my grandfather. But I remembered what he often said to me: *Courage.* And I went back on tour. I did it for him, for all of them. Before, I was very selfish. I played for me—to prove how good I was and to get fame and recognition. But after my grandfather died, every note I played was for him. And for my grandmother and my mother and father and brothers—for all the people on the boat that crept into the China Sea in the dead of night—for all the people in the world, living or dead, suffering or not. I finally understood what Mozart and Beethoven and Bruch and Sibelius and the rest of them were trying to say. It wasn't about the notes, or even about the beauty. It was about us. My music took on a new dimension, a new voice. I stopped playing the violin and started making music."

Hank reached a hand across the table.

Jackie put her hand on top of his. "Before, people came up to me and said how wonderfully I'd played, and 'aren't you amazing, playing those notes so fast.' But after, they'd come up and say, 'Somehow that made me think of my grandmother,' or they'd say, 'I listened to you, and I remembered that time I was so happy and in love.'"

"How did the critics react?"

"They adored me. And I enjoyed performing again. I was connected to the audience. I could feel their response, feel it on my skin. I draw energy …"

"… from the audience. You know what's working and what isn't."

Jackie nodded. "That's why I play a piece on the road before recording it. It drives my agent, Bertram Levy, to distraction. He wants me to do the recording first, then play the piece on tour. You sell more CDs that way. But I want to polish it on the road. I try different things. I might play three nights in a row, and each night will be a little different. After a season on tour, I know what works best. Then I'm ready to record."

"Ah, so that's why …"

"… why I don't want to have a recording career without a touring career. For me, they go together."

"But now you don't …"

Jacked bobbed her head. "Exactly. That burst of insight I had after my grandfather's death—that connection with the audience? I rode that wave for a long time. But the last few years it's faded. And my music has suffered. My days in front of a concert audience may be over."

"That would be a shame for the world—not to hear you play anymore."

"But I won't stand up there and just go through the motions. If it's not up to my standards, I'm not walking onto the stage."

"You're practicing two hours a day now," Hank said. "Every day."

"Practicing is going well. I'm pleased with my progress. But two hours a day isn't much." Her gaze shifted to a space beyond the restaurant. "I'm reluctant to go on tour. I could do three performances and find I don't have what it takes anymore. It's not something you ease into." She looked at Hank straight on. "You have to commit all the way."

"It's scares you."

"It frightens me to death—the thought of performing again."

Hank nodded. "How can I help?"

"You are helping. Keep doing what you're doing."

Hank shook his head.

"What?" said Jackie.

"Nothing."

"It's not nothing. Tell me."

Hank looked away from her. "My life seems so trivial compared to yours."

"Don't you ever say that!"

"It's true. What have I done? I tie some feathers and fur on a hook, and some guy goes and catches a fish. Big deal. Maybe he uses my fly to catch a wild steelhead, then kills it."

"Maybe he goes to the river and finds renewal and regeneration," Jackie said. "Maybe he goes out looking for fish but finds peace. Maybe your flies are an essential part of giving him the strength to keep going with a hectic and stressful life—just the break he needs. Have you thought of that?"

"Sometimes."

"If I go back on tour, you know what people will say to me? They'll say, 'Wow! That made me think about the first time I saw river otters.' Someone else will come up and say, 'You reminded me of that big trout I caught on an O Stone fly.'"

Hank gave Jackie a crooked grin and rolled his eyes. "I doubt that very much."

"There's truth to it. A lot of truth. Being with you—being on the river with you—has given me a new perspective and a new energy. I'm finding parts of myself that I didn't know existed."

~

AFTER LUNCH THEY WALKED UP the street to the local fly shop. Hank had tied three dozen flies in their room—the most extensive tying he'd done since meeting Jackie—and hoped to sell them.

They walked into the shop and spoke to the owner, who agreed to buy Hank's flies. While he was making out the check, a young man who'd been looking at fly reels came hesitantly to Hank. "Are you Hank O'Leary?" he asked.

"Depends," said Hank, smiling. "Do I owe you money?"

"No, dude, I owe you. A lot more than money."

Hank gave him a puzzled look.

"Your book, *True Flies: Practical Patterns for the Western Fly Angler*, saved my life."

"Did you hit a mugger on the head with it?" Hank said.

The man laughed. "No. It was after my tour in Iraq. I'm in the Army, 101st Airborne. Helicopter mechanic.

I leave for Afghanistan next week. Second deployment." He paused and put down the fly reel he'd been holding. "During Desert Storm I saw some nasty shit." He turned to Jackie. "Sorry, ma'am. Pardon my French."

The young soldier took another breath. "I was okay at first, but I had trouble after. I'd done some fly fishing and tied a few flies. My sister sent me a vise and some hooks and stuff. And your book. I ordered a bunch of tying material off the internet, and I tied every fly in the book. I tied nights, I tied days. When I wasn't sleeping, eating, or on duty, I tied flies. It was something to focus on, something to create. I'd dream about taking them to the river, about fishing with them. It got me through. Anyway, I just wanted to say thanks."

When they left the store, Jackie hung tightly on Hank's arm. They walked two blocks in silence; then she said, "If you ever think you don't do some good in the world, I'll … I don't know. I'll do something. You enrich people's lives and touch them in ways you can never imagine. Most of those people you'll never meet. You're my hero."

"Everything you just said? Back at you."

~

AFTER RETURNING TO THEIR ROOM, Jackie took out her violin, tuned it carefully, and started practicing. After an hour, she returned the violin to its case. She stood, hands on hips, looking at it.

"How's the arm doing?" Hank asked.

There was a pause before she answered. "Good," she said. "It's not the arm that bothers me." She seemed lost in thought. Finally she said, "Hank, honey? Come with me. Please." She put on her dark glasses and the battered straw cowboy hat she wore when they were floating rivers and when she wanted to look as little like Jacqueline Moreau as possible. She picked up the violin case.

"Where are we going?"

"Follow me."

They went onto the main street of Ashland, to a small plaza near the theaters. Jackie set the case on the sidewalk and took out her violin. She left the case open at her feet. "Sit on that bench," she said to Hank, "and just be there for me."

She began to play. People walked by, ignoring her. Then a few stopped and listened. Then more. Soon, a dozen people were around her. Some stayed awhile before moving on. Others stood rapt, unable to leave. Most put money in the violin case.

After half an hour she stopped playing, looking happy and satisfied. She peeked into the case and said, "Hey, Hank, I think I earned enough for dinner tonight! Not bad, huh!"

A middle-aged man came up to her and said, "Lady, you're really good! Have you thought about doing this professionally?"

Jackie smiled at him. "Maybe I will," she said. "Maybe someday I will."

30

August 23: On the Road to Beavertail

AN HOUR BEFORE DAWN ON Monday morning, Casey started down the access road north of Maupin. It would be a four-day steelhead trip, Beavertail to the mouth, with two couples. Casey was guiding Tom and Marilyn. Brandon Muckenhirn, Judd's other guide, had their friends Carl and Sheryl. Willie Hyde would row the bag boat and set up camp.

Casey couldn't stop yawning, and he was having a hard time keeping his eyes focused. He'd downed two cups of coffee and still felt like a zombie. "Not enough time in bed?" Marilyn said.

"That's the guide's life. At least during steelhead season. Don't worry, though. I'm fine." He was more than fine. He was over the moon. Just sleepy. He'd had plenty of time in bed last night, but sleep didn't enter into it: Megan had spent the night at his place. He hoped his grin wasn't too wide and obvious.

~

BY THE TIME HE REACHED BEAVERTAIL, Casey was starting to feel functional. After launching, they drifted to Cedar Island. He took Tom and Marilyn to the west side, while Brandon led his clients, Carl and Sheryl, to the east side. Willie kept going so he could claim a good campsite downriver.

Casey spent most of his time with Marilyn, who was the least experienced angler. This seemed fine with Tom, who was very focused on his fishing. Near the end of the run, Tom caught a seven-pound steelhead buck. Casey stood by him while he played it. "Not yet, Tom," Casey said when it looked like Tom might force the fish. "Wait until he can't get his head down any more."

After a few more minutes, the fish was close, and Casey grabbed it in front of the tail. He kept the fish in the water and passed it to Tom, then quickly snapped three photos. They released the steelhead, and it swam off briskly. Even though it was a hatchery steelhead and they could have kept it, Casey had convinced Tom that the meat would spoil before the trip was over. If Tom picked up a hatchery steelhead on the last day, he could keep it.

They finished the run with no more hookups, then floated downriver. Brandon and his two anglers had finished before them and were already into their next run. The two boats leapfrogged all morning, then met up for lunch in a shady spot.

Brandon's clients, Carl and Sheryl, were talking about the fish Carl had caught at their first stop below Cedar Island. "Brandon said it was the biggest steelhead he's seen on the river this year," Sheryl said excitedly. Carl looked very pleased with himself. "At least twelve pounds, maybe fifteen."

"Really?" Casey said, trying to keep the skepticism out of his voice. "Any photos?"

Carl handed him his camera. "That one and the next twenty shots. It was wild, so we had to let it go." He sounded like he regretted releasing it.

Casey thumbed through the photos. As he suspected, the steelhead was about eight pounds, not twelve, and was typical for this season. Brandon had exaggerated the fish's size to boost Carl's ego. Guides sometimes did that, although Casey didn't; Brandon seemed to take client-stroking to an extreme.

But what torqued Casey was that Brandon had taken photo after photo with the fish out of the water—overhandled and obviously stressed. Casey doubted the steelhead would survive, even though it had swum away when released. He was livid but didn't let it show. He handed the camera back to Carl. "Nice fish," he said evenly.

~

CASEY GOT SOME MUCH-NEEDED sleep on the lunch break; then they floated downriver and hit two more runs before reaching their campsite just below Macks Canyon. Willie had everything in order for them. There were two tents, one for each couple. A large tarp provided shade for the cooking gear and dining table. The guides would sleep on cots under the tarp. Brandon fixed dinner—excellent as usual—and the two couples fished until dark with one more hookup between them.

After the clients had gone to bed, Casey and Brandon walked to the river to clean up their boats and get things ready for morning. "Brandon," Casey said when they were away from the camp, "those photos you took for Carl? You shouldn't have kept the fish out of water that long."

"Aw, it'll be fine. Besides, Carl wanted lots of pictures. 'Give them what they want,' I always say."

"Instead of 'Give them what they want,' how about 'Do what's right'? Educate your clients about wild fish and proper fish care."

Brandon shrugged and rolled his eyes. "Whatever. I just think it's too bad it was a wild fish and we couldn't keep it."

"The meat would spoil before the end of the trip."

"So? He'd have been proud of his trophy." Brandon elbowed Casey in the ribs. "Hey," he said, "you know that photo album Willie keeps with him? I hid it. I thought we'd have fun watching the retard look for it."

Willie—a slight, dark-haired man a few years younger than Casey but with a perpetually boyish face—was desperately pawing through dry bags in the bag boat.

Over the summer, Casey had gotten to know Willie better. While he might be illiterate, he wasn't retarded. And in any case he didn't deserve this kind of treatment from a fish-abusing jerk like Brandon Muckenhirn.

When Brandon's back was turned, Casey opened a dry bag in Brandon's boat. He found the album and handed it to Willie. "Is this yours?" Casey said casually. "Looks like it got into the wrong bag."

Willie took it gratefully.

"What's in there?" Casey asked him.

"My family," Willie said.

Casey knew that Willie's parents were both dead, so he could understand why the album meant so much to him. "I know someone who can make a copy for you," Casey said. "As a backup." He figured Logan had the computer stuff to do it and probably wouldn't mind. Willie seemed grateful.

WHEN CASEY GOT READY FOR bed, he saw Brandon set up a small LED light next to his cot. Apparently he kept it on all night. It seemed odd, but everything about Brandon was weird.

Before, he hadn't trusted Brandon. Now he flat-out disliked the guy. Brandon was good enough with the clients, and he cooked great dinners. But his "give 'em what they want" philosophy could mean bad fish handling and maybe other things Casey didn't know about. His cruel treatment of Willie was the final straw.

Brandon was the last person that should have a voice in river management policy. Not that that was going to happen. The politicos were influenced by large groups, such as conservation organizations, and by people who owned river-dependent businesses. That left Brandon out.

Or did it?

Brandon had asked some questions about the burned-out Drift Inn. Casey knew Brandon had a trust fund. Did he have enough money to buy the Drift Inn property? Set up a rival to the OK and Judd's guide business? Learn the ropes from Judd, then go into competition with him?

Casey had another thought: what if Brandon had started the fire to force the Drift Inn out of business, so he could buy the land cheap? What if he was the one who had conked Ernie?

No, no. He didn't like Brandon, but he doubted the guy was capable of arson and attempted murder. It seemed far-fetched, and maybe he was letting his dislike cloud his judgment. But what if it was true?

~

CASEY SLEPT LIKE A ROCK ALL night. He awoke a half hour before dawn feeling refreshed in body but uneasy in spirit. Brandon was one source of his unease, but there was something much more troubling: Megan. Casey was having second thoughts. Was Megan really the right woman for him? Was he the right guy for her? She could be so uptight about things—especially money—and he was so easy going. She had a decent job, while he was barely supporting himself. What kind of provider could he be?

He wasn't sure which bothered him more: these concerns, or that he had any concerns at all. He'd wanted to get back with Megan for nine years, and not just for a good time in bed. She meant far more to him than that. So why did he feel this way?

It wasn't like he'd forced himself on her. She was as passionate for him as he for her. And yet … there was something there. Or not there. He couldn't make sense of it. Why was he wondering if she should be his one and only?

For the rest of the trip, he went through the motions of guiding, but his mind was somewhere else.

~

THE EVENING THEY RETURNED to Maupin, Tom and Marilyn treated Casey to dinner at the Imperial River Inn, the fanciest place in town, and after that it was getting late. Even so, he felt obligated to call Megan. But his boat and camping stuff needed cleaning. He was off the next two days, and could have done it later, but he felt compelled to take care of his gear now. He told himself that this was a sign of maturity and responsibility. Judd would be proud of him.

In the morning he thought about going to the OK for a mocha, knowing Megan would be there. But then he remembered he was running low on flies, so he tied four dozen steelhead patterns. This took five hours. He told himself that this, too, was being mature and responsible—taking care of first things first. He needed groceries, so he drove to The Dalles and did his shopping, returning to Maupin in the evening. He went straight to bed so he could rest up and be ready for his trip the day after tomorrow. It was the responsible thing to do.

CASEY ARRIVED AT THE OK AT 6:30 the next morning and ordered a mocha from Sam. Helen, Megan's sister, came in from the back. Casey greeted her cheerily.

Helen gave him a hard, thin look and shook her head.

Uh-oh, Casey thought. *Did I do something wrong?*

He sat at an outside table sipping his mocha. Megan's car drove in. She looked at him coolly, strode purposely to his table, and sat down. She looked at him like she expected something from him.

Casey felt he should impress her with his sense of responsibility. He launched into a long description of his last trip, dwelling on how he'd helped Willie. Megan liked Willie, he knew. After all, they were some sort of cousin. He figured Megan would approve of the way he'd handled things. Megan, however, seemed distracted and wouldn't look at him.

"There's a movie in The Dalles that I thought you'd like to see," Casey offered. "Would you like to go tonight?"

"Maybe you should take Willie," she said.

Why would I want to invite Willie? Casey wondered. Then he changed gears and asked Megan about her summer school classes. She began by complaining about Bobby Thompson, a fourth grader who was struggling with reading comprehension. She was describing her frustrations when Casey interrupted and suggested that Bobby might be dyslexic. Megan said he wasn't, and started to talk about how she wanted to help these kids, but sometimes they didn't get enough support at home. This made her both angry and depressed.

Casey interrupted again and said that sometimes dyslexia was hard to detect and they shouldn't rule it out.

Megan looked straight at Casey. "I'll tell you what the problem is with the … *little boy*," she said. "The … *little boy* … IS A CLUELESS ASSHOLE!" She stood up and left.

Casey sat stunned for a couple of minutes. Why would Megan talk about a student that way? Maybe she was having her period.

Helen came out to clear away some dishes. She leaned over near Casey. "Dumb ass!" She hissed.

It was dawning on Casey that maybe Megan's parting comment wasn't about Bobby Thompson. He looked around uneasily and saw Hank O'Leary's truck parked in front of Dave Tindal's fly shop. He walked there, hoping Jackie would be with Hank and could offer him some advice.

Hank was talking to Dave when he entered. "Jackie here?" Casey asked.

"She's in Portland getting some work done on her violin," Hank said. He turned to Dave. "She's got several. She keeps her best ones in a safe in New York and just takes a cheap one when we travel. I didn't think I could tell the difference, but she played them for me and—"

"When will she be back?"

Hank considered Casey for a moment, then said, "Ah. Megan advice. Problems?"

Casey hesitated, then described the morning conversation. "I guess maybe I should have called as soon as I got back," he concluded.

Hank nodded grudgingly. "Yeah, but she doesn't own you, man." He paused, and a flash of recognition showed on his face. "Oh. Ohhhh!" Hank pointed an accusing finger at Casey. "You slept with her, didn't you!"

Casey felt his cheeks flush. He wanted to deflect this but knew his face said it all.

"Oh, man. You slept with her just before you left. And when you got back you didn't call her right away."

Casey didn't respond.

"You idiot!" Hank said. He turned to Dave. "Imagine having a dick all these years and knowing so little about women."

"Said the pot to the kettle," Dave responded.

"I've learned a lot since I met Jackie," Hank said, speaking defensively to Dave. "We talk all the time. For one thing, I learned why I went through all those women. I always let Mr. Johnson do my thinking for me." He was pointing down. "And there was always some lady who was just fine with that. But we never connected at any other level, so it never lasted."

Hank turned to Casey. "You had second thoughts about her? That's why you didn't call?"

Casey chewed his lip, then finally nodded. "It bothered me. So I guess that's why I waited before I went to see her." He grimaced. "I don't know why I felt that way," he said softly.

"You felt that way because you're a guy!" Hank said. "It's what we do. We get where we want to be; then we wonder if that's what we really wanted. So we take a break and think about it. After that, we keep going. Or not."

"It's true," Dave said, like it was a revelation to him.

"You bet it's true. You might do this several times before your relationship smooths out." Hank ran his fingers through his thick hair. "How do you feel about Megan now? Do you want her back?"

Casey nodded. He wanted her back in the worst way. "What should I do?"

"Start with: 'I'm so sorry. I should have called—'"

"I could explain that I was cleaning my gear and tying flies and—"

"No explanations! They don't want to hear your explanations." Hank was speaking slowly and with exaggerated diction. "They want to hear you say you're sorry. Then they want to know that you know how you made them feel. It's all about their emotions. 'I'm so sorry. I should have called. That must have made you feel awful. I'm sorry I hurt you and made you feel bad. I'm such an unmitigated dipshit.' Am I right?"

Casey nodded. He'd call Megan right away.

"Am I right?" Hank repeated, this time to Dave.

"I don't know. I'm still stunned to hear you use a word like 'unmitigated.'"

"And another thing," Hank said to Casey. "When they're telling you how they feel about something? Shut up and listen. Don't wade in and try to fix their problem. Let them talk about their feelings. And agree with them. Even if you don't. 'Yes. I understand. You have a right to feel that way.'"

Dave was looking at Hank with his mouth open. "Who are you, and what did you do with Hank O'Leary?" He picked up his shop phone and spoke into it. "Hello? Air Force? I'd like to report an alien invasion! They've landed in Maupin, and one of them has taken over Hank O'Leary's body!"

"Yeah, funny," Hank said, like it wasn't. "But you know I'm right."

~

CASEY CALLED MEGAN AS SOON as he could. "I'm sorry," he said. "That was so stupid of me. I must have hurt you and made you feel like I didn't care. I do care. I—

"You are a clueless prick," Megan said angrily. "And a first-class bastard."

Casey paused. This wasn't going well. "You're right. I acted like a prick and a bastard. I'm sorry I made you feel bad. I was unfeeling and inconsiderate."

There was silence on the other end of the phone; then Megan said, "What was that movie in The Dalles?"

"Would you like to go? With me?"

"No, I want to go with Willie," she said sarcastically. "Yes, with you. Just the movie. Nothing more."

"I'm … I'm good with that. Pick you up at 6:30?"

"Bring flowers. And a box of chocolates."

31

September 18: Maupin

LOGAN MCCREA STOOD NEAR the stage at RiverFest, an annual Maupin event held on a large grassy area near the river. Hank O'Leary's band, Water Dawgs, was setting up. Rows of white plastic chairs were spread in front of the stage. Booths for food, arts and crafts, conservation groups, and government agencies ranged along the perimeter of the grassy area. On one side was a big galvanized steel tub with free beer. A large tent served as shade for sunny weather or shelter in case of rain. The sky threatened the latter.

Logan could hear Hank talking to Upper Dave, who played drums in his band. "Think of it as Italian country music," Hank said. Dave had questioned—not too politely—why Hank was wearing a blue baseball hat with the Portland Opera logo on it. *Evenings of Passion/No Regrets in the Morning* was stitched across the back.

"Look at it this way," Hank pressed. "What are the great themes of country music?"

"Um." Dave said, scratching his beard. "Love, cheating, feeling bad. Drinking. Trucks. That covers most of it."

"Every one of those was in *Pagliacci*, the opera Jackie took me to."

"There's an opera about pickup trucks? No way!"

"Well, they didn't actually sing about the truck, but they drove an old 5-ton onto the stage. It was a prop. Mostly, though, the opera was about love, cheating, and feeling bad. Especially feeling bad." Hank paused to see how this was going over with Dave. Not well. "People die in it," he said hopefully.

"I guess …" Dave conceded. "I still think it's a weird hat to wear while we're playing a gig."

"Well, Jackie bought me the hat. And I'm gonna wear it. Period."

"I guess we have to make allowances for someone of your advanced age who's regressed to reading comic books."

"It's not a comic book," Hank said strongly. "It's a graphic novel. *Persepolis*. It's pretty good, too."

The announcer introduced the members of Water Dawgs, finishing with "and on fiddle, the lovely *Jackie Riviera!*" The band launched their set with an upbeat tune, Jackie playing country-style fiddle.

The crowd was a mix of tourists and locals. As Hank's band played, a gray-haired lady in green sweat pants danced on the grass, a coffee cup in her hand. Her friends swayed rhythmically next to her.

Hank and Jackie did a harmonica-and-fiddle duet in "Dancing Caddis," a song Hank had composed just for them. Then Hank stopped while Jackie moved into a solo improvisation. The crowd cheered and clapped. Jackie bowed and was all smiles. Hank looked at her warmly and joined the applause.

~

LOGAN LISTENED AS WATER Dawgs played two more songs. Then he moved through the crowd, talking to people he knew: a fishing guide here, a store owner there, shuttle drivers. When Hank's band took a break, he asked Upper Dave about nymphing for steelhead. Logan had been working on the "Steelhead Tactics" chapter of his guidebook. He knew enough to write the traditional wet-fly swing part but was a shaky on nymphing tactics because he didn't fish for steelhead that way.

"I'd rather dig the Panama Canal with a garden trowel than nymph for steelhead," Dave told Logan.

"Casey said pretty much the same thing when I asked him."

Dave smiled knowingly. "Of course he would."

"There's something here that no one's telling me."

"Oh, you haven't heard the story. A couple of years ago—no, four years ago—one of those TV fishing show guys ... "

Logan made a face. He didn't like those shows.

"... yeah, I feel the same way. Anyway, this guy comes to town to do a piece on Deschutes steelhead. He wants Judd to go with him for the filming. Judd figures it would be good publicity for Casey, who'd only guided for a couple of years at that point and needed to build up his client base. So he gives the job to Casey."

"Generous of Judd."

Dave spread his hands and pointed both index fingers at Logan. "So anyway, the TV guy and his camera crew go out on the river, and he starts bugging Casey about nymphing for steelhead. Casey's strictly a 'swinger' and keeps telling him no way. After about the 499th time of 'When are we going to nymph for steelhead,' Casey turns to the guy and says, in this real disgusted voice, 'I'd rather row my boat with two plastic spoons than nymph for steelhead.'"

Logan laughed. "Well, that's not so bad."

"There's more," Dave said. "Then he says, 'I'd rather pick up a bobcat by its short stubby tail. I'd rather ...'" Dave paused and shook his head. "I don't remember everything Casey said. He was on a roll. He must have had ten things he'd rather do than nymph for steelhead—some colorful, some out-and-out profane. I've never heard the kid wax so eloquent. He finished with, 'I'd rather drop a goddam hornets' nest in my jockey shorts than nymph for steelhead.'"

"How do you know this?" Logan said. He had a flash of insight. "The camera was on!"

Dave nodded. "Yup. The show goes on cable TV and the internet. There's one minute of Casey in it: five seconds of casting, five seconds of holding a nice steelhead, and a whole bunch of what he'd rather do than nymph for steelhead. Someone posted a clip on YouTube. It went viral on the fly fishing discussion boards. You know how those guys carry on with their little religious wars."

"How did Judd react?"

"Irate. Yelling. 'You idiot. When will you grow up and learn to keep your goddam mouth shut? I hand you a golden opportunity to make something of yourself, and you flush it down the toilet!' Stuff like that. You know what Judd's like. When he gets amped up he can make your ears flap if you're anywhere near him. I think we heard him all the way up at the shop. Anyway, Judd damn near fired Casey. Casey was real hurt. He was going around like a puppy that somebody kicked. He idolizes Judd, you know."

"Obviously he kept his job."

"Well, Casey got so much publicity from it—though not the sort Judd had in mind—that his bookings went through the roof. Up sixty percent in one year. He was a hero to every die-hard 'swinger,' and they started setting up trips with him. And most of them came back the next year as repeat business. It made Casey's career. Business was so good that Judd shut up. Still, best not to bring it up around either of them."

"I'll keep it in mind."

"Dan Stephens, one of my guides? He nymphs for steelies in the late fall when the water's cold. We give him a bad time, but he's good at it. He's our token 'nympher.' I'll ask him to talk to you. He'll be in the shop tomorrow." Dave looked at the stage. "Time for the next set. See ya."

~

LOGAN WANDERED OVER TO the OK's booth, where Sam was making lattes. "Warm enough?" he asked.

"I'm fine." She leaned close to him. "Helen's pregnant!" she said in a low voice.

"Really? I'll have to rib Judd about being a granddad!"

Sam shook her head. "No one knows. Not even Kevin."

"Why did she tell you and not her husband?... Oh! She didn't tell you! She started ordering decaf!"

Sam nodded. "Your barista is the first to know. And there's a new shine in her eyes."

Steve Schultz, a local, came by and ordered a mocha from Sam.

"Hey, Steve," Logan said. "I saw you on the river a couple of days ago. Do any good?"

"Hooked one, but I lost it," Steve said.

"Too bad." Logan lowered his voice. "Say, I noticed you had a non-locking carabiner on the end of your anchor line. I've found through hard experience that those can pop open if they hit a rock. It could cause your boat to go adrift. Just thought I'd mention it."

"Probably a good tip," Steve said grudgingly. He raised his cup in a salute and walked off.

Sam looked at Logan and raised her eyebrows.

Logan shrugged. "I can't help it," he said. "I'm a pedantic know-it-all."

"Refresh me: what does *pedantic* mean?"

"Overly precise. Annoyingly predictable and fussy. A pedant is a teacher—a particularly tiresome one."

"Only a pedantic know-it-all would know the derivation of *pedantic*," Sam said. Then she laughed.

Logan laughed with Sam, then saw her smile fade and her face go tense. He felt something on his arm. It was Lisa Albright's hand. Logan was still occasionally having dinner with Lisa—formerly from Logan's old company, Med-Rec, and currently the fish checker on the road to Macks Canyon. She gave Sam a warm greeting. Sam was polite. Logan felt it best to leave Sam and went off with Lisa.

Lisa had a bit of Med-Rec news. She'd heard from Gary Sommers, the corporate counsel and part of the skeleton crew that was finalizing the buy-out by General Medical, Inc. Gary had gone to court over some patent issues and won, making the patents much more valuable. GMI would have to pony up more money if they wanted Med-Rec's technology or, equally important, if they didn't want a competitor to have it. Lisa said the buy-out price could go to sixty cents a share from its current five-and-a-half cents. She was excited because her stock would be worth enough to buy a new Subaru.

Logan calculated in his mind. Sixty cents a share would cancel his $237,000 debt to Med-Rec, with enough left over to send Sam to college. This was the best news he'd heard in months, if it was true. He decided not to get too excited until he'd gotten the story firsthand.

He and Lisa agreed to meet for dinner at her place next week, and she left.

~

LISA HAD BARELY DISAPPEARED when Casey and Judd came up with two other men. Judd introduced Ken Jones. "Ken's a biologist for the Warm Springs Tribes," he said.

"And this is my cousin Josh," Ken said. Josh shook hands but remained silent.

"The Tribes are starting some fall salmon surveys down below Macks Canyon," Casey said. "You may have seen their camp across from Nooky Rock. I thought you might want to talk to Ken. For your guidebook."

They talked a while about the river's salmon. To be polite, Logan asked Ken's cousin, Josh, if he was a biologist, too.

"Not me," Josh said. "I'm studying acting." He was about six foot seven and over 300 pounds, a mountainous man with a deep, resonant voice.

"Gotten any roles, yet?"

"Tribal stuff, of course. Some local theater. But mostly I do voice work for radio commercials."

"I knew I'd heard your voice!" Judd said. "You do those ads for the car races. And that big hotel in Bend, the one on the way to the ski area."

"That's me," Josh said. "I'm trying for movies and TV, too. My agent thinks I'd be good for some of those animated features."

Logan and Josh talked about his theater roles; then the two Indians moved on. "Hell of voice," Judd said, shaking his head after Ken and Josh left. "An Indian Darth Vader. If he played God on the radio, people would stop sinning in a heartbeat. We'd have world peace by Thursday."

Casey walked over to some fishing guide friends, leaving Logan and Judd together. "I wanted to thank you," Judd said quietly. "You made a copy of Willie's photo album for him. It's all pictures of his Mom and Dad and him growing up. His parents are dead, and he likes to be reminded of them. I didn't realize he was taking the album on his float trips. He'd have been devastated to lose it or have it get messed up. Now he can leave the originals at home and take the copy."

"No problem. It was Casey's idea, but he didn't have the right computer gear. I was glad to do it. And, Judd? I'm very grateful to you and Susan and Helen for being so kind to Sam."

Judd waved a hand. "Think nothing of it. She's a pleasure to have around the OK. Susan loves having a young person she can be 'mother' to."

"How long have you had the OK?"

"My dad bought it in the 50s from Oliver Klugman—that's where the OK comes from. Susan and I have run it since 1976, after Dad died. Same time he came to town." Judd pointed at Hank, whose band was now doing a ballad about lost love.

"Hank's a good guy," Logan said. "I like him a lot. And Jackie's great. They often come in and buy lattes from Sam. She's gotten to know Jackie very well."

Judd nodded and looked thoughtful. "Jackie's good for Hank. I tell you, Hank was one hard hombre when he first showed up in Maupin. He could tie flies and fish with the best, and he was always generous to a fault. I never met a man more honest and straightforward. But you didn't cross him. A couple of guys tried up at the tavern—you know how some of these country bucks can be after they've had a few beers. Anyway, it didn't take long for folks to figure out when to leave Hank O'Leary alone. It also didn't take them long to figure out that he spent a lot of time in the bar, but he'd nurse one or two beers for most of an evening. He told me once that he used to drink pretty heavily—especially when he first got out of the Army. But then he heard that alcohol kills brains cells. 'I need every one I've got,' he said. He's mellow in a way that makes some people think he's a boozer. But he isn't. He says too much drinking makes you unready."

"Unready for what?"

"To do whatever needs to be done. I think of him as a momma grizzly. Or a sheep dog; he's pack-oriented and protective of his 'herd.' I pity anyone who'd try to mess with someone Hank counts as a friend."

"He was in Vietnam, wasn't he?"

"He was a Lurp—Long Range Recon and Patrol. Green Berets on steroids. Weeks in the jungle tracking down the enemy. Those were tough dudes."

~

AFTER LEAVING JUDD, LOGAN ran into Bob Barkin, an old friend from Transcept. They hadn't seen each other for five years. In fact, Logan hadn't known that Bob had taken up fly fishing.

"Yeah," Bob said, "I spend all my time doing it and thinking about it. It's a real drag on my career." He shook his head. "But who cares?" he added with a laugh.

Logan invited Bob to float the river with him, and they picked a date a couple of weeks in the future. "I've been trying a new steelhead fly," Logan said. "The Plum Dandy—a Hank O'Leary creation. It's taken quite a few steelhead for me this summer. I'll bring some along."

BOB WAS BARELY OUT OF SIGHT when Logan was staggered by a slap on the back. *"Dobroe utro*, Logan!"

Well, well, thought Logan. *Sergei's back.* He hadn't seen the former KGB agent since July. "Whatever, Sergei. You having a good time?"

"Free beer!" He had a can in his right hand and one in each pants pocket. He pulled out one of the latter and handed it to Logan. "It's on me!" He clicked his can to Logan's. "To brotherhood!" he said. Clearly Sergei was on one of his periodic binges.

Sergei wandered off unsteadily, and Logan returned the unopened can to the big tub from which it came. He had some questions for Sergei but figured he'd better wait until he was sober— or at least less drunk.

~

THE NEXT DAY LOGAN LEFT ON a three-day float trip. When he returned to Maupin, he went into the OK to see Sam and get a latte. She asked him about the fishing, told him how the horses were doing, and gave him updates on town gossip.

"Oh," she said, "Some sad news. There was a drowning the day after you left."

"That's a shame. Rafting accident?"

She shook her head. "No one saw it happen, but they think he was drunk and just stumbled into the river. It was at South Junction. Looked like he went over the bank and fell into a big backeddy. Must have sucked him right down. Some rafters found his body on a gravel bar a few miles downriver. They tested his blood, and the alcohol level was pretty high. Russian tourist. Sergei something."

32

September 22: Maupin

ON A BACK EDGE OF TY DECKER'S property, up against a gravel bank, Hank O'Leary stapled a paper target to a wooden frame. He stepped back twenty feet and put on his safety glasses, then his hearing protectors. Last, he picked up his Smith and Wesson .38 revolver, his index finger resting alongside the trigger guard.

He nodded to Ty, who was standing near his side. Ty covered his ears. Hank took a steady stance, gripped the revolver with both hands, and moved his finger to the trigger. He squeezed, and a hole appeared near the center of the target. He fired four more times; the hole got bigger as each bullet hit near the first one.

As Hank reloaded the five-shot revolver, Ty said, "You always were good with firearms."

Hank nodded. He *was* good, and he knew it. But he also knew that frequent practice helped him stay accurate. "This little .38 is a great carry weapon," he said to Ty. "It has an enclosed hammer so it can't get hung up when you pull it out. Also, there's no rear sight, just a groove. It's small and lightweight. But it's hard to be accurate if you're more than seven yards from your target."

He reloaded and repeated the drill. The hole in the target's center enlarged slightly. Hank put up a new target, one with a life-sized outline of a person. There was a rectangle in the forehead and another in the upper thorax. Ty gave him a questioning look.

"When you need to stop someone, you have to hit the vital areas." He put a hand on his upper thorax. "Here …" he moved his hand to his forehead "… and here. Both places, because he might be wearing a Kevlar vest. You'd be surprised how many bullets a guy can take and keep shooting at you. So you need to do the maximum damage in the shortest time."

"You're the one who went to war," Ty said, shaking his head. "I'll stick with deer and elk and the occasional coyote."

Hank reloaded and fired four quick rounds: blam-blam, blam-blam. Two holes appeared in the target's lower rectangle and two in the upper. He walked to the target and put masking tape over the holes, then repeated the drill. Two fresh holes in the lower rectangle and ... only one in the upper. Where had the fourth bullet hit? In the target's lower right corner, far from where it was supposed to go. Hank stared in disbelief.

"Nobody's perfect," Ty said. "Not even you."

Hank's jar was tight. What a miss! Not just a little off, but a lot! He repeated the drill three more times, each one perfect.

"Don't let it get to you," Ty said. "Like I said, nobody's—"

"I know, I know." Hank opened the .38's cylinder and emptied the spent casings, then put the unspent round in the ammunition box. He handed the box and the revolver to Ty. "Take good care of my weapons," he said.

"I'll put them all in the gun safe. Except the .38. I'll keep that with me in the truck. Probably won't need it, but sometimes a steer ... anyway, it could come in handy. Too bad Jackie's terrified of firearms."

"I took her shooting once. It helped, but she's still not comfortable being around them. She's right to be scared. They're meant to kill."

After Ty left with his .38, Hank never felt so naked in all his adult life. The things a guy does for love ...

4: Dark Water

33

September 25, Evening: Deschutes below Macks Canyon

LOGAN STOOD IN THE RIVER casting for steelhead, feeling the gentle but steady wash of the current. The cast itself took all his attention, but after that—during the swing and hangdown—his mind split. One part watched for that tightening of the line that means a fish has taken his fly. But the other part contemplated the river and the canyon, both of which were gradually changing with the setting of the sun.

The changes were slow and subtle, but steady. First the light left the water on the west side, leaving Logan in the shadows while the canyon wall on the east side shone golden. The river took on the same hue by reflection.

As time passed, the shadow line crept slowly up the eastern wall. The sparse clouds took on more contrast. Occasionally a trout made a head-and-tail rise as it sipped an emerging caddis from the river's surface.

An hour before sunset, both sides of the canyon were in shadow, and the clouds glowed pink in a baby-blue sky. Caddis were thick in the air, and more trout were rising. Trees and rocks lost definition in the gathering dark. The wind, which had been strong when he'd started, gentled and nearly ceased.

A stillness settled on everything, and Logan felt like the last person on earth—or the first. Somewhere coyotes began their nocturnal hunt, their shrill yips echoing off the canyon walls. He imagined them coming out of their den, stretching, then pointing their heads to the sky as they announced their presence.

The air cooled, and crickets began to chirp. Their united sound modulated, the volume rising and falling with regularity. He'd once tried to analyze it mathematically. He suspected it was like the wave functions he'd studied in physics. But he didn't wonder about it anymore; he simply enjoyed it.

As it grew dark, bats flitted above the water, taking caddis. There were more and more splashes as trout rose to the accelerating hatch. The river was a rippling texture of dark fluidity. A canyon wren sang in descending notes. The pungent smell of sage filled the air. It was now nearly dark, almost too dark to cast. More crickets, more caddis, more trout, more bats.

During these times at the edges of the day—his mind cleared by the repetition of casting and his senses heightened to the life around him—Logan felt a peace and harmony that he found nowhere else. It wasn't the quiet. On the contrary, it was the energy: the canyon walls with their layers of lava pushed up from deep in the earth, the constant flow of water, the turning of the earth, the stars in the sky, the wildlife around him, the fish in the river, even the blades of growing grass and the rustling leaves of alders. Time collapsed, and all things merged into one vital, vibrant, instantaneous whole: the energy of Life. And he was connected to all of it, one with the river, one with the world around him. He drew energy from their energy, peace from their peace.

Logan lived for these sessions on the river. Trout fishing was fun, but it was only when casting for the invisible and elusive steelhead that he had these moments of awareness and connection.

The last few evenings he'd seen the river as a kind of Pool of Bethesda, drawing to it the sick and the injured: Sam with her gimpy leg; Casey and his yearning heart; Hank and Jackie searching for their deeper selves; himself, broken in spirit. The blind, the halt, the withered—they all came to the river, seeking healing from the moving of the waters.

Logan couldn't speak for the others, but he knew he'd made progress. The morning ritual of dry heaves was in the past. When he felt joy and happiness, the heavy weight of despair no longer dragged him back down. In May he'd sensed a hovering fate waiting to plunge earthward and sink its talons into his back like an osprey takes a trout. No more. He still had his bad moments, but they didn't rule his life as they once did. His mind was no longer drawn to his troubles like iron to the magnet.

The demon that sat on his shoulders and made him dance to its tune? Logan suspected it still lurked in the darkness, waiting for an unguarded moment to sneak back and see if it could run him around as it used to. But he'd think of these moments on the river and feel like he had the strength to shake it off.

He'd been broken, but the break was healing. And, like many such repairs, it seemed stronger than before. For the first time in many months, Logan had an abiding confidence in the future. He sensed, however, that a time of testing would come. The river's dark waters held secrets—deep and restless secrets, impatient to be revealed.

34

September 27: Maupin

TWO ANGLERS WERE IN A HEATED, if playful, argument when Logan came into Upper Dave's fly shop. One angler said he needed a new spey rod. His friend told him he felt inadequate, in a Freudian sense, and was trying to make up for it with a longer fly rod.

"Hey, man," his friend said, "if you just answered one of those spam emails, you'd get a bigger one. Then you'd save yourself hundreds of dollars on a new fly rod. You spent too much time waist-deep in cold rivers and shrunk your junk. Now you're overcompensating."

Good-natured banter followed, which Logan tuned out. It started him thinking though. Why did men have this concern? He decided it might be perspective. A guy looks down at himself, and what does he see? He's foreshortened: his concern is the hypotenuse of a triangle, but what he sees is the triangle's base, which is shorter. Logan tried to quantify it. If a guy's "hypotenuse" was ... what? six inches? five inches? He looked at the width of his hand. Four inches? He took the thumb away. Three inches? No, no, no.

Assume a forty-ish male, unexcited and at standard temperature/pressure: four-and-a-half inches, measured from the top. *The triangle's base is ... assume the hypotenuse is a straight line ... no, it's really more of a parabola ... but a straight line is a good first approximation ... what's the angle? ... assume 45 degrees, although its probably closer to 50, maybe 55 ... cosine of 45 degrees is .707 ... round to .7 ... times 4.5 ... that's 2.8 plus 0.35 equals 3.15 inches.*

So a guy looks across the locker room and sees someone else at four and a half, then looks down at himself and sees barely three.

That was it! All that male posturing was just a failure to understand mathematics. If the schools did a better job of teaching the practical aspects of trigonometry, men would settle down, and there would be world peace. Still, he felt that his own hypotenuse was shorter than average. The irony of this was not lost on him.

Dave was talking to him. "Hmm, what?" Logan said.

"What do you need?" Dave repeated.

"Leader tippet. Eight-pound."

~

AS HE LEFT THE STORE WITH HIS tippet spools, Logan wondered why this nonsense had popped into his head. Oh. Right. Lisa Albright, the fish check lady and last night's dinner companion. Logan was a long ways from being ready for a committed relationship with anyone and had made that plain to Lisa. She felt the same. That out of the way, one thing had led to another last night, with her doing most of the leading and him being a not unwilling follower. They'd made love.

Logan examined his emotions. How did he feel about this? Released. Guilty. Conflicted.

On one hand, he hadn't been with a woman for two years. First he was trying to win Trudy back. Then after the accident and his emotional collapse, sex was very far from his mind. But now he was coming to grips with his life, and yes, a roll in the hay with Lisa Albright felt pretty good.

On the other hand, there was his daughter Samantha—who knew he'd met Lisa several times in the past two months and grew silent and tight-lipped whenever her name came up, who knew he'd gone to Lisa's for dinner last night and hadn't come home until 3:00 in the morning, who knew how to put things together.

Was he setting a bad example? What if Sam said, "Hey, Dad, I met this guy at the OK. We like each other a little bit. I think I'll sleep with him." Logan couldn't exactly take the moral high ground, could he? He would be glad she was almost twenty and not fourteen. Even so ...

More importantly, was he jeopardizing his hard-won relationship with Sam? They were going to have to talk about it. Soon. But he didn't know how to bring it up. Use the preferred medium of youth and text her? "BTW IM SCREWG LISA. ITS GR8. HOW U FEEL ABT IT?" No, he was going to have to treat Sam like an adult and talk about it face to face. Someday.

He was also confused about what it meant. Did it signify more than an after-dinner romp? Did it mean something different to Lisa than it meant to him? The rules had changed in the last twenty-odd years. It was unsettling.

~

HE AND SAM HAD BEEN WORKING the horses in the evenings. Major, the two-year old, was coming along nicely. His ground training was excellent: Sam could lead him and back him, do haunch and forehand turns, side passes, and get him to walk, trot, and canter on voice command while free-lunging him.

Their next step was to train Major to work in harness. Ty Decker, their landlord, had a friend who would loan Sam a little two-wheeled cart. Major had a calm disposition; he should do well in harness, which would make the transition to saddle easier. So Sam had been working Major with a bridle and long reins, walking behind and getting him to turn, back, and go forward. In another week or so she'd fit the harness to him. When he was comfortable with that, she'd move on to the cart. She was excited, and Logan agreed that it was a good training program.

Sam was also doing a little roping. Ty had been a rodeo cowboy in his youth, and one evening he showed Sam how to swing a lariat. He let her practice on some of his calves.

She was now riding Mataan, and Logan worked with Gabe, the 15-hand bay gelding that belonged to Ty's friend Ron Bauer. Ron was delighted to have someone exercise his horse. Like Mataan and

Major, Gabe was a purebred Arabian. He was a good trail horse, and his lope was silky smooth. Logan couldn't say the same for his trot—he bounced like a bicycle with square wheels.

A couple of times a week Logan and Sam rode in the Criterion Hills or on Ron Bauer's property. Criterion was the steeper and more rugged of the two. It had a wildness that went straight to the soul. Ron's property was a little gentler. Both places had springs and creeks, if you knew where to look, so the horses could get water and their rides could be as long as they wanted.

Sam and Logan didn't talk much on their rides, but it was a shared experience that they both enjoyed. The rides seemed to be good for Sam, both physically and mentally. She was continuing her after-work walks up the hill from the OK into Maupin's main business district, so her leg was getting stronger. Sometimes you'd think there'd never been an accident.

It had been weeks since Logan had any feelings of deep depression or anxiety. For the first time in months he could look to his uncertain future without getting a tight, sinking feeling in his guts. He didn't know how things were going to work out, but he had faith that he and Sam were going to be okay.

Another cause for hope was his former company Med-Rec, to which he still owed $237,000. He'd talked to Gary Sommers, the attorney, and found that the situation was as Lisa had told him at RiverFest: the buy-out price for Med-Rec could go to around sixty cents a share. That would wipe out Logan's debt and leave enough for Sam's college. However, Gary told him, don't get excited yet; it wasn't a done deal.

~

EARLY THE EVENING AFTER HE'D bought his tippet from Upper Dave, Logan and Sam hauled the horses to Criterion for a few hours of trail riding. The sky was clear on their side of the Cascades. To the northwest, Mt. Hood poked gracefully through dark, heavy clouds; apparently Maupin's good weather was not shared with Portland. To the south, Mt. Bachelor and the Three Sisters loomed. Between lay Broken Top, Mt. Washington, and Mt. Jefferson. It was a majestic panorama of volcanic peaks that stretched a hundred miles across the horizon.

While grooming Gabe in preparation for saddling, Logan noticed some tangles in Gabe's mane—what horsemen call "witch's knots." He tried to work these out, but one was particularly stubborn, and he decided to cut the bit of mane just above the knot. "Can I borrow your hoofpick?" he asked. Sam always carried a folding hoofpick that included a knife blade. She handed it to him. As he started to cut the knot he said, "About Lisa Albright—"

"Done with my hoofpick?" Sam said abruptly.

Logan took the hint.

~

TO BEGIN, THEY RODE THE HORSES along a faint road. In places, the path was rough and rocky where the surface dirt had washed away. When they came to these sections, they moved to the side, which was easier on the horses' feet.

Saddles creaked, hoofs clopped, horses breathed hard but steadily. A cool, dry wind ruffled the sagebrush. Far below they could see into the river canyon as far as Two Springs Ranch. Beyond lay the Mutton Mountains and Whitehorse Rapids, the latter hidden from view by high hills.

After a couple of miles, Logan and Sam left the road and traversed a rocky slope until they were in a juniper grove. Coming out the other side, Logan had a clear view of the river. He pulled out his binoculars and looked for boats. He could see a couple—small dots on the distant water—but they were too far for any detail. He returned the binoculars to his saddlebag, and they rode on.

Logan loved these rides. They rarely saw anyone, and life seemed cut to the bone. You could see how the river had deconstructed the earth, revealing layer upon layer of ancient lava. It was a time to reflect, to contemplate.

As his thoughts settled into the ride, he tried to puzzle out the death of Sergei Kalinnikov, the former KGB agent. The incident was ruled an accidental drowning. What else? He was alone, there were no witnesses, and he was very drunk. Even so, it bothered Logan. For one thing, Sergei had always functioned at a certain level even when on a binge. He'd survived this long; why did he die now?

Logan re-thought his assumptions, starting with Sergei. He'd assumed his death was not accidental. Maybe it was. He'd assumed Sergei was working with Scarface, the guy with the pistol in the red-and-blue driftboat. Maybe he wasn't. Or maybe Scarface and Sergei were on opposing teams. But why, if the Russians viewed other Slavs as brothers? He'd also assumed Scarface was a Slav. Maybe he wasn't. Maybe he was … what? He didn't know.

Yet another assumption: he was looking for Middle Eastern Islamist terrorists planning something bad on the Deschutes. Every part of that assumption was open to question.

Logan dwelled on these issues for half an hour, then let his mind move on. He slipped into a natural rhythm with his horse, no longer thinking about riding but simply doing it. He and Gabe worked as one. His eyes took in everything but focused on nothing. Hills, canyon, river, horses, Sam—they were all connected, all in harmony. Analytic thought left him. Time did not exist.

~

THEY RETURNED TO THE HORSE trailer near dusk. As he and Sam were untacking the horses, a new scenario popped into thought: some Slavs were Muslims. Bosnia, for example, was Slavic but majority Muslim. Suppose Scarface and John Kincaid weren't drug dealers. Suppose they really were the Evil Doers he was looking for. Suppose what they had stashed was not drugs but something else; what, he didn't know. Suppose Sergei was with the FSB, the KGB's successor, and was sent to check things out.

This latter supposition annoyed Logan. If it was true, couldn't they have sent someone a little, you know, *swifter*, to be his counter-part? Yet if FSB had a low-priority intercept, not unlike the one NSA had passed to CIA, they wouldn't send their best agent. Logan could imagine someone in Moscow saying, "I doubt it's important, but let's send that clown Kalinnikov to Oregon and see if he finds anything. At least we won't have to look at him for a while." While it hurt his ego to be put on a par with Sergei, Logan had to admit that this was plausible. After all, whom had Langley sent? A broken-down bankrupt who didn't even work for them—a dial-a-spy, a temp.

~

As LOGAN AND SAM TRAILERED the horses back to Maupin, Logan's cell phone beeped. Bill Short had sent him a text message: "VIDEO TALK ASAP."

"B THERE 2.5 HRS" he texted back. He dropped Sam and the horses at the house and drove to Beaverton, arriving well after dark.

This time the receptionist didn't give him a bad time. Logan quickly passed the two checkpoints and entered the com room. Bill was already on the screen, and Logan had to admit it was good to see his face. He was beginning to like the pudgy bureaucrat. "What's up?" he said warmly. "You're working late, old buddy."

Bill grimaced at the familiarity and put on his strictly business face. "We just learned something that may or may not have anything to do with your assignment. I'll get right to the point. There might be four or eight M56 warheads missing from the Umatilla Weapons Depot."

Logan blinked twice and took a moment to digest this. He knew that the military stored chemical and biological weapons in Umatilla, a small town on the Columbia about two hours from Maupin. Obsolete missiles had been incinerated in a tightly controlled program.

"Let me make sure I understand this," Logan said. "These warheads *might* be missing? No one knows? And if they are missing, they don't know the exact number? I thought that was one of the most secure operations in the military. I thought they finished it over a year ago. How could they lose four—or eight—warheads? How could they not even *know* whether they were lost or not?" The more Logan thought about it, the more incensed he got. He was aware that his voice was growing shrill.

"Calm down," Bill said. "Don't blame me. I'm just the messenger." His head wiggled back and forth. He seemed almost as irritated as Logan. "We just found out today, so I'm relaying it to you in case it's relevant to your assignment."

"Tell me what you know."

"The M56 is the warhead part of the M55, a 115-millimeter rocket developed in the 1950s to deliver chemical weapons."

Logan computed 115 millimeters: about 4.5 inches—a bit more than the width of a hand.

"The missing warheads held VX nerve agent. The warhead is under a meter in length and holds 4.5 kilograms—about ten pounds—of VX."

"Refresh me about VX."

"It's the most toxic chemical in the world. Ten milligrams—one large drop—on bare skin will kill a person in less than thirty minutes. Causes convulsions. Stops breathing. Normally liquid, but will aerosolize when you apply an explosive force. If aerosolized, an unprotected target can take it into the lungs, where it works faster and with greater efficiency."

Logan felt a rising panic. The room was swimming around him. *Focus,* he told himself. *Try to stay focused.* "How much does the whole warhead weigh?" he asked.

"Around 15 pounds, with the casing and the burster."

"So 120 pounds for eight warheads. Eighty pounds of VX payload. Or half that. Or nothing."

"You got it." There was a pause; then Bill said, "It gets worse. A knowledgeable expert could remove the VX and repurpose it for terrorism. You could spray it from a crop duster over a crowded city. VX is heavier than air, so it would settle to ground level. It's virtually undetectable until it's used. You could feed it into an atomizer— these things are easily available on the commercial market—then put the atomizer in the back of a truck and drive down a crowded street spraying VX. Deploy a team of people and do it in several places at once. Put it in the ventilation system of a large office building ..."

Logan put up a hand. "Let me think a minute." *4.5 kilograms ... 4,500,000 milligrams ... divide by ten ... 450,000 lethal doses in one warhead ... could that be possible? ... as many as eight warheads ... enough to kill over three million people ...* He was sweating. His breath came quickly. *Focus! ... efficiency would be low due to methods of dissemination, difficulty of finding many people in one place, element of surprise, etc. ... even if the efficiency was ... what? ... one percent? 45,000 dead. Half of that? 20,000 dead. Per warhead. Four warheads ... maybe eight ... 80,000 dead ... maybe over 150,000 ... And that's figuring very conservatively.*

Logan rubbed his temples. Perhaps he'd run the math wrong. He got out his cell phone and used the calculator function. He came to the same answer. He could be wrong, but still ... anywhere VX would be used, tens of thousands would die, ground and water would be contaminated for years. Logan was stunned by the possibilities.

"I can see from your face," Bill Short said, "that you've grasped the implications."

Logan nodded slowly. "How difficult is it to transport?"

"The warhead is very easy to move. It was designed for field use, so it could bounce around in the back of a truck until it was deployed. And you used a small rocket to shoot it at your enemy; you didn't want it blowing up in your face. So, yes, very easy to move. Until the burster goes off, of course. At the time, it was a technical triumph."

"I'm so glad," Logan said sarcastically. "Any idea about a target?"

"It could be used inside the US. Or exported to another country. Or countries. You know how simple it is to bring things into the US? We can hardly check the smallest fraction of imported items. Well, it's even easier to get something out. You could put a suitcase with four warheads inside a container with a bunch of other items, load it on a ship, and send it somewhere with even less security than we have."

Logan exploded. "How the hell could they lose eight war-heads!"

"Keep in mind that we're not even certain they're missing. The records are … unclear. The person in charge of records—a civilian employee cleared at the highest levels—quit in January. A new guy came in. He found an old computer printout that had been misfiled. He compared it to current records and noticed a discrepan-cy. It may just be bad record keeping or a computer glitch. They're still working on it. I thought you should know."

"Have they talked to the man who left?"

"They're looking for him but haven't found him."

"Let me guess. He qualifies as a 'knowledgeable expert' who could repurpose the VX for terrorism."

Bill Short's face radiated concern. "Afraid so," he said.

Logan digested this, then said. "Um, Bill … "

"Yes?"

"Sergei Kalinnikov, the former KGB agent I told you about last July? I saw him in Maupin a couple of days ago."

"So he came back. Did you get anything out of him?"

"No. He was drunk, loaded to the gills. The next day he drowned in the river. It was ruled an accident."

"But maybe it wasn't."

"Maybe not. And one more thing. I saw a couple of suspicious guys on the river. They were talking about something they had stashed. I thought it was drugs. Maybe it wasn't."

"When did you see these two?"

"Third week of July, around the first time I saw Sergei. One was John Kincaid, who you checked out before and said was a low-level drug dealer; I confirmed that with someone in Maupin. The other guy spoke perfect English but had a slight accent—maybe Slavic, I couldn't tell. He was on the stocky side and had a shaved head. And a nasty scar across his forehead. They didn't fit the profile of who I was look-ing for, so I didn't pass it on. The guy with the accent was carrying an automatic pistol, but so are lots of people around here. I decided they had probably cached drugs and that if I stepped in I could blow my cover. And maybe get hurt."

"Your first guess was probably right. They sound like drug guys. The missing man from Umatilla doesn't fit that description. He's tall, a bit thin, and wears glasses. I'll send a photo and bio by encrypted email."

"What's his name?"

"Peter Bolton."

~

ON THE DRIVE BACK TO MAUPIN, Logan pulled over to the side of the road and poked the numbers into his phone calculator again. He hoped he'd done the math wrong, was off by an order of magni-tude. But no, he'd gotten it right the first time.

He was having what Dietz called an Iceberg Moment: the chilling realization that the little thing you're looking at is just a small part of a much bigger whole, most of which is hidden and will send you to the bottom of the deep blue sea no matter how unsinkable you think you are.

35

September 28: Maupin

"Good morning, Sunshine!" Casey said to Helen.

"If you want breakfast, you're a little early!" It was just after 6:00, and the OK wasn't officially open yet. "Sam will be here soon to fire up the espresso machine. I'm just helping Mom out. I'm off to the school in an hour."

"I know. I came early so I could congratulate you and Kevin! I heard the news last night. When's the little nipper due?"

Helen smiled warmly and said, "Thanks! The baby's due at the end of April. News travels fast. We just told Mom and Dad yesterday over lunch. I think Mom told everyone in town before dinner."

They talked while Helen worked. Casey had a day off—rare for this time of year—and was in no hurry to go anywhere. After ten minutes of easy conversation, he said, "So, do you get some sort of prize? For being the first of Judd's girls to get herself in a family way?"

Helen looked around, then dropped her voice and said, "Well, as you know, I don't get that prize. I'm just the first that Mom and Dad know about." She gave him a knowing look.

"What do you mean?" Casey said cautiously.

There was a long silence during which Helen looked increasingly uncomfortable.

"Megan," Casey said. "You're talking about Megan."

Helen looked everywhere but at Casey.

"Nine years ago," Casey said. "When she and I …"

Sam walked through the door, followed by Megan. Casey faced Megan. "Is that true? You were pregnant?"

Megan looked stunned. She eyed Helen, questioning.

"You told me that you'd told him," Helen said sternly. "Before you broke up."

"When we broke up?" Casey said. "You were pregnant? That's why you dumped me?"

"One thing at a time!" Megan said, raising a hand. She spoke to Helen, her face a mixture of anger, disappointment, and resolve. "I tried to tell him, but I chickened out." She sighed deeply and turned to Casey, "That's not the only reason we broke up."

"You lied to Helen?" Casey said. "And you lied to me?"

"I was nineteen and scared to death," Megan said, her voice stronger. "You have no idea how frightened I was. Or how much I wanted to tell you. I didn't know what to do. Then I lost the baby and didn't need to do anything. I didn't lie to you; I just didn't tell you the truth."

Sam looked around, hesitated, and went outside.

"All those things you said to me? Back then? They really hurt! They still hurt! And they weren't true? That wasn't how you felt? It was because you were pregnant? And even now, you wouldn't have told me if Helen hadn't … Did you think so little of me? Do you *still* think so little of me?"

Megan's mouth was set in a firm line. "It's complicated," she said slowly. "No, we didn't break up because I was pregnant. We broke up because—at that time—we weren't suited to each other. For the long term, I mean." She paused for another breath. "Think about it. If I'd told you, what would you have done? Gotten me to give it up? Arranged an abortion? Married me? How well would that have worked out?"

"We'd have gotten along."

"We would *not* have gotten along!" Megan said. "Anyway, I miscarried. There was no reason to tell you."

"There were lots of reasons to tell me! It might have helped me understand why you dumped me!"

"I'll say it again: we didn't break up because I was pregnant. We broke up because we weren't—at that time—ready for a long-term relationship."

"But all those things you said to me! You made me feel like I was the scum of the earth. A no-good screw-up! Do you know what I went through? What you made me think about myself?"

"Do you know what *I* went through? What I thought of *myself?*"

"I thought I was the most worthless person on earth. I went through hell! For years!"

"Maybe everything I said wasn't … I know I laid it on a little thick. I know it hurt you, and I've always regretted that. You have no idea how much! But I had to do something. And I … didn't have a lot of experience breaking up with boys."

"She didn't tell you she was pregnant," Helen said, "because you didn't need to know. Being pregnant made her rethink the relationship and where it was going. Remember how you were. She didn't see a future until—if—you grew up and made something out of yourself."

"That's about it," Megan said.

"You were so young," Helen said. "See it from Megan's point of view. She's nineteen, Little Miss Perfect, the straight-A student who never went to drinking parties, never got in trouble, always did what Mom and Dad said. You were her one bit of teenage rebellion. What would people have said if they'd known she was pregnant? Some would be nice, but plenty of others would pile on with dirty jokes and everything else. There are people who like nothing better than to see someone fall off a pedestal. With you, it would have been 'wink-wink, nudge-nudge.' With Megan it would have been, 'Who'd have thought? What a slut!' Maupin's a very small town. You know how it would have been."

Megan was nodding in agreement. "Casey," she said, "You meant a lot to me then, believe me. But remember who we were. Children! I was going to college. You were going—"

"Yeah, right. I was going nowhere. You told me enough times when you dumped me."

"You're not who you were back then," Megan said. "You're a

different person now. A fine, admirable person. But if I'd have stayed with you, I doubt either of us would be who we are today. Breaking up was the right thing to do."

Casey felt like he was wearing a straightjacket while locked in a tiny, airless closet. He turned on his heel and left the OK.

Sam was sitting at an outside table, hands in her pockets, staring at the river. Casey walked past her to his truck. His tires screeched as he turned left onto Highway 197 and roared up the hill to the south, away from Maupin. He didn't know where he was going, but he wanted the town and Megan and everything else as far behind him as he could make them.

As he drove, one thought played over and over in his mind. Nine years! It had taken him nine years to rebuild his self-esteem after Megan dumped him. She might never have told him the truth. Nine years of feeling hurt and wondering if he was as bad as she had said. Nine years! How could she have done that to him? She could have confided in him this summer. Why did it have to come out by accident? Nine years!

Anger and hurt feelings kept boiling to the surface, but occasionally other thoughts passed through. It couldn't have been easy for her. Helen was right: small-town gossip can be cruel and live forever. But nine years! It was true; he wasn't much of a prospect back then. Would he have done the right thing? Probably not. He might have blabbed, boasted even. And the tasteless jokes would follow Megan forever. Judd and Susan would have suffered, too. It was a long time ago. They were children, playing at being adults. But nine years!

Casey hurt all over, physically as well as mentally. Every muscle was tense, his throat ached, and his stomach felt like he'd swallowed a twenty-pound rock.

He was nearing Bend. He couldn't face the traffic and turned west onto Highway 20. After a few miles he came to the sign for the Metolius River. Casey hadn't been to the Metolius for years and felt compelled to go there now. He turned off the highway and drove down the quiet two-lane blacktop to the river.

He parked in a ponderosa-shaded spot near Wizard Falls. The air was cool but clearing. The blue sky was dotted with occasional clouds, dark in the center but edged in brilliant white. The forest smelled of settled dust and the mixed scent of pine and chaparral.

Casey walked to the bank and sat with his back against a cedar tree. He closed his eyes and listened to the Metolius, the biggest and purest of the Deschutes' tributaries. He breathed deeply and envisioned each exhale going downstream—the river carrying away his anger and his hurt, washing him clean.

He imagined himself as a nineteen-year-old Megan. What would he have done? Probably the same thing. So why did it hurt so much?

He dwelled on this for a long time. Eventually he saw that one part of him wanted Megan back because he craved her approval and acceptance. If she took him back, then it would cancel the rejection of their breakup. It would be a big RESET button, returning everything to its original state. Except that wasn't possible. He was a different person now; there was no going back. And that was a good thing.

As hard as it was to admit, he was a better person *because* Megan had dumped him nine years ago. Their breakup forced him to reexamine himself and to make a life independent of her. This was a foundation on which to build a relationship that would last.

New thoughts emerged. He decided he was a decent person and good at his job. And he didn't need anyone else's validation—not Megan's, not Judd's, not Helen's—no one's. He was who he was, and that was okay.

A burden was gone, carried away on the current. He'd lost that sense of someone looking over his shoulder and either approving or disapproving of everything he did.

He didn't need Megan to make him feel better about himself. If it worked for them, that was great. But if it wasn't a fit for both of them, they would move on and be better for it.

~

WHEN HE RETURNED TO MAUPIN, Megan's car was parked outside his house. She sat on the steps by the front door, head down, elbows on her knees. She looked up as he came down the walk. Her eyes were red, and her face was lined. She twisted a strand of hair around a forefinger.

She stood up, questions in her eyes. "I'm so sorry," she said. "I'm so sorry I hurt you."

He recalled something Jackie had said when he first met her—about women and secrets. "You had a right to tell me when— or if—you felt like it, " he said. "I'm sorry it came out this way." He opened his arms, and she came to him.

Casey had often seen thunderstorms rage through the Deschutes canyon. The tributary creeks would fill the river with muddy water as opaque as coffee-and-cream. Sometimes the storm is so intense and the current so strong that rocks move, old channels fill with gravel, and new channels are carved out. With time, the river carries away the mud, and the water clears. Then you can see which rocks have shifted and how the flow has changed.

He sensed that their relationship now flowed in new channels. They would move on. Separately or together, and to what, he didn't know. It would become clear, in time.

36

September 29: Southeast Portland

"Should we move the stuff back to my place in Antelope?" asked Zulfo. "Now that the Russian is dead?"

Peter Bolton shook his head. "You did your work well. Everyone thinks it was an accident. But we shouldn't move it yet. There are too many people on the river. We'll wait until the end of October. Then we'll move the cases to Antelope. But only for a couple of weeks. The Munich people have everything in place to ship it out in early November."

"But we're not shipping everything, right?"

"There's some for New York and Washington."

"Leaving enough for London, Paris, and Amsterdam." Zulfo smiled. "And Belgrade. They thought we were helpless. Ha! I still think the Serbs should get it all."

The thin man repressed a sigh. You had to explain everything to Zulfo three times. "It does no good to use too much in one place. You can't get that many people together. If you use less, but in several places, it's more effective. Besides, it's not just about the Serbs. NATO played a part, too."

"I'll let Kincaid know we'll need him in another month."

"Wait a couple of weeks; then tell him. Don't do it too soon. You don't know what could go wrong. And once we've got the warheads, you know what to do with him."

Zulfo smiled. "Oh yes!" Zulfo's smile turned to a frown. "I still worry about the guy in the blue raft."

"But you didn't find anyone in the trees."

"No. But he didn't come back to the raft that night. He could have been hiding somewhere."

"It could have been lots of things. Let it be a lesson: keep your mouth shut unless you're certain no one is around. And even if someone was in the trees, it's extremely unlikely they'd have known what you were talking about. No one knows the warheads are missing. It's hard to find something that you're not looking for."

"Kincaid was concerned."

"Kincaid is paranoid. That's been to our advantage."

The thin man fell silent. Fact was, he wished they'd never hired Kincaid, although he'd never admit it to Zulfo. He'd had to think of something too quickly. Given more time, he'd have come up with a better plan. But the Russian had forced their hand. Maybe they should take out Kincaid now. Zulfo had seen where everything was buried last July. All they needed was someone to row the boat. Hell, he could do that. He'd spent entire summers rowing boats at his family's vacation home on Lake Chelan, east of Seattle. Maybe they should eliminate Kincaid sooner rather than later.

Peter Bolton weighed the options but came to no clear conclusion. He'd think about it a little longer.

37

September 29: Maupin

JACKIE AND HANK SAT OUTSIDE the OK Cafe sipping lattes. Hank was telling a story from his youth—a hunting trip he'd taken with his father when Hank was a senior in high school. "I was a year or so younger than Sam," Hank said, pointing through the OK's window to the espresso machine where Sam presided. "We took two horses into the Ochocos and ..."

Jackie had heard the story before, but she didn't mind the

repetition. In the background she could hear the whoosh of pressurized steam as Sam made drinks.

Two women, clearly a mother and daughter, emerged from the OK. Each had a latte in hand. The mother was in her mid-forties; the daughter was maybe twenty. They were bright-eyed and enjoying each other's company. Something about this scene made Jackie uneasy.

Hank got to the part of the story when he and his father saw a cougar lurking in the forest as they dressed out an elk. Jackie glanced at the parking lot. The mother and daughter stood by their car. They laughed over a shared joke.

"It was on that trip," Hank was saying, "that I got some glimpse of my father as an actual human being, and not just 'my father.' It was a pity he died young. I wish I could have spent more time—"

"Excuse me, Hank," Jackie interrupted. "I want to check on something." She rose quickly and pushed open the OK's front door. Susan was gone, getting something from the freezer in back. Sam was by the espresso machine, staring out the window at the parking lot where the mother and daughter were now getting into their car. Her shoulders sagged, and her face was strained. Tears pooled in the corners of her eyes.

Jackie went to Sam and hugged her tightly. "It's all right, Sam," she said softly. "It's okay to miss her."

Sam hung limp against Jackie. "I'll never …" Sam said, her voice shaky. "I'll never …"

"I know," Jackie said. "That will never be you. And I know how hard it is. I understand. It's okay to let it out. Any time you want to talk, I'm here for you. We're all here for you."

Sam wept softly, but said nothing more.

38

September 30: Maupin

LOGAN SLIPPED THE HALTER off Major and loosed him into the fenced pasture. Sam was expected soon, and he wanted the young horse to let off steam before their evening training session.

Sam had been "driving" him from behind with long reins, and last night they'd fitted him in the harness for the first time, just to get him used to the idea. Tonight they planned to work him in harness, and next week move on to the cart. Saddle training would begin in the spring when he turned three.

The young horse loped quickly to join Mataan and Gabe. Logan leaned against the fence, arms folded atop a rail, and admired Major's smooth gait. Ty Decker, their landlord, came up and leaned next to Logan. "He's coming along well, isn't he?" Ty said.

"Yes. And it's been good for Sam. She's needed a project."

Major was now circling Mataan and Gabe, trying to get them to play. He stopped and kicked playfully in Gabe's direction, a horsey way of saying, "Come on, you old stick-in-the-mud, let's run around together." Gabe finally responded, and the two horses ran back and forth for a few minutes.

Gabe tired of the game and was soon head-down munching on hay that Logan had put out for him. Major kept running, sometimes at a slow lope, sometimes at a hard gallop, and sometimes doing a stiff-legged canter, neck arched, tail up, mane flying, nostrils flaring. He was a young horse feeling fit and proud.

It was during one of these latter displays that Major's right front leg suddenly went deep into the ground. His momentum carried him forward, and he flipped over onto his back.

Horrified, Logan was over the fence and running toward Major. Ty was right behind him. Logan heard Ty say, "Goddam badger holes!"

Major rolled over, put out his front legs, and tried to push himself up. He couldn't do it and fell onto his left side. By the time Logan got to him, the horse was on the ground quivering in pain. A bone protruded below the knee of his right foreleg. His cannon bone was broken.

Logan closed his eyes and hung his head. He was numb, and his breath came fast and hard. Was he looking at it right? Was there something he'd missed? He looked again. It was as he first suspected.

Ty arrived and looked at the horse. Logan turned to Ty. Logan's worst fears were confirmed by Ty's face: pain, resignation, determination. "I'm sorry," Ty said gently. "Damn but I'm sorry." He closed his eyes and sighed heavily. "Doc Evans is the nearest vet," he said. "I'll try to get him."

Ty pulled a cell phone from his pocket and called. After a couple of minutes he said, "He's in Condon on another emergency. It'll be an hour before he can get here." He tried veterinarians in Madras and The Dalles. The answer was the same for each: it would be forty-five minutes to an hour of drivetime before anyone could reach them.

Logan wanted to pound his fist into something, to rage against heaven, to wind back the clock to three minutes ago. His mind knew what had to come next, but his heart was breaking and didn't want to go along. *Focus. Focus on the immediate. Do your grieving later.* Major was in extreme pain. There was no fixing him. He had to be put down quickly and humanely.

"I have a revolver in my truck," Ty said quietly. "Hank O'Leary gave it to me for safekeeping; his girlfriend isn't comfortable around guns." He set off quickly and puffed back in a couple of minutes. "I put two rounds in the cylinder." He knelt next to Major. "I'll do it," he said softly to Logan.

"Thanks, but it's my job," Logan said. His head was swimming. Did someone have a backhoe? Could you dig deep enough to bury anything large out here? Did Ty have a plastic tarp they could cover the body with? Sam was going to be home soon. This needed to be done before she arrived. He had to take care of it and get himself together so he could deal with Sam.

Major was quieter now, though his sides still heaved with the pain and the effort of breathing. His eyes were wide, the white edges showing.

Logan reached out and took the revolver. It was cold in his right hand. He looked. Smith and Wesson snub-nosed .38 Special. He knew it. He checked the cylinder. Two rounds, the first in firing position. *Good. Pull once, make it count.*

"It's double action," Ty said softly. "You don't need to cock it."

"I know."

"Hollow point round."

Logan nodded. That was good.

"You know where to put it?"

Logan nodded again. He ran a finger from the inside corner of Major's left eye socket to the base of his right ear. It left a line of ruffled horsehair. He repeated on the other side. He laid his thumb on the intersection and put the muzzle above the thumb. It was near a little bump in Major's pretty white blaze. He put his finger on the trigger, pulled the revolver back two inches, then turned his head.

No. Double check. He took his finger off the trigger, removed the gun, and repeated the process of finding the right place. Then he triple checked it. *Do it right, do it once.* He put the .38 back on the spot.

There were sounds in the background—tires on gravel.

Logan's left hand was on Major's nose, partly to comfort the horse and partly to keep his head in place. "I'm so sorry, little guy," Logan said. "Forgive me." He put his finger back on the trigger.

A car door slammed. Running footsteps, a voice.

Logan squeezed the trigger. Major jumped under his left hand, gave a long sigh, and was still.

Sam was on him. "What have you done!" she screamed. She threw herself on the horse.

Logan felt for a pulse under Major's chin. Nothing. The nostrils were still. The eyes were open but dull and lifeless. *Good. Don't need the second bullet. Clean. No more suffering.*

"What have you done!" Sam screamed again. She was hysterical. Ty turned and left.

"He broke his right front cannon bone," Logan said evenly. "There was nothing we could do. You know that. He was in pain. It had to be done. I'm sorry."

Sam pounded him with her fists. "Why did you have to do that! You ruin everything! Everything you touch you turn to shit! I hate you! Goddam you! Goddam you to hell forever." Tears ran down her face. "I hate you! Go away! You destroy everything! I hate you!"

Logan tried to comfort Sam, to give her a hug, anything. She pushed him back violently. "Leave! Go away! I don't want you near me!"

Logan stood up heavily. He looked around. The rest of the world was going on as before. How could that be, when his life had just shattered? "You can see his leg," Logan said in a low, hoarse voice. "You know there was nothing that could be done. It was kindest thing we could do for him."

"*My* leg was broken. You helped me. Maybe you should have put a bullet in *my* head. Why couldn't you help him? Why couldn't you let *me* help him?" She was sobbing, distraught.

"You know how it is with horses," Logan said.

"Go *away*," Sam said. "I never want to see you again."

Logan sagged. He was tired beyond description, the old familiar tightness in his guts. Suddenly, he doubled at the waist. Dry heaves, again and again, worse than he'd ever had them. When the spasms quit, he walked slowly toward the back side of the barn.

Sam was right: everything he touched turned to shit—his work, his marriage, his life. Now his best chance to reclaim his daughter lay dead in blood-soaked dust. He walked in a trance, gun in hand, one round still in the cylinder.

~

IN A FEW MINUTES SAM STOPPED crying and wiped the tears from her face. Her right hand was in Major's mane, twisting it around her fingers. She hurt all over. All the good times she and Dad and Major had shared belonged to the past. All those good times they'd expected—would never be.

Sam tenderly patted Major's neck and stood up. She took a deep breath. Truth to tell, she was very disappointed in herself. Dad had done the right thing for Major. And her reaction? To have a proper old-fashioned teenage hissy fit. She'd hoped she was beyond that sort of thing, but sometimes she snapped and things came out that she didn't mean.

She needed to find Dad and say how sorry she was, that she understood why he had to do it. Where had he gone? Toward the back of the barn.

Sam was halfway there when she heard the gunshot. She stopped, put her hand to her mouth, then broke into a run.

~

WHEN SAM REACHED HIM, LOGAN was in a sitting position, back against the barn, eyes closed, motionless. The revolver was on the ground next to him but no longer in his hand.

Sam stopped, staring and shaking. She started to cry again. "I'm so sorry!" she said, barely audible.

At the sound, Logan turned his head toward her and opened his eyes. "Me too," he said.

She ran to him and threw her arms around him. Logan pulled her close. Her tears soaked into his shirt. "I didn't mean it," Sam sobbed. She was like a little girl again.

"Don't worry about it."

"I know why you had to … take care … of Major. You did the right thing. I'm sorry I said those things."

"It's okay. I understand."

"When I heard the gun I thought … I thought …" She pulled back and wiped her face, looking him square in the eyes. "Don't ever leave me. You're all I've got."

"I will never leave you. You're stuck with me forever."

"I love you, Dad. I know what you've done for me. And I've treated you … awful. Things just come out. I don't really mean them. I know I can be … It was such as shock to come on him like that … Sometimes I just lash out."

Logan was about to say, "Well, you're your mother's daughter." Trudy could be sharp tongued, then feel sorry. But he closed his mouth instead.

"Yeah," said Sam. "Kinda like Mom, sometimes. You don't have to say it. I know. I don't like it." She brushed back her hair. "That gunshot. I thought—"

"I wanted the bullet gone. That juniper over there? It's wondering what it did to deserve being shot at."

Sam laid her head on his shoulder. Logan put his arm around her. They were quiet together for a couple of minutes. Then Sam stirred and pulled back. She looked earnestly at his face. "Dad, there's something I need to tell you."

"Yes?"

"Don't hate me for what I'm going to say." Her voice was urgent, determined.

"Not in a million years."

"You're going to hate me."

"Never."

Sam took a couple of deep breaths. "It's about the accident."

Listen, Logan told himself. *Keep your big mouth shut. Let her talk.*

"It was my fault," she said.

Logan looked at her, head cocked.

"It was my fault," she said again. "If it wasn't for me, Mom would still be here." Another breath. "I was driving, not Mom. Everyone assumed it was her. I was in the hospital, out of it. When I came to, you'd already decided what had happened. So I never said anything."

Sam paused for another deep breath. "Mom was tired, so I drove. It was near dusk, getting dark. A deer jumped out from the woods, and I swerved to miss it. The car skidded off the road and we hit that tree. We were all right and got out of the car, but I was dazed and unsteady. I … I walked into the road. I keep having flashbacks to the accident, and that's what I see. Mom was calling my name, but it sounded like it was far away or in a dream. Then she ran over and grabbed me. There wasn't time to get me out of the way. She wrapped herself around me—between me and the car that was coming."

Sam's eyes were closed, and her voice was strained. "I'd have died if Mom hadn't … and she'd still be here …" Sam started crying again, the cry of a child when everything has gone wrong. "Now you'll hate me." She buried her head in his side. "I'm so sorry. You keep saying how much you loved her, what a saint she was. And I'm the reason she isn't here for you. I'm the reason you had to spend all our money. It's my fault everything went wrong for us." Her body shook against Logan as she gave over to her tears.

Logan held Sam close, trying to take in what she'd just confessed. The scene played in his mind. Sam in the road, looking lost. Trudy calls her name, louder each time. Trudy sees headlights coming and races for Sam, urgently calling her. The oncoming car swerves, goes into a spin, out of control, coming at Sam broadside. With no time to get them out of the way, Trudy runs between Sam and the car and wraps herself around Sam, hoping it will work out for Sam, knowing how it will end for herself.

Logan's throat and chest went tight; his breath was short. In an instant he saw that everything in his life—all his proud successes, all the agony of his failures—were trivialities, mere chaff, compared to Trudy's willing sacrifice.

He felt flattened, shattered. Putting Major down, Sam raging at him, and now this revelation about the accident and the burden Sam had been carrying for over a year—he wanted to run away and regain his equilibrium. But he couldn't. He had to respond to Sam. *Focus*, he told himself. *Grieve later. Do what you can for Sam. It's about Sam, not you.*

"You hate me!" Sam said. "You'll hate me forever!"

Logan waited, seeking the right words, trying to relax his throat so he could speak. At last he said, "Honey, it was an accident. There's no one to blame. Certainly not you."

"But I was driving! If I hadn't hit that tree … if Mom hadn't tried to save me … none of this would have happened. It was all my fault!"

"If I had handled things better," Logan said, "your mother and I would still be together. And none of this would have happened."

"If only I'd been a better driver," Sam pleaded. "If only I had more experience. If Mom had been driving instead of me—"

"It could have happened to anyone, Sam. It could have happened to Mom. Or me. That's the way it is with accidents."

"If I hadn't been … so out of it … had heard Mom … had gotten out of the way! I'm so sorry! You can't understand how bad I feel about it, how sick it makes me every time I think about it!"

"I understand a lot more than you think I do!"

"Why did Mom save me?" Sam said, her voice tight. "Why didn't she just let me go?"

Again, Logan waited until the right words came. "Because she's your mother," he said slowly. "Sam, you are loved more than you can imagine. When you have children of your own, then you will begin to understand. Until that day, you cannot comprehend how much your father and your mother love you. You are loved without conditions. You are loved forever."

Sam choked back tears. "What did I ever do to deserve love like that?"

"No one deserves that kind of love," Logan said, "but we get it anyway."

There was one more thing he felt he needed to say, and then he'd shut up. "Sam," he said, "your mother knew what she was doing. She's given you the gift of life. That was her first gift to you, and her last. What do you do when you get a gift? You say how much you're grateful. You don't have to be perfect. You can't be perfect. So just be grateful. And be patient with yourself."

Logan looked at the sky. "What a burden you've carried, Sam. All alone, for over a year. I'm so sorry. I had no idea what a load you had on your shoulders. Put it down and let it go. Or at least, let someone help you carry it."

"Can we help each other?"

Logan closed his eyes and nodded.

"Can you still love me?" she said.

"Forever. I will never desert you. That is my promise to you."

39

October 1: Maupin

"ARE THESE OUT OF YOUR 'RESERVE' bins?" Lower Dave asked Hank O'Leary.

"Nope," Hank said. He was in Dave's shop selling him flies. "Twenty dozen flies, fresh off the vise."

"So you're tying again?"

"Yes, and ..." he leaned close to Dave and lowered his voice "... take a good look." He arranged two Jonzies side by side. "I tied one, and Jackie did the other. See if you can tell the difference."

Dave examined the flies, then said, "You'd better be careful, or you'll be out of a job!"

"Well, she's good, but she's not very efficient. I can tie three for every one she ties. Still, it's a help. I'm getting caught up. It's fun to have someone to tie with."

The door opened, and Casey walked in. "Hey, Casey," Dave said. "Take a look at these flies. Jackie's helping Hank."

Casey looked at the flies. "Nice," he said. "Nothing like being taught by The Master."

Hank rolled his eyes.

"Did they give you the day off?" Dave said. "You look like you could use one."

"Half-day trip, starting in fifteen minutes," Casey said. "The Town Float. Then I'm busy every day for a while." He looked at the floor. "I am a little tired. I've been ... thinking about things. Not sleeping well."

"That's not good. I hope you're feeling better soon," Dave said.

Casey shrugged. "I need a little time to mull things over."

"Jackie's at the house," Hank said quietly. He suspected Casey's love life had hit a pothole.

Casey shook his head. "Thanks, but I need to work this one out on my own." He nodded a couple of times, like he was agreeing with himself. "Anyway, I was driving by and saw your truck parked outside. Could you do me a favor?"

"Sure."

"Old Ernie's out of the hospital and back in town," Casey said. "I've been looking in on him now and then—to see how he's doing after the fire and his head injury. But I haven't been able to get there for a few days, and I'm booked solid for the next week. Could you check on him?"

"No problem."

Casey chewed his lip, then added, "You might see if you can get him to tell you what happened during the fire. How he got hit on the head. I'm still not sure I believe the official version."

~

JOEY, ERNIE'S YELLOW LAB, MET Hank at the door, tail wagging. Hank patted the dog's head. Joey accepted the pat and licked Hank's hand. Then he padded across the room and flopped onto a dirty dog bed.

"Ernie, it's good to see you up and around," Hank said. They were in the living room of Ernie's tiny ramshackle house. Hank sat on the sofa, Ernie in an old recliner. The room held a hodgepodge of broken-down furniture that was cheap and tacky even when it was new a half-century ago. Cardboard boxes and newspapers were stacked against the walls; dusty curtains hung haphazardly over dirty windows. The carpet smelled like dog urine; Ernie probably had trouble getting Joey out to do his business. Hank made a mental note: *try not to end up like this.*

"What am I going to do now?" Ernie said in a fear-tinged voice. "The Drift Inn's gone. I've got no job." He wrung his hands.

"It'll work out, Ernie. You've got your Social Security and Medicare. You'll get by."

"How will it work out?" Ernie said like he hadn't heard. "What if those guys come for me again?"

"What guys?"

"I don't know who they are."

"Ernie, did anyone come into the Drift Inn and hit you on the head?"

"I don't remember nothing. I keep trying, but I don't remember." Ernie's voice trailed into a whine. His wrinkled face was twisted in worry, his eyes rheumy and distracted. He hadn't looked at Hank.

"What guys are you talking about?" Hank prodded again. "Did they attack you? Did they set fire to the Drift Inn?"

More hand wringing, but no response.

Hank worried that Ernie might be hitting the bottle again. Long walks with Joey had been Ernie's way of dealing with the urge to drink. "Ernie," Hank said, "do you think Joey needs a walk?"

Ernie brightened slightly, then sagged. "I can't walk very far. Not like before."

"Let's give it a try," Hank said gently. "Maybe just around the block. I'll go with you."

It was a slow walk, with Joey eager and Ernie unsteady. Hank took the leash so the dog wouldn't pull the old man over. "Ernie," he said, trying another tack, "how many guys are you worried about? Why are you worried about them?"

"They were up to no good, I'm sure. They thought I'd heard them talking, but I don't hear so good. I heard nothing." He started to whine again. "I heard nothing! Why did they want me?"

"How many guys?"

Ernie screwed up his face. "Three?"

"Where did you see them?"

A flash of recognition. "They were in the City Park. On the other side of Bakeoven Creek. Afternoon. It was raining a little. No one else there. When they saw me, they stopped talking. One of them came toward me. I didn't like the way he looked at me. Joey barked, and he backed off. Joey never barks at no one."

"When was this?"

"I don't remember."

"But it was three men."

"Maybe."

"Did three men come into the Drift Inn before the fire?"

"No. One … or … I don't know. I just don't know."

They'd finished their walk around the block, and Ernie seemed exhausted. Hank helped him inside and left him sitting in his decrepit recliner, head back, eyes closed, breathing heavily.

What had he learned? Not much. Ernie was worried about three guys, but maybe it wasn't three. He'd seen them in the City Park by the river—no idea when. Any other clues? Ernie said it was raining a little when he saw them. Was it was raining the day before the fire? Hank would pass this on to Casey.

40

October 9: Southeast Portland

ZULFO KNOCKED ON BOLTON'S door: two quick raps, a pause, and a final rap. As he waited, two young men walked by him. They were holding hands. Zulfo spat on the ground after they'd passed.

Peter Bolton opened the door. "I see from your demeanor that you've encountered my neighbors," he said with a thin smile. "They leave me alone, and I leave them alone. It's a good arrangement. Try it some time."

Zulfo felt vaguely put down, but he often felt that way around this man. *Well,* Zulfo thought, *I might not have as much education as him, but he'd be useless as a soldier.* So it all evened out. They each had their talents.

They sat at the kitchen table, Zulfo drumming his fingers while Bolton removed his wire-frame glasses and methodically cleaned them. "Are the arrangements complete?" Zulfo asked.

"Yes. We'll have all the VX in place before the end of the year."

Zulfo smiled, imagining the results of their efforts. He couldn't be there when the Serbs moved into Srebrenica. He'd vowed to protect her—to protect all of them—and he'd failed. But it wasn't his fault; he was following orders. Besides, the UN and NATO had said Srebrenica was a Safe Area, and everyone expected them to take care of the people who were trapped there. But this one act would set everything right. They would learn that you can't treat people like rats. "Will it take you long to get the VX from the warheads?" Zulfo asked. "And to get it ready to use?"

Peter Bolton examined his glasses for cleanliness. "Piece of cake," he said.

41

October 11: Deschutes River between Whiskey Dick and Maupin

"YOU'RE NOT GOING TO THROW it back, are you? The biggest fish I ever caught?" Brandon Muckenhirn's client looked at him sternly.

Brandon eyed the fish. It was a wild steelhead hen of about seven pounds. Then he looked at his client, a business acquaintance of his two brothers. "You want it for the freezer?"

"You bet! My friend from Bel Air said you'd fix it for me."

"Well, it's a fine steelhead, alright," Brandon said. "Twelve pounds, maybe even fourteen. Probably the biggest fish I've seen this year." He looked around. No other boats were in sight. He'd passed that Logan guy's blue raft, but it was around the corner. No one would see. He stuck his knife through the top of the fish's head and into its brain. It quivered and twitched. Then he ripped the gills out and held the fish upside down to drain the blood. He gutted it and threw the egg sac into the river. Then he put the fish on ice in the cooler.

It wasn't the first wild steelhead he'd killed this summer. *Stupid rule,* he thought to himself. A fish was a fish was a fish, and the difference between hatchery steelhead and wild steelhead was sentimental twaddle. Give 'em what they want. The people owned the fish, so let the people decide what to do with the fish. That's the marketplace at work. Keep government meddling out of it, and trust the people. You didn't need to educate them or explain things. They knew what was right. The river needed more fish that people could take home with them. Crank up the hatcheries and keep those babies coming. That would be good for everyone on the river, especially those who made their living there.

If his brothers knew what he was doing, they'd respect him for taking the initiative. Maybe they'd even let him back into the family's real estate business instead of shuffling him off with his trust fund. They thought they were so smart, so superior, always treating him like he was an idiot. They were the idiots—dickless idiots, who were jealous of him because he was the one the women wanted, the one who always scored.

~

ON A HILL ABOVE THE RIVER, Logan McCrea watched Brandon. Over the last month he'd formed a habit of going to a vantage point with the guidebook manuscript. He always picked a place that was away from his boat, so no one would suspect he was there. Once settled, he'd work on the book, glancing up now and again to see if anything was happening on the river.

He was looking for Kincaid and Scarface—and half hoping he wouldn't see them. They seemed to be absent from the river, so to keep himself amused he checked out all the boats and anglers.

To supplement his barely adequate binoculars, he'd dipped into his "cookie jar" fund and bought a high-powered spotting scope with a small tripod. He trained the scope on Brandon Muckenhirn.

He wanted to see whether Brandon's client had a wild or hatchery steelhead. And to see what Brandon would do with the fish.

When they're about five inches long, hatchery-raised steelhead have their adipose fin clipped; wild fish have an intact adipose. That was how anglers could tell them apart. With the spotting scope, Logan could tell from a distance whether a steelhead was fin-clipped.

Two weeks ago he saw Brandon kill a wild steelhead for his client and figured he'd seen it wrong. A week later the scene played out again, and he'd decided it was none of his business. This was the third time in two weeks, and Logan figured there were other incidents that he hadn't witnessed. He would tell Judd about it when he got back to town.

~

AFTER THE EVENING'S FISHING, Brandon started fixing dinner for his clients. In July it stayed light until well after 9:00, so the routine was to eat first, then fish. But by October it grew dark before 7:30, and they fished before dinner.

Brandon carried a powerful headlamp, plus a backup, when he was fishing in the evening. It could be quite dark when they were done. In camp, he kept a propane-fueled Coleman lantern going at all times. That bright circle of light was reassuring. If he had to go anywhere, such as to his boat or the outhouse, he took the lantern with him. For good measure, there was a big police-style flashlight in his duffle. It used four D cells and would back up the lantern and other lights if needed.

He'd grown up in tony southern California neighborhoods where there was plenty of light, even on the blackest of nights. Light, he knew, was part of the natural order of things, the way the world should be. Darkness was not normal. People weren't made to function without light, so take advantage of technology and bring light with you.

After all, you don't know what's out there. Wild animals with claws and fangs. Bad people. Maybe other things. Shadows moved and shifted; strange shapes came and went. You couldn't say for sure what they were. Those shadows could seem awfully human-like sometimes. And there were the noises. Mostly they were covered up by river noise, but if you listened carefully they sounded like … well, hard to say what they were. He didn't believe in ghosts. No, no. On the other hand, he didn't quite disbelieve in them, either. But light took care of those concerns. Shine your beam on anything suspicious, and all the doubts went away.

~

DINNER WAS OVER BY 9:30, and the clients retired to their tents. They would be up for the morning session in nine hours. Time enough for him to read. Brandon always took reading material with him: Stephen King novels, books about vampires, stories of the supernatural. Sometimes he brought his iPad and watched zombie movies and other horror flicks; sometimes he played Werewolf Invasion and similar computer games.

He read for an hour. Before turning off his lantern, he reached into his duffle and got out another light, a high-tech rechargeable LED job. He turned it on low and set it beside his cot. With one last reassuring look at the LED's blue brightness, Brandon turned off the big lantern and fell asleep.

~

THE NEXT MORNING BRANDON decided that killing wild steelhead and putting them in the cooler was not the right thing to do. He was ashamed of himself. Instead of putting fish in the cooler where some busybody might look for them, he'd put them in a dry bag. That was the smart way to do it. He'd wrap the fish in plastic and put it in the dry bag with some ice.

42

October 12: Maupin

CASEY WAS ELATED. AT LAST HE had Brandon Muckenhirn by the short hairs!

Logan had come by looking for Judd, but Judd was on a three-day float from Macks Canyon to the mouth, with Willie rowing the bag boat. They wouldn't be back until afternoon. Then Logan left to get his boat trailer fixed; he wouldn't be in Maupin when Judd returned. He'd told Casey about Brandon killing wild steelhead and putting them in the cooler, and said he'd speak to Judd when he got back. But Casey couldn't wait to catch Brandon red-handed. Maybe the shock of it would get him to admit he'd started the fire at the Drift Inn.

That afternoon Judd arrived at the OK's parking lot before Brandon. "Judd," Casey said after his clients left, "Brandon's killing wild steelhead for his clients."

Judd's jaw dropped, and his eyes narrowed. He looked like he was going to explode. Then Judd surprised Casey. "How do you know this?" he said. "That's a strong accusation. If it's true, he'll lose his guide's license. It won't help me much, either, if Fish and Wildlife and the BLM learn that one of my guides is killing wild steelhead. Are you positive he's doing this?"

Casey hadn't thought this part through. Logan would have credibility, having seen it. But Casey was telling the story second-hand; it was just hearsay. Even if Judd believed Logan, he'd still need proof because Brandon would deny it. After a long pause, Casey said, "You'll see. He keeps them in his cooler."

HALF AN HOUR LATER BRANDON drove up. His clients went into the OK for coffee while Brandon started straightening up his boat. Judd strode up to him, Casey right behind. Brandon had lifted up his cooler and was holding it over the side of his boat. He turned the tap to drain the melted ice. A red-tinged flow trickled out. Casey looked at Judd. Fish blood for sure!

"Brandon," Judd said in a commanding voice. "Casey says you're killing wild steelhead for your clients. Are you?"

"Me?" Brandon said, hand on his chest and looking indignant. "No way. Where'd Casey get such an idea?" He hoisted a dry bag out of the boat and tossed it into his truck.

"Look in the cooler," Casey said.

Brandon opened the cooler, looking disdainfully at Casey. Except for some half-melted ice cubes, it was empty.

Casey stared into the empty cooler like it was the gateway to Hell. "When he drained the cooler, the water ran red with fish blood," Casey said when he could talk again. "He's hidden the steelhead somewhere."

Brandon shook his head and looked at Casey like he had Alpo for brains. Wordlessly, he reached into his garbage bag and retrieved two empty cans. He tossed them at Casey's feet. "One of my guys likes V8 in the morning. He put a half-full can in the cooler, and it spilled." He paused dramatically. "I hope that's not against the law."

Judd gave Casey a look of mingled disgust and disappointment, then walked away.

Casey went to his pickup and sat on the driver's seat with the door open, his head in his hands. He'd been so sure, so positive that he'd be able to expose Brandon. Now Brandon knew someone was on to him, and he would be extra careful.

Two weeks ago Casey had decided he didn't need Judd's validation, and that he would do what he thought was right. Where had that decision gotten him? In the doghouse. He realized that maybe he still craved Judd's good opinion a bit more than he wanted to admit. It wasn't easy to change the way you thought about things.

Could things get any worse? Apparently they could. He saw Megan walk out of the OK and come toward his truck. He looked away, unable to face her.

"Dad's really pissed at you," she said. "How come?"

He told her the story.

"Well," she said, "You were right not to tell him that you hadn't actually seen it, that it was second-hand."

"I was so sure he had them in his cooler. He probably moved them. I didn't think to look anywhere else."

"Oh, Casey," she said with a sigh. She sat silently beside him for a while, then went back into the OK.

He sat alone in his truck for another hour, the most miserable wretch in the county.

~

CASEY HAD THE NEXT DAY OFF. Good thing, too, since he couldn't sleep. Judd was mad as hops, Brandon had gotten off scot-free, and Megan thought he was a flake and fool. And she was probably right.

About 6:00 a.m. he finally dropped into a fitful slumber. He was up and dressed by 9:00 and went to Lower Dave's to give him a fishing report.

"Well, you look like pureed rat crap," Dave said when he came through the door.

"Thanks. Good to see you, too." He did a neck roll. Man, his shoulders felt tight! They talked about steelheading. It was a ten-minute conversation that took almost an hour because people kept coming in to buy things and ask questions.

Logan came through the door. "Get your trailer fixed?" Casey asked.

"Two more days," said Logan. "I'm boatless till then." Logan lowered his voice and said, "I haven't had a chance to tell Judd about Brandon."

Casey took Logan by the arm and led him outside where they could talk without being overheard. Logan was silent while Casey told him what had happened yesterday.

When he'd finished, Logan said, "There's no question that he killed wild fish. I've seen him do it three times. He probably moved the fish from the cooler before coming back to Maupin."

"I wouldn't talk to Judd about it just yet," Casey said. "He's really mad at me. Megan's not happy either."

"She's caught in the middle between you and her dad." Logan smiled at him. "It'll get better. I'd bet Megan's on your side. And sooner or later Brandon will get nailed. Guys like that can't cover things up forever. Walk to the OK with me, and I'll ask Sam to make you a mocha. On the house."

"I hope Judd's not there."

"I saw him drive off a few minutes ago. Megan's at school. You're safe."

~

THEY HAD THEIR DRINKS AND walked back to Lower Dave's. On the way, Casey asked Logan what he and Sam planned to do over the winter.

"Sam starts college in January," Logan said. "She's going to Stanford. They've been holding a place for her." He hesitated a moment and said, "My old company, Med-Rec, was finally bought

out. And for a much better price than anyone expected. It left us
enough money for Sam to go to school." He paused again. "It took
care of some other financial issues, too. So I'm feeling pretty good."

Once inside the fly shop, Casey said, "Logan, at the end of
July you told me you had some photos of trout that you took from
deep in the alders. Do you still have them? I never got a look."

"I'll get them. Camera's in the truck." When he returned, Casey
and Dave crowded around him to look at the screen. Logan showed
some recent steelhead photos, a few scenics, and finally got to the
trout-in-the-trees shots from July.

"Sweet!" Casey said. "Don't you love fishing for them back
there?"

"I do like it," Logan said. "Real hunting."

"Any more?"

Logan pushed the button, and another photo came up. "Oops,
that one's no good," Logan said. " You've seen the best of the bunch."
He pushed the button and went to another photo.

"Wait, wait!" Lower Dave said. "Go back to that photo you
didn't like." Logan did, and Dave said, "I thought so. It's Nearly
Honest John. I didn't know he was back on the river. God help us all."

"I saw him last May," Casey said, "but not since then. That's
his boat. Red and blue and beat to hell. Kind of like its owner. "

"That's Kincaid, alright," said another voice. A customer had
come into the shop and was looking over their shoulders at the
photos. It was a local, Steve Schultz. "I didn't know he was guiding
again. Maybe he's cleaned up his act."

"I doubt it," said Dave. "Although you never know."

When Logan left, Casey followed him out the door. "Hey, Logan,"
Casey said in a low voice as Logan was poised to get into his truck.
"Hank talked to Old Ernie a few days ago and asked him about the
fire at the Drift Inn. Hank told me that Ernie doesn't remember a
thing, but he started going on about three guys he'd seen in City Park
last April. They thought Ernie had overheard them—he hadn't, but

they thought he had—and one of the guys threatened him. It was just before the fire. Ernie doesn't remember how long before, but he said it was raining a little when he saw them. I checked the weather, and there were showers the day before the Drift Inn burned down."

He shrugged. "Of course we were getting a lot of rainy days in March and early April, so it may not mean anything. But that fire always seemed suspicious to me. I think the door was locked from the outside. They never found Ernie's keys, and he wouldn't have locked it. Seeing that photo made me think: Kincaid is just the kind of lowlife that would do something like that."

"Let's print the photo on my computer," Logan said, "and we'll show it to Ernie."

~

"YES!" ERNIE SAID WHEN HE saw the picture. "It was John Kincaid. He was with two other men. That's who I saw in the park."

Logan asked Ernie, "The other guy in the photo—was he at the park with Kincaid?"

Ernie squinted at the photo. "Might have been. I can't tell for sure."

"It's not a very good shot, I know."

"Ernie," Casey said. "Think real hard. Do you remember anyone coming into the Drift Inn right before the fire?"

Ernie shook his head. "I don't remember. I just don't remember."

"Was Brandon Muckenhirn one of the three guys you saw?"

"Who?" Ernie suddenly teared up. "What's going to happen to me now?" He sounded pitiful.

Casey and Logan said some consoling words and left him alone with his dog.

~

"POOR ERNIE," CASEY SAID AS they climbed into Logan's truck. "I never paid much attention to him before. But since I pulled him out of that fire I feel responsible for him. I should stop in and see him a few times over the winter, but I'm not looking forward to it. I don't like being around unhappy people. That's one reason I like guiding. People are glad to be on the river."

"A lot of folks have stressful jobs," Logan said. "Getting away is good for them. They lighten up and go back refreshed. That's what I should have done when I was in high tech. But no, I was so damned important that I couldn't be gone for one day. Or so I thought."

Casey nodded. "I hear it all the time. About two months ago I guided a guy who's a consultant. He handles logistics for outfits that send doctors on mercy missions. He hears about nasty stuff all over the world. He was glad to have a break and think about something else."

"I'm sure."

"He couldn't totally turn it off, though. He told me an awful story. I've had a hard time getting it out of my head." Casey related Stan's story about the man whose fiancée was caught up in the Bosnian war and killed herself after being gang raped. "Stan said that guy was going to hate Serbs—all Serbs—until he died."

"That's … horrible," Logan said. He seemed deep in thought. Suddenly intent, he asked, "Did your client say where the guy was from? The Serb hater?"

"Pendleton."

Logan gave a noncommittal response and relaxed, like it wasn't the answer he expected.

Casey thought some more. Several images passed quickly through his mind: Pendleton; two men in a bar, one of them Stan and the other indistinct; then an image of the indistinct man in Umatilla; then an image of a forearm with a tattoo.

"No, I got that wrong," Casey said. "It was Pendleton where Stan heard the story. In a bar. The guy who told it was from Umatilla, but they were in Pendleton. Stan said he had a tattoo: *Never Forget. Never Forgive.* On his right forearm. Kept it covered most of the time, but he showed it to Stan. Stan figured it must have been about the girl."

"You're positive your client said Umatilla?"

"Pretty sure. Yeah, Umatilla."

"Did Stan say if anyone was with the man he talked to?"

"Hmm. I don't remember." Another image popped to mind: the advertising icon Mr. Clean. "He said the guy went off with a tough-looking dude who had a shaved head or was bald." Casey thought for a moment. "Kincaid's passenger—the man in your photo—wasn't he bald?"

Logan shook his head. "You can't tell much from the photo, but I had a good look at him. His head was definitely shaved. But there are a lot of guys like that. It's not unusual." Logan seemed to be still thinking. "Do you remember the name of the medical aid outfit?" he said.

"I never heard it," Casey replied, "but I can get you Stan's phone number. It's at home."

They drove to Casey's place and retrieved the number, then Logan dropped Casey at the fly shop. "You've been a wealth of information today," Logan said as Casey got out. "I'll tell Sam to give you free mochas for the rest of the fishing season."

"Thanks!" Casey said as Logan left. But he didn't think his steelhead report was worth that many mochas.

43

October 12: Maupin

AFTER DROPPING OFF CASEY, Logan went home and unlocked the drawer where he kept a thin manila folder of items related to his mission. He pulled the photo of Peter Bolton and returned to Ernie Doyle's.

"Ernie," he said. "Was this one of the people you saw in the park?"

Ernie peered at the photo, then shook his head. "Could have been, but I don't know." He scrunched his face in concentration. "One of the men had his back to me, and I couldn't see him. Or … I don't know. I just don't remember."

Logan then went home and called Stan, Casey's client. He told Stan he was a writer working on an article about the Balkan wars. Stan gave him a contact name. Logan followed up and confirmed the story. The name of the woman who'd killed herself was Adina Osmanović.

Armed with this information, Logan drove to Beaverton and called Bill Short on the secure phone link. He told Bill the Adina Osmanović story and gave him the contact in the medical aid group in case Bill wanted more details. "It may not mean anything," Logan said. "But it's worth investigating."

"There might be a connection," Bill Short said, "with the missing warheads. It's worth checking out. There could be a motive there, as well as the means. We'll follow up and let you know."

"Any sign of the missing chemical weapons expert?"

"Peter Bolton?" Bill said. He shook his head. "Nothing. No credit card charges, no anything. He doesn't want to be found."

"That's not a good sign. Is there anything that links him to Kincaid?"

"Nothing."

TWO DAYS LATER LOGAN FELT pent-up and on edge. First, he
wanted to hear from Bill Short about the Bosnian lead—whether
it was going anywhere or not. Second, he was supposed to meet his
friend Bob Barkin, whom he'd run into at RiverFest. They'd made
plans to float the river from Trout Creek to Maupin, but that had been
ruled out because Logan's raft trailer was in the shop with a broken
weld and a damaged axle. Plan B was for them to meet at South
Junction tomorrow morning; Bob was already there.

Having everything up in the air made Logan anxious. He wanted
to stay close by, but he also needed to work off his nervous energy. So
at 2:00 in the afternoon he loaded the horses in the trailer, then went
to the OK to fetch Sam for a ride in the Criterion Hills.

Logan and Sam had become very close since Sam's confession
about the accident that killed her mother. Sam had finally opened up,
and the two of them talked naturally and easily. Mostly they talked
about Trudy, Sam's mother. Both of them felt a burden of guilt,
although for different reasons. Logan told Sam she shouldn't feel
responsible for the accident. Sam told Logan he'd been overwhelmed
by work stress.

They'd been riding for an hour when they came to a spring and
let the horses drink, reins loose and hands resting on their saddle
horns. Logan took a breath and said, "I'm having dinner with Lisa on
Friday. At her place."

Sam's face went tight, then relaxed.

"Look, Sam," he said. "I don't know where things are going
with Lisa. Probably nowhere. But I've got to … *we've* got to … move
on with our lives. You know how much I loved your mother. She was a
saint. Kind, generous to a fault …"

"… upbeat, full of life …"

"… loved animals and being outdoors …"

"… made the worst meatloaf I've ever tasted."

Logan flinched. "You didn't like her meatloaf?"

Sam made a finger-in-the-mouth gagging gesture.

"I hated it, too! I thought I was the only one! I had to smother it with ketchup before I could eat it. And she was so proud of her recipe." He thought a little more. "She couldn't sing, could she?"

"Tuneless. And when she lost her temper, she could say anything."

"When she was tired, her brain would fall asleep, but her mouth would keep talking."

"I tried to keep my friends away when she was like that. It was embarrassing."

The horses finished their drink. Logan and Sam turned them from the spring and rode side by side along the faint dirt road. "I guess she wasn't perfect," Logan said.

"She was a really good person," Sam said. "And we can still love her and be grateful? Even if she wasn't perfect?"

"Yes." Then Logan saw what Sam was struggling with. If they treated Trudy like a saint—carved an image in mental marble and put it in a niche—they would separate her from her humanity. Her willing sacrifice of herself would be trivialized, because after all, isn't that what saints do—selflessly sacrifice themselves for others? But to see Trudy as she was, with flaws and weaknesses, made her someone they could admire and even emulate. Because how many of us are born to perfection and sainthood?

"You don't have to be perfect," Sam said, "to be loved. Do you?"

"No. We can try to understand each other. Be forgiving. And hope to be forgiven."

Sam said, "Are there things that can't be forgiven?" Sam didn't wait for his response. "Dad?" she said. "Mom slept with other men."

Logan was stunned. *Trudy? Other men?*

"I mean, after the divorce. She was … she was lonely. I think she needed acceptance. She felt so abandoned."

Logan took a minute to digest this. Finally he said, "I was not a nice person to your mother. At the end." He grimaced at the memory of himself. "She deserved so much better than she got from me.

I always thought that somehow I'd get myself together and win her back. So we'd be a family again."

"Dad, you and I are a family. Let's make the most of what we've got and stop wishing things were different."

"I won't do anything that puts a wedge between us. I'll stop seeing Lisa if it bothers you."

Sam shook her head. "No. It's hard to see you with someone else, but I'll get used to it. I've got to. Anything else would be unfair." She smoothed Mataan's mane, then said, "I just thought you should know how it was with Mom. And Dad? It was only one or two guys. It wasn't like she went nuts or anything."

~

WHILE LOGAN AND SAM WERE riding, John Kincaid—Nearly Honest John—passed through Maupin on his way to Madras. He needed food, so he stopped at the Maupin grocery store to buy some cigarettes and a twelve pack of Bud Light to get him through the next few days. As he left the store, he ran into Steve Schultz, the local man who'd seen Logan's photos two days ago. Steve said, "Hey, John! I see you're guiding again."

John shook his head, his long stringy hair rubbing the collar of his dirty shirt. "Not me."

"Huh. I thought you were. I saw a photo of you in your boat. You were with another guy. Your client was bald or had a shaved head. Couldn't see his face because his head was turned. The photo was shot through some trees last July. "

"Oh, yeah. Bald dude. I guided him during the caddis season. I forgot. Who did you say had the photo?"

"That guy Logan. You see him around town and on the river a lot. He's always asking questions because he's working on a guidebook. Drives a silver GMC. Has a blue raft. Lives up the hill at Ty Decker's place—in his rental house."

"Logan. Blue raft. Got it." Kincaid left in a hurry.

THEY FINISHED THEIR RIDE AND were back in Maupin by 5:00. Logan dropped Sam at the OK and took the horses home. Then he checked his email.

There was one from Bill Short that had arrived an hour before. He went straight to it. "See attachment" was all it said. He tried to view the attachment, but it was gibberish. He decrypted the file, and a photo of a pretty young woman appeared. It was Adina Osmanović. She was the nurse that had been raped in Bosnia. Adina was so beautiful, so lively looking, with kind, compassionate eyes. Logan winced, and his shoulders sagged. From the records, it was clear that she and Peter Bolton were in Boston at the same time. It was entirely plausible that they'd been lovers, but there was no proof.

The third photo chilled him to the bone. It was Scarface. His name was Zulfo Osmanović. He was Adina's older brother.

A brief bio followed. Zulfo, Adina, and their parents had moved from Yugoslavia to San Jose, California, when Zulfo was thirteen. Their father was an electronics engineer, born in Belgrade but with roots in Potočari, six kilometers northwest of Srebrenica in what was now Bosnia. Zulfo had a green card, so he qualified as a resident alien, if not a US citizen. When the war began, Zulfo went to Bosnia and fell in with Naser Orić, one of the most effective commanders in the Bosniak militia. Srebrenica was their base. Zulfo had been wounded in a skirmish with the Bosnian Serbs: a bullet had plowed across his forehead, nearly killing him and leaving a prominent scar. Orić's group left Srebrenica before the massacre and weren't there to defend the helpless residents when the Serbs moved in. After the Dayton Peace Accords, Zulfo returned to the US, ending up in Pendleton, Oregon, where he worked as a diesel mechanic. For some reason, he'd recently bought 40 acres in Antelope, a town not far from Maupin. At the bottom of his bio it said in boldface, "Known to be ruthless and extremely dangerous."

Logan printed the photos and bios. He retrieved the manila folder from the locked drawer and put the photos in it. Then he drove to Ernie Doyle's and showed him the picture of Zulfo. "How about this man," he asked Ernie. "Have you seen him before?"

Ernie's eyes grew wide, and he started to shake. His lips were quivering, but he couldn't speak. That was all Logan needed to know.

After Logan left Ernie's, a car followed him from a distance. He didn't see it.

~

WHEN HE REACHED HOME, LOGAN immediately called Bill Short on his cell phone—there was no time to drive to Beaverton for a secure line.

"Bill," he said, "I just got a positive ID on Zulfo Osmanović. He's the guy I saw on the river, and it looks like he started the fire in the Drift Inn and tried to kill Ernie Doyle. No ID on Peter Bolton, though."

"So we've tied together Zulfo and Kincaid, who had stashed something—we don't know what—on the Deschutes. And we've tied together Zulfo and Adina. And put Zulfo at the scene of the fire ..."

"But we don't know if that had anything to do with the missing warheads."

"Or if Bolton was involved with Zulfo. But he was in Boston at the same time as Adina. They *could* have been lovers, but we don't know for sure. And he *might* have been the guy in the bar in Pendleton. Or there's no link at all."

There was silence for several seconds; then Bill Short said, "I'm going to get Dietz involved. I think we need to send an agent out there ASAP, but it's his decision." There was a further pause, and Bill asked, "No one suspects why you're there, do they?"

"I don't know why they would. I'll keep my eyes peeled, though."

"Be cautious. Stay close to town. We could have someone there tomorrow morning."

LOGAN PLANNED TO FOLLOW Bill's advice. However, he was supposed to meet his friend Bob Barkin tomorrow morning. Bob was already camped at South Junction. There was no cell phone coverage, so Logan couldn't tell him there had been a change of plans. He didn't want to leave his friend in the lurch. Tomorrow would be too late; if they sent an agent, Logan would probably be showing him around all day and wouldn't have time to meet Barkin.

Logan pondered this dilemma and decided to drive to South Junction right away and tell Barkin he wouldn't be able to fish with him. After all, Bill Short had told him to stay *close* to town. South Junction was close—in country terms. Besides, he'd only be gone a couple of hours; what could happen in that amount of time?

He made himself a sandwich, then locked the door and headed out. It was 7:15 and getting dark.

~

AFTER LOGAN'S LIGHTS DISAPPEARED around the corner, a car pulled out from a side road and drove into his driveway. A man got out and walked up the steps onto the porch. With a practiced move, he opened the locked door and went inside. He looked around, hands on hips. He spied the laptop and walked to it. He hit the Shift key. The screen went from dark to light, but a password was required.

Next to the computer was a manila folder. He casually opened it. A photo of Peter Bolton was on top. His eyes narrowed. He moved Bolton's photo aside and saw Adina. His jaw went tight. He lifted her photo. Underneath was a third photo—a younger version of himself. Zulfo Osmanović left the house at a run and got into his car. He didn't bother to close the folder or relock the door.

LOGAN DROVE TO THE OK. HE SAW his raft and trailer were
in the parking lot they used for shuttles. Apparently the repairs had
been made. He parked next to the trailer, then entered the OK to
check on Sam. She was chatting with Helen.

"Can I get you anything to eat?" Helen asked.

"No thanks. I've got a sandwich, but I'd like that pretty young
lady to fix me a latte while I walk down the street and get some flies
from Dave. He's working late tonight." He turned to Sam, "I told Bob
Barkin I'd bring him some Plum Dandies to try. I'm going to drive
to South Junction and give him the flies—and tell him I can't fish
with him. I'll be back in a couple of hours."

"How come you're not going to fish with him?"

"Oh, just a change in plans. I've got things I need to do here
tomorrow."

~

ZULFO PARKED ACROSS THE street from the OK and turned off
his lights. He watched Logan walk out of the OK and disappear into
the fly shop. Zulfo left his car and walked to Logan's raft. He circled the
boat, examining it carefully. Then he went into the OK. "That man
who was just in here?" he said to Helen, "Is that his raft trailer parked
over there?" He pointed in the general direction. "The blue raft with
the white rope?"

"Yes," Helen said. "That's Logan's. Are you looking for him?"

"I saw him drop something on the river today. A box of flies.
I want to put it in his truck. Is he parked next to his raft? The silver
pickup?"

"Silver GMC? That's his. Better get there quick, though. He's
leaving for South Junction right away."

"Ah, South Junction. Is the fishing good there? How do you
get to it?"

"Fishing is excellent. You go south on 197 to the Highway 97 junction. Take the road on the right. It starts as pavement, then turns to gravel in a couple of miles. Just follow the gravel till you get there. There aren't any places to turn off once you're on the gravel."

Zulfo left the OK and went to Logan's truck. He picked up a rock, looked to see that no one was around, then smashed a hole in the lens over the left taillight. He cleaned out the plastic so the bulb was exposed and returned to his car.

~

LOGAN REENTERED THE OK. Helen handed him his latte. "Sam went to the lady's room a few minutes ago," she said.

"I need to head out," Logan said. "Tell her 'thanks a latte' and I'll see her about 9:30."

He got into his truck and headed south on Highway 197. He saw headlights a few hundred yards behind him, but there was nothing unusual about that. He thought no more about it.

44

October 14: Maupin

HANK O'LEARY COULDN'T STOP worrying. He told himself he was being foolish and paranoid, but he couldn't shake the feeling that something wasn't right. He'd been driving back from Portland when he'd seen an unfamiliar car leave Logan's driveway. But Logan's house was dark, so Hank had turned in to check on things. He'd found the door unlocked, which he knew was unusual for the normally cautious Logan.

He went inside and looked around to see if anything was amiss.

An open manila folder lay atop Logan's desk, next to his laptop. Hank wasn't one to pry, but there was something familiar about the official-looking appearance of the top photo; it reminded him of his Army days. He looked at the photo and the two others with it. He read the text that accompanied them. That's when his nagging sense of concern shifted to out-and-out worry.

Hank went quickly to Ty Decker's house, which was also dark. He tried the door, but it was locked. Hank was desperate for a weapon—just in case—and he'd stored all his firearms in Ty's gun safe because of Jackie. But he couldn't break into Ty's house just because he felt uneasy. He looked around. Ty's car was gone, but his pickup was there. Something clicked, something Ty said when he took his Smith and Wesson revolver.

Hank trotted to Ty's truck and opened the glove compartment. Bingo! His .38 was inside. He grabbed it and checked the cylinder. Empty. He reached back into the glove compartment and found a box of hollow point ammunition. He loaded the revolver and put the ammo box in his pocket.

Feeling more secure, Hank drove to the OK. When he got out, he saw a few plastic shards on the ground near Logan's raft trailer. Fender bender? Something else? He strode briskly into the OK.

"Hank!" said Sam. "What can I get you?" She looked around. "Where's Jackie?"

"Portland," Hank said quickly. "Where's your dad? I need to talk to him pronto."

"You just missed him. He went to South Junction. There's someone he needs to talk to. He'll be back in a—"

"How long ago did he leave?" Hank interrupted.

"Five minutes."

"Was his truck parked next to his trailer?"

"I guess."

"He's a popular man tonight," said Helen. "There was another guy in here looking for him. He said Logan dropped a fly box on the river today. Wanted to put it in his truck."

"But he didn't fish today," Sam said, puzzled. "We went riding."

"The guy who was asking about him," Hank said. "What did he look like?" His voice was now in command mode.

"Medium height," Helen said. "Round face. Shaved head. Scar across his forehead. Good English, but foreign accent."

Casey walked in. "Hank, you snake! What's—"

"Casey," Hank said, "help Helen and Sam close the OK. Then go with them to Helen and Kevin's house, and stay there until I get back."

"What's going on?" Sam said. "Is Dad in trouble?" Her face was tense with fear.

"It's just a precaution," Hank said. "But do it now."

"You got it," Casey said.

"Don't leave me out of this!" Sam said. "Take me to my dad!"

"Later. This is best for now," Hank said. He sprinted for his truck.

~

SINCE HE'D LEFT MAUPIN, LOGAN had occasionally seen headlights behind him. It may or may not have been the same car; there was no way of knowing in the dark. But now the car was closer and didn't want to pass him. Three miles back, another pair of headlights had appeared, moving fast, but then slowed down and stayed behind the first car.

None of this was unusual; the road was twisty, and most drivers were cautious about passing, especially in the dark. Still, Logan's suspicions were roused. Was he being tailed?

However, before he reached the turnoff, the first car swung out and passed him, then made the turn onto the South Junction road. It accelerated and quickly disappeared.

Logan made the turn, then thought to check his rearview mirror for the second car. He didn't see its headlights anymore. *Must have gone on to Madras,* he thought. His concerns allayed, he kept going.

In a couple of miles, the road became gravel, and he rounded a turn. A car was crosswise in the road. *Serves him right for spinning out,* Logan thought. *Shouldn't go that fast on gravel.*

Logan stopped. A man walked from behind the other car. Logan stepped out of his truck. "Can I help you?" Logan asked. He couldn't see the man clearly—too much glare from the headlights. "Do you need help?" he repeated.

"Was that your blue raft at the OK? The one with the white rope?"

Odd start of a conversation. Suddenly on alert, Logan said nothing. He reached into his truck and turned off the headlights. Now there were only the parking lights. It was enough for him to see that he was talking to Scarface, the Zulfo guy in the photo. Logan's blood ran cold. He tried to fake more nonchalance than he felt, and said, "Looks like you're okay. I'll be going." He started to get back into his truck.

"Don't move."

Logan turned. Zulfo was twenty feet away and pointing a gun at him. Logan slowly put his hands up; he hadn't been asked, but it seemed the thing to do. "Look," Logan said, "I'll give you my wallet. Take all the money and the credit cards. I'll keep my mouth shut." He figured he'd try to make it look like he knew less than he did.

"Quiet! You know this isn't a stickup. I was in your house tonight and saw what you left in a folder."

I'm such an idiot! Logan thought. *I forgot to put it back in the locked drawer!* But he'd been in a hurry, and he was only going to be gone two hours. He'd do it when he got home. Except … it was dawning on him that this guy was about to kill him.

"Step away from the truck."

Logan slowly complied.

Zulfo walked behind him. Suddenly Logan fell to his knees. Zulfo had kicked him behind the kneecaps, buckling his legs.

"Keep those hands up!" Zulfo said.

Logan couldn't focus. *Do something!* he thought. But he couldn't think what to do. Sam's face came to mind. He closed his eyes. This would be devastating to her. All he could think about was Sam and how he'd let her down. He'd promised to always be there for her, and now she'd be alone. Tears started down his face. He tried to say a prayer for her, but all that came out was "Sam … Sam … Sam …"

Logan sensed movement behind him. Zulfo had changed position, maybe even lowered the gun.

"You goddam queer," Zulfo said with disgust. "All you can think about is your boyfriend!" He switched to a wheedling voice. "Sam, Sam, come and save me, my pretty boy Sam." Zulfo sighed loudly. "What a country! People like you are everywhere! No wonder America is so weak and useless."

Logan heard the sound of spitting.

"Americans make me sick!" Zulfo went on. "Cowards! You see trouble, and you scatter like mice. The Serbs raped and murdered their way through our country, and you stood by saying, 'now, now, mustn't be naughty.' We didn't need you to do it for us. We could have defended ourselves against those swine, but you wouldn't even let us buy arms. And the Serbs had warehouses full of them! What did you think was going to happen?" He spat again. "You see what needs doing and run the other way. Or you use your money to get other people to do the dirty work. Like that Russian buffoon."

During Zulfo's tirade, Logan began to get control of his thinking. *Trudy had the presence of mind to save Sam,* he thought. *You can too. Stall, and think of something to do.* "We didn't hire Kalinnikov," Logan said. "He was working for the FSB. You killed him, didn't you?"

"Like drowning a cat. No, a cat's harder. He was too drunk to resist. He was getting too close to finding the stuff—already poking around my land in Antelope. That's why we had to distract him, then move it quick. I never liked that idiot Kincaid, but he said he knew where to stash something so no one would find it. Then the old man came along."

"You started the fire in the Drift Inn, after hitting him with the frying pan."

"He heard us making plans in the park. He had to be stopped."

While Zulfo was talking, Logan had slowly dropped his hands. Zulfo was so involved in his rant that he hadn't noticed. Logan quietly gathered a fist-sized rock in his right hand. His left fingers were under another rock. "Why kill so many innocent people?" he said. "People who weren't involved, people who didn't do anything."

"*Because* they didn't do anything! They stood by doing nothing and let it happen." Zulfo's voice started to crack. "My sister was the kindest, gentlest person on earth. An angel of mercy! She helped everyone. Serbs. Croats. Muslims. It didn't matter to her. And how did you repay her? You raped her in every way possible! Then you sent her down the road with blood and filth caked on her legs and nothing but a torn shirt to cover her. Do? You did nothing! That's why not one of you deserves to live!"

"So you honor her memory by killing thousands? Is that what she would have wanted?"

"I am her family, all that's left, and that's what *I* want! It's what Bolton wants. Everything is in place now. We will get the VX, and they will hear from us in Washington, London, Paris, Amsterdam, the UN in New York. And Belgrade. You can't stop us."

Zulfo fell silent. Logan sensed the gun pointing at the back of his head. It was now or never. He flipped the rock in his left hand. It clattered into a sagebrush. He didn't know if the sound momentarily distracted Zulfo, but he took the chance and pushed himself backward to where he thought Zulfo's legs were. He met solid resistance. Zulfo crumpled on top of him. Logan rolled over and had him flat on his back.

The gun was in Zulfo's right hand. Logan held it down with his left hand, and with his right he smashed the other rock onto Zulfo's wrist. Zulfo's hand sprang open, and the gun fell into the dust. Logan reached for it. Before he could get to it, Zulfo heaved, and Logan rolled off. Logan scrambled onto his hands and knees for the gun. Zulfo was up and kicked it away from him, then ran after it. Logan sprang forward and tackled Zulfo.

They rolled in the dusty road. Zulfo was on top of Logan, hands on his throat. Logan brought his knee up and nailed Zulfo in the crotch. It slowed the Bosniak down just enough for Logan to get out from under him.

They were ten feet apart. *The gun! Where's the gun?* Logan saw it. And saw that Zulfo was next to it. And that Zulfo saw it. Zulfo reached down and picked up his pistol. He was starting to straighten up. *It was only a small chance,* Logan thought. *But at least I tried. I'm so sorry, Sam.*

"Put down the weapon!" The voice was behind Logan. He saw Zulfo look up, startled. "Drop the weapon! Now!"

Zulfo was still slightly bent over, hand gripping the pistol, finger on the trigger. But it was pointed at the ground.

"If you move, I will shoot!" The voice was Hank O'Leary's, and it was pure steel. "Logan!" Hank said. "Get behind me, and hang onto my belt so I know where you are!"

Logan scrambled behind the big man and grabbed the back of his belt tightly. They were twenty feet from Zulfo.

"Do not let any part of yourself show!" Hank said to Logan. Then to Zulfo: "I am a trained soldier and a marksman. I have killed before. I will not hesitate to do it again. If you do anything but drop the weapon, I will shoot you. If you make any move, if you lift that weapon one inch, I will shoot, and you will die."

Zulfo spoke. Logan imagined the man as he'd last seen him: bending over, right hand holding the pistol. "Every soldier misses," Zulfo said. "Even marksmen. Especially," he sneered, "the old ones."

"I will not miss," Hank said. "You will die. Drop the weapon!"

"I don't want you. I want him. Step aside!"

"Never! Drop the weapon!"

There was silence for the space of half a minute. In his mind's eye Logan could see the two men staring at each other, gauging their chances. Then the air exploded in sound. Logan couldn't tell who was shooting or how many shots were fired. He felt Hank's weight shift forward. Was he hit? Was he falling?

"You can let go now," Hank said calmly. "He's down."

Logan let go of Hank's belt. His hand felt stiff from gripping it so tightly.

Hank moved slowly forward, his revolver still aimed at Zulfo. Zulfo sprawled in the dust, face up. Logan could see two closely spaced red splotches in his upper chest. There was a dark spot in his forehead and a mess where his left eye had been. His right eye was open but not seeing. He looked really really dead.

Logan watched, mesmerized, as Hank picked up Zulfo's semi-automatic and put it in his waistband. Still keeping the revolver aimed at Zulfo's head, Hank reached over with his left hand and flicked Zulfo's staring right eye. There was no blink, no reaction.

Hank stood up. Logan saw him eye Zulfo's wounds with what could only be described as professional detachment. "Old soldier, my wrinkled ass," Hank said with disdain.

The big man coolly opened the cylinder of his revolver. He emptied the spent brass cartridges into the palm of his hand and dropped them into his left pants pocket. Then he reached into his right pocket, pulled out a box of shells, and reloaded. "It's no good when it's not loaded," he said. "I need to remind Ty Decker of that."

Logan nodded absently. All he could think was, *He's dead. I'm not.* Suddenly he staggered to the side of the road and vomited. When he was done, he croaked, "Sam?"

"Safe with Casey."

Relief flooded through Logan.

"We gotta get rid of Mr. Bad Ass before anyone comes down this road," Hank said. "I'll get my rig."

Hank strode up the road, darkness swallowing him. In a few minutes Logan heard a truck start; then Hank was back. He reached behind the front seat and pulled out a blue plastic tarp and some duct tape. "Help me wrap him in this, and we'll put him in the back."

"How—"

"I saw the photos on your desk. I hope you don't mind. I'll bet you've got some people in Portland who can come up here and make it all right—and keep you and me out of the news. I did clandestine work for the Army, in Asia. I know how these things work."

Logan's mind had settled somewhat from its shaken state. He had a few questions. "Hank—"

Hank interrupted. "He broke your taillight so he could follow you in the dark. It's an old trick. I drove until I could see your rig— one red light, one white. You stood out like a neon trout. I drove past the road junction, then shut off my lights and doubled back. I parked when you stopped so he wouldn't hear my truck. Then I snuck down here. Just in time, too, from the look of it. He was talking so much he couldn't hear me coming. Then you toppled him. You were pretty spunky! I'm proud of you. It gave me time to get close." He patted his front pants pocket. "These popguns aren't too accurate from a distance. Another ten steps back and who knows what I'd have hit."

"Uh, Hank. Before we … you know, with the tarp … I need to take care of something." Logan reached into his truck and got a clean pair of pants out of his duffle bag. "This is kind of embarrassing …"

"You crapped your pants. That happened to me in Vietnam. More than once. It's something they don't put in war movies."

Logan changed his pants, then went to help Hank, who had

spread the blue tarp on the ground. As they rolled Zulfo's body onto the tarp and wrapped him up, Logan saw that Hank was wearing his Portland Opera baseball cap.

Hank spiraled tape around the tarp. "Duct tape," he said. "Don't leave home without it. Now take his feet, and we'll sling him into the back of the pickup."

Logan picked up his end, and they carried the body to the truck. Hank muttered, "'I'll lug the guts into the next room.'"

It was Hamlet's exit line from Act III, after he'd killed Polonius, and it was the last thing Logan expected to hear from Hank O'Leary. "You know Shakespeare?" he said, trying not to sound as amazed as he felt.

"Jackie took me to Ashland for the plays," Hank said. "*Hamlet* was my favorite. I'm quite the cultured buckaroo. Now heave." They swung the body. The blue tarp and its contents thudded into the pickup bed.

"You shouldn't drive," Hank said. "Leave your truck here, and we'll get it later. I'll move it up the road so no one will see the scene if they stop to check out your truck." He pointed at Zulfo's car. "I'll move it, too."

Once the vehicles were moved, Hank motioned Logan to get in his truck. "Ride with me until we get to cell phone range and you can call whoever needs to be called."

They'd driven as far as the Highway 197 junction when Logan said, "I'm wired! I can't slow down!"

"Count out eight seconds," Hank said.

Logan tried.

"Slower."

Logan forced himself to slow down.

"Now keep doing it. Breathe deep on the one-two. Hold it for three-four. Exhale on five-six. Wait seven-eight. Just keep doing it. It helps."

Logan did this for a while. It calmed him down.

"You sure had a tight grip on my belt," Hank said. "Drop the weapon," he said in a deep voice. Followed by "Drop the weapon!" in a falsetto. He played the joke over several more times.

Logan smiled thinly.

"I don't want to have to explain to Jackie why I went from a baritone to a boy soprano."

"When I was hanging onto your belt," Logan said, "I kept thinking, *Let the Wookiee win!*"

Hank laughed. "Don't ever forget it!" His laugh trailed off, and he fell silent.

Surreal, Logan thought. He'd escaped death because a gunman went on a homophobic rant, giving a Shakespeare-quoting Wookiee fly tyer in a Portland Opera hat enough time to sneak up and save him. Now they were making jokes. He saw that it was a release, a kind of gallows humor that helped them cope with the stress. But still.

Then his mind turned to Adina Osmanović, Zulfo's sister. And he wondered: if it had been his sister—or his daughter—would he turn to violence and vengeance? Would he seek to make the whole world pay for the degradation and death of a good and innocent person—a kind, caring, compassionate woman who deserved so much better?

He didn't have an answer for that. Or a joke.

45

October 15: Portland

"HANK, HONEY, WOULD YOU fasten these for me?" Jackie sat on the edge of the bed at Portland's Heathman Hotel. Her hands were around the back of her neck, holding a string of pearls.

Hank came behind her wordlessly.

"You're quiet tonight," Jackie said. "Does this dinner bother you? Anthony's quite easy to get along with. He's very funny and outgoing."

"No, that's not it. I'm just, you know, thinking about things."

"What things?"

"Things."

"My, you're going to make me think you've got another woman on the side."

He fastened her necklace, kissed her ear from behind, and stood up. "Nope. You're all the woman I can handle," he said.

Jackie had been in Portland for two days before Hank arrived. He hadn't told her anything about last night's confrontation on the South Junction road. He hoped to keep it that way.

They were going out for an early dinner with Anthony Ishimaru, an old friend of Jackie's from Julliard. Tonight and for two nights after, he was the headliner with the Oregon Symphony Orchestra, performing the Elgar cello concerto.

~

AT THE RESTAURANT, JACKIE walked quickly to an Asian man and threw her arms around him. "Anthony!" she said. They kissed each other on both cheeks. Hank was worried he'd get the same greeting and was relieved when Anthony shook his hand instead.

Anthony was dressed entirely in black: black pants, black blazer over a black turtleneck, black-framed glasses. His black hair was cropped close on the sides, with a ridge down the middle—not a mohawk, but suggestive of one.

They took their table. Jackie and Anthony were animated, talking about musicians they knew, funny incidents from Julliard, and other items of interest to them but not to Hank. As Jackie had said, Anthony was outgoing, talkative, and good humored. His family had come to America when he was eight; like Jackie, he had a slight

accent. Hank was pretty sure Anthony was gay, not that it mattered
to him.

"Hank, do you do anything musical?" Anthony asked during
a lull.

"Hank plays in a group," Jackie said, encouragingly.

"Really?" said Anthony. "What do you play?"

"Harmonica," Jackie said before Hank could answer. "He's
quite good at it."

Anthony started to laugh, like they were playing a joke on him,
then stifled himself as it became clear that Jackie was serious. There
was an awkward silence; then Anthony said, "Harmonica is good!
Very democratic. An instrument of the people. I never understood
how you play it. I had one as a child, and all the notes came out at
once. How do you do it, Hank?"

"You use your tongue to cover the notes you don't want," Jackie
said.

"Oh," said Anthony. "Your tongue."

More awkward silence, then Jackie said, "I've played with his
band. I played fiddle."

"Jackie, you surprise me! I thought you'd given up performing.
Are you going to tour with Hank's band now? Bertram will be very
disappointed." Bertram Levy was an agent; he represented both
Jackie and Anthony. "Have you met Bertram?" Anthony said to Hank.

"No," Hank said, shaking his head.

"He drives a mean deal," Anthony said. "Maybe you should get
him to represent your band."

Jackie gave Anthony a warning look. Hank said, "I doubt he
does people like us."

"I'd like to hear your band sometime," Anthony said. He said it
in a way that made Hank think he actually meant it.

"Anthony's very eclectic, musically," Jackie said in a hopeful
tone. "He borrows ideas from everywhere. You never know what he's

going to do next, especially for a cadenza or an encore. There are conductors that dread him."

Anthony looked pleased with himself. "Never be predictable," he said to no one in particular.

Jackie and Anthony were back on Julliard stories for a few minutes; then Anthony said, "I'll tell you what I'd like to do, Jackie. I'd like to play the Brubanini with you—like old times at Julliard. We wowed them!"

"We did," Jackie said, smiling. She turned to Hank, "We took a theme from one of Paganini's caprices and reimagined it as a jazz piece, in the style of Dave Brubeck. We called it "Brubanini. It was very showy."

"There was room for improvisation and flashy solos," Anthony said. "Jackie's an amazing improviser."

"I know," said Hank. "She's famous for it in my band."

"You should do more crossover work, Jackie," Anthony said. "It keeps you fresh."

Jackie had no reply, but looked thoughtful.

"But of course you're not performing anymore," Anthony said. "Except in Hank's band."

"She's practicing five hours a day now," Hank said. "And not with my band."

"Practicing for whom?" Anthony said, hands spread wide. "The world mourns the loss of your wonderful music."

"I … I haven't decided what I'm going to do next. One way or the other."

"She's marvelous," Hank said. "I could listen to her for hours."

"So could we all, and here she is—hiding in Oregon, floating down rivers and playing fiddle in country bands."

"Don't knock it, Anthony," said Jackie. "Whether I go back on tour or not, I'm a new person. Breaking my arm and meeting Hank are the best things that happened to me in twenty years. I've had time to think about things and get some perspective."

"I can tell," said Anthony. He turned to Hank. "Hank, you've been good for her. Make her play the Brubanini with me after dinner, in your suite."

Hank shook his head. "I don't *make* Jackie do anything."

"Buy me dessert, Anthony, and I'll play it with you," Jackie said, like it was a dare.

~

JACKIE ORDERED CRÈME BRÛLÉE for dessert. As she was cracking the topping with her spoon, Anthony started in on American attitudes toward guns. "These people scare me to death," Anthony said, "walking around with guns in their pockets. Like they're going to shoot a terrorist or something and be a hero."

Hank looked at the table, lips tight.

Jackie cocked her head and gave Hank a curious look. "Hank was in the Army," she said. "In Vietnam. He took me to the pistol range once. He gave me a safety course, and I fired at a target."

Anthony put his hand just below his throat. "Jackie, you are amazing! Catching fish, rowing boats, and shooting pistols!" He reached for his wine and took a sip. "I shall be careful not to offend you!"

Hank and Jackie went back to their room after dinner. In a couple of minutes there was a knock at the door. It was Anthony with his cello. "I bought you dessert, Jackie. Now it's Brubanini time."

Jackie wordlessly opened her violin case and got ready. She and Anthony had a couple of false starts, then got into the swing of the duet. After an hour, Anthony announced that it was just like old times.

THAT NIGHT WAS THE FIRST OF Anthony's three concerts. Hank and Jackie had tickets in the balcony, but Anthony wouldn't hear of it and scored them seats on the main floor near the aisle.

Anthony and the Elgar concerto followed the intermission. As the last notes ended, the audience clapped and bravoed enthusiastically and gave Anthony a standing ovation. In the orchestra, some violinists clapped the back of the hand holding their instrument; others waved their bows. Even the conductor rapped his baton on his music stand. Anthony bowed, left the stage, came back to more applause, left the stage again, came back again, and finally took up his cello to play an encore. The audience immediately quieted and resumed their seats.

Instead of playing, Anthony thrust a finger at the audience and beckoned. He'd pointed at Jackie.

Jackie shook her head, "No way. No way," she said quietly.

Anthony gave her a coy and encouraging look. "Jackie" he mouthed.

Jackie kept shaking her head but was bright-eyed and smiling.

Hank looked at her, then whispered in her ear, "Do it. Play it for me."

Jackie got hesitantly from her seat and made her way onstage. The audience was puzzled. The conductor stared coldly at Anthony. Anthony conversed briefly with Jackie, then announced loudly. "Ladies and gentlemen, this is my good friend, Miss Jacqueline Moreau."

The audience divided into thirds: one third gasped and started to clap; one third sat politely still; and one third apparently sided with the man behind Hank, who said, "Who the hell is Jacqueline Moreau?"

A violinist in the orchestra's front row handed her instrument to Jackie. Anthony and Jackie checked their tuning, Anthony nodded his head, and they launched into the Brubanini. It was fun, upbeat, and the audience was into it. Near the end, Anthony stopped playing and let Jackie go solo. When she saw she was on her own, she started improvising. She played the theme, then shifted into a country fiddle-style version, which merged into "Dancing Caddis," the tune Hank had created for them. Then she nodded at Anthony, and he joined in for the finale. They finished with a flourish, and the audience erupted in applause. Even the conductor looked pleased. Jackie bowed again and again, all smiles.

~

BACK IN THEIR ROOM, JACKIE was effusive and radiant. Hank told her she was wonderful. Conversation was easy. It was a little after 11:00. In the background a local news hour droned on the TV. Hank and Jackie weren't paying attention, but then the station showed a map. The highlighted cities were Bend, Portland, and Maupin. There was an inset with South Junction on it, and the Deschutes River.

"The Deschutes River is a popular Oregon destination for whitewater rafters and fly anglers," the reporter said, "but last night it erupted in gunfire as federal agents attempted an arrest on a lonely gravel road. One man, an unidentified foreign national, was killed …"

"Oh my God!" Jackie said. "The South Junction road …"

Hank made a sign for quiet. He wanted to hear what they said and, more importantly, what they didn't say. There was more talking, but no more information. It was portrayed as a drug arrest gone violent. They'd closed the river to the public while federal agents checked for a drug cache. Hank relaxed.

"Hank, did you know about this?"

Hank nodded slightly.

Jackie was thoughtful for a few seconds, then said quietly, "You more than knew about it."

Hank looked away.

"You were the 'federal agent' weren't you," said Jackie. "That's why you've been so quiet tonight."

Hank looked at the ceiling. Damn, but it was hard to hide anything from Jackie. "He had Logan on his knees and was about to shoot him. I showed up and did what I had to do."

"Logan!" Jackie said, shocked.

"I'm sorry," Hank said.

"You saved his life!" She put her hands on her cheeks. "What would have happened to Sam? Thank God you were there." She went to him and held him tight, her head buried in his chest. "What could you be sorry for?"

"Not sorry I did it. I'm sorry he didn't drop the gun and surrender. I gave him every chance I could." He shook his head. "Sorry that I had to do it."

They talked no more about it that night.

~

THE NEXT MORNING OVER BREAKFAST, Hank said, "Jackie, I've been thinking. Maybe you ought to take that gig in Europe." Bertram Levy, Jackie's agent, had called a couple of days ago. A prominent violinist had fallen ill, and Levy was desperate to find a replacement, starting next week in London; there was the promise of more engagements. Jackie had told him to give her two days to think about it.

"Are you trying to get rid of me?" Jackie asked, mocking.

"Never. But I would be the most selfish person on the planet if I kept you to myself. Try it. It's only a few weeks. If you don't like it, you're done. If you find it suits you, stay on for the longer—"

"Come with me!"

"Can you see me trotting around Europe? Having dinner in fancy restaurants with the Anthonys of the world?"

"Bring your fly tying things! Stay in the hotel and tie flies!"

"I need to test new patterns. Here. I can't do my thing in Europe any more than you can do yours in Maupin."

She reached across the table and took his hand. Her lips were tight, and she was fighting tears.

"I can't keep you from being who you are," Hank said. "You know you need to do it. Just to find out what comes next."

"It's not fair!" Jackie said. "Without you, I wouldn't have gone back to the violin, and my career would be over. You got me back on my feet. And the reward for us? To be separated! That's not fair at all!"

"It's not forever. Do it. See how you feel about it. Then tell me how it's going. You know it's the right thing to do."

46

Two FEDERAL AGENTS MET LOGAN shortly after midnight on the night he was waylaid by Zulfo Osmanović. By morning they'd put out a story about a major drug bust on the Deschutes. That was their excuse for booting everyone off the river and closing all the roads. Serious-looking people arrived with high-tech "sniffers" and other fancy gear.

Logan helped them search for the warheads. Never in his life had he felt so ragged and tired. Around noon they found a gray military-style case buried in a grove of trees half a mile downstream from where Logan had seen Zulfo and Kincaid last July.

The gray case had some tricky-looking hardware on the outside that made the federal agents think it was booby-trapped. Further investigation showed it wasn't. They opened the case and found four M56 warheads, each with a payload with VX.

Frank Kovak, a burly man in his late fifties who was the agent in charge, told Logan the warheads appeared to be intact. "We wouldn't have found them so quickly," he said, "without your input. The world owes you big-time, son."

The federal agents now had a dilemma. They needed to keep searching, in case there were more warheads—they still weren't sure if they were looking for four or eight. But river-based businesses and agencies were pressuring them to reopen the Deschutes. "It's only drugs," was their theme, "but this is our livelihood. Do what you have to, but reopen the river!"

Of course the feds couldn't tell the world what they were really looking for. "Remember," Kovak told Logan, "how a lone sniper panicked DC a few years ago? What do you think would happen if we told the public we were looking for enough nerve agent to kill a million people?"

Kovak said they were "95 percent certain" there were only four warheads missing from Umatilla, and those had been found. Their focus was now on locating Bolton and Kincaid, figuring that one of them could lead the feds to the remaining warheads—if there were any. Bolton and Kincaid were both missing, and Kincaid's red-and-blue driftboat was gone.

So the federal agents agreed to reopen the river, but they posted law enforcement officers at the boat ramps and on the roads. In addition there was aerial surveillance.

By evening, Kovak recognized that Logan was exhausted and insisted he go home. "It's up to us now," he said. "Your job is done. Get some rest."

An assistant drove Logan home in his truck. He collapsed into bed, but sleep was elusive. Finally, near 10:00 at night, after being up for thirty-six hours, he drifted into blessed sleep.

~

LOGAN AWOKE FOURTEEN HOURS later feeling refreshed and wonderfully free. His "mission" was over. All his debts, including the

$237,000 he owed Med-Rec, had been cleared. He had a little money to live on, and Sam had enough to go to college. He'd been useful. And he was alive.

He was eager to do something with Sam, so he loaded the horses and tack in the trailer and drove to the OK, planning to pull her out for a ride. They took the horses to Ron Bauer's, the friend of their landlord. Ron's property was similar to the Criterion area but not as steep.

Logan had told Sam a few details about the other night, but he'd left out the worst parts. He said he'd stumbled into a drug deal and had been rescued by federal agents who'd happened along at just the right time. He credited Hank O'Leary with alerting the feds. It was all white lies, of course, but the truth would only have made Sam fearful.

Hank knew more than Sam, but even he didn't know everything. Casey, who had provided the vital link to Adina Osmanović— the key that opened all subsequent doors—knew nothing. In Casey's mind, Brandon Muckenhirn was the baddest person on the river. Logan was happy to let him think that. He wasn't too keen on Brandon either, but at least the guy wasn't bent on mass murder.

Logan and Sam were silent as they saddled the horses. The only time Logan spoke was when he asked Sam for her folding hoofpick, the one with the knife blade.

The silence continued as they rode. Sam seemed lost in thought, and Logan was pondering a long conversation he'd had with Bill Short. Bill told him that the CIA had contacted the Russian FSB, and between them they'd pieced together most of the story.

Apparently Bolton had stashed the warheads for months— possibly at the Weapons Depot, possibly not; it wasn't clear. What was clear was that he and Zulfo had everything set up last fall. The warheads were on a 40-acre farm that Zulfo bought in Antelope. As near as the CIA could tell, an Islamist cell in Michigan had channeled the purchase money to him. The cell was going to help smuggle the

VX warheads to their final destinations. The CIA's working hypothesis was that some of the VX would then be given to Middle Eastern terrorists for their own purposes.

Last fall the FBI arrested two of the Michigan cell's key members on other charges, and the rest scattered. Bolton and Zulfo scrambled to find another cell to help them. Through Zulfo's contacts they located one in Munich. The NSA intercept was from them.

The Russian FSB got involved due to intelligence they'd received. Like NSA's intercept, the Russian intel was ambiguous at best but hinted at a Bosnian connection. The Russians were paranoid about Chechen terrorists; peripherally they were concerned for the Serbs. So they dispatched Sergei Kalinnikov to poke around Oregon. Sergei stumbled onto Zulfo, got wind of his Antelope property, and was prowling over it in the night. That's when Bolton and Zulfo linked up with Kincaid and shifted the warheads to the Deschutes.

Logan asked Bill Short why Bolton and Zulfo didn't just kill Sergei. Short explained that that would have confirmed FSB's suspicions. The working assumption was that Bolton and Zulfo decided to move the warheads and let Sergei sniff around Antelope all he wanted. They killed him when they finally had everything in place. Because Sergei was on a binge, they could make it look like an accident.

Bill Short said it was too soon to write the history of the incident, and there were still details they didn't understand—and might never understand until they found Bolton and Kincaid. LOGAN AND SAM PAUSED IN their ride. Logan rose in his stirrups and took a deep breath. The fall day was cool, with low clouds and a gentle breeze. Fog hung in the low places and obscured the river. Grass that had been a vibrant green in spring, and golden in summer, was now a faded tan. Soon the grass would turn black with winter frost.

With each passing day, fewer ospreys were on the river; they wintered in Costa Rica and other tropical destinations. Along the riverbank, the alder thickets were thinning out as the trees dropped their leaves. Chinook salmon were spawning in the river. Mornings were cold, and any wet thing left out overnight was likely to be coated with ice by sunup.

Logan settled back into his saddle, and they resumed their ride. His thoughts turned to Peter Bolton. Logan had learned from Bolton's bio that he was born the same month and year as Logan. Like Logan, he'd been an Eagle Scout. Bolton went to the University of Washington, majoring in chemical engineering and graduating with honors a year after Logan finished *magna cum laude* at Oregon State with a computer science degree. Bolton was accepted to graduate school at Stanford and MIT but chose MIT. Logan was accepted at those two schools but went to Stanford. After graduate school, Bolton took a job with a defense contractor, then moved into a civilian job with the Army. Logan had followed a similar path before going into private industry.

Logan felt like he and Peter Bolton were twins separated at birth. But things went awry for Bolton, probably after Adina Osmanović's death in Bosnia. Logan tried to imagine how he would have felt. What if it had been Trudy? What if it had been Sam, God forbid? Would his heart have turned to stone, alchemized by a lust for revenge? He liked to think not. But could he be sure?

As he and Sam rode, Logan tried to put himself inside Bolton's mind. *I know this man* he thought. *I could have* been *this man.* He tried to imagine how it would be: hatred and vengeance fester in the mind, dominate all thought, kill all conscience. Each day, he comes a little closer to the edge. Then one morning there's nothing left but the urge to make someone—anyone, everyone—pay the price.

If he were Bolton, how would he approach it? A hazy notion at first, more fantasy than plan. A job opening comes up at the Umatilla project. He seizes the opportunity to be close to a means of mass destruction. He lusts to be around all that potential for agonizing death. Then one day he sees a loophole in the system, a way to diddle the records—to steal warheads and conceal the theft.

He thinks about it for weeks, maybe months, perfecting the method in his mind, embellishing the fantasy. Then he steps on the other side of the line. He contacts Zulfo, Adina Osmanović's brother. Like the upward spiraling flames of a wind-whipped fire, each man's hatred feeds the other's. The plan is put in motion.

It was clear to Logan that patience was Peter Bolton's greatest asset. He needed to be smart and clever, of course. But without patience he might have acted rashly. It was patience that let him wait and perfect his plan. Patience that got the warheads out. Patience to cache them somewhere no one would think of looking. And when the first Islamist cell was blown, it was patience and persistence that linked them up with a second cell. Eventually patience would be rewarded: they would quietly get their cache of horror and carry it out in an ordinary driftboat. Who would even suspect?

How will Bolton react when he realizes Zulfo is dead and his masterful plan has been compromised? It occurred to Logan that John Kincaid was the weak link. His only role was to row the boat and find a hiding place for what he probably thought were drugs. If caught, he would plea bargain and tell the federal agents where to find the cache. Logan wondered: *What would I do if I had no conscience?* The answer was obvious, and Logan doubted that Kincaid was still among the living.

Kincaid out of the way, what would Bolton do next? Be patient and wait? No—time is not on his side. He would risk everything and make a dash for the warheads.

But the river is closed. And when it is reopened, it's clear that the feds have found his stash. It's over. He's been snookered, boxed in.

"You're awfully quiet," Sam said. "What are you thinking about?"

"Boxes," Logan said.

"You're weird." They rode a few more steps; then Sam turned in the saddle and asked, "I've been wondering about something, and

I bet you know the answer—since you're such a pedantic know-it-all. Where did that expression 'think outside the box' come from?"

"It's an old corporate training thing, something to get people to expand their thinking. You put nine dots in three rows—in a square—on a piece of paper. Then, without lifting your pen from the paper, you try to draw four straight lines that go through all the dots. The only way you can do it is with diagonals that extend past the box. You have to 'think outside the box.' It's hard to describe. I'll show you when we get home."

They rode a little farther, and Sam asked, "When are Hank and Jackie coming back?"

"I don't know. They're in Portland. Jackie wanted to take Hank to a symphony concert."

"Hank's getting his horizons broadened, isn't he?"

"So's Jackie," Logan said. "A couple of weeks ago I went to Lower Dave's to get some fly tying advice. I was trying to tie Hank's new steelhead fly, the Plum Dandy. Dave was busy, and Hank was uptown on an errand. But Jackie was there. She showed me the right way to tie it. Turns out she's been tying flies for Hank for the last few months. She's good at it!"

"Amazing! She told me about her first trip down the Deschutes with Hank, how much fun it was. She said she saw you up on a rock above Buckskin Mary Rapids."

"I remember." That horrible day seemed light-years away.

"She liked seeing the animals, but she said Hank was upset about some guy. John something. He had a funny nickname."

"John Kincaid? They call him Nearly Honest John. He's a lowlife." *And now,* thought Logan, *probably a no-life.*

"Yeah, that was it. Nearly Honest John. His boat was mostly covered by a camo tarp. Like he was trying to hide something."

"Near South Junction, I'll bet." Logan didn't want to let on too much, but it sounded like it might have been when Kincaid was stashing the VX for Bolton and Zulfo.

"No. Not near South Junction. She said it was on the Indian side. By a big rock, not far above Whiskey Dick."

"Whiskey Dick? Are you sure?"

"Positive. I remembered it because Whiskey Dick is seared in my memory."

"I guess it is. Sorry."

"I'm over it," Sam said. "Take me there again sometime, and maybe I'll have a better experience."

"Couldn't get worse."

They rode on, Logan deep in thought. He visualized the Reservation lands near Whiskey Dick. He'd drifted through there almost a dozen times since May. A big rock? He remembered such a place: a prominent feature maybe seventy feet high, with a thick grove of trees on the north side—a good hiding place.

Something clicked in Logan's mind. He raised himself in his stirrups and urged Gabe into an extended trot.

Sam followed suit. "Where are we going in such a hurry?" Sam asked.

"Whiskey Dick!"

47

AS THEY RODE, LOGAN THOUGHT it through again to see if there was anything he'd missed. Now that he thought about it, he was convinced that Peter Bolton wasn't in a box at all. Being a cautious methodical man, Bolton wouldn't have just one cache; he'd have a backup in case one was discovered. The ambiguity about the number of missing warheads was a deliberate ruse, a red herring. Masterful! Logan had heard Kincaid and Zulfo talking about one cache and hadn't twigged that there was a second one. He cursed his stupidity for not seeing it before.

After Zulfo doesn't return, Bolton knows it's up to him. He takes Kincaid's driftboat so the agents would think that's what they should look for. But it's a feint. He hides Kincaid's boat and steals another one; they are all over the place, in people's yards and driveways. You could take a boat from a vacation home, and it wouldn't be missed for days or even weeks. He didn't need an oarsman; he probably knew how to row, being from boat-crazy Seattle. Probably had the rowing merit badge when he was a Boy Scout. Figured if a lowlife tweaker like Kincaid could manage a driftboat, a smart guy like him could do it.

But once he'd retrieved his stash, how would he get it out? How would he launch the boat, with all the ramps and roads being watched? What about the aerial surveillance that the feds had in place?

It hit Logan that you didn't need a ramp to launch a driftboat. They were designed so you could slide them down a steep bank; many coastal launching sites were crude dirt slides. No one did that on the Deschutes because it could cause erosion and was illegal. But what did Bolton care about that?

As for the roads—there were dozens of obscure dirt roads around the river. Most were on private property and behind locked gates or barbed wire fences. The public wouldn't use them, but Bolton could cut through a gate or fence. The fed's ace-in-the-hole was aerial surveillance. But the clouds were low today, and the river was shrouded in fog.

When Logan thought it through, he could think of a dozen ways

Bolton could slip through and get a boat to the river. But how would he get away? Again, a dozen different scenarios came to mind.

In each case, the probability of success was low, maybe less than ten percent. But if he succeeded …

Logan squeezed Gabe into a lope. Sam did the same. They traversed the hillsides, slowing to a trot when going down a steep section, and sometimes shifting to an efficient extended trot to give the horses a break. The trail passed through a juniper grove; Logan and Sam ducked and twisted past the branches. They came to a spring and gave the horses a drink, then moved on. After an hour of hard riding they reached a private gravel road by the river. Logan tapped a heel on Gabe's flank, gave the horse his head, and they thundered on at a full gallop.

Five minutes later their path was blocked by a gate. A barbed wire fence went both directions, and the gate was padlocked. They were just opposite the big rock on the Indian side. Logan pulled his binoculars from the saddlebag and scanned the area. The fog had thinned enough for him to see that some tree branches were at an odd angle, like someone had been in there. He looked downstream. There was a driftboat with one person in it. It was Peter Bolton. Bolton then picked up his own binoculars and looked at Logan. As Logan watched, Bolton put down his binoculars and rowed downstream, fast.

Logan was stymied. No phone line, no cell reception, take too long to get back to the main road. Peter Bolton was getting away with four VX-tipped warheads, and Logan had no solution. He was stuck in a box. The horses grew antsy and hard to keep in place.

"Do you need to catch that guy?" Sam said. She looked like he felt—concerned and frustrated, thinking.

"Yes!"

Sam trotted Mataan back thirty feet, turned him in a half circle, then urged him into a canter—straight at the gate. She'd done some jumping with him, but never anything over three feet high. The gate was four feet. Logan held his breath as Mataan barely cleared it.

Now what? Logan had never jumped a horse. Gabe danced around, moving left, then right, barely controllable. His herd had just left him, and he didn't like it one bit.

Logan gave Gabe his head. The horse shifted his weight backward, lifting his front feet off the ground; then he ran straight at the gate. He pushed off and sailed up. Logan heard a slight "ping" as Gabe's hind feet ticked the gate on the way down. Logan almost fell off as the horse landed. He righted himself, looked at Sam, and they galloped on.

What next? Logan thought as they drew closer to Bolton's boat. Then he saw another driftboat anchored near some trees. A couple of anglers were nymphing for trout in the riffle upstream. Logan could see long spey rods in the boat—apparently a combination trout and steelhead trip.

Logan reined Gabe to a halt and jumped off. He quickly released the cinch and dropped the saddle. He slipped the bridle over Gabe's ears and tossed it near the saddle. Gabe sidled off, then stood breathing hard. Logan started for the river.

"What are you doing!" Sam asked.

"Stealing a driftboat."

"Not without me you're not." She was unsaddling Mataan.

"No! Stay here and take care of the horses."

"Is this important?"

"Yes!"

"Then you are *not* leaving me behind!" She threw Mataan's bridle next to his saddle and walked quickly toward Logan.

"No! Stay here!" Logan ran for the bank, Sam close behind. He sloshed through shallow water to the boat. He unclipped the carabiner that held the anchor: *non-locking—what fools!* He jumped in, grabbed the oars, and started rowing. After two strokes the boat rocked violently. Sam had climbed in. "We're in this together!" she said.

"It's too dangerous! I won't put you at risk!"

"I won't put *you* at risk! We are a team!"

The anglers upstream had figured out that someone was hijacking their boat. They ran through the water, yelling obscenities. One of them tripped and fell down with a splash.

Logan rowed as hard as he could. "It's too much weight!" he said to Sam. "I can't go fast enough. You need to get out!"

"I don't need to get out to lighten the boat," Sam said. She picked up the cooler and heaved it over the side. A fishing bag followed, then another. Rain jackets. Life jackets. Camping gear. A bag of Fritos and two thermos bottles. The obscenities behind them grew louder.

The front seat doubled as a dry box. Sam opened it and started tossing more stuff. Then she loosened the knobs that held down the front seat, picked it up with a grunt, and pushed it over the gunwale. She looked around. A couple of spey rods were stashed along the side. She scooped them into her arms.

"Not the rods!" Logan said. He'd seen the tackle: high-end Burkheimer rods with Danielsson and Nautilus reels. Premium gear. Sam held them over the water, then dumped them. Logan closed his eyes as they splashed into the river. If he was wrong about this guy … well, he'd have to find another place to fish because he'd never be able to show his face on the Deschutes again.

Everything was out of the boat except the anchor rope. Sam sat on the floor of the boat, facing forward, looking intent. The good news, from Logan's point of view, was that Sam was now down low where Bolton couldn't see her. Maybe he didn't even know she was in the boat.

Logan was slowly gaining on Bolton. His first thought was that Bolton would stop at Whiskey Dick. But his second thought was that Whiskey Dick was too accessible; Bolton was probably headed for the Reservation's roadless area below Whitehorse. Could this guy get through the rapids? Maybe, maybe not. Then he saw a difference between him and Bolton: Bolton was a plodder; he was smart and methodical over the long run, but he probably got rattled if he had to act quickly.

By the time they reached Whiskey Dick, Logan was 150 yards from Bolton. He could see him clearly. A gray military-looking case, like the one they'd found near South Junction, was strapped to the seat in front of Bolton.

They were into the straight stretch before Whitehorse Rapids. The line of rocks reached out from river-right. Noise from the rapids grew louder. Logan saw Bolton stand up to see it, then row to river-left and pass through.

Logan followed, now close enough to see relief on Bolton's face. Then it hit him—Bolton probably thought he'd just passed through Whitehorse Rapids. Another flaw: he was intellectually arrogant. Bolton probably wouldn't get the difference between reading a book about whitewater boating and being able to do it. Logan was willing to bet Bolton didn't have a clue how to run Whitehorse or know exactly where it was; Zulfo was the one who went with Kincaid.

Logan was less than fifty yards away. They were in the slow section before Whitehorse.

Bolton suddenly shipped his oars. Was he giving up? Logan doubted it. Bolton reached in front of him, then stood and faced Logan, pointing at him. A shot echoed in the canyon. Then several more.

Sam turned to Logan. She was still sitting on the floor where she couldn't see or be seen. "Is he shooting at us?" she said indignantly.

Logan nodded. "He's going to have a hard time hitting anything from a rocking boat. Keep your head down. I don't think he knows you're in here."

"What are you going to do when you catch him?" Sam asked.

Logan shrugged. He hadn't worked that one out yet. All he knew was that he had to stay close and not let Bolton get away with the VX. "I'll think of something," he muttered.

Sam looked around and spotted the anchor rope, the one thing she hadn't thrown overboard. She pulled her folding hoofpick from her pocket. She flipped out the knife blade and cut off the carabiner, then jerked the rest of the rope, about forty feet, to her. She busied herself doing something that Logan couldn't see.

They were now a hundred feet from Peter Bolton. Another shot, and a hole appeared in the driftboat near the bow. Another, and Logan heard a bullet snap past his head. He saw Bolton drop the clip and slide in a new one.

The two boats came around the corner, and a roar filled the air. Bolton turned to the noise. They were just above the entrance to Whitehorse. Bolton looked right and left, obviously surprised. He put down his gun and took up the oars. His actions were quick, all herky-jerky. Logan was convinced that Bolton was now panicked. He was at the trickier, center entrance. Logan was in a better position and gained distance. The boats were twenty feet apart, but both oarsmen were pulling hard—Logan to stay in one place above the rapids, Bolton to get into position to run the rapids.

"Is he still shooting?" Sam asked.

"No! He has to row. We're at Whitehorse. He's twenty feet in front of me."

Sam nodded, then stood up. She was swinging something around her head. In an instant Logan knew what it was: Sam had fashioned a lariat from the anchor rope. She threw it at Bolton. The boat rocked; the loop missed and fell onto his lap.

Sam cursed and pulled back on the rope for another try. As she pulled, the loop slipped up past Bolton's arms and around the handle of his left oar. Sam yanked. The oar jerked upward, then splashed into the water and floated downriver.

Bolton now had only one oar. He slid into the V-slick at

Whitehorse's center entry. At the mercy of the river, his boat was pushed left and dragged on the rock known as The Canopener. He spun counterclockwise. Logan heard Bolton say, "Oh shit!" as he hit the next rock. The driftboat went on its side and filled with water. He was in the river, hanging onto the boat with one hand and the gray case with the other.

Logan saw a life jacket in front of the gray case. He saw Bolton look at it, but he wouldn't let go of the case to get it. The life jacket soon washed out and floated away.

Logan had been pulling hard on his oars, delaying his entry into Whitehorse, on a treadmill of river current. He was slowly slipping downstream into the rapids. His arms ached, and he was breathing hard. He let his boat go.

As Logan entered the rapids, he saw Bolton's boat disappear, pulled under by the river's powerful hydraulics. Bolton was adrift, looking desperate, his head turning every direction. He was swept to the right of House Rock. He grabbed a ragged rock sticking up from the river. Logan saw him swing into the eddy behind, safe for the moment.

Logan was now nearing House Rock. He was out of position and couldn't get to the safer left passage. He decided he'd have to deal with it and pulled to the right. He slipped through a narrow passage. He could see Bolton downstream from him, clinging to his rock.

There was a loud groaning noise coming from the river. Something was moving underwater, just to Logan's right: a large shape, shiny but tinted green by the water. It shot suddenly upward. With a whoosh, Peter Bolton's driftboat, now twisted, punctured, and bent, exploded from the river. The boat arched five feet into the air and splashed down just downstream from Logan. Half full of water and barely afloat, it drifted sluggishly toward the right bank.

Bolton let go of the rock and swam for his boat. The current caught him and spun him in a circle. His downstream movement suddenly stopped. He was flat in the water, head downstream. It was every angler's horror: a foot had wedged between two boulders. The river poured over Bolton, holding him down. He twisted and writhed to free himself, but to no avail. Then he was still, arms extended, body waving in the current.

Logan pulled hard for Bolton. He slammed the oars inboard and reached over the gunwale to grab his right arm. Sam leaned over to help him. Logan could see the tattoo: *Never Forget. Never Forgive* on his forearm. The current was too strong, and Bolton's arm slipped from Logan's grasp. He slid the oars back into the water and rowed for shore.

"What have I done?" Sam said, her hand to her mouth. "I killed him!"

"Two minutes ago," Logan said, "he was shooting at us. He'd have killed us both if he could have. And a lot more people besides. He was safe; then he swam for his boat. It was his choice, his risk. It's not your fault."

"Why would he do that?"

Logan didn't reply. "Get out and hang onto the boat," he yelled to Sam when they reached shore. He jumped out and ran up the bank to where Bolton's shattered driftboat had stopped. The gray case was still in it, securely strapped to the seat. Logan undid the straps and wrestled the case to the bank. As he carried it to their boat, he tried to gauge the weight. *Four times fifteen. Sixty pounds. Figure another fifteen for the case. Does it feel like seventy-five pounds?* It did.

Logan laid the case flat on the bank. He stared at it for a moment, then flipped the latches. Sam watched over his shoulder. He opened the lid. Inside, surrounded by foam packing, were four shiny metal tubes, pointed at one end.

He looked at Sam. Her eyes were huge. "Those are M56 warheads," Logan explained. "Each one has eight pounds of VX nerve agent. Enough to kill many thousands of people. Enough to start a cycle of death and revenge that could last a century or more." He closed the lid and latched the case, then put it in their boat and pushed off.

As he maneuvered through the rest of Whitehorse Rapids, Logan gave Sam some of the background. "I guess I don't feel so sorry for that guy," Sam said after hearing the story.

"I wouldn't dwell on it," Logan said. "You're a hero and saved a lot of innocent lives."

"We did it together, didn't we?"

"We did."

"Would Mom be proud?"

"She would be very proud of you."

As they floated under the North Junction railroad bridge, Sam gasped. "Oh no! All that stuff I dumped over the side of the boat! What will we do about it?"

"I've got this guy I talk to," Logan said. "He works for Walter Dietz. He'll make it right with them. Probably buy them a boatload of shiny new fishing gear. Make them sign a secrecy agreement: 'Button your lip, or a G-man will break your spey rods.' They'll be okay. The feds will say it was part of a drug deal. The last thing they want is people going nuts about a case full of VX on the Deschutes."

At North Junction, they found an occupied house. Logan stayed with the boat and the gray case while Sam hitched a ride into town. She told the man that a boat had been lost in Whitehorse and there had been a fatality. Logan gave her contact information for Frank Kovak, the federal agent.

Logan sat alone in the boat trying to catch his breath. He stared at the gray box in front of him. He'd spent half a year looking for foreign religious zealots concocting a terrorist plot. Instead, the Bad Guys were two Americans—or an American and a half, since Zulfo was a resident alien, not a citizen—trying to avenge the death of a young nurse in Bosnia.

Doubtless there were Serbs whose ancestors had been treated no better by Bosnian Muslims. Or Croats. Or Albanians. Or … the list went on. Some of them may have felt justified in Adina Osmanović's rape and degradation. It was easy to put Zulfo and Bolton in the context of the Balkans, to blame it on ancient animosities. But he knew that the easy answers were seldom the right ones. Hatred and revenge had no geographic boundaries.

There were questions behind his questions. How do you break the cycle of vengeance? If you don't stand up for what's right, do you just encourage evil? Is it enough to not seek vengeance but still hold hatred in your heart—the desire for vengeance, if not the act of it?

Which led to the biggest questions of all: *How much can be forgiven? And what happens if you don't?*

~

SAM WAS BACK IN LESS THAN an hour. She'd borrowed a car from Helen at the OK. Two unmarked white vans came with her. Frank Kovak emerged from one of these and walked over to Logan. He pointed at the gray case. "In there?" he asked.

Logan nodded.

Kovak opened the case. He gingerly hoisted each warhead and looked it over. "Looks like it's all here," he said to Logan. "And it looks like they haven't been tampered with. We'll do some testing in the lab, but I think it's all good."

Logan nodded. As he watched them load the warheads into the white van, he was aware of the crunch of shoes on gravel. Another man had come up to him. "Not bad work," said a familiar voice from the past, "for a pedantic know-it-all."

Logan turned to confirm the source; then he laughed thinly. "Dietz, if there's one thing I've learned this summer ... it's the astonishing depth of my ignorance."

Walter Dietz nodded approvingly. "Then you know more than most people."

"How are you, you old crow?"

"I can't complain. Or when I do, no one listens. Just like they wouldn't listen to me when I said they should be looking for eight warheads instead of four."

Logan rose to his feet and extended a hand to Dietz. Dietz grabbed his hand, then pulled him close and gave him a bear hug.

"Dietz?" Logan said. "How did this happen?"

"A computer guy at the Umatilla Depot had a bad gambling habit and was heavily in debt to some very nasty people."

"And they threatened to break his kneecaps unless ..."

"Not *his* kneecaps. They threatened to cripple his six-year-old daughter if he didn't come up with the money he owed. One day at work he broke down and confessed to Bolton, who paid off his debt. In exchange, the man told Bolton how to twiddle a few bits. The guy didn't do it himself; just told Bolton how it could be done. He convinced himself that Bolton was doing a security review. So Bolton hacked the system, shredded the old hard-copy reports, and replaced them with new ones. Everyone believed what the computer said."

"Ah. 'A few bits.' That's why it was four warheads or eight. Change a 'one' to a 'zero,' and thousands of people nearly lose their lives." Logan shook his head.

"The computer guy knew Kincaid," Dietz added. "That's how they linked up with him."

"When did you figure this out?"

"This morning. We started questioning people in Umatilla. Bolton's accomplice cracked and told us everything he knew. We still haven't figured out how Bolton got the warheads off the Weapons Depot. We're working on it." Dietz nodded in the direction of the white van. "The world thanks you."

"Do a good deed daily."

"You're such a Boy Scout," Dietz said, shaking his head. "I'm sorry this turned out to be so dangerous. I had your compensation adjusted for 'hazardous duty,' retroactive to the start of your assignment. Don't get excited. Money's tight, and our Congressional overseers view virtue as its own reward. But it'll keep you in turnips for a week or two."

"Thanks."

Dietz nodded, then cocked his head. "Our hiring freeze is over. I have a job opening, if you're interested. Take advantage quick; I'm retiring in less than a year."

"A job in Langley? No thanks. I'm going to stay here, by the river."

"Doing what?"

"I've got this guidebook. It's almost done. I think I'll look for a publisher. Then maybe I'll do some computer consulting."

"In Maupin? I doubt you'll find much high-tech business there. It's not exactly Gotham, is it?"

"Give me broadband and a laptop, and I can do anything for anyone from anywhere."

The van with the VX pulled away. Logan and Dietz were both silent as they watched it disappear down the road.

"We need to catch up," Dietz said. "Know any place with good coffee?"

"The OK Cafe has espresso. The barista is a lovely young woman who knows her way around the beans."

"It's the funky little place at the end of the road?"

"That's it. You go ahead, and I'll meet you there. Then Sam and I need to pick up a couple of horses."

Dietz drove off, and Logan was left alone with Sam. She came near and put her arm around his waist, then leaned her head against his shoulder. He wrapped an arm around her.

"Shall we move on?" Sam asked.

"Yes," Logan said. "Together."

5: Tailout

48

October 21: Maupin

"How do you feel about *Hamlet*?" Megan asked.

"A hamburger?" Casey replied. "I'm game."

"Not the food. The Shakespeare play."

"I knew what you said the first time. I'm just winding you up. I could go for *Hamlet*. And a hamburger. How do you feel about *The Legend of Sleepy Hollow?*"

"The old Disney cartoon? Halloween's almost here, so that would be 'seasonally appropriate,' as they say."

"And a *Mission Impossible* episode?" In his teen years, Casey got hooked on reruns of the old TV series and had the complete set on DVDs.

"Hmm, let's see how we do with the others. If we still feel like it, we can watch one of those."

With the guide season winding down, Casey only had day trips—about three a week. This gave him more time with Megan, and they were spending a cozy evening watching videos at his place.

Megan's senior English class was reading *Hamlet*; then they were going to see a movie version on DVD. She wanted to preview it before showing it to her students. Casey flipped a coin to see what they'd watch first. *Hamlet* won the toss.

Casey was dubious about *Hamlet*. He'd read the play in high school, of course, but had forgotten what it was about. He remembered parts of it as they watched, however, and by the end he admitted that he enjoyed it, sort of.

The Legend of Sleepy Hollow was more his speed. He identified with Brom Bones, the local swain courting the lovely Katrina. Ichabod Crane, the newcomer to town, reminded him of Brandon Muckenhirn.

Casey hadn't seen the cartoon since he was twelve. When Brom Bones was telling the story of the Headless Horseman—and scaring the pants off the superstitious Ichabod—Casey suddenly paused the DVD. "It's the same as *Hamlet!*" he said.

"What?"

"I never understood that before. There was no 'Legend of Sleepy Hollow.' Brom Bones made it up at the party so he could frighten Ichabod. That was Brom Bones on the horse *pretending* to be the Headless Horseman. He was trying to run Ichabod out of town."

"Well, yes … I get what you mean. When I was a kid—which was the last time I saw this—that went over my head, too. I see it now. But what's it got to do with *Hamlet?*"

"The play … " Casey said.

"'The play's the thing wherein I'll catch the conscience of the king.' Right! It's a made-up story to force someone to reveal his true nature!" She nodded approvingly at Casey. "Very insightful!"

"And," Casey said, "think about this: it's the same as most *Mission Impossible* plots: a kind of elaborate practical joke to trap the bad guy."

He restarted the DVD but was lost in thought the rest of the evening.

A WEEK LATER THE OK HELD its end-of-season party for the staff and friends. Judd and Susan were there, as were Helen and her husband Kevin. Diana, Willie, Brandon, Casey, and about a dozen others including Sam and Logan also attended. Ken Jones, a biologist for the Warm Springs Tribes, had stopped by earlier in the day, and Judd invited him, too.

It was a beers-and-burgers shindig, with reminiscences about the season and plans for the next year. The lights of the OK shone warm and bright in the cool night air. Trees rustled in a gentle wind, and the river added its background song.

About 10:00, as the party wound down, Casey walked up to Brandon. "Have one on me," he said, handing Brandon a fresh beer. "How was your Warm Springs to Trout Creek yesterday?"

"Hammered 'em!" Brandon said. "Especially by Memaloose." Memaloose was a large island at the end of that stretch, just above Trout Creek. It was a favorite spot for Brandon.

"Swinging flies or nymphing?"

"All on nymphs, of course. That's the only way to do it when the water's cold."

"Really? I'm still picking up fish on the swing. With a floating line."

Brandon looked disdainful and pointed an emphatic finger at Casey. "You want to catch steelhead in the fall? Nymph! But," he smirked, "I guess we all know what you'd rather do than nymph for steelhead."

"I bet I could get just as many on the swing as you could nymphing."

Brandon gave him an oh-you-country-bumpkin look. "No way."

Heated discussion followed. Finally, Casey said, "Tell you what. Put your money where your mouth is, and we'll have a fish-off. Warm Springs to Trout Creek. You nymph, I'll swing. First light to dark. We'll see who does better."

"You're on!" Brandon said. "How much?"

"You know me. I don't have money lying around."

"So you're not really serious."

"Yeah? I'll bet you my driftboat against yours."

"You got it, man!"

"Shall we ask Judd and Megan to referee?" Casey suggested. "One in each boat?"

"Deal!"

They went to Judd and explained the contest. Judd shook his head and looked at Casey like he was the dumbest kid in the county, but agreed to do it. He took Casey aside and said, "How are you going to make a living if you lose your boat to this guy?"

"I'm not worried about losing my boat."

"Boat, hell. You've already lost your mind."

~

MEGAN HAD THE SAME CONCERNS as her father. Casey betting his driftboat? What was he thinking? She began to wonder if she'd made a mistake about him. Maybe he hadn't matured as much as she thought.

Near the end of the party, she saw Casey lead Ken Jones outside. She could see them talking, and every now and then she caught snippets of conversation: Casey saying things like, "Just back me up," and Ken saying, "Don't mess with my culture, man. Leave the Indians out of this." Then Casey said, "Your cousin Josh would be perfect."

After they came back in, Casey asked Megan, "What's 'ersatz' mean?"

"A cheap and inferior imitation. Why?"

"Oh, Ken used the word. I just wondered."

AS THE PARTY BROKE UP, CASEY followed Brandon out the door. "Hey, Brandon, Ken was telling me a story that I thought you'd find interesting. It's about Memaloose Island."

Brandon looked at Ken, "Oh, yeah? How's it go?"

Ken looked at the ground like he was he was trying to memorize what dirt looked like. "Oh, I think Casey tells it best," he said.

"I think I can remember it," Casey said. "Long ago, before the white man came, the Indians had a village on the Deschutes ..."

"Several villages," Ken said. "And a hell of a lot on the Columbia."

"Yes, but this happened on the Deschutes. Anyway, a young man named Red Beaver was the best hunter and fisherman in the village. He prayed to the Steelhead Spirit to make him worthy to catch fish. He prayed to the Elk Spirit to make him a worthy hunter on land. He learned the ways of the elk and the ways of the fish. He became the best provider in the village." Casey looked at Ken, who was staring into the darkness. "Isn't that how it starts, Ken?"

"What?" Ken said.

"How the story starts. Red Beaver is the best fisherman in the village. He prays to—"

"The Salmon Spirit," Ken said.

"Steelhead, wasn't it?"

"Him, too," Ken sighed.

"One fall," Casey went on, "at the time when the steelhead—"

"And salmon," Ken said.

"Right. When the steelhead and salmon return, the other young men decided to be better than Red Beaver. But they didn't pray to be worthy of the fish. Instead, they invented new dip nets and better spears. They were so good at getting fish that they soon had more than the village needed for the winter. Red Beaver pleaded with them to stop. 'You do not show respect,' he said. 'Your methods are not worthy. You are killing fish when you shouldn't. The spirits will

be angry. The fish will not return to us, and our village will be punish-
ed.' But they wouldn't listen. Red Beaver pleaded with the elders.
'Make them stop!' he said. The others could see that the elders were
almost convinced, so they ambushed Red Beaver and cut off his head
with their knives. They said some enemy Indians had done it."

Casey glanced at Ken. His eyes were closed, and he looked like
he had a headache coming on. Casey continued. "The village mourn-
ed Red Beaver and laid his body on Memaloose Island."

"Well, thanks for the story," Brandon said, zipping up his
jacket. "Can I go now?"

Casey raised a hand. "Almost done. Coyote saw what they'd
done and took pity on Red Beaver. He gave Red Beaver's spirit—that's
his *ghost*—strong medicine, great power. Red Beaver's spirit became
the guardian of the fish, especially the steelhead. If—"

"And salmon," Ken said.

"Especially the steelhead and *salmon*. If anyone takes fish
when they shouldn't, Red Beaver's spirit comes to them in a canoe
paddled by …" Casey paused and counted on his fingers "… by four
spirit-warriors. Coyote then gave Red Beaver's spirit—his *ghost*—a
magic knife. Red Beaver doesn't have to touch the offender. He just
raises his knife and slashes it through the air. If the offender hasn't
repented, his head falls off. Red Beaver's spirit lives on Memaloose
Island, your favorite fishing water."

"Yeah, well, whatever." said Brandon. "See you at the fish-off."
Brandon was headed for his truck when he suddenly turned around.
"What does 'Memaloose' mean?" he asked.

Casey looked at Ken.

"Place of the dead," Ken said, still gazing into the dark.
He turned to Casey and shook his head before leaving.

AT 7:00 THE MORNING OF OCTOBER 31, Casey and Brandon stood by their driftboats at the Warm Springs ramp. Their rods were strung, and they were ready to go.

Casey's last guide trip had been two days before—a day when the wind howled, and every type of cloud in Nature's inventory scudded across the sky. Fishing had been poor. Today's weather, however, promised to be mild, with calm winds and better fishing conditions. A thin crescent moon hung over the eastern rimrock. A few trout rose to a minor hatch of small mayflies.

Casey waded into the river to measure the water temperature: fifty degrees, the low end of effectiveness for swinging flies on a floating line. Still, with the warmer weather and low winds, fishing could be good.

At 7:15 Judd crunched across the gravel parking lot and said, "It's light enough to fish. Let's roll."

They'd agreed that Brandon and Casey would leapfrog down the first three miles until Dry Creek. Then Casey would stay on river-right, and Brandon would fish river-left. The left side is Reservation land, but from Dry Creek to Trout Creek it can be fished if you have a permit. This was the last day for fishing on the Reservation side.

By the time they broke for lunch at Grassy Camp, Casey had hooked and landed two steelhead, and Brandon had caught one.

Over lunch, Casey pointed at a bankside alder that had lost its leaves and said, "Don't those branches remind you of skeletons? They're like long bony fingers reaching out to get you. Gives me the creeps now that I think about it." He said this to Megan, but Brandon stood nearby.

As they set out to resume fishing, Casey said, "A big chinook salmon swam past me in that last run—probably forty pounds. Spawned-out and covered with brown fungus. Died last week and doesn't know it yet. A zombie chinook. If one touches you, do you join the living dead?" He said it in jest to Judd, but again, Brandon was close enough to hear.

About 4:00 Casey pulled into a favorite run. Another angler was already fishing there. It would be bad etiquette for Casey to fish, too, and he was ready to move on when he noticed that the angler was using a spinning rod, not a fly rod. So Casey waited. After fifteen minutes in one place, the other angler left.

Judd grinned knowingly at Casey. "Some guys go to one spot and never move their feet," he said. "They leave a lot of fishing water for the rest of us."

Casey started high in the run, and within ten minutes he hooked a steelhead. Unfortunately it broke off before he could land it. "Tough luck," Judd said. "Doesn't count if you don't land it."

A little after 5:30 they passed Brandon. Megan held up two fingers: it was tied at two fish each. Casey looked at the sky, which had clouded over. Judd joined his upward gaze. "Looks like a long, slow slide into darkness," Judd said. "No chance of strong light."

Casey nodded. He knew what Judd meant: Brandon's best water, the stretch near the lower end of Memaloose Island, flowed east, so any steelhead would be pointing west. If the light was strong, Brandon would have a harder time hooking a fish because the sun would be in its eyes. But today there was nothing to prevent steelhead from jumping on his fly.

In confirmation, they heard a whoop as Brandon hooked another fish, and a few minutes later a loud, "That's three!"

Judd rowed Casey over to confirm the score. Darkness was coming on. The crickets had started their undulating chirp, trees were now indistinct dark masses, and shapes were losing detail and color. Brandon was still fishing. The river hissed as it flowed past his knees. "Giving up?" he said to Casey. "It's quitting time. First light to dusk, you said."

"First light to *dark.*"

Brandon scowled. "Whatever."

"I can still get a fish," Casey said.

"Where?" Judd muttered. It was too shallow for steelhead on Casey's side of the river.

Judd went to talk to Megan. Casey lingered near Brandon. A coyote howled. "What was that?" Casey said.

"Coyote?" said Brandon.

"Didn't sound quite like a coyote," Casey said. "Deeper, more human. But not human. Kind of inhuman. Never heard anything quite like it before." He listened, but there were no more howls. "Maybe it was a zombie chinook," he said with a grin. "Don't let it get you!" Suddenly Casey ducked. "Whoa!" he said. "Bats are thick tonight! I wonder if any of them are *vampire* bats?"

He left Brandon and went back to other side of the river with Judd.

~

TEN MINUTES AFTER JUDD AND Casey left, Megan said, "I hear something coming."

Brandon stood still and listened. "What's that?" he said in a high-pitched voice. A large shadow was moving toward them. A voice called Brandon's name. "Who's there? Who are you?" Brandon said.

"It's Judd. Who else?" Both voice and shape resolved themselves. Judd was rowing Casey's driftboat. "I left Casey on the other side." He shook his head. "He took three casts and reeled up. Said it was hopeless and sent me over here to tell you he was done." Judd rested on the oars, looking tired.

"Sounds good to me," Brandon said. He reeled in quickly and stowed his rod.

They rowed for the Trout Creek boat ramp, both boats close together. As they reached midriver, a large shadow glided swiftly across the water toward them

"Judd, is that you?" Brandon called out.

"I'm over here," Judd said. His voice was nearby, but downriver.

Brandon dropped his oars and grabbed his big flashlight. He pushed the ON button, but nothing happened. He banged it against his hand several times and tried again. No light came.

Megan could see that the shape approaching them was a large canoe. Four paddles dipped in unison. The paddler's faces were obscured, their heads covered with something like monk's hoods. Only the lower parts of their faces could be seen, lit by a faint light. The paddlers were chanting: "Brandon, Brandon, Brandon ..."

"Holy Mary, Jesus, and Joseph," Judd said. "What the hell is that?" He rowed his boat to stay in one place in the river. The current was slow and steady, and the two driftboats floated together near the canoe.

From the center of the canoe, a huge man rose, wearing only a breechclout and a headband. The canoe rocked when he stood, and the paddlers stopped and held onto the gunwales. "I am Red Beaver," said the standing figure in a deep and resonant voice, "Guardian of the Fish. Brandon Muckenhirn, you have sinned. Your head ... *is mine!*"

Brandon dropped the flashlight and grabbed his lantern. It worked no better than his flashlight. He cast it aside. He made a cross sign with his fingers, but the paddlers were heedless and kept stroking toward him and chanting, "Brandon, Brandon, Brandon ..."

Brandon jerked an oar out of its lock and held it like a baseball bat. "Don't come any closer," he yelled. His voice was high and cracking.

Megan looked carefully at the canoe. Her eyes narrowed, and she turned to Brandon. She put on her schoolteacher voice and said, "Brandon Muckenhirn, stop being stupid. We're coming up on fast water. You put down that oar and row your boat to shore this instant."

The paddlers were no longer powering the canoe, but their chant was even faster: "Brandon, Brandon, Brandon ..." The standing figure raised his arms. A long, machete-sized blade was in his right hand. It glowed in the dark. "Brandon Muckenhirn," the deep voice repeated, "YOUR HEAD IS MINE!"

"Oh God oh God oh God," Brandon said. "I'm sorry about the fish! I won't do it again! Don't hurt me! Oh God! Please don't hurt me! I'll never kill a wild fish again! It was that guy from El Segundo. I'm sorry about the fish! And the guys from Northridge."

"When?" boomed the standing figure. "When did you sin like this?"

Upstream, Judd shouted, "Brandon, you poaching sonofabitch. You'd better hope they get you before I do."

Brandon was still pleading, "Since August. They made me do it. Oh God, I'm sorry! And that couple from Dallas …"

"Save yourself and confess your sins," the deep voice said.

Megan heard Judd say. "I know that voice." Megan had already recognized it but kept her mouth shut.

"… and those three guys from New Jersey …"

Red Beaver bent toward one of the paddlers, who seemed to be talking to him. He straightened and said in his commanding voice, "And did you start the fire at the Drift Inn?"

"No," Brandon said, perplexed. "That was a grease fire." Then he said suspiciously, "Say, who are you?"

The huge man raised his arms higher. "I am the Guardian of the Fish. Your head is MINE!"

"No! No!" Brandon croaked. He dropped the oar into the water and jumped out of the boat. He splashed quickly to shore.

Judd rowed after the retreating Brandon. "They won't take your head, you fool! They're fakes. But your worthless butt is *mine*!"

The current was gathering speed, and the canoeists backpaddled to stay in one place. In Brandon's boat, Megan picked up the remaining oar and tried to reach shore, but it was tough going. She drifted around a sharp right bend and into fast water. She heard a thunk as the boat's chine hit a rock. The boat stopped, but the upstream side lifted from the pressure of the current. Megan tried to get to the high side but was too late. The boat tipped over. She spilled into the water and was swept downstream. She could feel the bottom but was moving too fast to get to her feet.

Suddenly she was in deep, slow water. She recognized the place: it was the big backeddy just past the boat ramp. She tried to swim for shore but seemed never to reach it. A current surge pulled her under, then let her back up, gasping.

The river was cold, and she felt incredibly tired. She seemed to have no breath or strength and couldn't lift her arms to swim. Then there was a tightness around her chest and a voice in her ear saying, "Hang on, we're almost there." Her heels dragged the bottom, and she was on the shore. Megan rolled over, resting on her hands and knees.

"Are you all right?" an anxious voice said.

Megan took two deep breaths and looked up. Casey was next to her, soaking wet. "That idiot Brandon," she said, breathing hard. "I could have drowned."

Casey helped her up the bank. She sat at a picnic table and closed her eyes. She felt herself shivering uncontrollably.

"I'll be right back," Casey said. He ran off and quickly returned with a couple of bundles. "Change into these dry clothes," he said. "Then wrap up in this space blanket. I'll build a fire. There's hot coffee in the thermos."

Ten minutes later Megan could honestly say, "I'm doing better." She took a good look at Casey. He was wearing shorts and was shivering. She held open the blanket. "Come on in and get warm. Have some hot coffee."

Casey sat next to her, and she held him tight. "Did you engineer this?" she said.

"I wasn't planning on you getting dumped," he said. "I'm sorry."

She could hear Judd's voice nearby, overpowering a weaker, whining voice. She giggled. "I think Dad's really giving it to Brandon."

"You don't think he'd—"

"Hurt him?" Megan said. "No, but by the time Dad's done yelling at him he'll wish Red Beaver got him instead. Where did you come up with this scheme?"

"It's *Hamlet*. And *Sleepy Hollow*. And *Mission Impossible.*" Casey told her the Red Beaver story.

"That is the dumbest, fakest 'Indian legend' I've ever heard," Megan said.

"Ken Jones didn't think much of it either. But when I told him Brandon was killing wild fish he went along. Reluctantly."

"It did the job. I don't think we'll see Brandon Muckenhirn on the Deschutes again." She took a sip of coffee. "How come his flashlight and lantern didn't work?"

"I reversed the batteries when we broke for lunch."

"You're sneaky. But in a nice way." She put her head on his shoulder.

Other people joined them at the campfire: Hank, Willie, and Logan, who had been the other paddlers; Ken's cousin Josh, who'd played Red Beaver; Judd and his family.

Logan left for a bit and came back with his truck. Sam and Lisa got out with him. He had a load of wood in the back, and everyone brought a log to the fire. Laughter flowed for an hour, then eased. The fire died to embers. People began drifting away. Cars and pickups drove off.

Nearly everyone was gone when Casey and Megan left, wrapped in their blanket of mutual warmth. Willie went with them.

Logan stood by the fire between Sam and Lisa. "I think it's time for us to go," Logan said.

"I'll tend the fire," a voice replied.

HANK O'LEARY SAT ALONE BY the dying embers. He pulled a harmonica from his shirt pocket and played the melody from "Dancing Caddis," the song he'd written for Jackie and himself. After the last notes echoed off the canyon walls, he tapped the harmonica on his palm and slid it back into his pocket. There were no duets with fiddlers in his immediate future.

From his jacket, he took out two sheets of paper. The first was a well-worn clipping from a London newspaper—dateline eight days ago. He read it again, especially the last part, which had been underlined: "This reviewer has heard Miss Moreau many times, but she has never sounded better than at last night's concert. Her music has a new energy and freshness that is simply breathtaking. I asked her about recent retirement rumors. She said she has no plans to retire, but is scheduling fewer public engagements than in the past and will curtail her concert schedule. When asked what she would do in her free time, she smiled enigmatically and said she planned to row a boat. She would not elaborate."

Hank chuckled, then opened the other sheet of paper. On it were five squares, labeled May, June, July, August, and September. A fishing fly had been taped to each square: Soft Rock, O Stone, XYZee Caddis, Jonzie, and Plum Dandy. He examined the workmanship of the flies. Not bad. Not bad at all.

He stood up and returned the papers to his jacket, then doused the fire. Before leaving, he counted on his fingers: November, December, January, February, March, April. Then May.

Not long. Not long at all.